S0-AIP-674

Chloe tilted her head to look at his shuttered face. "I've offended you."

Nik arched an eloquent brow.

"Sorry."

He bowed slightly from the waist. "Accepted." A glimmer appeared in his eyes. "Friends again?"

Chloe looked at the hand extended to her as if it were a viper. It was news to her that they ever had been friends, but she reached out.

He took her hand but not to shake it. Without his seeming to exert any overt pressure, she found herself colliding with his body.

His dark face lowered to hers. "It's all about sleight of hand and distraction," he whispered before his mouth came crashing down on hers.

Kim Lawrence lives on a farm in Anglesey with her university-lecturer husband, assorted pets who arrived as strays and never left, and sometimes one or both of her boomerang sons. When she's not writing, she loves to be outdoors gardening or walking on one of the beaches for which the island is famous—along with being the place where Prince William and Catherine made their first home!

Books by Kim Lawrence

Harlequin Presents

A Ring to Secure His Crown
Surrendering to the Italian's Command
One Night with Morelli
Captivated by Her Innocence

Wedlocked!

One Night to Wedding Vows

One Night With Consequences

Her Nine Month Confession
A Secret Until Now

Seven Sexy Sins

The Sins of Sebastian Rey-Defoe

Royal & Ruthless

The Heartbreaker Prince

At His Service

Maid for Montero

Visit the Author Profile page
at Harlequin.com for more titles.

Kim Lawrence

—

THE GREEK'S ULTIMATE CONQUEST

Recycling programs
for this product may
not exist in your area.

ISBN-13: 978-1-335-41912-5

The Greek's Ultimate Conquest

First North American Publication 2018

Copyright © 2018 by Kim Lawrence

Printed in U.S.A.

THE GREEK'S ULTIMATE CONQUEST

CHAPTER ONE

WHEN HAD HE actually last slept…?

The medication that the medic had administered to him in the field hospital had only taken the edge off his agony and since he'd got on the military air transport to Germany it hadn't even done that, despite the copious amounts of alcohol he'd downed in an attempt to self-medicate.

But now he was finally about to fall sleep, the moment was delayed as a half-burnt log in the open grate disintegrated, sending a star burst of sparks outwards and pulling him back from the brink. He watched through heavy half-closed eyes as the flames flared briefly before fading, leaving dark specks on the sheepskin stretched over the wood floor.

The woman lying across his arm stirred gently before burrowing into his shoulder. He flexed his fingers to relieve the numbness that was creeping into his hand, and with his free hand pushed back a hank of hair tinged silver by the moonlight shining through the open window. He glanced down, the soft light caressing her face revealing the smooth curve of her cheek.

She was, simply, beautiful. It wasn't just the bone structure and the incredible body, but she had something else about her…a *glow*, he decided, smiling at the uncharacteristically sentimental thought as he rubbed a strand of her hair between his fingertips. She was the sort of woman that at any other time in his life he would have gravitated towards. But even though he'd picked her out immediately when she had entered the bar earlier—with a noisy, youthful après-ski group oozing the confidence that came with privilege and intent on having fun and spending money—he had not reacted. Instead shutting out the sound of upper-class voices, he'd turned back to the drink he'd been nursing as he'd sunk once again into his black thoughts.

Then she'd come over to him. Up close she was even more spectacular, and she clearly had the self confidence that went with knowing it as she approached him. A real golden girl complete with golden glow, long gorgeous legs, her lithe body lovingly outlined in tight-fitting ski gear that was suited to her sinuous, athletic body. Her fine-boned face had perfect symmetry, the full lips and the deep blue of her wide-spaced eyes made him think of an angel, a sexy angel with a halo of lint-pale hair that glittered in the reflection of the beaten copper light shade suspended over his table.

'Hello.'

Her voice was low, accentless, and had a slight attractive husk.

A flicker of uncertainty appeared in her eyes when he didn't respond, then after a moment she repeated the greeting, first in French and then Italian.

'English is fine.'

She took the comment as encouragement and slid onto a stool beside him. 'I saw you from...' Without taking her eyes from his face—*they really were the most spectacular eyes*—she nodded towards the group she had arrived with, who seemed to be involved in a noisy shot-downing game. The sight of the bunch of spoiled socialites giving the bar staff a hard time twitched his lips into a contemptuous sneer.

'You're missing the fun,' he drawled.

She glanced back at her friends, giving what appeared to be a wince before training eyes that were a shocking shade of blue on him. 'It stopped being fun about two bars ago.' Her soft lips still smiled but a quizzical groove appeared between her brows and her head tilted a little to one side as she continued to stare at him. 'You look...*alone.*'

He gave her a look then, the one that made ninety-nine out of a hundred people back off. The hundredth was generally drunk, although it was obvious this woman wasn't; her blue stare was clear and candid, unnervingly so. Or maybe what unnerved him was the electric charge he could feel in the air between them, a low-level thrum but undeniably present.

'I'm Chloe—'

He cut her off before she could introduce herself fully.

'Sorry, *agape mou*, I'm not good company tonight.' He wanted her to go away, he wanted to be left alone to slide back into the darkness, but when she didn't, he wasn't really sorry.

'Are you Greek?'

'Among other things.'

'So what do I call you?'

Nothing worse than he'd called himself. 'Nik.'

'Just Nik?'

He nodded and after a moment she gave a little shrug of assent. 'Fair enough.'

When her friends had left she had stayed.

This was her room, an apartment in an upmarket chalet—not that they'd made it as far as the bedroom. A trail of their clothing traced their stumbling path from the door to the leather sofa where they lay.

He had always enjoyed the physical, sexual side of his nature but last night... Nik still couldn't quite believe how raw it had been, a true sanity-sapping explosion of need, and for a few moments he had felt free, free of grief, guilt and the oily taint left by the things he had witnessed.

He trailed a hand down her back, letting his fingers rest on the curve of her smooth bottom. As he breathed in her scent he desperately wanted to close his eyes, but for some reason every time he thought about it his glance was drawn across the room to where, he knew, even though the light was too dim to see properly, his phone lay after it had fallen from his pocket.

How did he know it was about to vibrate?

Then it did.

He glanced down to see if the sound had disturbed the sleeping woman and every muscle in his body clenched violently in icy horror and shock, trapping the cry of visceral terror in his throat. He was staring down, not at a warm, beautiful woman, but at the pale, still face of his best friend. The body he held was not warm and breathing but cold and still, the eyes not closed but open and staring up at him, blankly empty!

When he suddenly awoke, gasping, he was not in his bed but beside it on the floor on his knees, shaking like someone in a fever, sweat dripping from his body as he gulped for air. The effort of drawing oxygen into his lungs defined each individual sinew and muscle in his powerful back as he rammed his clenched fists against his rock-hard thighs. The scream that clawed at the edge of his mind remained locked in his raw throat as he struggled to reclaim reality from the lingering wisps of his dreams.

It finally came, and when it did he felt...well, he felt no better or worse than he had on any other of the countless times previously he'd woken out of exactly the same nightmare.

Slowly Nik got to his feet, the normal fluidity of his actions stiff, the athletically honed body so many envied, and even more lusted after, responding sluggishly to commands as he lurched across the room to the bathroom, where he turned on the cold tap of the washbasin full blast and put his head under the stream of cold water.

Fingers curled over the edge of the basin hid the fact he refused to acknowledge, that his hands were shaking, but as he straightened up he was unable to avoid a brief view of his own reflection in the mirror before he turned away, knowing that although the blinding visceral fear was temporarily back in its box, the shadow of it remained in his eyes.

The shower did not entirely banish the shadow either, but it did revive him. He checked the time; four hours' sleep was two hours too little but the idea of returning to bed, probably only to relive the nightmare yet again, held little appeal.

Five minutes later Security buzzed him out of the building, the concierge dipping his head and wishing him a good run when he exited, while privately probably thinking that the guy from the penthouse who regularly took a pre-dawn run was insane. Maybe, Nik reflected grimly as he pulled up the hood of his sweatshirt against the rain, he had a point.

The exercise did the usual trick of clearing his head so by the time, shaved, suited and booted, he skimmed through his emails the night horrors had been banished, or at least unacknowledged. He had other things to focus on, things that were nothing to do with the message on his phone. After noting the caller identity with a grimace, he slid it into his pocket.

He knew without looking at the content that it would be a reminder about the dinner party his sister was hosting that evening, the one he had agreed to attend in a moment of weakness. With Ana it was easier to say yes, because *no* was not a word she understood, neither was single or unattached, at least where her younger brother was concerned.

He slowed as he reached another set of traffic lights that had sprung up overnight, and smothered a sigh as he struggled to push aside the thoughts of his evening entertainment and the inevitable candidate for the position of wife, or at least serious girlfriend material, who would be seated beside him.

He loved his sister, admiring her talent and the fact she juggled a career as a designer with being a single parent. He was ready to admit she had many good traits but unfortunately conceding defeat was not one of them!

Part of his mind on the increasingly heavy traffic he was negotiating, he tried to put the evening ahead out of his mind, but maybe due to his disturbed night the prospect of being polite to one of the perfectly charming women his sister produced on a regular basis to audition for the role of potential mate weighed more heavily on his mind.

He knew that as far as Ana was concerned all his problems would be solved the moment he found a soul mate. He still couldn't decide if she really believed it and though there were occasions when he found her rosy optimism sweet, usually after a bottle of wine, mostly it was intensely irritating.

Hell, if he'd thought love was a cure-all he'd be out looking for it now, but as far as Nik was concerned the search would be in vain. It was a stretch but he was prepared to suspend disbelief and concede that it was possible that there was such a thing as true love, but if this was the case, the way some people were born colour-blind, he was love-blind.

It was a disability he was prepared to bear. At least he was never going to be in the position of having to experience the falling *out* of love process. It would be hard to find two people more civilised, more genuinely nice than his sister and her ex, but he had watched their break-up and eventual divorce and it had been toxic! The worst aspect of the split had been the child stuck in the middle. It didn't really matter how hard you tried to protect them from the worst, and they had tried, a kid had to be affected by it.

Give him plain and simple lust any day of the week, and as for growing old alone, surely it was better by far than growing old next to someone you couldn't stand the sight of!

He was prepared to concede that there were happy marriages around but they were the exception rather than the rule.

The car moved five yards before he came to another halt, and someone farther down the line of stationary cars sounded their horn in frustration. Nik raised his eyes heavenwards, the frown lines in his brow smoothing out as his glance landed on the neon-lit face on the advertising billboard across the road.

The advertising agency had clearly gone old school. There was nothing subtle about the message they were sending, just a straightforward fantasy for men to buy into. Use the brand of male face product clutched to the generous bosom of the woman in the bikini and you too would have similarly scantily clad and gorgeous women throwing themselves at you.

Not this one... His mobile mouth twitched into a sardonic smile; he was probably one of a handful of people who knew that this particular object of male fantasy was in a secret same-sex relationship. Secret, not because Lucy was concerned about any negative impact on her career, but because of a deal the couple had struck with her partner Clare's soon to be ex-husband. The guy wouldn't contest the divorce if the women waited to go public with their relationship until after he had landed the contract worth multi millions he was in the middle of negotiating with a firm who had built their brand on family values and a squeaky-clean image.

Maybe, Nik mused, if the guy had spent as much time on his marriage as he did on nurturing business deals he might still be married...? After all, if you believed everything you read, maintaining a good relationship took time, energy and hard work. Well, he definitely didn't have the time. As for energy, he was quite prepared to be energetic, but not if the sex seemed like hard work... No, marriage really was not for him.

He was jolted from his reverie by another blast on a horn, from behind him this time. It had a knock-on effect…not *quite* a eureka moment but pretty damn close and, like all good ideas, it was perfectly simple. Actually he couldn't quite figure out why it had not previously occurred to him to counter his sister's relentless matchmaking by turning up with a date of his own choosing and acting like a man in love.

He smiled up at the inspiration for the idea looking down at him…was Lucy Cavendish in town? And if she was, he wondered if the idea would appeal to her sense of humour; failing that he'd appeal to her conscience. After all, she did owe him one as he was the person who'd introduced her to Clare.

The caterers were carrying boxes through the open front door when Chloe arrived. Tatiana had asked her to be early but maybe this was *too* early?

'Go through to the office. Mum's in there.'

Chloe did a double take and realised that one of the caterers holding a box was Eugenie, Tatiana's teenage daughter.

The girl saw her expression and nodded. 'Yeah, I know…not a good look, but Mum insisted I work at least half the holiday to reduce the danger of me being a rich spoilt brat who thinks money grows on trees. You look great!' she added, her eyes widening as she took in the full effect of the sleeveless silk jumpsuit Chloe wore. 'Of course, you have to have legs that go on for ever to get away with it.'

Chloe laughed as the girl whisked away.

The door of the study was open and after a brief tap Chloe went inside. The room was empty except for the dog that was curled up on top of a designer silk jacket that had been flung over a chair. Even crushed and underneath a Labrador the distinctive style of the design made the label it bore unnecessary. *Tatiana* had become famous for her use of bold, brilliant colours and simple wearable designs.

The animal opened one eye and Chloe went over, drawn by a silent canine command. As she stroked his soft ears she looked curiously at the drawings set up on the massive draftsman table that took centre stage in the room.

'Oh, don't look at those. I was having a bad day,' Tatiana exclaimed, walking into the room. In one of her own designs, the petite brunette projected an air of effortless elegance. 'Down, Ulysses!' She gave a little sigh when the dog responded by wagging his tail and staying put. 'Nik says a dog needs to know who's master, but that's the trouble—you already do, don't you, you bad boy?' she crooned.

Chloe gave a smile that she hoped hid the fact that her first thought whenever she heard the name of Tatiana's younger brother was, *Oh, God, not brother Nik again!*

Nothing Tatiana said about her brother challenged Chloe's growing conviction that the man thought he was an expert on everything—and was not shy about sharing his expert opinion.

But then, being reticent and self-effacing were probably not the most obvious characteristics for someone who was the head of a Greek shipping line, and though Chloe knew that Nik Latsis had only stepped into his father's shoes relatively recently, it sounded to her as though they fitted him very well indeed!

Tatiana didn't seem to question or resent the fact that her younger brother had inherited the company simply because he was male, so why should Chloe?

Maybe because she wasn't Greek.

And there was no doubt the Latsis family considered themselves Greek even though they had been London based for thirty years. They were part of a large, well-heeled Greek community that had settled in the British capital. Rich or nouveau riche, they all had the rich part in common, that and being Greek, which seemed to be enough to make them a very tight-knit community where everyone knew everyone and traditions were important.

As she gave the dog one last pat she caught sight of her reflection in the mirror that made the generously sized room appear even larger, and made a conscious effort to iron out the frown lines that the thought of Tatiana's invisible brother had etched in her forehead.

The invisible part was no accident. It was eighteen months since his father's stroke had brought forward the younger brother's ascension to the 'throne' of Latsis Shipping and he had kept a very low profile, something you couldn't do unless you had loyal family and friends, limitless resources and, she supposed, an inside working knowledge of how the media worked that being an ex-journalist would bring.

The point being, Chloe, she told herself sternly, *is that he is invisible. You've never met the guy, and yet here you are making all these judgements on the basis of a few comments and gut instinct.* Something that she'd have been the very first to condemn in anyone else.

'You're being a hypocrite, Chloe.'

The softly voiced self-condemnation caused Tatiana, whose eyes had drifted with a distracted expression to the fabrics pinned on one of the boards, to look up. She directed an enquiring look at Chloe, who shook her head.

'Those colours are beautiful,' Chloe said, nodding to the fabrics, and lifted a finger to touch one piece of silk that was a shade or two deeper than the blue wide-legged jumpsuit she was wearing.

'It would suit you, but I'm not sure…' Tatiana stopped and shook her head. 'Sorry, I just struggle to switch off sometimes.'

She smiled ruefully as she moved to kiss Chloe warmly on her cheek.

'The trials of being artistic,' Chloe teased.

'I don't know about that, but I do know that I am a bit of a workaholic…the work-life, home-life balance always did elude me.' A wistful expression crossed her face. 'Maybe that's why I got divorced…' She shook her dark sleek head slightly and smiled. 'But never mind about that tonight…just look at you!'

Hands resting lightly on Chloe's slim upper arms, she pushed the taller woman back a little. The sombreness of earlier drifted across her face when her glance stilled momentarily on Chloe's legs covered in loose folds of sky-blue silk, but it was gone by the time her eyes reached Chloe's face.

'You look stunning, as usual. I'm not saying it's all about a pretty face, but it definitely helps when you're trying to get men to open their wallets for a good cause…and before you ask you have my permission to put the hard sell on everyone here tonight.'

'People are usually very kind,' Chloe said.

'Especially when they are being guilted into it by the sister of a future queen. But why not use your connections? That's what I always say, and, while I might not have the right sort, your sister certainly does.' She sketched a curtsy and Chloe laughed. Her sister might be a princess and one day destined to be the Queen of Vela Main, but Chloe could not imagine anyone less *royal*. Both sisters had been brought up to believe that what a person did was more important than their title.

'I'll do my very best for the charity,' Tatiana continued in earnest now. 'In my book, I owe you.' She walked across to the mantel where the marble surface was covered with framed photos. She selected one and held it up in invitation for Chloe to see it. 'For what you did for Mel,' she finished, looking fondly at the photo she held.

Chloe shook her head, uncomfortable with the praise. As far as Chloe was concerned, the young Greek girl was her inspiration. 'I didn't do anything.' She took the frame that Tatiana offered and looked at the photo it held. It was a snap taken the previous month in a pavement café on a girls' trip to Barcelona. 'She's a brave girl.'

Chloe had known Tatiana by sight and reputation before the other woman had boosted Chloe's career by mentioning her blog in an interview she'd given covering London fashion week, two years ago now, Chloe realised, though it seemed more like a lifetime. Back then the interview was pretty much responsible for her blog becoming a profitable overnight success.

Chloe had contacted Tatiana to thank her for the plug and they had exchanged the odd email but they had never met in person.

That had happened in a very different context a year ago, after the designer's god-daughter was moved into the room next to Chloe's own in the specialist burns unit. Chloe had already been in there for three months; she'd known every crack in the ceiling and had been living vicariously through the love lives of the young nurses designated to her care.

Though the burns Chloe herself had received in a road traffic accident had been severe and painful and the healing process long, her own scars were easy to hide from view under her clothes. But the young woman in the next room had not been able to hide the damage done to her face by the fire caused by a gas explosion. Then, as if life hadn't already thrown enough rubbish at her, the day after she had arrived at the burns unit her boyfriend had dumped her, at which point Mel had turned her face to the wall and announced she didn't want to live.

As she'd listened through the partition wall

Chloe's heart had ached for the other girl. Their first conversation later that night shouted through the wall had been a one-sided affair, but it had been the first of many.

'You got her through it, Chloe,' Tatiana choked. 'I'll never forget that day I arrived and heard her laugh—you did that.'

'Mel helped me as much as I did her. Did you see the information sheet she put together for me on make-up techniques?' she asked, placing the photo back on the shelf. In doing so she accidentally nudged the one next to it and straightened it, admiring the frame; it was an antique one, the ebony wood delicately carved and rather beautiful.

Chloe was admiring the craftsmanship, running her fingers across the smooth indentations, when her glance drifted across the photo it held. Her mouth tugged into a smile; with a white-knuckle ride in the background, a younger Eugenie smiled back at her, complete with braces, from under the peak of a baseball cap with the logo of an adventure park emblazoned on it.

The jeans-clad man crouched down beside her in the shot was wearing the same cap, and he was... Chloe's smile vanished like smoke as brutal stinging reality hit her like a slap across the face. Pale as paper now, she stared at the male in the picture, wearing jeans, a tee shirt, and a teasing, carefree expression on his handsome face, a face that bore no signs of a tortured soul. There were no shadows that she felt the need to banish; he was just a regular guy...well, only if the *regular* guy in question was more handsome than any man had a right to be with a body that an Olympic swimmer might dream of possessing.

She stood like a statue staring at the photo she held in a hand that quickly developed a visible tremor—the tremor penetrating past the skin level and moving deep inside her.

By sheer force of will she released the breath she was holding in her lungs, but not the avalanche of questions whirring in dizzying succession through her brain. She felt as though a dozen people were inside her shouting so loudly she couldn't make out the individual questions.

Obviously it couldn't be him but, equally obviously, it was! The man in the photos was the same man who she had spent a never-to-be-forgotten night of lust with. If all learning experiences were as brutal as that one had been, it would not be worth getting out of bed in the morning—happily they weren't and she had moved on.

But that didn't mean she'd forgotten any of it. Forgotten the feelings of emotional hurt and humiliation that had made her physically sick the next morning when she'd realised he'd slipped away during the night. And the worst part was, she had no one to blame but herself. Because she had been the one who had followed her instincts when she'd approached him in that bar, telling herself that what she was doing was somehow meant to be... If they had been handing out awards for naivety and general stupidity that night, she would have walked away with an armful of prizes!

She'd wondered if his name really was Nik. It seemed utterly incredible to her now that she'd ever thought it part of the romantic fantasy element of their night together that she hadn't even known his full name! Time had stripped away the romantic gloss and revealed it for what it truly was—a cheap and tacky one-night stand, even if the sex had been utterly incredible.

Keeping her voice carefully casual, she half turned to Tatiana, as yet unable to tear her eyes from the snapshot. 'How old was Eugenie in this one?'

Tatiana came across and looked at the photo of her daughter and she gave a nostalgic sigh. 'Oh, that was taken on her tenth birthday, although just five minutes afterwards she was throwing up. Nik let her eat a bag of doughnuts then took her on some white-knuckle ride.'

Chloe's own knuckles were bone white where her hand was pressed to her chest. Her poor heart was vibrating against her ribcage, her insides were quivering as she told herself sternly to get a grip, not to mention a sense of proportion. It was only a photo after all, and he was old history.

Note to self, she castigated herself, *the next time you decide to make love, don't do it with a complete stranger! No, Chloe, let's be grown up and honest here—it wasn't making love, it was having sex.*

It hadn't been until she'd accepted that particular fact and realised that what they had shared that night had had absolutely nothing to do with a spiritual connection but everything to do with blind lust that she had been able to move on.

Move on—really? So why was she shaking?

She put the photo down carefully and smoothed her hands down over the fabric of her jumpsuit. She would not let that man do this to her again; she was not that silly naive girl any longer.

It had been a painful learning experience, but once her pride had stopped stinging and she had stopped feeling basically stupid she'd understood that while empty sex with anonymous strangers could obviously be physically satisfying, it probably wasn't for her. She wasn't exactly holding out for the love of her life, but she did think maybe a bit of mutual respect might be nice.

'So that's your brother Nik,' she said flatly. Sometimes it seemed as if fate had a very warped sense of humour.

Her eyes skimmed the mantel. The same man, she recognised now, was in several of the photos. It wasn't just the time difference that made him look younger, it was the absence of the cynicism and dangerous darkness she had sensed in him that night they'd had sex. What had happened to the man in these photos to turn him into the one she'd met only a few years later?

She dug her teeth into her plump lower lip as she squared her shoulders. Nik Latsis, *her* Nik—it was *so* weird to finally be able to put a full name to the man who had introduced her to sex and the fact it really was the only thing that some men were interested in. Well, his name was actually pretty irrelevant and she couldn't care less what had happened to turn him into such a cold bastard.

Not that she wasn't totally prepared to take her fair share of the blame. After all, 'naive closet romantic meets utter bastard'—it was never going to end well, was it? But she was not that person any more.

'I forgot, you haven't met Nik…have you?' Tatiana asked.

The truth or a lie?

Chloe settled for somewhere in the middle. 'He does look a little familiar…'

It's the clothes that threw me.

She brought her lashes down in a concealing sooty curtain and fanned her hot cheeks with a hand, causing the bangles she wore around her wrist to jingle. 'I think summer might finally have arrived,' she commented, ignoring the house's perfect air-conditioning system.

'You might have seen him on the television, perhaps?'

'Television?' A puzzled frown drew Chloe's brows together above her small straight nose. 'I don't think so…' Then it clicked; Tatiana wasn't talking about the present day but her brother's previous life. 'Oh, when you said he was a journalist I thought you meant he was in print…'

His sister nodded. 'He started out in print journalism but Nik was a war correspondent, and he was on the telly quite a lot actually. He won awards.' Tatiana's pride in her brother's achievements was as obvious as her distress as she enlarged. 'He spent the last two years of his journalistic career embedded with the military, in the worst war zones you can imagine. Nik has always been the sort of person who doesn't do half measures.'

He had certainly been no half-measure lover or, for that matter, halfway callous!

'On his last assignment his cameraman, his best friend, was shot.'

Chloe blanched in shock. 'Did he...?'

Tatiana nodded. 'He died in Nik's arms, but the worst part—at least for the families—was that for three days we knew that there had been a fatality. There were about ten journalists, all from different media outlets pinned down, but we didn't know their identities or who had died.'

Chloe gave an empathetic murmur of sympathy and touched her friend's hand as the older woman closed her eyes and shuddered. 'We all loved Charlie, he had just got engaged...but at the same time we were all so incredibly relieved that it wasn't Nik. It made everyone feel so guilty.'

'Survivor's guilt,' Chloe said, thinking of her sister who, after the accident from which she had escaped unscathed while Chloe had not, had been helped by a therapist. Well, Nik Latsis could afford the best help money could buy.

'You've probably seen him, although professionally he used Mum's maiden name, because he didn't want to be accused of using the family name. Does Kyriakis ring a bell...? Nik Kyriakis?'

Chloe shook her head. 'I've never watched much TV. There was a rule when we were growing up, half an hour's television a day, and then when I could decide for myself I suppose it had become a habit I never really broke. Even now I listen to the radio rather than switch on the box. It must have been hard for your brother going back to work after what had happened...?'

She had gone back to the spot where the accident had happened—had it been therapeutic? Only in the sense that she had proved to herself that she could do it?

That had been how she had privately charted her recovery: the things she was able to do, the things she could move past—looking at her scars, showing them to her family, getting into a car, driving a car... going back to the winding mountain road where the accident had happened.

'He didn't go back. A day after he returned, our dad had his stroke and couldn't run the company any more; the plan had always been for Nik to step up when the time came.' She stopped, an expression of consternation crossing her face. 'Nik doesn't ever talk about what happened to Charlie, so don't mention it tonight, will you?' she finished anxiously.

If he wanted to bottle things up in a stupid manly way, that was fine by her; she definitely wouldn't be getting him to unburden himself to her. In fact, the idea of seeing him, let alone passing the time of day with him, made the panic gathered like a tight icy ball in her stomach expand uncomfortably.

Ironically there had been a time when she would have paid good money to confront her runaway lover, but that time was long gone; she had no intention of having any sort of conversation with Nik Latsis.

He was history, a mistake, but not one she was going to beat herself up over any more, and one she really didn't want to come face to face with, but, if she absolutely had to, she was going to do it with pride and dignity.

Well, that was the plan anyway.

'I won't,' she promised as the voice in her head reminded her once again that her plans often had a habit of going wrong…

CHAPTER TWO

'You're late.' Tatiana kissed her brother's lean cheek, grimacing a little as the sprinkling of designer stubble grazed her smooth cheek before one eyebrow rose. She struggled to hide her surprise as she shifted her gaze from her impeccably turned-out brother to the woman who stood with one hand possessively on his dark-suited arm.

'You know Lucy Cavendish?' Placing a hand across her shoulders, he drew the model, her famous dazzling smile firmly in place, close into his side. The redhead tilted her head. Unusually for a woman, in her heels she topped his shoulder.

'I did Tatiana's last catwalk show in Paris. What a lovely home you have.' Lucy's expertly made-up green eyes moved admiringly around the entrance hall with its chandeliers and dramatic staircase.

Tatiana inclined her dark head and delivered an air kiss. 'Thank you. You're looking well, Lucy...' Tatiana looked up at her brother. 'You growing a beard, Nik?'

'With your views on facial hair, Ana, would I dare?'

'Oh, I just *lurve* the moody, broody look.' Lucy's eyes sparkled with teasing amusement as she stroked his cheek, letting her red fingernails slide familiarly over the stubble.

Nik removed the hand firmly from his cheek where it had lingered and whispered so only she could hear him, 'Don't overdo it, angel.'

As they moved across the hall the sound of voices and laughter drifted out through the open double doors of the drawing room.

'Anyone I know here?' Lucy asked.

'Just a small gathering of friends.'

Letting Lucy go ahead of them, Nik fell into step beside his sister. 'Hope you didn't mind me bringing Lucy.'

'Why should I mind?'

'I thought you might have had me paired off with some good breeding stock…?'

'I don't—' Tatiana stopped and gave a shake of her head, admitting ruefully, 'I suppose I do, but I just want you to be happy and…like you used to be…before…'

Impelled by an inconvenient spasm of guilt, Nik stepped in to hug his sister as suddenly the charade with Lucy seemed less of a good idea. 'I am happy.'

'I like Lucy. Are you two together?'

Nik's glance slid away. She looked so hopeful that, although this had been the idea, he felt reluctant to raise her hopes, knowing full well they were false ones. 'Early days,' he prevaricated slickly.

'I just hope Lucy won't be bored silly,' Tatiana

fretted, glancing towards the model who was walking through the double doors. 'It so happens that there is a woman here who might interest you—'

'Just when I thought I might have misjudged you,' he began sardonically.

'Not in that way!' Tatiana cut back. 'She's a good friend of mine.'

'And you wouldn't wish me on a friend?'

She slung him an irritated look. 'I just want you to set a good example when you meet her, and give a *really* generous donation to the charity—set a good example for the others.'

'Another of your worthy causes, Ana?'

'This is important to me, Nik.'

'Fine, I'll be generous.'

Chloe glanced at the clock…maybe he was a no show? Annoyed with herself for caring one way or the other, she turned her back on the doorway and focused her attention fully on the man beside her, a middle-aged Greek man who ran a property development company and seemed genuinely interested in the charity.

'I admire your enthusiasm but, and I don't want to be negative, aren't you being a little overambitious? Have you costed it up properly? The premises alone would—'

'Yes suitable premises, especially here in London, will be difficult.'

'Which is where I come in?'

Her smile glimmered. 'Your specialist knowledge and advice would be much appreciated.'

'And my money?' he added shrewdly.

Chloe's dimples appeared. 'I know that Tatiana has already spoken to you about…sorry, I really can't do this.'

The recipient of her half-empty glass of champagne looked startled and then amused as Chloe popped the finger food she had been holding into her mouth, swallowed, then smiled. 'That's better!' she said as she held out her hand for her glass.

Tipping his head, her companion replaced the crystal wine cup in it.

'Mostly I can multitask,' she told him cheerfully. 'I can do food or drink but not both at the same time. You wouldn't believe how many outfits I've emptied glasses of wine down, which makes it sound as though I always wander round with a glass of pinot in my hand, which I don't.' She delivered another smile. 'I can assure you that your donation will be in sober and sensible hands.'

The older man gave an appreciative chuckle at her tactics. 'Nice try, but I don't recall saying yes.'

Chloe conceded his point with a nod. 'But you didn't say no either and I'm an optimist.'

This time the man's chuckle was loud enough to divert some of the attention currently being given to the model who was making her entrance. 'So let me get this right, you'd like me to let you have the lease on several buildings for a fraction of what they are worth, and what do I get?'

'A warm glow knowing you've done the right thing? Or, failing that, the sort of publicity that money can't buy? The sort of publicity that comes from having your company represent the caring face of capitalism,' Chloe said, thinking wryly that she was getting quite good at this.

The man gave her an approving look tinged for the first time with respect. 'I think we should schedule a meeting, Lady—'

'Call me Chloe,' she cut in quickly.

He tipped his head in acknowledgment of her request. 'Right, Chloe, how about...?'

As the man's eyes moved over her head and his voice trailed away Chloe turned to see what had snatched his attention. The answer was immediately obvious in the shape of a glamorous redhead in a glittering gown more suited to a red carpet event than a dinner party.

Immediately tolerant of her companion's distraction, she turned to study the new arrival with some curiosity. In her experience people you had only previously seen beautifully lit on the screen or airbrushed in magazines rarely lived up to expectations, but Lucy Cavendish did and then some.

She looked beyond her hostess and the model to see if Lucy had come with someone. The woman's past boyfriends had included not one but two Hollywood A-listers, a Russian oligarch and the heir to a banking fortune, so Chloe was expecting a handsome face or serious money, someone who might be interested in donating to a good cause, perhaps?

She got neither...or rather actually what she got was both!

What she also got when she saw that Lucy's date was Nik was a jolt similar to the occasion her hair-dryer had given her an electric shock, times a hundred. A home-made and dangerously uncontrolled defibrillation that felt as if a hammer had landed on her chest and made her limbs feel weak.

But this was fine; she could totally deal with it...

Not dealing with it, Chloe!

Ignoring the mocking voice in her head, she took a deep breath, straightened her slender square shoulders, cleared her throat and readjusted the chunky necklace of raw amethyst slices that hid the pulse pounding at the base of her throat.

Breathe...she told herself, so she did, and for good measure she focused on the positive.

The worst was over and, as *worsts* went, seeing the man you'd made the mistake of sleeping with without knowing his full name was, on the scale of things, pretty low-key. A couple of minutes and her nervous system would catch up with the message and by tomorrow she'd be laughing—all right, maybe *smiling* about it.

But that was tomorrow; being realistic today, as in the next sixty seconds, she was aiming for a less ambitious goal. Her legs stopping shaking would be a good start.

She stifled a stab of impatience; her nervous system was getting this situation way out of proportion. After all, what was the worst that could happen?

And what was the worst anyway: him remembering her or him not?

Her mobile lips quirked into a smile as she considered the alternatives. An awkward reunion or a hit to her ego?

Did it really matter?

The fact that she could even ask herself the question was a sign of how much she'd changed in a little over a year. There had been a time when, despite the outward confidence she projected, what people thought about her had mattered, and she wanted the right people to like her...she wanted to fit in.

The journey to where she was today had not been easy, but everything had changed. Well, maybe not *everything*, she conceded, watching the new arrival above the rim of the glass she raised to her lips. Still, even at a distance, he had the ability to make the muscles deep in her pelvis quiver...so it was lucky she could consider this phenomenon in an objective way, wasn't it?

She might not be able to achieve total physical indifference to the male magnetism he oozed, but she was more than a bundle of hormones...despite the fact that he was, she thought, studying him through the protective sweep of her lashes, just as incredible-looking as she remembered.

They said you always remembered your first and it turned out they were right. The self-mocking glint in her wide-spaced sky-blue eyes faded and a tiny pucker appeared between her darkly defined feathery brows as she realised how intact her memory of him was, not just the way he looked, or moved, but the texture of his skin...the smell of his... She took a shaky breath and straightened her shoulders, slamming the door on that particular memory. *It was just a lapse of judgement, ancient history, Chloe,* she told herself. *Do not revisit.*

'What a stunning woman!'

Chloe started slightly at her companion's comment and tore her eyes from the tall figure whose dominant presence had made her forget about the woman he'd brought with him, although they made a pretty magnificent couple. 'Yes, she is.' Stunning was probably an understatement.

'But I'd say she's high maintenance, and I can't see her climbing Kilimanjaro.

The comment startled a laugh from Chloe. 'It sounds to me like you measure all women by some pretty high standards.'

He smiled and nodded. 'My wife is an extraordinary woman.'

Chloe stood and listened as the man launched into what was clearly his favourite subject. An emotional lump settled in her throat as he talked about his wife. What would it feel like to be the centre of a man's universe? she wondered wistfully.

Nik walked past his sister and moved to where Lucy stood.

'Maybe this isn't such a good idea,' he muttered.

'I was the one who told you that,' the model reminded him. 'But you've been my beard on more than one occasion, darling, so I kind of owe you. Do you realise how much money is in this room tonight?'

His eyes moved over the heads of the fellow guests assembled; most were members of the Greek expat community, and all of them would have considered not having a private yacht as being poverty-stricken. 'That figures. Ana is raising money for one of her causes again.'

'So you're not in danger of meeting Ms Right here. Does that mean you're dumping me already, darling?'

'Funny... God, I need a drink.'

He placed a guiding hand under Lucy's elbow, and she immediately exclaimed mockingly, 'Ooh, darling, I do so love it when you're masterful. Ah!'

She staggered a little as Nik suddenly released her arm without warning.

It was an automatic response to a soft peal of laughter that made Nik turn his head. Although it hadn't been loud, there was something attractively infectious about the sound that tugged his lips into a smile.

As his eyes surfed across the heads of the other guests to the source of the sound, his smile snuffed out as recognition crashed through his nervous system like a tsunami, and for several seconds his mind went a total blank, the effect of sheer shock colliding with serendipity.

He took a deep breath and decided he'd call it something more mundane—*convenient*. Or he would once he got his rampant, raging libido under control. It took another few deep breaths to think beyond the heat that had streaked down his body and settled painfully in his groin.

His cognitive powers were clearly working on the reserve battery. He had no idea how long he stood there paralyzed, it could have been a second or an hour, before, like a man waking from a trance, he finally shook his head.

The air trapped in his lungs hissed out as in a single urgent sweep his dark, penetrating stare took in every single detail of her. The soft shiny blonde hair falling from a slight widow's peak down her back and cut shorter at the sides to frame a vivid beautiful face, the sinuous curves of her lush body outlined by the flowing lines of blue silk.

She was stunning.

He'd sometimes wondered, generally around two a.m., if he exorcised the woman, would he finally exorcise the nightmare? The two seemed so intrinsically linked, maybe they were interdependent? It had been an intellectual exercise he'd never really taken seriously as he hadn't expected their paths to cross again.

Well, it was no longer intellectual, and neither was the roar in his blood, and he knew that not to explore the theory now that he had the opportunity would be insane!

Chloe knew Nik was standing there even before Spiros's glance moved past her, alerted by the fine invisible downy hairs on her body rising in reaction to his invisible presence.

She emptied her glass carefully, wiped her expression of anything that could be interpreted as a desire to dig a big hole and jump in it and mentally circled the wagons against attack.

If she refused to be defined by the scars she wore, she was definitely not going to be defined by a past mistake, even if he was six foot three and sinfully gorgeous!

Her defensive stance wasn't against anything he might say or do, as there was a very strong possibility that he wouldn't even remember the night they had spent together, but against her own indiscriminate hormones, which still, it seemed, responded independently of her intellect to his rampant animal magnetism.

Oh, for God's sake, Chloe, you need to get a life!

While she was silently chastising herself Nik had moved level with her. 'Spiros.'

His voice had the same rough velvet, almost tactile quality she remembered…but this time she was only shivering because she was standing in a draft, she told herself stubbornly.

They were actually standing level, side by side as he stretched out a hand to the older man, but Chloe didn't turn her head. She didn't need to, because she could already feel the sheer physical power of his tall, muscled frame.

'No Petra tonight?'

'No, she's resting up. She sprained an ankle during training.'

Nik made a sympathetic noise in his throat. 'For *another* marathon?'

The older man gave a rueful nod. 'I think it's addictive.'

'You not going to join her?'

'I know my limitations.' Chloe, who felt as though her *casual* social expression could do with some work but needed all her focus to control her too rapid breathing, took encouragement from the fact that Spiros didn't seem to notice anything amiss as he touched her arm and looked at Nik. She was still working her way up to it. 'Do you know Chloe?'

She held her breath.

'Of course; we go way back,' Nik said smoothly.

'Royal connections—you kept that quiet, Nik.'

No longer able to delay the moment, Chloe turned her head, her features arranged in a smile that was intended to project polite indifference, although she had a horrible feeling that a touch of the hunted animal had crept in!

Her first hope had been that he wouldn't remember her; the second was that up close he would have some flaw she had forgotten, but again her fairy godmother had not granted her wish.

So Plan B it was, then: be polite, be distant, be… Oh, God, on an intellectual level the dark, predatory, raw animal magnetism stuff did nothing for her, only it seemed the message hadn't filtered through to the non-intellectual parts of her that were only listening to the hormonal clamour—but then it was pretty loud.

His male beauty, and beauty was no exaggeration,

hit her at a purely visceral level. She had never experienced anything like it before—well, just the once.

His high knife-sharp cheekbones, strong aquiline nose, and angular jaw even dusted with stubble gave his face a patrician cast, though this was offset by the overtly sensual outline of his mobile mouth, twisted at that moment into a faintly cynical smile. The same emotion was reflected in his eyes, his quite simply spectacular eyes; deep set and heavy lidded, and fringed with dense, straight, spiky lashes, they were a stunning dark chocolate brown.

Pinned by those dark eyes, she experienced a 'rabbit in the headlight' moment and froze.

'How are you… *Chloe*?' He seemed to roll the word over his tongue as though he were tasting it.

As *he'd tasted her…* Chloe pushed the thought away but not before her body's core temperature had raised a few uncomfortable degrees. She lifted a hand to her neck to feel the dull vibration of her heavy pulse, and she fingered the uncut gemstones that felt cold compared to her skin.

From somewhere she manufactured a smile but the effort made her cheek muscles ache while she silently struggled to keep the door locked against forbidden memories. It wasn't about wanting to forget him, she thought, but more not wanting to remember and be reminded of the things she strongly suspected she might never experience again.

And maybe that was a good thing, she rationalised. Yes, head-banging, uninhibited sex was good— it was pretty excellent—but so was waking up with someone who actually cared for you, or for that matter was physically still there in the morning.

Refusing to acknowledge the sense of loss that still lay like a heavy weight in her chest, she reminded herself that she was looking, or she would be when the time came, for more in a man than his knowledge of the female anatomy... Hell, clumsy with feeling was infinitely preferable to the refined torture of a skilled touch with no emotion behind it.

'How long has it been?' he asked coolly.

'I'm not sure,' she lied, thinking, *Eighteen months, eight days and thirty-one minutes...not that I'm counting.*

She stiffened when without warning he bent his head and brushed her mouth lightly with his. His lips were warm, reminding her of when they had been even warmer, when he had tasted of her... The muscles low on her pelvis cramped as she stood as still as a statue, fighting with all her might the shameful urge to lean in and kiss him back.

The gasp she locked in her throat ached as she breathed in the warm male scent of him through flared nostrils.

It wasn't until he lifted his head that she realised she was holding his sleeve, though she had no memory of grabbing it. Disturbing, but there was no point reading too much into it, she decided as she let it casually fall away, ignoring the tingling sensation in her fingertips.

Nik smiled. The quiver he'd felt run through her body as he'd kissed her reminded him of just how receptive she'd been that night…how *giving* she'd been. And he'd taken… He countered the irrational slug of guilt with a reminder that she was the one who had taken the initiative that night, she'd made all the running and she hadn't acted like a woman who would take no for an answer.

His smile, the glimmer of dark danger glittering deep in his eyes, elicited an involuntary spasm of excitement in her belly that made Chloe feel ashamed.

'You look well.' She looked incredible, though up close there was less of the outdoorsy golden glow he remembered. Her skin was creamy, the faint touch of colour in her cheeks highlighting the smooth contours, the freckles along her cheekbones paler too, but she was, if anything, even more delicious than he remembered.

'Thank you, and how are you—sorry, Nik, wasn't it?'

The composed words aimed somewhere close to his left ear were prim, but the message shining in her deep cobalt-blue eyes as they glittered up at him was neither prim nor polite.

They said quite clearly, *Go to hell!*

Her reaction threw him off his stride, in the same way he realised he'd have been thrown if he'd reread a favourite book and found a main character had suddenly been given a different personality.

Except the woman in his dreams had never had a personality beyond being warm, giving, passionate and available when he had needed her, and he had not been curious about what lay beyond those qualities.

Realising that there *was* a beyond came with a sense of shock as Nik struggled to consider her negative reaction to him dispassionately, but got sidetracked by his own reaction to her.

The problem being there was very little room left for dispassion after the explosive blast of primal desire that obliterated everything else when he looked at her. It was like walking…no, *running* full pelt into a ten-foot wall of lust.

The time it took his stupefied brain to push past this fresh blast of raw hunger was only moments but it felt longer, and the mere fact that he *had* to make the effort deepened the frown lines in Nik's broad forehead.

In his previous life, he had cultivated dispassion until it required no effort, and it was second nature. He'd seen men and women in his old line of work who hadn't managed to do that, and the personal toll it had taken on them had not been good to see. You needed to be able to keep an emotional distance.

He had witnessed acts of bravery and self-sacrifice that were humbling, but for every one of those inspiring acts there were a hundred acts and images of suffering and inhumanity. You carried those nightmare images around with you and they ate you from the inside.

The sheer absurdity of comparing a war zone to a dinner party where people were toting glasses of wine instead of automatic weapons almost dredged up a smile. *Almost.*

CHAPTER THREE

'I'M—'

'With Lucy Cavendish…' Chloe paused, head tilted in challenge, to let the reminder sink in and had the satisfaction of seeing an expression of shock chase across his handsome face.

'Lucy…hell, I forgot about her!' A quick glance located the model, who was deep in conversation with another guest. Nik dragged a hand across his hair-roughened jaw in annoyance; he must have left her standing there looking like… He gritted out a curse. 'I'm never going to hear the end of this.'

The wrathful, choking gasp of sheer disbelief that escaped Chloe's lips drew his attention back to her face.

If there had been even the *faintest* suggestion of guilt in his reaction, she thought it would have gone some way to redeeming him…actually, no, it wouldn't!

Wanting to make excuses for him made her even angrier—as if there could be any excuse for a man who arrived with one woman and then came on to another with all the subtlety of a sledgehammer!

It made her wonder whose bed he had walked straight into after being in hers.

There had been a time when the thought would have hurt...now it simply made her stomach quiver queasily.

'It's so inconsiderate of a woman to expect you to remember that you came with her.' She produced a saccharine-sweet sympathetic smile, waiting until he frowned slightly in response to her comment before slinging out sarcastically, 'I suppose she even expects you to be there when she wakes up in the morning.'

The words hung there, every syllable oozing with exactly the sort of subtext Chloe had wanted to avoid. She sounded just like what she hated most: a victim.

Someone to pity.

Her narrow-eyed glare dared him to show it, but, although her comment had surprised a flicker of re-action, it was something else she saw move at the backs of his eyes. Fine, she could deal with something else, actually *anything* else, but *pity*.

'You were asleep.' This was the reason he avoided one-night stands; there was the potential for the stranger you went to bed with assuming that one night of sex connected you in some deep and mean-ingful way.

'I'm not talking about me.' She lifted her feathery brows in an attitude of mild surprise that he should think otherwise, then, willing herself not to blush, she pronounced bluntly, 'We had sex but we were not in a relationship. Although it would have been useful if you had woken me as I had somewhere I needed to be.' She wrinkled her brow, giving the impression she was trying to recall the sequence of events—events that couldn't have been more indelibly imprinted on her had someone branded them into her soul. 'I'm pretty sure I was late.' In her head she clutched the invisible award to her chest as a voice pronounced, *And the award for most convincing liar goes to... Chloe Summerville!*

The dream had once more become a nightmare before he'd ever reached the moment where he'd made the choice to leave her sleeping, not that waking her had ever really been an option. Good manners versus getting to his dying father's bedside after receiving the call about his stroke had been a no brainer.

And yes, he'd been relieved not to have to speak to her again.

Relieved to avoid the potential morning-after awkwardness and recriminations. It hadn't been his first one-night stand, but those other encounters had all been with fellow journalists, and there had been some mutual respect on a professional level between him and the smart, independent women who had shared his bunk. There had been no need to explain the desire he had felt to escape the sights and sounds of war for a few hours and let passion drown it all out. The connections had been brief, pleasurable, but nothing deeper remained.

He wouldn't have cared if any of them had forgotten his name, or implied that the memory they'd walked away with after sleeping with him was that they'd had somewhere else to be but had overslept!

His ego took a few startled seconds to recover from the blow while recognising the irrationality of his reaction. Chloe Summerville's cool attitude was *exactly* what he looked for in women he gravitated towards. Women who had a male approach to sex; women who did not expect or even welcome sentiment in their liaisons, but enjoyed sex in an uncluttered and simple way.

'Sorry, I had someplace I needed to be too…but unlike you I wasn't too late.'

His father's prognosis had been grim. The doctors had been all for calling time and letting nature take its inevitable and cruel course, but his mother had insisted they try a third lot of clot-busting drugs. When Nik had walked into the room, his father had been sitting up with nothing but a slight hesitation in his speech to show he'd even had a stroke and people had been talking about miracles.

'Well, it's…nice to see you again, lovely to catch up…' Chloe said absently, adopting the tone you used when you bumped into someone whose name you kept forgetting. 'But if you'll excuse me, tonight is about work and I need to circulate.' Giving her best impression of a woman with her priorities firmly sorted, she flashed him a generic smile and turned back towards where Spiros stood talking to a small group of guests.

Even if he'd taken everything else out of the equation the dismissal would have awoken his interest, if only for the fact that it was new territory for Nik. Women did not usually walk away from him. His curiosity overcame his irritation… So, all right, it was something a lot stronger than irritation, but he didn't need to waste energy trying to identify it as it morphed seamlessly into the much easier to deal with lust and his eyes became riveted on her long, sinuous curves and the gentle sway of her hips.

If sleeping with her again was the way to finally lay his nightmares to rest, great. If not, the trying was going to be fun. Not trying at all had stopped being a possibility the second he'd set eyes on her.

The frustration raging through his veins made it hard for him to formulate a plan of action, as there had been no plan required in his dreams. On a conservative estimate he'd been making love to Chloe every other night for the past year…except this wasn't a dream, it—*she*—was the real deal! And Chloe Summerville was *more* in every way than the woman he remembered. A halfwit could have worked that out in thirty seconds.

And Nik was accounted to be quite intelligent.

She had been pulled into a group several feet away from where he stood alone, and he watched like a hawk as she lowered her lashes over a smile in response to something Spiros had said. In profile he could see the little quiver of the fine muscles in her throat and along the delicate line of her jaw, and he wondered why he found it so fascinating.

Was he finally losing his mind?

Chloe's legs were still shaking but, as there was no longer any imminent possibility they would give out beneath her, she let go of the image of herself lying on the floor and people staring down at her. Sad, they'd say, she used to be able to stand on her own two feet... She suddenly realised a moment too late to avoid awkwardness that the extended silence was one she was meant to fill. Chloe gave an apologetic smile.

'Sorry. I wasn't following; I was just trying to remember if I put an aspirin in my bag.' She delved into the limited depths of her bag, her hair falling in a concealing curtain around her face.

Still she couldn't quite escape the conversation replaying in her head... When he had asked her how long it had been since they'd met, she'd had a nasty shock. Up to that point she hadn't known that she knew the answer even to the day and hour, but she clearly did... God, but it was terminally depressing.

What, she asked herself, had she ever seen in him?

Beyond of course the face, the body, the high-voltage charge of raw, scalp-tingling sensuality he had oozed... Beyond that, nothing at all!

Other than the dark brooding aura tinged with danger and a touch of vulnerability.

Well, he wasn't vulnerable now and she was no longer the romantic little fool she had been, but, considering her reaction to Nik just now, it was lucky that she had decided celibacy was the way to go... Not for ever—just short term. Who knew what the future held?

But one of the advantages of celibacy was that she

could stand here now and look at this incredibly...
really incredibly sexy man, and remember, in a way
that sort of felt as if it had happened to someone else,
how it had felt to have his warm, no, *hot* flesh slide
over hers and it wasn't a problem.

God, you are such a liar, Chloe Summerville.

In fact, if she had truly believed she was cut out
for celibacy long term, it would have simplified life
in general, she concluded, studiedly ignoring the
scornful voice in her head.

'You have a headache?' a woman whose name
Chloe couldn't recall, despite being normally good
about that sort of thing, asked.

'It's not that bad.'

Then Nik touched her arm. She knew it was him
without even looking at his long fingers brown
against her skin, and suddenly it was *extremely* bad.
The thump, thump in her temples was keeping time
with her heartbeat as Chloe felt a primitive thrill
run along her nerve endings. Deeply ashamed, she
waited for the fluttering inside her to subside and,
under cover of looking in her bag again, calmed her
breathing.

'Lost something?' he asked.

'Just an aspirin; I'm getting a headache.' *And
I'm looking at it.* But she wasn't. She looked everywhere but at the tall dynamic figure towering over
her, which was not something that happened often
when you were five feet ten.

Eyes she had control over, but not her thoughts that
drifted back to the moment she had first seen him,

as if she were stuck in some sort of mind-destroying time loop. The last thing she had anticipated when they had crowded into the almost empty bar was that she would leave with a total stranger. She'd never been a person who was led by her hormones and, while she'd had any number of male friends, she'd not had a lover.

She had dated, obviously, but things had usually ended in an *it's me not you* sort of way. And she had started to think it was—that she was simply one of those women who weren't highly sexed.

Until that night.

Whatever had been lying dormant within her had surfaced with a vengeance!

'Oh, Chloe, have you met Olivia?' Spiros asked, oblivious to any atmosphere, drawing a striking middle-aged woman into the group.

Chloe shook her head, welcoming the opportunity to turn her back on the biggest mistake of her life to this point.

'Olivia, this is the young woman I was telling you about. Olivia was very interested when I told her about your project; her husband, who isn't here tonight, is a plastic surgeon.'

Chloe beamed. 'That's why you look familiar!' she exclaimed. 'I've seen the photo of you that your husband has on his desk at work.'

Listening to her, Nik twisted his lips in a cynical smile. The plastic surgeon must be very good at his job because you really couldn't tell Chloe had had any work done at all. Whatever it had been, he decided, watching her expressive face as she chatted with animation to the older woman, it hadn't been Botox.

Though now he thought about it there were changes, though not those he associated with surgical intervention. Some of the youthful softness he remembered in her face had gone, had become more *refined*, revealing a breathtaking bone structure. As he continued to study her the therapeutic benefits having sex with her might bring to him slid to the back of his mind, leaving having sex with her as soon as possible just because he wanted to very much in the forefront.

'So sorry,' he interjected.

This time with the touch of his cool hand on her wrist Chloe couldn't stop herself turning towards him; the intention was defensive, the result was not!

He was standing very close to her and she stiffened, her chest lifting as she took a deep breath and held it while, inside her ribcage, her heart rate climbed like that of an athlete waiting for the starter's pistol.

Fighting the impulse to cover her mouth with her hand as his eyes drifted to her lips and stayed there, she waited until he had stepped back far enough for her to escape the heat from his body to release the air trapped in her lungs, but unfortunately his aura of sexuality had a wider radius.

'You don't mind if I steal Chloe, do you?' he asked, taking her elbow. To an observer his attitude as much as his body language was suggestive of a long and intimate relationship with her.

The suggestion might have drawn a smile from her if her facial muscles were not locked in what she sincerely hoped was an expression of indifference. What they had shared had been little more than a collision! Granted, an extremely *intimate* collision... As a series of freeze-frame images flashed through her head they had an almost out-of-body quality to them.

She had fallen asleep in his arms, and as she'd drifted off she'd found herself thinking that she had never felt more comfortable with anyone in her life.

Comfortable was something she didn't feel right now as he half dragged her across the room; if she could, she would happily have crawled out of her skin. But pulling away would have made her look even more conspicuous.

He came to a halt in one of the deep window embrasures where the half-drawn curtains gave it an element of privacy that Chloe could have done without.

She immediately pulled away, retreating as far as physically possible. He countered her action by raising one sardonic brow.

Chloe embraced the anger that prickled through her with something approaching relief, while simultaneously ignoring the worrying excitement that popped like champagne bubbles in her bloodstream, making her feel light-headed, which probably made the little head toss with attitude she gave a mistake, but she did it anyway.

'What the hell do you think you are you doing?' she muttered under her breath.

The silky fair hair that streamed down her slender back settled into attractive waves around her face. As he watched the process he suddenly remembered it had taken a long time to gather it all up in his hand and each time his fingers had brushed her skin she had shivered.

Good question, Nik. What the hell was he doing?

He said the first thing that came into his head. 'So you're a royal of where?'

'Do you mind? I was having an important conversation back there!'

He shrugged his magnificent shoulders. 'So have a conversation with me.' *So I can look at you.* 'And if by important you mean you were about to get a donation for whatever charity it is... I'll double it,' he said casually.

She expelled a hissing sigh. 'Am I meant to be impressed by your altruism, seeing as you don't even know what the money is for?'

'Does it matter?'

She gritted her teeth and fought the impulse to slap him—anything that would break through his armour of sheer selfishness.

'Clearly not to you!' she countered contemptuously.

'You still haven't told me...'

'Told you what?'

'Royal how?'

She gave a growling sound of aggravation through

her clenched teeth. 'My family,' she said finally in a bored, reading-the-telephone-directory voice, 'lives on East Vela; it's an island.' Most people didn't have a clue where it was, though most had watched the recent royal wedding on the television.

Nik proved a little more informed.

'The Vela that has just been reunified.'

She nodded.

'So where do you fit in?'

Chloe used her stock reply. 'I'm the sister who hasn't married the future King.'

'Lucky you.'

It was not the usual stock response and Chloe bristled defensively at the slightest suggestion of criticism of her brother-in-law. 'Lucky me? Most people envy my sister!'

'Do you?' The speed with which she had jumped to the man's defence made him wonder if there wasn't a personal element to her reaction, and the possibility tugged his lips into a cynical sneer.

The sheer unexpectedness of his response made Chloe blink and shake her head. 'What sort of question is that?'

He ignored the spiky question and reverted to his original comment. 'I meant lucky because a queen with any kind of history has to be a nightmare for the PR people-lovers with kiss-and-tell stories coming out of the woodwork,' he explained, pointing out the obvious.

She was tempted, but only for a moment, to retort that her *only* lover was more concerned about keeping a low profile than she was, so that was problem solved. But what would he say if he knew that? The question circling in her head jolted her back to her usual common-sense mode.

Unable to adopt a sufficiently *shallow socialite* tone while she was looking at the outline of his disturbingly sensual mouth, Chloe switched her focus to his hard, stubble-covered jaw. 'Yeah, it really was a lucky escape for me,' she began, and then stopped, her eyes darkening as the memories of feeling cheap and used, still fresh and raw, surfaced once again. Why was she pretending to be someone she wasn't? She didn't care what he thought of her and her chin lifted a notch in defiance. 'Oh, why don't you just call me an easy lay and have done with it?'

His half-closed eyes lifted from the heaving contours of her breasts and collided with her blue shimmering glare. She pulled in a deep breath and, lower lip caught between her white teeth, took a moment to control the quiver in her voice before she drove home her point.

'Just because you treated me with zero respect, Nik, do not assume that I don't respect myself!'

She was lecturing him! Nik was too astonished to immediately react to her accusation and too ashamed to admit anywhere but in the privacy of his own thoughts that he probably deserved it.

'And for the record this is the twenty-first century; nobody expects a prince to marry a virgin bride these days!'

'Again, that's lucky or the European royalty would

be a doomed species...' As he spoke the gaps between his words extended as he almost lost track of what he was saying. Her currently outraged attitude meshed with the images and little snatches of memory from that night in his head, flickering faster and faster until he could hear his own thoughts from back then—*so deliciously tight,* so *excitingly shocked...* As if everything *was* new to her, shockingly new! Had she been a virgin?

'We are a doomed species anyway, I suspect,' she was saying. 'They call it evolution, but I suppose royals are a bit like dinosaurs. In the future there will be entire floors of museums displaying our fossilised remains in glass cases.'

'Evolution is preferable to revolution... How didn't I treat you with respect?' he suddenly shot at her, trying to catch her by surprise so she would answer him truthfully.

She said nothing.

'So you *did* have a problem with me walking out on you?'

Her eyelids half lowered. 'It was a first for me, I admit.'

A first? A first of what, exactly? The idea that she could have been a virgin, considering the way she'd approached him that night, was totally crazy, and even if it were true, did he actually want to know? Didn't he have enough guilt in his life without adding any more? The problem was that now the idea was out there, swimming around in his brain, he had to voice it, even if he did end up looking like a fool.

'The first time you'd woken up with the pillow beside you empty, or the first time for you full stop?'

She felt a trickle of sweat trace a sticky path down her back and decided to deliberately misunderstand him. 'First one-night stand? You really haven't read any of the surveys in the magazines, have you? Everyone's doing it.'

'The thing about those surveys is that people lie.'

His intent stare made her feel as though he were looking directly into her head and she could feel the blush she was willing away materialise until she felt as though every inch of her skin were on fire.

'And I'm not talking about one-night stands,' he added flatly.

Pushed into a corner, she reacted with cool-eyed hauteur. 'I really don't think there's any need for a post-mortem...but if you're asking what I think you're asking, I don't think I owe you any explanation.'

'So you *were* a virgin.'

'Weren't we all once...even you?' Hard as it was to imagine. 'How old were...?' Her eyes flew wide. 'Oh, God, I said that out loud, didn't I?'

'I was sixteen and she was...older.' The glamorous, bored stepmother of one of his friends at boarding school, and he'd been very willing to be seduced. 'But even at sixteen I would not have thought it the greatest idea in the world to pick up a total stranger in a bar and have sex with them.'

'It wasn't exactly planned!'

'Look, I'm fine with youthful rebellion. I've been

there and done that, but I sure as hell don't much like being the unwitting partner of it.'

Chloe felt her embarrassment slip away, incredulous anger rushing in to fill the vacuum; his hypocrisy was staggering. 'So now you're the victim and *I* should apologise? Not that there is a victim, I mean… I just saw you that night and…' She met his eyes and looked away. 'Oh, for heaven's sake, it's not as though you were fighting me off with a stick, is it?'

A laugh was wrenched from Nik's throat before he closed his eyes and wondered how a man could feel like a defiler of innocence and incredibly turned on at the same time.

'I guess I crushed a few of your romantic illusions,' he said heavily.

She sucked in a deep breath. 'Well, it had to happen sometime so relax; after the therapy I'm totally fine.' She stopped suddenly, remembering that she was talking to someone who might really have needed therapy for something more than making a poor choice. She'd slept with the wrong man; he'd seen his friend die in his arms. 'Not that there is anything funny about therapy…in fact, it's a very useful tool,' she told him earnestly.

A nerve began to slowly clench and unclench in Nik's jaw, and it had a mesmeric effect on Chloe.

'What has my sister been saying to you about me?'

Chloe began to shake her head, thinking his sister's opinion of him proved that love really *was* blind… *Lust*, however, was a completely different proposition… She tilted her chin and refused to acknowledge the shameful ache of arousal she felt just looking at him, but in her own defence this man took the term eye candy to a whole new level! 'Absolutely nothing…except of course that you are an expert on just about everything. To be totally honest with you, I'd got sick and tired of hearing the sound of your name.'

All the time she had been ripping up at him he'd stood there looking at her in that disturbing way. When she finally stopped talking he placed a finger against her lips just to make sure he was not interrupted. 'You are really, truly *perfect*! Hell, I so want to take you to bed right now.'

The raw driven declaration, barely more than a husky whisper, made her catch her breath, the air between them shimmering with suppressed sexual tension. She could only stand there, her eyes wide as he moved his finger down her cheek, the light touch, barely there, making her shiver with delicious sensation.

Her eyes had half closed in drugged pleasure when from somewhere a sliver of sanity shattered the sensual haze.

What the hell are you doing, Chloe?

'Does that line really work for you?' She was pretty sure it did, and she'd have been yet another of the women who'd fallen for it if it hadn't been for that one word…*perfect*! He still saw her as the woman with the perfect body she remembered from eighteen months ago.

The ugly reality would surely have him running for the hills.

'It isn't a line.' His heavy-lidded eyes moved in a slow approving sweep from the top of her glossy head to her feet in kitten-heeled slingbacks. 'You look fantastic.'

'Yes, I know.' But *looks*, she reminded herself, were cruelly deceptive. Even if she had been tempted to accept the offer he was making, she knew that it wasn't about her; it was only the perfect body that he wanted.

The body that no longer existed.

Loss was something she didn't normally allow herself to feel but it slammed through her now.

'I'd forgotten how direct you were. It's really refreshing,' he said.

The memory of how direct she'd been brought a flush to her face. If she ever regained the sort of confidence she'd once had, then it wouldn't be with a man like Nik Latsis. It would be with a man who could see beyond her scars, and who would want her for the woman she really was.

'Ah, well, I'm so glad to have refreshed you, and speaking of which, if you'll excuse me, I'm going to refresh my glass. I'm not interested—is that direct enough for you?'

'I'd be devastated if I believed you,' he returned with a level look.

'Believe me, you are the *last* man in the world I would be interested in!' Interested, no, she was *fascinated*…but equally she recognised it was an unhealthy 'moth to the flame' sort of fascination. One that would only lead to her being burnt up, and not in a good way.

'Never mind, Nik. If I was interested you'd be the first man to know…or maybe the second,' Lucy Cavendish corrected. 'My dentist has the loveliest eyes.' Her smile deepened as she looked at Chloe. 'So have you.'

Chloe's face burned with embarrassed heat.

Just how long had the model been standing there listening to them? And yet she didn't seem even a jot put out by what she'd heard… Maybe because she had heard it all before? Chloe speculated. Maybe she was fine with sharing her man? Or even…? *None of my business,* she told herself, swiftly closing down this lurid avenue of speculation.

'Dinner is served and I'm starving,' Lucy drawled, then, turning to Chloe, she added, 'I loved your blog, by the way. If you want to know any of the dirty details on this one, I'm the girl to come to.' She gave her a conspiratorial wink before leading Nik away.

CHAPTER FOUR

DAZED AND BEWILDERED, Chloe experienced a quite irrational sense of abandonment as she watched the couple walk away arm in arm. She hung back as the guests made their way through the double doors, which had been flung open revealing a long table covered in white linen and groaning with antique crystal and fine china. The last to enter the room, Chloe saw that Eugenie was directing guests to their places. As she watched Nik bent down and kissed his niece's cheek.

'I'm working, Uncle Nik,' she remonstrated, kissing him back despite her protest.

Chloe watched him throw a quizzical glance at his sister. 'Child labour, Ana?'

'Laying the foundations for a healthy work ethic, you mean,' Tatiana shot back.

'You were right the first time.' Eugenie raised her voice as her uncle moved away. 'No, you're down that way, Uncle Nik,' the girl called, pointing in the opposite direction from where her uncle was heading.

'No, kiddo, I think I'm sitting here.' Nik picked

up one of the place cards and held it up to show her his name.

His niece frowned, pulling a slim tablet from her pocket. 'But I thought…'

Her mother leaned in and closed the tablet. 'It's fine, love,' she said drily, picking up a card from the floor and, glancing at the name on it, placing it at a gap on another table.

Her brother reacted to the pointed look she sent him with an unrealistic innocent expression.

Watching the interplay, Chloe had a sinking feeling, and so she was unsurprised when the teenager smiled at her and directed her towards where Nik was holding out a chair next to his place.

Chloe's eyes brushed his and her stomach vanished completely!

The prospect of spending the entire meal next to him made her feel nauseous. *Oh, get over yourself, Chloe,* she told herself sternly. *What's the worst that can happen—you get indigestion?*

'Now, isn't this nice?' The innocence was gone and instead there was a feral gleam of challenge in his steady stare as he stood behind the chair waiting for her to take her seat. 'So cosy,' he murmured, pushing in the chair neatly behind her legs before taking his own seat.

Cosy? Huh. Chloe decided, nodding to the woman seated to her right, that was the last word she would use where Nik Latsis was concerned, so she didn't voice any of the half-dozen sarcastic responses that trembled on her tongue. The best way to cope with this situation was simply not to rise to the bait; instead, she would rise above it.

'Thank you,' she murmured, rather pleased with her aloof little nod, a nice combination of condescension and coldness. Yes, she decided, the high ground was *definitely* the route to take in this situation. Right but not very easy when even without looking at him she could feel the male arrogance he was radiating.

He set his elbows on the table and looked at her. 'You're dying to ask me, so go ahead.'

She squared her shoulders, and took a long swallow of the very good wine, looking at the plate that had been put in front of her; it smelt fantastic but she had virtually no appetite. 'Sorry, I don't know what you mean.'

'I'll put you out of your misery, then. You're right, Lucy and I are not a couple, just, as they say, good friends.'

'Well, that's a relief. I wouldn't have been able to sleep tonight if you hadn't explained that to me.'

Far from annoying him, her sarcastic riposte drew a broad grin. 'Ana often invites potential mates to her cosy little dinners.'

'This dinner isn't little or cosy or, as it happens, all about you.'

A smile quivered across his lips. 'Ouch!'

'You could always try dating agencies, which would be a bit more scientific than relying on your sister to set you up,' she suggested.

'I've always thought a sense of humour is overrated, especially when I'm the joke. Ana wants to see me settled down; she thinks that marriage is the magic bullet that will solve all my problems. She means well but it can get…tiresome. But you don't want to know all that; the point is… Lucy isn't my girlfriend.'

'Why are you telling me this?'

'Because I want you to say yes when I ask you to come home with me tonight.'

Having delivered this conversational dynamite in the same manner a normal person would discuss the weather, he calmly turned to the man on his right and inserted himself into the conversation concerning the most recent banking scandal.

Chloe couldn't hear what they saying, because she couldn't hear anything much beyond the static buzz inside her own head. Of course, she was going to say no to him.

She rested her hand on her thigh, running her fingers lightly across the raised damaged skin under the fine blue silk. The outline of the ugly ridges beneath her fingertips had an instant mind-clearing effect, and the doubts fluttering around in her head vanished. A man who hadn't bothered hanging around to say goodbye the morning after they'd had mind-blowing sex wasn't interested in her emotional journey; he only wanted perfect.

'I used to be a fan of your blog…is there any chance of you resurrecting it?'

Chloe snapped clear of her reverie before it reached self-pitying territory and smiled at the woman sitting across from her who'd just asked her a question. 'Well, never say never, but at the moment I can't see it happening.'

The woman looked disappointed. 'You were very successful and you had so many followers, but I suppose you've got your hands full at the moment.'

Nik had disengaged from the conversation he was involved in and took an indulgent time out to study Chloe, watching as the fine muscles along her firm jawline quivered beneath the smooth creamy skin. Her long fingers tightened around the stem of her wine glass, and he noted the absence of rings.

'So what is this blog I keep hearing about?' Nik asked curiously.

He had just announced his intention of inviting her to spend the night in his bed and now he was making small-talk! Did he compartmentalise his life as neatly as he did his conversations? she wondered, envying him the ability.

'It was a fashion blog. I started out just writing about things that caught my attention, fashion tips, current style trends, that sort of thing, and it took off after your sister—' she glanced towards Tatiana '—gave me a plug.'

'Was?'

She nodded and directed her gaze to the wine swirling around in her glass. The crystal caught the light of the chandelier that hung over the table, sending little sparks of colour through the flute. 'I've moved on to other things.'

Dreams were not reality, they were an exaggerated, distorted form of it, and Nik had assumed his memory had been guilty of making some editorial cuts, smoothing out the flaws and adding a rosy tinge to the reality of the woman who had shared her body with him. *Sharing* hardly seemed an adequate description for the lack of barriers that had existed between them—but actually sitting beside her now, he realised that the reality was even better than his memory. And she'd been a virgin—her cagey reaction had virtually confirmed his stab in the dark—but it still didn't seem possible.

'I suppose a lot of people would get bored quickly if they didn't have to worry about paying the rent, *Lady* Chloe.'

His efforts to needle her into a response were rewarded when she slung him an angry glare and drained her glass in one gulp.

It was not the first time that someone had added the title and her background together and come up with the totally inaccurate conclusion that she was a lady of leisure who didn't have to work for a living.

They weren't to know that, although her family had the aristocratic family tree and the castle that came with it, they didn't have any money, which accounted for the holes in the roof, the ancient plumbing and the fact she and her sister had always been expected to work for their living. Of course, it didn't make them poor by most people's standards but the man sitting there judging her was not *most* people.

Even at this table, where conservative estimates of all the guests' wealth were eye watering, he was probably worth more than them all combined.

Her indignation fizzed hot under the surface as she fixed him with a smile of dazzling insincerity and batted her lashes like the social butterfly he seemed to think she was.

'Oh, and how I envy the *little* people with their *simple* lives… I've even heard that some people don't bathe in ass's milk or have anyone to put toothpaste on their brushes for them.'

'Did I say something to annoy you?' His glance slid from her blazing eyes to her tightened lips and his body stirred involuntarily as he remembered kissing them, tasting her… The need to do so again as soon as possible made his body do more than stir.

She shuddered out a breath and their gazes connected. Chloe was aware that she was breathing too fast as she fought to escape the message that seemed to vibrate with a palpable force in the air between them.

'You breathing annoys me!' *Too much honesty, Chloe,* she thought, aware she had lost her moral high ground the moment the childish admission left her lips, but at least she was no longer thinking about kissing him, which was good. Taking a deep breath, she glanced around to see if anyone had heard her comment. Greatly relieved when it seemed they hadn't, she directed a straight look at him. 'Look, Tatiana is a friend and I don't want to be rude to her brother.' *Or go to bed with him.*

'Or alienate a potential donor?'

Chloe realised guiltily that the sobering reminder

was necessary. She *was* in danger of forgetting that tonight was about getting the charity off the ground. Tatiana had done her bit, inviting people with deep pockets who were sympathetic to Chloe's aims, but the rest was up to her.

It was a crowded market; there were so many good causes around Chloe knew that she needed to make a positive impression on these people if she was going to make a difference.

'True, and all donations are gratefully received.'

'You already have Ana on board, so how long have you two known one another?'

'She took an interest in my fashion blog, but we'd never met. We actually met in person only a year ago, a few months after the—' She stopped abruptly, her lashes lowering in a protective sweep.

'After what?' Against his better judgement, her sudden impersonation of a clam made him curious, and, even though he knew on one level that this should be an exercise in exorcising his demons, he found he really wanted to know what made her tick.

'After I got bored with it,' she countered, deliberately not analysing her reluctance to discuss the accident with him. She applied herself to her starter, trying to simulate an interest in her food, which she couldn't even taste.

Nik, who continued to ignore his own food, propped an elbow on the table and studied her. 'So what do you do now, besides selling raffle tickets?'

'I'm working to raise the profile of the charity.'

For *working*, Nik translated, she had probably arranged a charity fashion show or a masked ball, which was fine, but hardly enough to stimulate someone of her obvious intelligence. His dark brows flattened as he recognised but struggled to explain a sense of disappointment.

It wasn't as though he had any expectations of her, and God knew she wouldn't be the only titled socialite who didn't hold down a real job. Maybe it was just that he was surrounded by strong, driven women. His mother was a partner in a law firm, who had raised brows when she had continued to work after she was married, and his sister juggled a successful career with motherhood. Ana might be in the fashion industry, but he knew that his sister would have been appalled if her daughter had thought being decorative was more important than getting an education, which made this friendship with Chloe all the more puzzling. He really couldn't see what the two women had in common.

'I don't have my wallet with me, but I do have my chequebook and I am a dutiful brother,' Nik said.

Before Chloe could react to the patronising undertone that brought a sparkle of annoyance to her eyes, across the table an elderly silver-haired Greek businessman began to laugh.

'I wouldn't be so quick to give her a blank cheque, my boy. If that young lady gets you in a headlock, she's relentless.'

Nik elevated a dark brow. 'I thought that was just a rumour.'

'She's cost me more than my wife.'

'Which one, Joseph?'

The question caused a ripple of laughter around the table.

'It's all in a good cause,' Tatiana said, patting his hand. The soft murmur of agreement that followed her words left Nik feeling excluded, as he seemed to be the only one who didn't have a clue what the old man was talking about.

'And what *cause* would that be?'

The rest of the table had returned to their own conversations and Nik's curiosity was the only thing left to distract himself from the ache in his groin. Messing with the seating arrangements had seemed like a good idea at the time, but he really hadn't factored in the painful strength of the hard throb of need, which was becoming increasingly impossible to think past.

Insane... When had a woman made him feel like this? He looked at her mouth, remembering how it had tasted, and wondered. Last night about three a.m. she had vanished from his dreams like mist, as she always did. What if he woke up with her in his arms for real? Would she and the nightmares be gone for ever?

Chloe shifted in her seat before looking up from her contemplation of her empty glass. Strands of blonde hair fell across her cheek and she brushed them away, puzzling at her own reluctance to discuss the subject so passionate to her heart. It struck her as ironic considering she'd spent the evening selling the cause, and in all honesty she felt she was pretty good at it.

'Helping burns victims. Originally the idea was to raise money for specialised equipment for the NHS that under normal circumstances they can't afford.'

It was the last thing he had expected to hear. 'And now?'

'Oh, we'll still do all those things, but, in conjunction with that goal, we are also aiming to set up centres where there is access to physical therapy like physiotherapy, rehabilitation and so forth, alongside psychotherapy and counselling, plus the practical stuff like learning how to apply make-up to cover scarring and job retraining. In essence it will be a one-stop shop where people can access what they need or just come in for a cup of coffee and a chat.'

He watched her face change as she spoke and the animation was not something that could be faked. She was truly passionate about this charity. 'That is a very ambitious scheme for someone so young.'

She lifted her chin. 'I really don't see how my age has anything to do with it, and I was always brought up to aim high.'

'So you're saying positive thinking works miracles?'

'I'm not after miracles. Everything we are aiming for is achievable and I have the facts and figures to prove it. As for positive thinking…well, that is helpful, but there comes a point when action is needed. This isn't some sort of game to me.'

'I can see that.' His admission came with some reluctance. He didn't want to admire her; he wanted to bed her. *Liking* was not a prerequisite for compatibility in the bedroom. In fact, it was a complication.

'So why this particular cause?' he asked.

'I met someone in hospital...'

'You were ill?' He visualised an image of her lying in a hospital bed and didn't dare analyse the emotion that tightened in his gut.

She dodged his interrogative stare and looked down at her fingers, watching as they tightened around the stem of the wine glass she held. She had recovered her composure by the time she responded, explaining in a quiet measured voice wiped clean of any emotion, 'I parted company with a motorbike.' The shaky laugh was less planned. 'Or so they tell me.'

The how and why remained a blank to this day. In fact the only thing she remembered that might not have been a dream was climbing on the bike calling to her sister to follow her, and then nothing until the smell of burning and sirens. If it hadn't been for her brother-in-law she wouldn't even remember that.

She wouldn't be here at all.

Some people needed their drug of choice to be happy, but she was alive and that was all the buzz she needed. The knowledge that life was so fragile had made her determined to do something with her life that would leave something tangible behind.

'I hope the driver didn't get off scot-free.' The corners of his mouth pulled down in disapproval as he imagined her slim arms around some leather-clad idiot, her lithe body pressing into him.

'I wasn't riding pillion.' It occurred to her that her pride was misplaced; after all, how well had the going-solo scenario been serving her so far?

The problem with being so independent was that when you messed up there was no one else to share the blame with.

'So you like to be in charge?'

'In charge? If by that you mean do I like to make my own decisions, then, yes, I do,' she told him calmly. 'It's never been my fantasy to be dominated by a male chauvinist.' *Just a bit too much protesting there, Chloe!*

'You're a risk taker, then?'

Holding his gaze and reacting to the challenge glittering in the ebony depths was about the most dangerous thing she had done in a long time. 'I'm not the one who made a living dodging bullets.'

He stiffened, and their eyes connected once more. The shadows in his gaze belonged to a man who had seen far too much trauma for one lifetime. A moment later his expression shuttered and the change was so abrupt that Chloe was momentarily disorientated.

'It's a phase I grew out of.'

It was the bleakness in his voice that made her realise she hadn't imagined it. For a few seconds she was back in the bar, turning without really knowing why and seeing him sitting there, the most handsome man she had ever seen or actually imagined. In the confusing mesh of emotions—attraction colliding with empathy—she'd felt the pain he was unconsciously emanating.

Dragging her thoughts back to the present, she extinguished the ache of empathy with a large dose of objectivity. *You don't need another cause,* she warned herself, *and you definitely don't need this man.*

'So was anyone else hurt in the accident?'

'Several people, including my brother-in-law, though he wasn't then…my brother-in-law, that is. Apparently there had been an oil spill earlier on a blind bend and…it just happened. There was no one to blame but me and fate.'

He tipped his chair back to look at her, though it was hard to read his expression thanks to the thickness of his long lashes. 'So you believe in fate?'

She shrugged. 'I believe you make choices and have to live with the consequences.'

'Well, you don't seem to have suffered too many long-lasting consequences.'

He really had no idea. She struggled not to touch her leg again, and instead let her eyelids lower, shading her expression with her own long, curling lashes. 'I was very lucky,' she agreed quietly.

'So what else do you believe in?' He believed in very little and he found himself almost envying her her idealism, but equally he was disturbed by the idea that it might have been some form of this idealism that had first led her to his bed, or him to hers…

Had she seen him as some sort of romantic hero or had it meant nothing to her beyond a rite of passage?

He wasn't actually sure which possibility disturbed him more.

'I believe in the resilience of human spirit, I believe that you should never take anything for granted and I believe...' She gave a sudden self-conscious laugh, her eyes sliding from his. 'I believe that I'm in danger of boring you.'

It came as a shock to realise that they had reached the coffee stage.

'I'd prefer to be dead!'

The horrified exclamation by one of the female guests coincided with a lull in the conversation.

'So what is it you prefer death to, my dear?' The man to her right voiced the question on everyone's mind.

'Being a size fourteen!' She gave a theatrical shudder. 'Can you imagine?'

Chloe sat there and imagined what this woman would say if she saw the scars on her thigh. She knew full well that her reaction would not be unique.

'She's an eating disorder waiting to happen and the sad thing is she has a daughter who she'll probably pass on her neuroses to.'

Anger struck through Chloe; while she might have agreed with the sentiment Nik had privately voiced in her ear, she doubted he had ever dated a woman who carried any extra weight.

'So I suppose appearances don't matter to you,' she charged bluntly. 'You'd date someone who wasn't perfect, would you? You honestly wouldn't care if your wife gained a hundred pounds or suddenly went bald.'

His brows lifted at the heat of her accusation. 'That sounds rather personal. Were you an ugly duckling before you became a swan? A fat child with acne…or is that a wig you're wearing…?'

She reared back as he went to touch her hair.

'You switched the place cards, didn't you? So you could sit next to me and drive me around the bend.'

'You didn't answer my question.'

'You didn't answer mine.'

He tipped his head in acknowledgment. 'I have some skills,' he admitted modestly. As he spoke he held out his hand and turned it over, extending his long brown fingers. Then with a flick of his wrist he produced one of the place cards from the sleeve of his opposite hand. 'Distraction and sleight of hand. I have other skills.'

She compressed her lips and made a point of not asking him what they were.

'Have you thought about what I said about you coming home with me tonight?'

She choked gently on her mouthful of wine before giving him a direct look. 'I assumed you were joking.' She was quite pleased with the compromise; it was a way of saying no without injuring his male ego.

Unfortunately, he didn't appear to appreciate the favour she was doing him. 'Then I'll have to think of a way of showing you that I'm not.'

Her nerve ends tingling in response to the throaty purr of his challenge, she gave a little gasp and knocked over a glass as she bolted to her feet. Aware that people were looking at her, she calmly folded her napkin and dabbed at the damp spot on the snowy cloth. 'Send me the dry-cleaning bill,' she joked.

People responded to her quip with smiles and barely looked at her as she walked around the table to where Tatiana sat.

'I promised to ring the palace to check on...'

Tatiana's sympathy was instant. 'Of course. Use my office if you want some privacy, then join us for coffee in the drawing room.'

CHAPTER FIVE

SHE LISTENED TO her sister, who spoke at some length on the joys—*not*—of morning sickness. It wasn't until she hung up that Chloe identified the odd achey tightness in her chest as envy, but she refused to acknowledge it. Her sister deserved her happiness; it just made her aware of the things she didn't have and maybe never would.

Catching the self-pitying direction her thoughts were taking, she got to her feet, but halfway to the drawing room she chickened out and slipped into the bathroom, where she spent a great deal of time admiring the decor.

Sometimes discretion was *definitely* the better part of valour. Hoping no one had sent out a search party for her, she waited there long enough to be sure that her arrival would coincide with people leaving. Hopefully she could slip away unnoticed without any further confrontations with Nik.

She had just stepped out into the hallway when she heard Lucy's voice and ducked back into the bathroom. It was instinctive and she felt foolish the moment she locked the door. It wasn't Lucy she was hiding from, but that didn't matter; it was the fact she was hiding at all that filled her with self-disgust.

With a sigh she turned, dumped her bag on the vanity unit and, palms flat on the marble surface, she looked at herself in the mirror.

Her face illuminated by the spotlights above looked pale and her eyes were too bright. She leaned in and touched the fine skin under her eye; the make-up helped but did not quite conceal the blueish half-moon, which was the result of a week of disturbed nights that had preceded her decision not to continue with further surgery.

The decision had felt liberating, she'd felt completely in control and yet what had it taken to throw that equilibrium into chaos? One single encounter with Nik Latsis. She made a sound of disgust in her throat and turned her back on the mirror.

She sighed. She hadn't felt in control tonight, she'd felt… She shook her head, unable…unwilling to examine her emotions as she turned, taking care not to look in the mirror, and twisted the cold tap onto full.

She stood there with her wrists under the running water, waiting for her heart rate to slow, wanting to reject outright the idea that she was attracted to Nik Latsis. The lie would have been easy, easier than admitting a man like him would never want someone less than perfect, but she couldn't.

It was a fact.

She turned off the tap, lifted her chin and looked at herself in the mirror.

'It is what it is, Chloe.'

She made her way back downstairs, where the hallway was empty but the door stood open. There was no sign of Tatiana, so she decided to call for a cab before saying goodbye to her hostess.

She had started to punch in the number when a voice at her elbow made her jump.

'Have you been hiding?' Nik asked.

'What?'

He was wearing a long tailored dark overcoat that hung open, his hair glistened wet and the same moisture glistened on his face. He had brought the smell of outdoors and rain into the room.

Chloe struggled to hide her dismay and the illicit excitement that made her stomach muscles quiver. 'You haven't gone yet.'

'Ever the gentleman, I have been escorting the ladies to their cars.' He held up a large umbrella.

Chloe clenched her fingers over her phone, ignoring the little ribbons of warm electricity making her aware of the tingling nerve endings in her skin. 'I'm just ringing for a taxi.'

He watched as she began to punch in a number, noticing that her face had a fresh scrubbed look as though she'd taken off her make-up. She still looked good, very good, but she looked more vulnerable... delicate, even. He felt an emotion swell in his chest but refused to acknowledge it as tenderness.

'You don't need a taxi.'

The harshness in his voice drew her glance upwards. 'Thanks, but no, thanks,' she said firmly, ashamed of the moments of self-pity she had indulged in.

'You're still here!' Tatiana's relieved voice rang out before Nik could respond.

Chloe was glad of the interruption but puzzled by the older woman's sense of urgency. 'I was just ringing for a taxi before I came to say goodbye, but did I forget something?' She nodded to Lucy who had appeared behind her host; the redhead was wearing a denim jacket over the slinky red dress and carrying off the contrast in considerable style.

Tatiana shook her head. 'Spiros just rang to warn anyone left not to try taking…well, just about any road, I think. The peaceful protests apparently turned out not to be so peaceful, and the police have closed down half the streets. Spiros is stuck, and he saw a car alight too. I really think it would be better if you all stay here for the night. There are reports of the disturbances spreading and even looting.'

'I'm walking home, so it's no problem,' Lucy said.

Tatiana looked alarmed.

Lucy put her hands on the older woman's shoulders. 'Relax, I'm not going to my home, I'm booked into the new boutique hotel around the corner. It's only a hundred yards, so I think I'll be safe.' She air-kissed Tatiana and thanked her, landed a kiss on Nik's cheek and waved to Chloe. 'Interesting night.'

Chloe didn't even try and translate this cryptic utterance.

'And I'm going Chloe's way so that's her problem solved,' Nik announced in a tone that brooked no argument.

Not from where she was standing!

'How do you know which way is my way? That is,' she continued, lowering the levels of antagonism in her voice, 'I wouldn't dream of bothering you.'

'Nonsense!' Tatiana sent her brother a warning glare. 'He's fine with it, aren't you, Nik?'

Chloe clenched her teeth as, with a totally unconvincing display of meekness that made him look even more like a wolf, he tipped his dark head.

'Absolutely.' Slower than Tatiana to jump back squealing when he shook the umbrella, sending a spray of cold water droplets that hit everything in the immediate area, Chloe was the only one close enough to hear his not at all meek-sounding addition. 'My way is whichever way you're going.'

She brushed her ear where the sensitive flesh still tingled from the touch of his warm breath and glared at him, while he continued to look smugly satisfied with himself.

'Well, that's sorted, then,' Tatiana said, looking relieved. 'You will text me when you get home safely?'

Chloe promised.

She gave a sigh and rubbed the tip of her nose with her finger. The truth was, there was a part of her, a clearly twisted part of her, that had…*enjoyed* their flirtation. No, that was the wrong word. It hadn't been flirtation; that was far too gentle. Combat probably better described the heart-thumping, skin-tingling adrenaline charge of their exchanges tonight.

She had felt what…? *Like a woman.* Her eyes flew wide with shock as the recognition of her too-long-suppressed sexuality crashed through her.

'Are you all right?' Nik asked.

'I'm fine!' she lied.

She read criticism in his eyes as they swept her face. 'You look like you're in pain.'

'The only pain around here…' at the last second she managed to apply the brake to her runaway tongue and lowered her eyes, muttering '…is a slight headache.'

Actually pain was pretty accurate for what she felt, as though the circulation were returning to a limb deprived of blood. It hurt and so did this—the part of her that had been in hibernation since the accident had finally woken up and it was tingling!

She wasn't ready yet; she wanted that part to go back to sleep. It was such awful bad timing! At this point an affair of any kind, let alone the sort of superficial no-strings fling Nik Latsis had in mind for them, was the last thing she needed.

She lifted her chin, defiance sparking in her eyes, as she thought, *I deserve more than that! I deserve better than Nik Latsis!*

Even if she had been in the market for a man, which she wasn't, he would not have made the shortlist. If she had needed reminding, and she didn't, how shallow he was, tonight would have driven the point home to her.

Yes, she was attracted to him, it was actually too exhausting to try and pretend otherwise, but in her defence he had more sexual charisma in a single hair follicle than most men had in their entire bodies. Although *attraction* hardly came close to describing the visceral reaction he evoked just looking at him… *Then don't look!* she told herself.

She needed to stop over-analysing everything. Nothing was going to happen between them because it couldn't. She brushed her leg with her hand, not that the numbed scar tissue registered the touch. She found herself wishing fiercely for a moment that the numbness went even deeper, that she could anaesthetise the emotions that tonight had reawoken in her.

She squared her shoulders. If he had been the Nik who had vulnerabilities, and not this insensitive, slick predator, she might have been in trouble, but he wasn't, so she was completely safe.

As safe as being circled by a tiger, she thought, injecting as much grateful insincerity into her smile as she could.

'I hope it's not too far out of your way, Nik.'

It was Tatiana who replied. 'Don't be silly, Chloe…'

'Looks like that's settled, then.' Nik walked ahead and left Chloe to walk beside his sister. When they reached the open front door she realised with a stab of shame that she didn't have a clue what the other woman had just been saying to her.

This had to stop, she told herself. Nik Latsis was

the past, not a mistake because the last few months
had taught her that thinking about mistakes meant
you couldn't move forward. She had moved forward
and she would continue to do so.

'It's stopped raining.' Nik, who had walked outside ahead of the women, lowered the umbrella
he had raised and held up his hands to the sky. He
grinned, twirled the umbrella and stamped in a puddle.

Fighting the urge to run out and join him, Chloe
was conscious of an ache in her chest. She snatched
a quick breath, knowing that the image would stay
with her, but not knowing why...or at least not asking herself why.

'You're welcome to stay over if you like.'

Her friend was looking concerned as she reit-
erated her offer; if Tatiana had picked up on her
distress, Chloe just hoped she hadn't picked up on
the cause! She was tempted, she really was, but accepting the offer would mean she was afraid to be
alone with Nik. And she wasn't, because nothing
was going to happen between them. Chloe gathered herself and turned with a smile that felt stiff
and forced, although she was unwilling to admit
that even to herself.

'Thanks, but no, it would be good to get home.'
She raised her voice a little to make sure that Nik
could hear what she was saying and get the message.
'I'd like to sleep in my own bed.' The way her mind
was working overtime she doubted there would be
much sleep for her tonight.

After a pause, Tatiana nodded and kissed her cheek. 'Take care...and drive carefully, Nik,' she called after her brother, who lifted an arm and waved.

Chloe trudged on head down, Nik beside her, not touching her but close, close enough for her to be aware of the tension that stopped him dead in his tracks at the sound of distant sirens.

He stood there, head sharply angled, his lean, tense stance making her think of a wolf sensing danger, nostrils flared, scenting it in the air.

The sound retreated and he shook his head as though clearing it before glancing down at her. 'I'm parked over here.'

It took Chloe a moment to recover from the expression she had glimpsed on his face before she fell into step beside him.

'Are you all right?' she asked softly. Haunted; he had looked haunted.

He glanced down at her, the sounds of war, the explosions, the disembodied screams and the discordant staccato peal of shells still sounding in his head. 'The silences in between the shelling were the worst. Somehow they tapped into a man's primitive fears... the calm before the storm.' He stopped and the street light above them showed the shock reflected on his face...as if he'd only just realised he'd spoken his thoughts out loud.

Then it was gone, as quickly as it had appeared.

Another time his car, a low, gleaming monster, would have drawn a sarcastic remark from Chloe about macho power statements, but all she did was slide into the passenger seat when he opened the door.

She ached for his pain but she knew she couldn't let him into her life…every instinct of self-preservation told her this. The memory of that morning waking alone, when she'd waited for him, imagining the reasons for his absence—he'd stepped out for coffee, he'd gone to find a red rose—made her cringe, but even worse was when the penny had finally dropped and she had acted like someone heartbroken.

The memory she filed away as water under the bridge. Mistakes were fine—it was repeating them that was unforgivable! He was a fragment of her history and, after all, you were never supposed to forget your first lover. Well, only time would tell and she was an optimist.

'I need to stop off at the office first…there are some contracts I must sign tonight,' he said.

Any delay, any reason to prolong the time she spent in this enclosed space with him filled her with dismay, although it was mitigated with a relief that he was sounding normal again. If he was acting she was glad…she simply couldn't deal with his trauma and her own reaction to it. A vulnerable Nik was a very dangerous Nik to her peace of mind!

'At this time of night?' Her voice sounded calm but her agitation revealed itself in the smooth stroking motion of her hands as she moved them up and down over her silk-covered thighs.

'I think they'll let me in,' he said, thinking about

how her legs had wrapped tight around him as he'd thrust inside her.

'Of course,' she said, feeling stupid…then something more uncomfortable than stupid when she realised his eyes were following the mechanical motion of her hands. She stopped and folded her arms defensively across her chest.

He cast a glance across her face and was distracted for a moment because she was chewing her plump lower lip and all he had to do was bend in a little closer to taste it for himself.

'Look, Nik, tonight I think I might have… If I seemed like I wanted you to…' She swallowed and stopped; if she really hadn't wanted Nik to flirt with her, why hadn't she just told him straight out about the scars that remained after the operations, the puckered, discoloured patches of flesh on her right thigh? It would have been amusing to see how fast he retreated.

Except it wouldn't have been *amusing*.

She told herself that people's attitudes to her scars were their problem, not hers, and most of the time she believed it, but there was a world of difference between theory and fact, not to mention a world of humiliation, and she wasn't ready for that yet.

'You were saying…?' he prompted, wondering if she knew how expressive her face was. The drift of emotions across it was almost like watching a silent film.

'I think it's a very bad idea to try and relive some-

thing that happened in the past. Much better to remember it as it was.'

'So am I a happy memory or a bad one?'

'A bit of both,' she admitted, thinking that she
had reached the stars with him and discovered the
depths of despair. She buckled her belt, reminding
herself that self-pity was for people who did not have
a life and she did. She was not going to waste her
time thinking about what she'd lost; she was going
to celebrate what she had.

Nik watched her, the knot of frustration in his
belly tightening the muscles along his jaw. He enjoyed a challenge as much as the next man but this
was different... He swore under his breath as he
started the engine.

'So how long have you lived in London?' he asked
in an attempt at a normal conversation.

'I went to college, but I wasn't very academic...'

'You dropped out?'

'More like I was invited to leave, which was fine
because I had begun to make money with the blog,
which seemed so amazing at the time. I've always
been lucky.'

'And accident prone,' he commented.

'People died in that accident so I was still lucky,'
she retorted.

'I'm guessing you are a glass-half-full kind of
person.'

'I really hope so...' She turned her head to look
at the glass-fronted building he had pulled up in
front of.

* * *

'I won't be long.' He leaned across and snatched the phone she was nursing on her knee.

A moment later he tossed it back to her. 'My number's in it, and if you see or hear anything, call me,' he directed sternly.

It took her a few moments to realise what he meant. Some of her antagonism faded, but she remained sceptical that his caution was warranted.

'I think Spiros might have been exaggerating the danger.' Other than the initial couple of distant sirens, which was not exactly unusual, they had encountered nothing that suggested widespread rioting.

'You might be right.' He gave a concessionary nod and slid out, closing the door behind him with a decisive click.

Chloe leaned back in her seat, relaxing enough for her shoulder blades to actually make contact with the leather, and she watched him walk away, his hands thrust deep in his pockets, up the shallow steps to the building. He paused for a moment and she heard the decisive click of the car doors locking.

'I don't believe it!'

There was no one to hear her exclamation, and her angry bang on the window went unnoticed. Then there was nobody but the uniformed security guard, who'd come out when Nik went in, who just stood there ignoring her, his eyes constantly scanning the areas to left and right.

When Nik reappeared exactly three minutes fif-

teen seconds later, the two men shook hands and exchanged a few words before the man walked back
into the building and Nik got into the car.

Chloe stared stonily ahead as he flung some files
onto the back seat. 'You locked me in.'

'I didn't want any looters stealing my car.'

She compressed her lips. 'That man ignored me—'

'That man is an ex-marine. He knew what you
were doing.'

'Oh. Do you have a lot of ex-marines working
for you?'

'The transition is not always kind to men who
have given their lives to protect us. Dave, back there,
flung himself on a landmine and saved three others
in his squad, but he lost a leg below the knee.'

Their eyes connected and in his dark gaze she
saw something she didn't want to acknowledge. In
seconds the heat banked inside her burst into life,
starting low in her pelvis and spreading out until her
entire body was suffused by the same blazing fire.
The instant conflagration scared her witless… It was
a warning, she told herself, a warning that said if she
had an ounce of self-respect she'd get the hell out of
that car right now.

Panic hit her hard. 'Stop the car.' She used the
anger when he ignored her to drag herself free of
the last of the dangerous languor that lingered in her
brain. 'I said, stop the car,' she said calmly.

He took his eyes off the road to briefly glance at
her face and she could hear the irritation in his voice.
'Don't be stupid.'

The only stupid thing she had done so far was getting into this car with him and Chloe had every intention of keeping it that way.

'You're acting as though we have unfinished business, but that's not the case. Look, I spent the night with you, end of story. It is not something I have any wish to repeat.'

'So you want to pretend it didn't happen at all.'

The suggestion, his tone, his attitude they all struck a jarring note inside her, so she counted to ten and fought to dampen the resentment she knew she had no right to be feeling.

'I'm not pretending it didn't happen; I'm admitting it shouldn't have.'

'I—'

'Get down!'

It was the tone as much as the terse instruction that made her stomach clench. 'What's wrong?'

'Just do it. There's a blanket there, cover yourself with it and duck down.' The odd instruction was delivered in a light, calm tone, but when she leaned forward and saw what he had already seen, she didn't feel very calm at all.

Ahead of them the road was filled with crowds of people. Some had banners and some carried dustbin lids, which they were banging.

He wound down the window and the suggestion of noise became a loud, discordant din.

'They sound mad.' Fear fluttered in her belly.

'They are a mob.' And it was the nature of the beast, anger and unpredictability, the pack-animal mentality, that could make the whole group do things that as individuals they would never dream of doing.

'I don't like this,' she said, once again gnawing at her plump lower lip, a nervous habit she'd never managed to break.

'I would be more concerned if you did. Duck down and pull the cover over your head.'

If he had faced this situation alone he would not have broken a sweat, not because he was brave or fearless, but because he had been in far worse situations, and as far as he could see the only thing he stood to lose was a car.

But he wasn't alone, and knowing that Chloe's safety was his responsibility changed everything. He had talked his way out of much worse situations, but with Chloe here he wasn't prepared to take even a calculated risk.

'No, I'm not hiding and leaving you exposed,' she stated, but her fists were clenched tightly.

'Why does beautiful so often go with stupid?' He sighed.

Her wrathful gaze met his in the mirror and he smiled. If she was angry, at least she wasn't afraid. 'Relax, *agape mou*, I will not let anything hurt you.'

She believed him, although it seemed that she ought to be more concerned about her mental well-being than her physical! She caught his arm and he paused, his eyes going from her fingers curled into the fabric, to her face. 'You're not going to do anything stupid, are you?'

'Could you be more specific?' he asked.

'I don't know…like fight them.'

He let out a loud throaty laugh. 'Me against fifty, sixty people? I don't much like those odds, but I'm sorry if I disappoint you in the hero stakes.'

'I promise you I never thought you were a hero.'

One corner of his mouth lifted in a lopsided grin and there was something about him…a combustible quality that made her think it would have been a brave person who bet against him, even if the odds were stacked against him.

'But I do think you're capable of doing something stupid.'

'Like they say, a good general chooses his field of battle. I am not good or a general but the concept holds true.'

'Are you going to drive on through them?' she asked nervously.

Nik had been going to reverse, but a glance in the rear-view mirror made it clear this was a now-or-never choice. The street on one side—he adjusted the mirror and silently corrected himself—on both sides of the road were full of people streaming towards the main artery road. It was hard to be accurate but he suspected that their options would close in seconds, not minutes.

'Hold on, this might be a little bumpy.'

She connected with his eyes and made a shocking discovery. 'You are enjoying this, aren't—?' She let out a shriek and closed her eyes as the car went into sudden reverse, travelling at what felt like the speed of light. It continued backwards even when it hit obstacles, objects in the road flung down by rioters.

The banner-waving maniacs followed initially, but they quickly fell away and by the time the car reached the gaggle of police cars the protestors were nowhere in sight.

'Wait here.'

She narrowed her eyes, tilted her stubborn little chin and thought, *Oh, yes that is* really *going to happen!* Who did he think he was, issuing orders to her? She opened her door and got out.

Two uniformed officers were already moving towards the car, and Nik walked towards them, looking calm and confident.

By the time she was within hearing distance, the police were complimenting Nik and shaking his hand.

'Thank you, sir. If all witnesses could be so clinically precise it would make our job a lot easier.'

'More resources,' the younger one said, 'would too.'

In response to a look he received from his colleague, he added a defensive, 'It's no secret that we're overstretched.' Then he stopped as he saw Chloe coming towards them, his eyes widening.

Before he could speak to her, Nik moved, cutting off her approach. With a firm hand on her elbow, he turned back to the men. 'We won't get in your way, officers, and thank you. Come on, Chloe.'

She was hustled back to the car with equal ruthless efficiency. 'You didn't let me say a word to

them! What did you think I was going to do?' she
demanded as Nik folded his long length in beside her.

'Distract them from their job,' he replied suc-
cinctly.

'So what happens now?' she huffed.

'Now I take you home. The police have given me
a route that should be clear and, before you ask, the
Tube stations are closed, so don't even think of asking me to stop the car again.'

The rest of the journey was completed without
incident and in total silence.

She waited until he had neatly reversed the car
into a parking space clearly marked reserved outside
her building before releasing her seat belt.

'I should thank you.'

'But you won't.'

'That's not what I...' A sound of irritation rattled
in her throat. He drove her insane! 'All right, I *do*
thank you.'

'It was my pleasure.'

He moved to open his door and she shook her
head. 'No, don't get out; I'm fine.'

'I will see you to the door.'

'I'm not going to be ravished or kidnapped between here and there,' she said, nodding to the Georgian building behind them. Once it had housed one
family; now it was split into twenty one-bedroom
apartments, a bit down at heel, or, in estate-agent
speak, ripe for improvement. Chloe had no cash to
improve hers as she had poured all the money her
blog had made into buying the place.

'Looking like that, I would not be so confident.'

'You mean I would be asking for it?' she countered crankily.

His exasperation increased. 'I mean that you are a very beautiful woman, this is a fact, and it is also a fact that a man who forces himself on a woman is no real man.' His nostrils flared in distaste. 'And a man who excuses the actions of such a person is no less of an inadequate loser.'

He got out and walked around to her side of the car, standing there silently as she got out.

She tilted her head to look at his shuttered face. 'I've offended you.'

He arched an eloquent brow.

'Sorry.'

He bowed slightly from the waist. 'Accepted.' A glimmer appeared in his eyes. 'Friends again?'

Chloe looked at the hand extended to her as if it were a viper. It was news to her that they ever had been friends, but he had got her home so she reached out.

He took her hand but not to shake it. Without his seeming to exert any overt pressure, she found herself colliding with his body.

His dark face lowered to hers. 'It's all about sleight of hand and distraction,' he whispered before his mouth came crashing down on hers.

The kiss was hard, hot and hungry as he plundered her mouth with ruthless efficiency. For a split second, shock held her immobile, then as his dark head began to lift something snapped inside her.

Chloe felt it, even heard it, as she dragged his dark head back down to hers, parting her lips to invite a deepening of the slow, sensual exploration.

It was an invitation that he accepted, driving his tongue deep into the warm recesses of her mouth.

She was distantly conscious of the throaty, mewling little sounds but didn't make the connection between them and herself. Her hands curled into his jacket to stop herself falling as tongues of flame scorched along her nerve endings, and she felt a deep shudder ripple through the hard, lean body pressed close to her.

'Oh, God!'

Her shaken gasp seemed to break the spell.

The thud that Chloe heard when she fell back to earth seemed almost as real as the searing humiliation she felt as, still shaking, she looked up at him, to see that he was perfectly fine. Standing there as though nothing had happened, she thought, her indignation going supernova…then cooling slightly as she noticed the streaks of colour along his cheekbones and the fact he was breathing pretty hard.

At least he had put enough distance between them to make the basic stuff like breathing a whole lot easier. She tilted her head but it was impossible to make out his expression. Even with her eyes narrowed, his face was just a dark blur, which was probably a blessing of sorts because he no doubt looked as smug as a man who had just had his point proved could look.

She took a deep breath. 'I am not sure what that was meant to achieve.'

'Achieve?'

She ignored the interruption and didn't even register the odd strain in his voice.

'I already knew that you were a good kisser.' He was a good everything, that was the problem.

'So the problem is…?'

Arms crossed over her chest, she rubbed her upper arms with both hands. 'I enjoyed the night I spent with you, but I happen not to be quite as casual about sex as you are. That's not a criticism,' she hastened to assure him. 'I mean, as far as I'm concerned, each to his own.'

'So now you have developed a puritanical streak?'

She slung him a look of simmering dislike. 'Last time you looked…hurt…lost…' *And what's your excuse this time, Chloe?* 'I don't know, but—'

'You are saying you had pity sex with me.'

'No.'

'So are you looking for a deep and meaningful relationship?'

The sneering tone of his voice set her teeth on edge and tightened her expression into a glare, though she fought to keep the edge of antagonism from her voice. 'I'm not actually looking for any sort of a relationship just now, but when I am… I'd like to find a man who will accept me for who I am inside, and not care about the way I look.'

He gave a hard, incredulous laugh. 'Well, if that's the kind of man you're looking for, I'd start looking for a couple of nice cats instead, if I were you. What's so wrong with being beautiful? It's not exactly a curse; women spend their lives and fortunes trying to look like you and they never will. How is noticing you're beautiful an insult to you?'

She stuck out her small determined chin. 'I'm a hell of a lot more than that, not that you're ever going to know, and, believe you me, that's your loss!' she flared, secreting the security card she'd extracted from her bag in her palm.

She widened her eyes and looked into the middle distance. 'Oh, my!'

As soon as he turned his head to see what she was staring at, Chloe ran to the door. Her security card swiped first time and she stepped into the foyer, slamming it shut a split second before he reached it.

She pressed the button on the intercom. 'It's all about sleight of hand and distraction.'

A reluctant smile fought its way to his lips. 'I thought you never hid.'

She might not know about distraction, but she understood about odds. Her father owned the leg of a racehorse and she knew the odds were good that if Nik kissed her again and she got another taste of that raw power, if she felt the impression of his erection grinding into her belly, instinct would take over and reason would fly out of the window.

And everything would be hot and marvellous until he got an up-close-and-personal look at the part of her that once had been perfect and now wasn't. Did she want to carry the memory of his look of disgust or embarrassment as he pulled away from her? That was a no brainer.

'I'm not hiding from you. I'm walking away. There's a difference.' The moment she turned away from him the tears she had been holding back began to fall, and, running up the stairs, she swiped at them irritably.

Just sex was really not worth it!

CHAPTER SIX

IT WAS NOON when Chloe got back to her flat, but the first thing she did was strip off, push her clothes in the linen basket and step in the shower. The act of washing was purely symbolic; she knew the scent of hospital was in her mind, because the only thing the doctor's consulting room on the top floor of the rather beautiful Georgian building it occupied had smelt of was his expensive aftershave.

Hair still damp, she tightened the belt of her robe around her waist and flung herself down on the sofa, keying in her sister's number on her phone...but it went straight to voicemail.

With a sigh she dropped the phone in her robe pocket and padded barefoot over to the kitchen. Of course, if her sister had known about the hospital appointment she would have been waiting for the call—no, she would have come with her—but she didn't know. Chloe deliberately hadn't told anyone about it, *especially* her family.

They had been through enough during the long months after the accident—not that her choice not to tell them was entirely selfless. She knew that they, or at least her parents, would struggle to understand her decision not to have further cosmetic surgery. Down the line who knew how she'd feel about it? While it certainly was an option, right now she'd had enough of hospitals and she felt that to go through all that again was unbearable, especially as there were no guarantees regarding exactly how much improvement there would be, as the doctor would not give any promises.

She had taken a sip of her scalding coffee when her phone rang, and she lifted it to her ear and said hello.

It was not her sister who replied and, stifling a surge of disappointment, she said, 'Can you just hold on a second?' and reached out to shut the door of the fridge, which was buzzing to remind her she'd not closed it. 'Hi, Tatiana.'

'S… Sorry, is this a bad time?'

Chloe's reaction was immediate; elbows on the counter, she leaned forward, concern furrowing her brow. 'No, it's fine…is anything wrong?' When they had spoken earlier today, Tatiana had sounded relaxed and happy, issuing an invitation that Chloe had refused, which had been to join her on the family estate on the Greek island of Spetses. But now, only a few hours later, she was obviously close to tears.

'I told you, didn't I, that I agreed to Eugenie spending the first week of the holiday with her friend Pippa in Hampshire…?'

'Yes…has something gone wrong?' Chloe asked.

Tatiana gave an unamused laugh. 'You could say that. Pippa's parents in their wisdom decided that two fifteen-year-old girls were mature enough to be left alone in the house while they went away for the night.'

'Oh, dear!'

'Oh, yes, definitely *oh, dear*. The girls decided to have an impromptu party with supposedly just a few friends but, to cut a long story short, it was gate-crashed by lots of other kids, the place was wrecked and the neighbours called the police! Eugenie has been cautioned by the police and she is waiting at the local police station to be picked up. Pippa's parents have decided she is a bad influence—can you believe it? The problem is, my grandmother has a really high temperature, so I can't leave her, and my brother's not picking up his phone and no one seems to know where he is.'

'What can I do?'

A sob of relief echoed down the line. 'Could you pick her up for me and take her to the airport?'

'Of course.'

'The Gulfstream jet was in Frankfurt; I have no idea what my parents are doing there. Anyhow, I made some excuse up to say I needed the plane, but I really don't want them to know about this. It should be there by the time you arrive.'

'Don't worry, I'll drop her off safely.'

'Drop her off? Oh, no, Chloe, I need you to travel with her to Spetses, and sit on her if necessary! I'm not risking her pulling another stunt.'

It was only the rising hysteria in her friend's voice that stopped Chloe pointing out that there seemed little possibility of her daughter coming to any harm on a private flight to a Greek island. 'Fine, I'll sit on her.'

'I knew I could rely on you. Thank you so much, Chloe. I'll never be able to repay you.'

Actually, Chloe realised as she picked up her car keys, it was Tatiana who was doing her a favour. Left to her own devices she'd have spent the evening brooding over her decision and planning how she broke the news to her parents. Instead, she had plenty to distract her.

A cloudburst proved to be one of the distractions she hadn't figured on.

Chloe was drenched to the skin as she sat in the police station studying a poster on the wall that proclaimed in large letters *Don't be a victim,* a sentiment she agreed with wholeheartedly, when Eugenie appeared walking alongside a fresh-faced policewoman who barely seemed older than the teen.

The girl's face dropped when she saw Chloe.

'I thought Uncle Nik was coming to get me.'

'Your mum couldn't contact him.' Chloe struggled not to sound judgemental about that as her imagination kicked in, supplying a slide show of selfish reasons for Nik being off the grid, all revolving around beautiful women and bed.

Well, you declined his offer to spend the night

with him, Chloe reminded herself. *Did you expect him to go back home and weep into his beer, or did you expect him to pursue you?*

He clearly hadn't done either, which reinforced the obvious: it had been an opportunist offer, made in the heat of the moment, and when she'd refused he had chalked it up to experience and moved on.

A circumstance she told herself she was relieved about.

'Uncle Nik would understand…*he* wouldn't lecture me,' the girl said, her defiant expression suggesting that Chloe couldn't even begin to do so.

In contrast to the girl's dramatic pronouncement Chloe kept her voice light and friendly. 'I'm not here to lecture you,' she returned, thinking, *Thank God, it's not my job.* 'Just get you to your mum.'

The girl pouted and tossed her head. 'Well, you took your time.'

Chloe smiled and counted to ten. 'Yes, I thought I'd take the scenic route as it's such a lovely day for a drive.' She gestured to the window, where the rain was falling from a leaden summer sky. 'And obviously I had nothing better to do.' Without waiting for the girl's response, she turned to the policewoman. 'Thank you very much for looking after her.' She glanced at Eugenie. 'Ready…?'

The girl nodded. Minus the truculent attitude, she looked so miserable and very young standing there shifting her weight from one spiky heel to the other that it was all Chloe could do not to hug her.

Instead she slipped off her jacket and draped it over the girl's bare shoulders. 'It's a bit chilly out there.'

Eugenie turned her head to look up at Chloe. 'Is she really mad? Mum, I mean?' she muttered.

'I'm afraid I'm just the chauffeur.' Chloe hesitated, choosing her words with care. 'I've zero experience of being a parent, but I have been a daughter and when my parents were angry with me it was usually because they were worried about me.'

'There was no reason for her to be worried.'

'If you say so.'

'You don't believe me, do you?'

'I'm parked just over there.'

'Uncle Nik would believe me—he'd understand.'

Well, bully for Uncle Nik, Chloe thought, keeping her lips sealed over her resentment. Uncle Nik, who would no doubt have beautiful babies, and was, as far as she knew, somewhere right now trying to make one.

She frowned, rubbing her upper arms through the silk of her already drenched blouse, and pushed the accompanying image away. Wherever he was too busy to pick up his phone, it was bound to be some place nice and warm while she was drenched to the skin and walking on eggshells with a teenager who made her feel about ninety!

Just as she was on the point of deciding that parenthood was clearly a mug's game, her sulky charge stopped. Impatient, Chloe turned back.

'Thank you for coming for me,' Eugenie said in a small quivery voice.

'You are very welcome.'

Chloe fished her keys from her pocket and opened the passenger door of her own utilitarian hatchback. 'Sorry you're slumming it today.'

'*That* is your car?' The girl's astonishment was almost comical, as was her horror. Chloe strongly suspected that the idea of being seen in anything so uncool worried her more than the idea of parental ire or a jail cell.

'So what does it do, thirty with the wind behind it?'

'If we're lucky.' *Speed* had not been a priority when she had first got behind the wheel of a car after the accident, but safety had. Not that she expected the girl, or anyone else for that matter, to understand that this car represented a personal triumph for Chloe.

She could have rationalised it and it would have been easier than admitting her fears. Far easier to pretend that she was doing her eco bit for the planet by using public transport, asking how convenient actually was it to have a car in the City?

Instead she had admitted she had a problem, and her family had been proud when she had conquered her fears, but the truth was her honesty had certain limitations. She'd never told them that her hands still got clammy when she slid into the driver's seat and her heart rate took a few minutes before it settled into a normal rhythm.

Time, she hoped, would eventually finish the healing process.

'I thought you were meant to be royal or something...'

'Or something,' Chloe admitted with a laugh. 'You can always duck down if you see anyone you know—'

The sound of a car that was neither safe nor slow made them both turn as a limousine complete with blacked-out windows drew up behind them.

The girl's pale face lit up. 'It's Uncle Nik.'

Chloe already knew that. As he got out of the car her minor palpitations suddenly became critical.

'He'll understand.' The relief in the girl's face faded away to uncertainty as she realised what Chloe already had. The man striding towards them was furious.

His face set in hard lines, his dark brows drawn into a straight line above his hawkish nose, he stopped a couple of feet away from them. He was breathing hard and looked like a well-dressed version of a dark avenging angel as the wind caught the hem of his long coat, making it billow out behind him.

'What the hell did you think you were doing?'

As the teenager shrank into her side Chloe wondered if Nik knew he had gone from hero to villain in just one short sentence.

Nik's narrowed eyes followed the protective hand Chloe slid around the girl's shoulders, and his jaw tensed as he flashed her an arctic glare.

'Thank you for your…*help*.' The word emerged reluctantly through his clenched lips. 'I'm assuming that Tatiana contacted you?'

Her chin lifted in challenge. He had managed to make the statement sound like an accusation. *No, I just happened to be passing.*

It took an effort but she managed to keep her lip buttoned on the snarky retort that hovered on the tip of her tongue, and she dipped her head in acknowledgment, reflecting that surely *one* of them had to act like an adult in front of Eugenie.

'Well, I'm here now.'

As if that could have slipped anyone's notice! So this was Nik in business mode; impressed hardly covered her reaction. His designer-cut business suit didn't disguise the hardness of the body it covered, but it did emphasise the effortless power he exuded.

Nik dragged his eyes away from the outline of the lacy bra covering Chloe's breasts, clearly outlined beneath the drenched silk, just in time to see her roll her eyes at him. He wondered why, of all the people she could have turned to for help, his sister had chosen this woman, who was nobody's idea of a responsible adult. Hell, she didn't even have the basic sense to leave the house with a coat in a storm!

'Get in the car,' he ordered his niece.

'I'm not going anywhere with you!' was the response.

If his scowl was any indicator, he only saw the surly expression on Eugenie's face, and not the fact that her defiance only went about a cell deep despite the dramatic pronouncements. Clearly it wasn't his incredible insight into female behaviour that got him the girls, Chloe thought sourly.

'I hate you!'

Chloe sighed. It was a long shot, but she felt obliged to at least make an attempt to smooth things over.

'Look, clearly you're both feeling pretty intense...'

Two pairs of antagonistic eyes zoomed in on her face.

She cleared her throat and attempted a smile. As far as feelings went, her own were pretty much all over the place and had been from the moment she'd identified the person getting out of the car and her heart had started fibrillating madly. It had not even begun to calm down when he'd stalked towards them looking deliciously sexy, hard and... She gave her head a tiny shake. This wasn't about her, or her hormones; it was about Eugenie and Tatiana.

'Maybe now...' she continued, channelling sweet reason and calm while wondering if it was all right secretly wanting to do the wrong thing just so long as you actually resisted the weakness.

'Now what?' he bit out.

She dragged away her eyes, which were showing a disastrous tendency to drift up and down his long, lean, loose-limbed frame without her permission, and cleared her throat. What she needed right now was cool thinking, logic and maybe a bit of inspiration. What she didn't need or, for that matter, want was this animal attraction, insane sexual chemistry or a vivid imagination supplying her with memories of how he'd looked naked.

'Now is not the right time to—'

The teen shrugged off the arm across her shoulders and, with hands on her hips, took a defiant step towards her uncle. 'It wasn't my fault.'

Chloe sighed and wondered why she had even bothered to try. If she had any sense, which she did, she would get in her car, drive off and let these two slug it out, but then she reminded herself that Tatiana was her friend, and she had promised her she'd look after Eugenie.

Nik felt his grip on his temper slipping, but he breathed through the moment.

It had not been a good morning. He'd had a breakfast meeting with a guy the normally reliable firm of headhunters had sent, and in the space of thirty minutes the candidate had broken every unwritten rule in the book: drunk too much, confided personal problems, bad-mouthed colleagues and talked politics. Then Nik had returned to the office and found all the messages on his machine his stand-in secretary had not seen fit to respond to.

But compared to his present situation, faced with a niece who appeared to loathe him while challenging his authority, and the woman who hadn't been out of his head for more than three consecutive seconds ever since they'd parted company nearly forty-eight hours ago, he was extremely frustrated and close to snapping point!

He'd spent the last two days considering the best

way to seduce Chloe Summerville. Seduction had never had much to do with the kind of recreational sex he enjoyed; usually it wasn't about anything but slaking a hunger and for a short space of time blocking out everything else. Mutual attraction was certainly involved, but comparing it with what had sparked into life between himself and Chloe would have been like comparing a light shower with a monsoon!

And the attraction between them was mutual, he knew that without question, which made her rejection of him all the more teeth-grindingly frustrating.

He didn't make the mistake of reading anything deep and meaningful into their attraction; it was more to do with the timing and circumstances of their first meeting than anything else. Those circumstances had just intensified the chemistry that existed between them, that was all—a chemistry that would inevitably fade.

If when it did, so did his nightmares, that was only an added bonus. Getting her into bed was definitely going to happen; it was just a matter of when. His instincts could not be that far out, surely?

'Get in the car,' he repeated to his niece, digging into reserves of tolerance that had already been seriously depleted.

Chloe took a deep breath and came to a decision. Stepping forward, she put herself between the angry male and his niece. 'Actually, I promised Tatiana that I would deliver her personally, so, Eugenie, get in my car.' The slam of the car door told her that the girl had obeyed. Chloe felt a stab of relief; she would have looked pretty silly if Eugenie had ignored her.

Nik growled. He wasn't used to having his decisions challenged or his instructions ignored and suddenly the emotions that ran rampant through him had nothing to do with their natural chemistry and everything to do with the fact that Chloe was a pain in his backside! He made to move past her but Chloe mirrored his move.

She held up her hands, her expression determined. 'You think my niece needs protection from me?' he demanded incredulously, his voice pitched to a low, private rumble.

Not half as much as I do, Chloe thought, despising the part of her that couldn't help but notice how incredibly good he looked clean-shaven. 'Don't be absurd!' she snapped, fighting the urge to follow his lead and respond in kind. Instead she modified her tone. 'Of course I don't! It's just that in a situation like this—'

'And how many times have you been in a situation like this, *Lady* Chloe?'

'You might be surprised,' she retorted, but as the antagonistic glitter faded from his eyes she admitted, 'Fair enough, I've never been arrested, but I think you're the last person in the world to be throwing my life of imagined privilege in my face.'

'You're encouraging Eugenie to think this is a joke.'

She flung him a pitying look; for an intelligent

man he was being pretty dense. 'She doesn't think it's a joke. She was scared stiff. I just think you're making a big thing out of this when—'

'My niece has been arrested. I call that a big thing!'

'She was only cautioned, and according to the sergeant I spoke to—'

A hiss of impatience left his clamped lips and she changed tactics.

'Look, Tatiana wants to keep this low-key, so you could force Eugenie to travel with you, but what would be the point? I mean, do you even know what you're letting yourself in for? Teenage girls tend to have a taste for melodrama and, I can assure you, she'd make the journey hell for you.'

'Is there a problem here?'

Chloe turned to see the policewoman from earlier standing looking at them. Well, actually she was looking at Nik and her mouth was ajar.

Chloe cleared her throat and gave the girl time to recover, as she had some sympathy for her dilemma.

'You know what it's like—you wait for a bus and two come along at once. This is Eugenie's uncle and we were just discussing it.' She turned to Nik. 'So is it OK if Eugenie comes with me?'

He didn't miss a beat. 'Absolutely and we can catch up on the way. Fred, my driver, can follow us.'

Her air of complacence vanished in an eye blink. 'You want me to give you a lift to the airport?' she squeaked, forgetting to avoid his eyes. They were shining with malicious amusement as if he knew perfectly well that the very thought of being confined inside her car with him for an hour was already making her break out in a cold sweat.

She closed her eyes and breathed out through her nose as she subdued her panic; he'd called her bluff and now she'd have to live with it. An hour was only sixty minutes, she reminded herself, yet somehow the maths wasn't particularly soothing so she decided not to work out the seconds as she watched him speak to the driver of the car.

Maybe it was wishful thinking but lately she liked to think that she was not quite as tense behind the wheel, but either way this journey was going to put her back months.

Nik was not a relaxed passenger; she could feel the tension rolling off him. Maybe he didn't like women drivers…or perhaps it was just her… He certainly couldn't be comfortable as he had to draw his long legs right up in order to squeeze himself into the space.

Served him right, she decided uncharitably as she stared doggedly ahead, ignoring him and the subtle spicy notes in the male fragrance he used.

The expression on her face when Nik had invited himself had seemed worth it at the time…but the decision had come back to bite him. The physical discomforts aside, and there were several—he had intermittent cramp in his left leg, and was losing the feeling in his foot, and the torture didn't look like being over any time soon, if ever—she drove at a maddeningly slow speed that he found at odds with her personality.

He suspected that if he mentioned it she'd go even slower just to annoy him, but when a caravan overtook them he lost the battle with exasperation. 'You drive like an old woman.'

'Sexism and ageism in one sentence…wow, impressive.'

'You haven't even got out of second gear yet.'

'Enjoy the scenery. Is he going to follow me the entire way?' She glared into the rear-view mirror that reflected the limo that was following close behind.

'That's the idea.'

'Is your driver ex-army too?'

The question startled a surprised look from him. 'What makes you say that?'

She shrugged. 'He has that look, you know, tough, hard…the catch-a-bullet-in-his-teeth type.'

Nik grinned, thinking Fred might quite like the description. 'He's a veteran.'

'You do employ a lot of ex-servicemen.'

'I'm not being charitable…'

He said it as if being considered charitable was an insult.

'I simply employ people I can rely on.'

And where he'd lived and worked, she supposed, you had to trust and rely on the people around you. 'Do you miss it…?' She bit her lip. 'Sorry, I didn't mean to remind you of…anything…'

'So Ana has been talking.'

'She mentioned what you used to do and—'

'Relax, you haven't reminded me. Losing a friend is not something you ever forget.' *Or forgive,* he thought as once again the familiar sense of guilt settled its suffocating weight over him.

She glanced in the rear-view mirror again. Eugenie had her eyes closed, and even over the engine the muffled bass boom coming from the music she was playing through her earphones was audible. 'Of course not…sorry.' She winced—the response to what he'd said seemed painfully inadequate and she pressed a hand briefly to the base of her throat where a blue-veined pulse was pounding in the hollow.

The action drew his eyes to the vulnerable spot, and the arrow-piercing thrust of raw desire caught him off guard and fed into the resentful anger he was feeling. 'If Ana has recruited you to her cause, please don't bother—'

'What cause?' She felt the suspicious brush of his dark hostile eyes over her bewildered face.

'It doesn't matter,' he said after a moment. 'My sister is overprotective and a great believer in *talking* about everything.'

Comprehension dawned. 'Oh, she wants you to talk through your…experiences with…someone.' And for a proud man, a man used to being in control all the time, that would be anathema. She wished Tatiana good luck with that endeavour, but she didn't envy her the task of persuading her macho brother it was not a sign of weakness to talk about his feelings.

Nik's lips twisted into a cynical smile. 'How delicately put,' he mocked. 'But I don't want to forget.'

'Therapy isn't about forgetting. It's about living with the memories.'

'What would you know about it?' he jeered.

'We plan to use the services of therapists in our centre; it's an intrinsic part of the recovery process.'

'An *intrinsic* part of *my* recovery process is a glass of whisky and a night of f—'

'Nik!' Pretty sure what he'd been going to say and equally sure he wouldn't want to risk his niece hearing him say it, she jerked her head towards the back of the car, her eyes wide in warning.

Dark strips of colour stood out darkly against the uniform gold tones of his olive skin, emphasising the slashing angle of his high cheekbones.

In the back Eugenie began humming off-key to her music, her eyes still closed. The sound broke the awkward silence that had settled in the front of the car. 'She'll probably be deaf before she's twenty. I don't know why Ana allows her to use those things,' Nik muttered.

'Maybe you won't sound quite so disapproving when you're the parent of a teenager.' Her smile faded. The idea of Nik with children of any age was quite a depressing thought.

'Ana's a great parent,' he agreed.

Chloe was surprised to hear an unusual tone of humility in his voice, and she was even more surprised when he added, 'So is Ian.'

'I've never met him.'

'He's a nice guy, and they made a great couple. If

they couldn't make it work I really don't know why anyone tries.'

'Love, maybe?'

His laugh was hard and cynical…leaving little doubt in her mind about his opinion of love.

For some reason the sound brought back a memory of another laugh, soft instead of harsh, a laugh she'd heard when her tongue had been moving across the hard pebble of his nipple, his fingers tangled in her hair, his body hot as he'd collapsed onto the bed, pulling her on top of him.

Then a minute, an hour, a lifetime later—time had stopped having much meaning—that laugh had come again as he'd rolled her onto her back, pinned her hands above her head with one hand and slid the other between her legs…

'You should be careful—you almost hit forty miles an hour then.'

His voice jolted her free of the images playing in her head and she drew her bottom lip over her upper one to blot the beads of moisture there. She felt the heat that suffused her body travel up her neck, threatening her with the mother of all blushes, so she dealt with it by choosing to pretend it was happening to someone else and it was this anonymous person who was feeling the shameful ache between her legs, not her.

'I'm trying to concentrate,' she snapped, glancing guiltily in the rear-view mirror, relieved when she saw that Eugenie was busy texting on her phone.

He looked at her fingers, which were locked,

knuckles bone white, on the wheel. 'Do have you points on your licence or something?'

'Or something,' she said in a flat little voice.

He glanced in the mirror. 'She's texting again.'

'You don't know many teenagers, do you?'

'It's a day for new experiences, it seems. Is there a reason you drive this old thing?'

'Reliability.' A very underrated commodity.

'I have a reliable lawnmower but I don't go to work on it.'

'You could always get out and thumb a lift with your friend Fred.'

'That's a difficult choice. He has terrible taste in country and western music…anything involving heartbreak and tragic lives and he's happy. But if I stay with you, I might never walk again.' He grunted as he attempted to stretch out one leg in the confined space, while beside him she released her death grip on the steering wheel long enough to push a strand of hair behind her ear. Though her hair was almost dry now, the scent of her shampoo still permeated the enclosed space.

Seeing the action out of the corner of her eye, Chloe permitted herself a smirk, which she suddenly doused, feeling ashamed. Maybe she should have allowed him to take Eugenie; after all, he was her uncle.

Had she done the right thing?

The obvious thing would have been to check with Tatiana, but the thought vanished as a sharp pain made her wince and she moved her head to try and ease it. Reluctant to take her eyes off the road, especially as they had just passed a road sign that announced they were approaching a series of tight bends, she twisted her head sharply in the hope that the action would free the earring that had got tangled in her hair, but instead it just tugged harder, bringing tears to her eyes.

'Let me help...'

'I'm fine!' she snapped, unable to keep the note of panic from her voice, but then his long fingers brushed her neck and she flinched, desire clenching like a fist low in her belly.

It was crazy, she knew that, but recognising this fact did not lessen the physical impact, although she didn't have to embrace it!

'These things are lethal,' he said, lifting the weight of her hair to lessen the tug of the earring on her earlobe.

One element of her discomfort eased, Chloe stared straight ahead. Having her earlobe torn or her hair wrenched from her scalp would have been a hell of a lot more comfortable than feeling the warm waft of his breath on her cheek.

'They're one-offs, hand forged, the silversmith is a friend...' She spoke quickly, trying to distract herself.

She remembered reading somewhere that the ear had a lot of nerve endings, and all of hers were definitely screaming right now.

His brows drew together in a dark line of disapproval. 'Your earlobe is bleeding; you must have one hell of a high pain tolerance.'

An image floated into her head of her in hospital, repeatedly pressing the pain-relief button that for weeks had never left her hand. 'Not really.' Actually, not at all, she corrected silently, thinking of the lovely floating feeling after she'd pressed that button. The pain had still been there in the background, but she had been able to float above it.

She felt rather than saw him looking at her.

'I fainted when I had them pierced, although that might have been the…ouch, be careful!'

'Sorry. Hold on, I've almost finished…'

Almost was not soon enough. It seemed to take for ever for him to unwind the silver spiral. Her relief was so intense when he gave a grunt of triumph and leaned back in his seat that she would have punched the air in triumph had she not had such a tight hold of the steering wheel. Instead, she contented herself with heaving a huge sigh.

'Cool!' Eugenie, her earphones now dangling around her neck, leaned forward and snatched the silver spiral that dangled in her uncle's fingers. 'Where did you get them from? I'd love a pair.'

'A friend of mine makes them.'

The girl moved forward asking eagerly, 'Boyfriend?'

Aware that beside her Nik was now sitting with his head bent, fingers pressed to the bridge of his nose, she shook her head. 'Her name is Layla.' She slid Nik a sideways glance and lost the fight against her concern. 'Do you have a headache? There should be some painkillers in the glove box and a bottle of water—'

'I'm fine.' He let his hand fall from his face and exhaled slowly. The headaches hit without warning, but he never took medication. Perhaps he deserved the pain, not that it ever left him feeling cleansed of his sins.

'Uncle Nik is never ill. He's bulletproof *literally*,' she enthused with awe. 'He never got a scratch when he was working in war zones,' she chattered on, lifting the earring to her own ear and craning her neck to admire the effect in the rear-view mirror. 'Mum says the only thing he's got is survivor's guilt...' She stopped abruptly as her uncle caught her eye. 'Well she might have said something like that but I don't quite recall.'

Chloe couldn't see Nik's face but she could feel the raw tension vibrating off him.

In the back seat Chloe gave a sigh. 'How much longer? It's not mine,' she added when the audible sound of a vibrating phone suddenly echoed through the car.

Nik swore. His phone had fallen in the gap between the seats and, eyes still closed, he reached out a long arm for it.

Chloe gave a grunt as an elbow landed in her ribs.

'Sorry,' he muttered and, delving further, he gave a grunt of triumph as he managed to get his fingers around it.

'Your mother,' he said to Eugenie after reading the text message, before switching his attention to Chloe. 'Telling me not to bother, not to worry, that she arranged for someone else to pick you up… I contacted her when I started out but she must have sent this straight away. Looks like you're calling the shots here.'

Embarrassed, Chloe shook her head. 'You're Eugenie's uncle.'

'My sister must really trust you, but it might take me a while to work my way back into her good graces.'

'She'll understand.'

He huffed out a laugh. 'Why should she?'

'It's what family do. Where were you anyway? Not that I have any right to ask, I know…'

'My secretary has the flu and her stand-in hadn't charged my phone.' Louise always did it for him. 'And when I said I didn't want to be disturbed I made the mistake of assuming she would know that didn't include family emergencies. She let all Ana's calls go to the messaging service and when I tried to ring her back there was no signal. Then when I asked her why she hadn't put the calls through she just burst into tears.'

'Poor woman, she was probably scared of you.'

He gave a snort of disbelief. 'Then she'll be much happier working elsewhere.'

Chloe was shocked. 'You didn't sack her!'

'My father would have, whereas I'm a much more tolerant employer and, employment laws being what they are, I just shipped her back to the department she came from.'

'You're afraid to let anyone see you have a heart,' she charged and, expecting to see him discomfited by her discovery, she turned her head to look at him, but found a very different expression on his face.

She looked away quickly, but not before the need she had seen shining in his eyes had awoken the same feeling in her belly.

He shot a quick furtive glance in the back before announcing very quietly, 'I have a heart and I am very anxious to prove it to you.'

'It's not your heart you're offering me.'

'All parts of my anatomy are on offer.'

She shivered and stared ahead. 'I'm not discussing this with you now.'

'Later, then.'

A hissing sound of frustration escaped her clenched teeth.

'Chloe...'

Chloe started guiltily at the sound of the curious voice from the back seat. 'Do you live in a castle?'

'My sister does, but where my mum and dad live is more properly termed a fortified home.'

'Normal people do not live in castles.'

'Normal people do not have a rota for the shower because there's never enough hot water to go around! Trust me, we are not at all glamorous—in fact, we're just a little bit last century. I was at college before I ordered my first takeaway pizza.'

'God!' Eugenie breathed.

'Take the next exit,' Nik said suddenly as they approached the roundabout. 'You just went past it,' he said with an air of resignation.

'Roundabouts are made for going around.' On this note of logic she did so for the third time.

CHAPTER SEVEN

THEIR PROGRESS THROUGH the private airport was swift. Once they were on the plane one of the male attendants drew Nik apart as Chloe and Eugenie were seated.

Their conversation in rapid Greek lasted a few moments.

'I'm travelling up front,' he said to Chloe as he moved past her.

'Can I come too?' Eugenie cried in the act of unclipping her belt.

'You're grounded, or I'm assuming you will be, so no…behaving badly doesn't get rewarded, kiddo.' He flicked her nose affectionately with his finger and walked on, vanishing through the cockpit door.

'I'm going to get my pilot's licence as soon as I'm old enough. Uncle Nik got his when he was seventeen.'

Did that mean he was flying the plane now? Chloe wondered, tensing a little as the plane started taxiing; she was fine with flying but the take-off and landing always tied her stomach in knots.

Once they were in the air, Chloe accepted the offer of tea but refused anything to eat. Eugenie, who seemed to have recovered from her brush with the law, tucked into some hot beef sandwiches.

She finished and sighed in pleasure. Chloe pointed to her chin and the teen wiped away the spot of relish there.

'So how long does it take to get to Spetses airport?'

The girl looked surprised by the question. 'Oh, there isn't an airport on the island. We land at the small private airport just on the mainland opposite and then we'll fly over on the helicopter.'

Questioning her decision not to simply hand Eugenie over to her uncle when she'd had the chance, Chloe took a sip of her tea. The return flight might not be as simple to organise as she had imagined.

On the helicopter trip over from the mainland Chloe sat next to Eugenie, who went into tour-guide mode the minute they took off. By the time they landed Chloe felt pretty well informed about the island of Spetses and its aristocratic heritage; she could have written a paper about the colourful mansions, the history of blockade running, its significance in the Napoleonic wars, and its long association with the master sailors.

While Chloe was being educated, Nik sat next to the pilot in the cockpit. The two men obviously knew one another pretty well and, with his sleeves rolled up and his dark hair tousled, Nik looked relaxed and very different from the man she remembered from that night in the bar.

Or for that matter from any time since.

It would be very easy, she mused, to let her defences down with this Nik. Just as well she was only here to chaperone Eugenie.

She turned her head at the sound of a phone ringing, struggling to make itself heard against the noise of the helicopter.

'It's Mum, for you,' Eugenie said, holding her own phone out for Chloe.

Chloe pressed the phone close against her ear, raising her voice above the background noise. 'Hello.'

'How can I ever thank you, Chloe?'

'No thanks required. I'm glad I could help.'

'How is she?'

'Fine.' She gave the worried-looking teenager a thumbs-up signal. 'I know a great deal about Spetses now. Did you know that Spetsiots were heroes of the War of Independence?' Chloe was pleased to hear the older woman laugh, then listened to her friend launch into another fulsome apology for imposing on her. 'Eugenie was no problem,' she said honestly, adding when Tatiana made sceptical noises, 'It was good practice for when I have my own children...' She lifted the phone away and waited for the static crackle to subside before shouting, 'I said it was good practice for when I have my own children!'

It was only when she realised the signal had cut

out and she lowered the phone that she realised Nik was standing right beside her, so there was zero chance he'd not heard every word she'd said. But if she'd had any doubts his first comment dispelled them.

'Thinking of starting any time soon?'

Working on the assumption that if she ignored her blush he might not notice, she managed a small laugh. 'My body clock is not ticking too loudly just yet.'

'Just wanted to say, another five minutes and we'll be landing.' He turned away and moved back to the cockpit.

Once he'd gone, Chloe closed her eyes and pushed her fist against her mouth to stifle her loud groan. The other hand was pressed to her chest, where her heart was performing all sorts of life-threatening gymnastics.

It was ridiculous...bewildering and humiliating. Why did she react this way to him? What was it about him that seemed to tap into something inside her...a *need*...a *hunger*...? An image of the answering hunger she had glimpsed in his eyes flashed into her head and her heart gave a heavy traitorous thud then started cantering crazily again.

She was complaining a hell of a lot, Chloe reflected, but if she really didn't want Nik chasing her, throwing temptation in her way, why hadn't she done something about it?

She could.

And she knew it. There was a fail-safe way, a

one-hundred-per-cent-guaranteed method to make him back off at her disposal… It wasn't as if she'd even have to show him; just using the words would have the desired effect. She could casually throw into the conversation that she had some ugly scars and always would have.

In Nik's head she was perfect. She inhaled and lifted her chin, a little smile playing across her mouth. She had been perfect and she had taken it for granted. Strange how you didn't appreciate something until it was gone.

The smile vanished and along with it the enduring sadness; she'd been lucky and she knew it. She no longer wallowed in self-pity or asked herself why it had to happen to her.

She contented herself with imagining that one day there would be a man in her life; of course, he might not make her think of passionate, all-consuming sex the moment she saw him but there were other, more important things in a relationship…deeper things that lasted the test of time.

It would be nice to have both, but she was a realist and she knew few people were that lucky.

They had disembarked the helicopter when Nik joined them, his tall, broad-shouldered figure drawing glances from the handful of fellow travellers that hovered nearby. Watching his approach through the shield of her lashes, Chloe had to admit it was not surprising he drew every eye; he might be the most irritating man on the planet with an ego to match, but he was also the most supremely elegant and by far the sexiest.

'If you don't mind I'll hang around for a bit and hand Eugenie over to her mum personally,' she said.

There was a slight time delay before he responded and the enigmatic smile that briefly tugged at the corners of his mouth troubled her, but as she'd been geared up for an argument his non-reaction was a bit of an anticlimax.

'The car should be waiting; it's this way.' His gesture invited Chloe to step ahead of him.

The waiting car was another long, shiny monster, and as they approached the driver jumped out, a Greek version of Fred.

Nik called out to him in Greek, the man called something back in response and walked around to the passenger door, but before he had a chance to open it an open-topped Jeep driven at speed drew up behind it. Chloe stepped back from the cloud of dust it threw up, but before it had even settled Tatiana, wearing a cotton shirt over a tee shirt and shorts, her shiny bell of dark hair pulled back off her make-up-free face in a severe ponytail, jumped out.

Chloe felt the teenager beside her tense and heard her sharp intake of breath, before she stuck out her chin and quavered out defiantly, 'Before you say anything—'

'How could you?' her mother ground out.

'I…' Without warning the youngster's belligerence vanished and she started to sob heartbrokenly. A second later she was in her mother's arms being told everything would be all right. Chin resting on her daughter's head, a shiny-eyed Tatiana shot a look of gratitude in Chloe's direction.

'We are so, so grateful to you, Chloe.'

'It's fine. I'm glad I could help.'

The image of Chloe sniffing into a tissue at the scene in front of her while she blinked hard made something tighten in Nik's chest, but he ignored it and drawled out sarcastically, 'Are you going to cry too?'

'I am not crying!' Chloe snapped back, blowing her nose hard.

'Do you mind travelling back with Nik?' Tatiana asked, glancing at her brother for the first time. 'I could do with talking one to one with this one.' She kissed the top of her daughter's head. 'Alone.'

Chloe minded very much. In fact, the idea of sharing the back seat of the limo with Nik filled her with horror, but she hid her feelings behind a smile and shook her head.

'Actually I don't mind waiting here to catch a lift straight back to the mainland.'

Tatiana looked blank and then shocked. 'You don't think we'd let you go straight back, do you? Heavens, you're here as our guest for as long as you like.'

'I couldn't possibly stay.' Chloe tried to sound firm, but all she sounded was tired as she lifted a hand to her ticcing eyelid.

'Perhaps Chloe has other places to be.' And other people she'd rather be with, he thought sourly, and the silent addition caused the line between his dark brows to deepen.

'You can't fly straight back,' Tatiana argued.

'Not unless she sprouts wings,' Nik inserted drily. 'Marco is refuelling the jet and then heading straight off to Düsseldorf.'

He slid effortlessly into Greek as he added something to Tatiana, who nodded in agreement.

'Well, that settles it, then, you'll stay with us…at least for tonight…to let me say thank you…?'

'But your grandmother is unwell…' Chloe began searching desperately for a legitimate reason to refuse their hospitality, or at least a reason that wasn't, *I really can't be around your brother because I don't want to be reminded of something I want but can't have, and shouldn't even want to begin with!*

It sounded convoluted even in her own head, but then so was her relationship with Nik. Except she didn't have a relationship with Nik. She closed one eye as the eyelid tic started up again.

'She's a lot better.'

'Yaya is a tough old bird,' Nik said gruffly, the warmth in his voice when he spoke of his grandmother unmistakeable.

And I'm sure there are some serial killers who love their grannies too, Chloe reminded herself as she fought hard against any lowering of the levels of antagonism that she felt were essential to maintain. Bad enough that she lusted after him, liking him as well would be too, *too* much to take.

'Well, that's settled, you'll follow us,' Tatiana announced.

Chloe, who was pretty sure that she hadn't agreed to anything, not that that seemed to bother anyone in the Latsis family, opened her mouth to protest but Tatiana was telling Eugenie to throw her bag in the back. 'Or, better still, Nik can take the scenic route and show Chloe…oh, no!' Her eyes slid past her brother and her enthusiasm morphed into dismay. 'Get in the car,' she said sharply to her daughter, then, after adding something urgent-sounding in Greek to Nik, she climbed in beside the girl and slipped back into English, saying hastily, 'Sorry, Nik, but I don't want Eugenie to get caught up in this.'

Nik, who had turned to follow the direction his sister was looking, nodded. 'You get going. Chloe, get in the car.'

Tatiana was already starting up the engine and Chloe couldn't help turning round to see what had caused her friend to rush off.

There was a woman approaching them, about fifty feet or so away now, who was by turns running then walking, or rather stumbling, towards them, her uncoordinated gait suggesting she'd been drinking.

Chloe didn't have a clue what was happening, but she was the only one, it seemed. Even the driver, who had murmured something in Greek to Nik and got back behind the wheel after receiving a nod in response, seemed to be in the know, but she did recognise an order when she heard one. She told herself she wouldn't have obeyed him on principle, even if she hadn't been eaten up with curiosity to discover what was going on!

'I said—' Nik began, still not looking at her, but Chloe could feel the tension coming off him in waves. His taut profile looked grey and grim, and the muscles along his clenched jawline were set like iron.

'I heard you, which isn't the same as obeying you,' she said calmly.

He turned his dark head then, flashing her a look of seething impatience, and ground out, 'I really don't have time for this now.'

The woman was close enough now for Chloe to see that she was correct in surmising that the woman was drunk; she could smell the alcohol from yards away. So, it seemed, could Nik, who set his shoulders and turned back with an air of forced resignation as he waited until she was within hearing distance.

'Hello, Helena.'

The woman was probably pretty when she remembered to comb her hair and her eyes weren't lost in black-smudged circles of mascara that had been washed by tears running in dark rivers down her face.

The sound coming from her was half sob, half breathless pant as she walked straight past Chloe, her attention totally focused on Nik, her eyes burning with hatred.

Nik didn't move an inch as the woman staggered up to him, glaring.

'I wake up every morning wishing you were dead!' she slurred. 'I wish I was dead!'

The mixture of venom and despair in her voice sent an ice-cold chill down Chloe's spine but Nik just stood there. What made it all the more bizarre was that he didn't look angry, he looked…sad, compassionate and, most telling of all, guilty.

Chloe's imagination went into overdrive. What had he done to this woman?

'I'm so sorry,' he said finally.

The woman's face screwed up and an anguished high-pitched shriek left her open mouth as she pulled back her arm and aimed a closed-fisted blow that made contact with Nik's cheek.

Chloe gasped in alarm, her hand going to her own cheek, but he just stood there and continued to do so as the woman started to pound his chest with her flailing fists, shrieking hysterically the whole time.

As the frenzied attack showed no sign of abating, although God knew where the woman got the strength from, the shock that had held Chloe immobile abated.

'No!' She wasn't even aware that she'd voiced her protest or had moved forward until Nik looked at her and moved his head in a negative motion.

It was the total absence of anger in his austere, strong-boned face that hit her, that and the profound sadness. It added a deep ache of empathy to the already present confusion and horror—too many layers of emotion for Chloe to comprehend.

His headshake coincided with the woman running out of steam and she finally slumped her head against Nik's chest, weeping in a way that hurt to listen to.

After a moment Nik lifted a tentative hand to her head, smoothing the tangles of hair down in a gentle stroking motion.

'I'll take her.'

Her focus totally on the tableau before her, Chloe hadn't heard the approach of a man wearing a harassed expression. 'Come on, honey, that's it. I didn't know where you'd got to.' The woman lifted her head slightly at the sound of his voice.

'The bastard should be dead!'

For all the reaction Nik showed to this venomous declaration he might as well have been, the skin drawn tight across the prominent bones on his face giving them the appearance of stone.

The stranger took the weeping woman, who reminded Chloe of a puppet whose strings had been severed, and pulled her against him, wrapping a supportive arm around her ribs as he half dragged, half lifted her away from Nik. 'Sorry, you know she doesn't mean it; she doesn't know what she's saying.' The woman continued to weep uncontrollably as she slumped up against him.

The stranger looked from the woman he held to Nik with an expression that brought a lump to Chloe's throat. 'It's not always this bad, but it's particularly hard today…'

Nik nodded, his face still granite.

'She's been drinking all morning. I thought maybe being here with family would help.' He stopped and shook his head. 'Bad idea. I stopped for gas and she must have seen you… I had no idea that you'd be here.'

'Neither did I. It was an unexpected visit. Is there anything I can do…?'

The woman's head lifted at that. 'Haven't you done enough already?' she slurred, before pressing her face back into the man's shoulder as he turned and began to walk away down the road.

Nik watched for a few moments before he looked at Chloe. Some of the rigidity had gone from his tense posture, but not the lines of tension bracketing his mouth or the shadow in his eyes. 'Have you seen enough now?'

She flinched, but didn't react to the unspoken accusation, which was both harsh and unjust, that she had taken some voyeuristic pleasure at the scene she had witnessed.

'Are you all right?' she asked, wincing inside at the crassness of her words, and she wasn't surprised when he just flashed her a look.

The muscles along his taut jaw tensed as he turned away. He didn't want or deserve Chloe's sympathy.

Are you *all right*? she'd asked. Well, he was certainly more all right than the man who would have been thirty-five today if he'd lived. An image floated in his head, of Charlie grinning as he delivered the punchline of one of his terrible jokes, Charlie looking guilty when he explained this would be the last time they worked together because he was letting his lovely Helena finally make an honest man of him.

Nik remembered feeling pleased that he'd managed to guilt Charlie into one last assignment, though he hadn't succeeded in planting a seed of doubt in his friend's mind when he'd predicted that Charlie wouldn't be able to live without the adrenaline buzz.

You know when it's time to quit, Charlie had said.

CHAPTER EIGHT

CHLOE WAS LEFT standing there when without a word Nik got into the front seat of the car beside the driver. She blew out a breath and for once in her life wished someone would tell her what to do or at least what to think.

A reel of the terrible scene still played in her head. She had only witnessed it and she felt shaken and physically sick; she couldn't begin to imagine what Nik was feeling and she had the distinct impression he wouldn't be telling her any time soon.

She gave her head a tiny shake and slid into the back seat. In the front Nik was speaking to the driver, issuing instructions, she assumed, but she didn't know for sure because it was literally all Greek to her.

Apart from that, they drove in absolute stony silence. A couple of times Chloe cleared her throat to ask how long it would take to reach their destination or for that matter where they were heading but chickened out at the last moment. So silence reigned until about maybe ten minutes into the journey when Nik suddenly spoke in Greek once again.

The driver responded in the same language and pulled onto the side of the road. The car had barely stopped when Nik flung himself out, and, leaving the door open, he strode off into the scrub at the side of the deserted road up an incline, immediately disappearing from view as he went down the other side.

So what did she do now?

Did she sit here and wait, or did she follow him…? She caught the eyes of the driver in the rear-view mirror, and his expression was sympathetic but he just shrugged.

'I think I'll stretch my legs,' she said, not sure he understood her or if he'd try and prevent her from leaving the car.

He didn't.

Grateful her shoes only had moderate heels, she stumbled her way across the steep slope of the rough ground, waking up tiny little things in the undergrowth as she picked out a path between the rocks, following roughly—she hoped—the route she had seen Nik take. The linen trousers she wore were of a loose style that ended mid-calf, protecting most of her legs from the razor-sharp ends of the long tough grass that poked through the rocks. But her calves already ached; the incline was steeper than it looked.

She had lost track of time today but the sun overhead was still high in the sky that was a uniform blue. It was very hot and she became uncomfortably aware of rivulets of sweat trickling down her back. Pausing to rest, she turned her head to make sure that she had not lost sight of the car.

Getting lost really would add the finishing touch to this day. Nik had seemed to vanish from view after only moments, so either he was astonishingly fit or she had somehow gone off course and attacked the slope at a wider angle.

Probably both, she decided, pausing again, this time just below the top of the incline. She ran her tongue over her lips; they felt dry and she was thirsty. Without the crunch of her footsteps, she could make out a distant whooshing sound above the softer constant buzzing of the bees that smothered the sweet-smelling wild thyme that filled the air with a deep sweet fragrance.

She closed her eyes and inhaled.

What are you doing? she asked herself wearily. *So you find him—what then? Does he strike you as a man who needs a shoulder to cry on?* Like a wounded animal, he'd gone away to lick his wounds; he clearly wanted privacy and she was going to crash it. It had seemed like a good idea at the time—but *why* exactly?

She puffed out a gusty sigh. This was starting to feel like a very bad idea, but, torn between turning back and pushing on, she hesitated only momentarily before tackling the last few feet of slope.

As she crowned the hill her efforts were rewarded by a view that made her catch her breath. In contrast to the steep slope she had just climbed, the other side was a very gentle incline, the vegetation spare where it grew out of the sandy ground, but she barely noticed as her eyes went to the horseshoe curve of a bay ringed by rocks. Alternating stripes of pebbles and silvery sand ran down to the water. Beyond the gentle waves that frothed white as they broke on the beach, the blue of the sea deepened, interspersed with iridescent swirling areas of deep green and dark turquoise before it met the sky.

The view was so unexpected and so soul-soothingly beautiful that for a long moment all she did was stare, but the moment of spiritual peace shattered into a million shards as her eyes reached the figure standing at the farthest point of the beach before the rocks rose up out of the water.

Nik stood, his tall, remote figure a dark silhouette against the backdrop of bright blue. The strength of the empathetic sympathy that swelled in her chest took her by surprise, and, without pausing to examine it or the need to be with him right now, she began to jog towards him, the downward journey on the smooth, gentle slope far less taxing than the climb up it.

Once she reached the sand she slowed until finally pausing to remove her shoes. Swinging them from the fingers of one hand, she continued slowing as she picked her way across the bands of smooth stones that were sandwiched between the wider bands of powdery sand.

The closer she got to the water, the more she felt the breeze, warm but very welcome as it lifted the damp strands of hair from her neck. She stopped a few feet away from Nik, suddenly unsure what to do next, which seemed to suggest she'd ever known. The thought that she actually knew what she was doing or had any sort of plan when it came to Nik tugged her lips into an ironic, self-mocking smile.

Blind instinct had got her this far and if she had any sense, Chloe reflected, it would take her straight back the way she had come.

She never had had much sense.

'It's very beautiful.'

He didn't react to her comment, so she assumed he already knew she was there. She took a few more steps towards him, in the shade cast by the rocks, which meant it was pleasantly cooler underfoot. But not as cool as standing ankle deep in the water, which Nik was doing in his beautiful handmade leather shoes, although he seemed utterly oblivious.

'Don't worry; I'm not going to ask you if you're all right.'

'Are you moving on to *you probably deserve it*?' he tossed back, thinking grimly that if so, she was right. Digging his hands deep into the pockets of his tailored trousers, he stared sightlessly in front of him, eyes narrowed at the horizon, trying to remember what it felt like not to carry this constant weight of guilt around with him.

He swivelled around, his short hair catching the breeze as a sudden spurt of stronger wind made it stick up in sexy tufts.

As their eyes connected it struck Chloe with the force of a blow that his expression was exactly the same as the first time she had seen him, dark and tortured. The sight made her heart squeeze in her chest.

The expression he caught on her face stung his pride into painful life, but he didn't want her concern, genuine or otherwise. He didn't deserve concern, and certainly not from her... Hell, life had been easier when she had been filed in his memory banks under the heading of a typical shallow, narcissistic socialite. He had used her once to distract himself from his past and he was doing the same thing now; why didn't she seem able to recognise a lost cause when she saw one?

'No, I don't think you deserved it.' Chloe's first thought had been that she was seeing an ex-lover he'd done the dirty on seeking revenge, and to her shame she had been prepared to be the cheering squad, but the impression had only lasted for seconds as it had almost immediately become obvious that she was seeing something much more complicated.

An expression she couldn't interpret flickered across his face. 'Well, I do.' He flung the words at her like a challenge.

'You must have done something really bad, then,' she said calmly.

A sense of deep self-loathing rushed through him with the force of a forest fire. His chest heaving, he heard a roar inside his skull before the feelings he'd kept locked inside for years finally exploded out. 'I killed a man—my best friend.'

'I'm sorry.'

His head came up with a snap.

'*Sorry!*' he echoed as he began to walk out of the

water towards her with slow deliberate steps. Confession was supposed to be good for the soul but he didn't feel good or cleansed; he felt furious with himself for losing control, especially in front of the last person he wanted to see…see what?

The question brought him to a halt when he was six inches away from her, so close that she had actually closed her eyes to shut out the awe-inspiring image he presented.

She could feel the heat of his body through the narrow gap between them but it was nothing compared to the anger and frustration that the air was practically coloured with that rippled off him in almost tangible waves.

He dragged a frustrated hand roughly across his forehead, but as he scanned her face for a clue to what she was thinking his own expression was cloaked. 'Did you hear what I just said?'

'You said that you killed your best friend. I have no idea what actually happened but, as they put people in jail for murder and you are not there, I'm assuming—'

He interrupted her, speaking through clenched teeth. 'He is dead.' His shoulders sagged as the anger drained away leaving a desolate hollowness inside his chest. 'I am here.'

The emptiness in his flat delivery brought an ache to her throat. Watching him through her lashes, Chloe struggled to hide the dangerous rise of emotions that made her chest tight.

'I know, Nik, I'm not deaf or blind.'

The hand he was dragging back and forth through his hair stilled at the mild reproof. He shot her a look and wondered for the tenth time in as many seconds why, if he was going to have some sort of meltdown, he had to do it in front of this woman who did not seem to have any concept of personal boundaries.

'I am not one of your charity projects!' he snarled, the very idea offending his masculine pride deeply.

Taken aback by the outraged charge, she just blinked.

'Has it ever occurred to you that people who put so much of themselves into worthwhile causes are compensating for something that is missing in their own lives?'

Anger at this outrageous statement replaced her bewilderment. Face flushed, she compressed her lips and arched a brow. 'Let me guess what you think is missing in my life—a man,' she drawled. 'Why do all men assume that they are essential for a woman's happiness and fulfilment? If there is anything missing in my life I'll get myself a dog. They're far more reliable.'

Eyelids half lowered so that all she could see was a glitter of dark brown, he let the silence that developed between them stretch out taut before breaking it with a thoughtful, 'I obviously touched a nerve there.'

He'd managed to change the subject from his own trauma, she realised, which she was assuming had been his intention all along. 'Your friend is dead and I'm sorry. You might feel responsible, you might *be* responsible in some way, I have no idea, but I do know for definite that you didn't kill anyone.'

'How can you possibly know that?' he jeered. 'You don't know me.'

She found herself wondering if anyone did. Did he push the world away or was it just her? 'Who was that woman?' she asked quietly.

He turned to look at the sea again. 'Her name is Helena and she was engaged to Charlie, my best friend.'

'Do you mind if I sit down?' Without waiting for him to respond, she brushed a piece of silvered driftwood to one side with a foot, set down her shoes and sat down on the sand, stretching her long legs in front of her, crossing them at the ankle.

Nik turned as she was leaning back on her hands, just as the breeze lifted her hair, blowing it across her face before it settled in a fine silky mesh down her back except for a few errant strands that stuck to her face. Wrinkling her nose, she pursed her lips and huffed them away.

There was something about her beauty that could touch him in a way he hadn't known he was capable of even at a time like this. He made an effort to resurrect a scowl but gave up on the attempt, deciding instead to sit down beside her.

'Charlie was a cameraman, the best there was. People often forget when they see some correspondent standing there in the middle of a gun battle that there's a man behind the camera too, taking the same risks without the same recognition. We'd worked together for two years in the sort of environment where…well, let's just say that you get to see the best and worst of people.'

Chloe glanced sideways at his face…and wondered what he was seeing as he stared out to sea. For a while there was nothing but the hissing sound of the waves breaking a few feet away, and she had the impression he had forgotten she was there.

When he finally spoke his deep, strong voice held a rusty crack.

'He met Helena through me. Her family are part of the London Greek expat community too, but like us they have relatives who still live here on the island. When I was a kid staying with my grandparents I used to hang around with her brothers. That was one of them with her back at the airport—Andreos. Helena used to tag along with us,' he recalled. 'A nice kid.'

And the nice kid had grown up to be a beautiful young woman with everything to live for, except now she didn't want to live.

'She and Charlie hit it off straight away. I was surprised as they were total opposites. Charlie was an extrovert and she was thoughtful, quiet and…' He swallowed hard, the muscles in his brown throat working.

It really hurt her to see him struggle. 'So it was a whirlwind romance?'

'Actually more of a slow burner,' Nik recalled. 'They had an on-off thing that lasted eighteen months or so, the sort of thing that often fizzles out.

But then something changed… I don't know what it was, but they got engaged.'

She watched as he silently wrestled with the emotions inside him. Finally, she prompted softly, 'You were surprised.'

He turned his head, his dark eyes glittering with self-contempt as he contradicted her. 'I was irritated. We were a team and Charlie had announced that he was quitting and moving to a safe job where there was no risk of being kidnapped or shot.

'It was me who persuaded him to take that one last assignment together. I was convinced that he'd realise that he couldn't survive without the adrenaline rush, that he'd resent Helena if he gave up a life he loved for her. Oh, I was a *really* caring friend.' Nik squeezed his eyes closed, still seeing Charlie's dead eyes, his nostrils flaring at the remembered metallic iron scent of blood. 'So it did turn out to be his last assignment after all, and he was only there because of me.'

Chloe swallowed the lump in her throat and turned her head to hide the tears that filled her eyes before picking up a handful of sand and letting the silver particles slide through her fingers, watching them vanish into the billions of identical grains. Risking a look at him through her lashes, she saw his expression was completely remote as though he'd retreated to another place entirely.

She didn't attempt to react to his words until she had full control of her emotions again. Nik didn't want her tears or her sympathy; he'd made that obvious. The only thing he wanted from her was her body, which rather begged the question as to why she was getting involved with his problems, seeing as it was the one thing she couldn't give him.

'What happened was a tragedy.' She winced at the triteness of her comment. 'But how exactly is it your fault?'

He vented a hard laugh and looked at her incredulously. 'Have you listened to a word I said?' He still didn't know why he'd said those words—any of them.

He was already regretting it.

He was a private man living in a world where people were tripping over themselves to expose their innermost thoughts and feelings, mostly for public scrutiny. You couldn't turn on a television or a computer, or open a newspaper, without finding some celebrity *revealing all*, but the idea of turning your personal tragedies and failings into entertainment for the masses made his blood run cold.

Getting to his feet, he brushed the sand off his clothes and stood there looking down at her. 'Tatiana will be wondering what has happened to us.'

Chloe uncrossed her legs and raised herself gracefully to her feet. 'Do you think you're honouring your friend in some way by beating yourself up for being alive? The way you talk about him, it doesn't make it sound as though your friend Charlie would have approved.'

'Helena might disagree.'

'Come on, you're an intelligent man—it doesn't

take a professional to see that the poor woman needs help. She's attacking you because she wants someone to blame.' She shook her head in disbelief as he turned and walked away. 'Nik!' Cursing softly under her breath, she picked up her shoes from the sand and ran after him. 'Fine,' she said, falling breathlessly into step beside him. 'Deal with it by ignoring the problem. That always works, doesn't it? It's very adult of you!' How the hell could you help a man who was too stubborn to admit he needed it?

He stopped and swung around to face her, feeling a twisting feeling in his chest as he looked down into her angry face. 'I did not invite you into my head, so stay out!'

'Or what?' she charged, pitying the woman who one day actually wanted to reach him, whose heart ached to help him.

He reached out and cupped a hand around the back of her head, drawing her up onto her toes until their lips were a whisper apart. 'Or this.'

Her gasp of shock was lost in the warmth of his mouth as it came crashing down hard on hers. He kissed her like a man starving for the taste, kissed her as though he'd drain her. One big hand slid down the curve of her back, coming to rest on the smooth curve of her bottom, dragging her up against the grinding hardness of his erection. His free hand moved to the back of her head to hold her face up to his as the kiss continued on and on until her head was spinning.

Her body arched against him as her shoes fell

from her nerveless fingers. Mouths still sealed, they took a few staggering steps together as the ferocity of their desire intensified. Chloe's knees were on the point of buckling when without warning he suddenly let her go.

She slid down to the sand and sat there, arms wrapped around herself as she looked up at him, her big eyes wide and shocked. Bleeding control from every nerve ending, Nik's hands clenched by his sides... He wanted to shed the pain, lose himself inside her—but he knew he would be using her in exactly the same way he'd used other women...using sex to gain a few moments' oblivion.

Why couldn't he bring himself to use Chloe?

'*That's* my way of dealing with it, *agape mou*,' he told her harshly, staring at the pouting line of her lips, which were still swollen from his kisses. 'So if you're feeling sorry for me and fancy a bit of pity sex...?'

Even as she winced at the deliberate crudity of his suggestion, shameful excitement clenched low in her belly.

'It was just a thought,' he drawled.

She watched him stalk away, wondering how anyone managed to look rock-hard, tough and vulnerable all at the same time, but then he was a man of massive contradictions. Her energy levels felt as though they'd moved into negative territory as she began to slowly slog her way through the sand after him. It wasn't until the car came into view with Nik standing beside it looking impatient that she realised what the tight feeling in her chest was—fear. She had never felt more scared in her life, which was saying something.

She couldn't be in love with Nik. She lifted her chin in defiance at the idea… She *refused* to be in love with him.

As she approached he opened the back door for her.

She tipped her head in acknowledgment and murmured sarcastically, 'What a gentleman,' before slamming the door behind her just in case he thought he was going to ride in the back with her.

CHAPTER NINE

'DO YOU LIKE IT?'

'It's beautiful,' Chloe said honestly as she walked around the room that Eugenie had guided her to. 'What a view,' she exclaimed, walking over to the open French doors. Three steps away was the infinity pool and beyond that the sea.

'It used to be a little tiny cottage, and Granny was born here,' the teenager confided. 'She was poor. That must be awful, I think. When she married Grandpa he wanted to knock it down but she wouldn't let him so he built around it. There wasn't any beach here then, so he brought the sand and made one.'

'What about the big place on the hill?' It had looked Venetian and just gorgeous set against a backdrop of pines.

'Oh, we own that too. Grandpa bought it but Yaya wouldn't live in it and he preferred modern so...' She gave a shrug that made Chloe think of her uncle. 'It's pretty much falling down now.'

'That's sad,' Chloe said, glancing through the doors of a walk-in closet, realising that she didn't have even so much as a toothbrush with her.

The girl seemed to read her thoughts. 'Don't worry. Mum will organise you some stuff.'

'No, really—'

'It's fine. She has closets full of samples.' She looked at Chloe with envy. 'They wouldn't fit anyone else here. Are you sure you won't join us for dinner?'

Chloe resisted the pleading tone and gave a firm shake of her head, adding, 'I'm really whacked.' She escorted Eugenie to the door and closed it behind her reluctant-to-leave guest.

She released a sigh and leaned back against the wall, willing the images that were flashing through her head to stop or at least slow down because they made her dizzy.

Finally summoning the energy to kick off her shoes, she flopped onto the bed and lay there staring at the fan that was whirring silently above her head.

She had pleaded exhaustion when she had been given the option of a tray in her room, which suggested she looked as bad as she felt. The bone-deep weariness felt as if it were crushing her; even lifting a hand to her head was an effort, as was closing her eyes. But when she'd managed it, opening them again was just not an option.

She suspected her weariness was as much emotional as physical. Lack of sleep was the reason, she decided, unwilling to admit the truth even to herself.

She touched her lips, a silent sigh rippling through her body as she remembered the moment Nik's eyes had dropped to her mouth and she'd known he was thinking about kissing her... Had he been able to feel how much she wanted him to? Oh, God, why was she even wasting her time thinking about it? It was just a damned kiss; there was nothing deep and meaningful about it!

She sighed, thinking, *I'll get up in a minute and shower the day and the memories away...* There was no hurry.

Fighting her way out of sleep was like fighting her way through layers of gauze, convinced when she finally broke through the veil of sleep that she had heard someone crying out.

She lay there listening but it was silent except for the sounds of the night coming in through the open door.

Night!

She sat up abruptly, looking around the room. It was dark but not inky black, as the sky outside the door was tinged faintly with red. She reached for the lamp switch and found it, illuminating the room and revealing a tray on a table, the food covered by domes.

She swung her legs over the side of the bed and the first thing her glance lighted on was a full-length silk kaftan hanging on a hook of the door to the bathroom. She smiled as she got stiffly to her feet. She picked up her phone and glanced at the time, her eyes widening as she saw it was five-thirty in the morning!

She picked up one of the domes and looked at the food, but she was not hungry enough to be tempted by the sad, cold remains of what had, she had no doubt, been a delicious meal.

There were more clothes neatly folded and stacked on the shelves in the wardrobe and hanging on padded hangers. Tatiana had clearly crept in while she was asleep like a petite Greek Santa. She yawned and stretched, wondering about Greek Christmas traditions.

She spent a long time in the shower and emerged feeling half human. Laying out a towel on the bed, she sat down and began rubbing the oil one of her physiotherapists had recommended into the tight tissues of her scars with light but firm strokes.

Maybe its effects were just a placebo but it smelt good and, while it was no magic cure-all, her skin always felt more supple after she'd applied it. She had got into the habit of carrying it in her handbag.

She waited for it to dry before she put on the kaftan, enjoying the feel of the silk against her skin. She lifted an arm and performed a swishing motion, smiling. Tatiana really was talented. Drawn by the smells and sounds of early morning, she wandered to the open door and pulled aside the mosquito curtain that someone had pulled across while she slept.

Eyes closed, she breathed in deeply before she walked out, the soft scented breeze blowing the kaftan against her body. A tiny lizard disturbed by her tread emerged from a crack in the stone and vanished beneath the glossy, well-trimmed shrubbery.

The swimming pool lit by underwater lights that reflected the mosaic tiles drew her like a magnet;

she loved water. She'd learnt to swim at school and if she had been prepared to put in the sort of dedication that involved a relentless early morning training schedule and no social life she might have been able to compete at a high level.

Physical ability and natural talent were no good unless you had the dedication that went with them and Chloe didn't…but she really loved to swim. Apart from the times she had stayed with her sister, as camera lenses and shocked stares were really not an issue in the royal palace, she had not ventured into the water since the accident.

She liked to think that one day she would be brave enough to swim in a public pool and not care about the stares, but that day had not yet come.

Walking to the edge, she hitched the folds of silk around her knees and sat down, dangling her feet in the warm water, thinking about the lovely feeling of it on her skin.

It was tempting to go in for a swim, it really was… Who was around to see?

Nik had been swimming lengths for ten minutes, pushing his body to the limit in an attempt to wash away the personal devils left in his head after the nightmare had visited him yet again. He neared the wall at the deep end, flipped over and had lifted his head to gulp in air when he saw Chloe approach the pool through a watery haze.

He paused, his head just breaking the surface as he trod water, the shimmering image solidifying. He was unable to take his eyes off her as she walked towards the water, the thin floor-length robe she wore blowing tight against her, outlining every supple curve of her long, luscious body.

She obviously wasn't wearing a stitch underneath.

The sound of blood drumming in his ears became deafening as in his head he saw her opening the garment and slipping it off, then standing there naked on the side before diving in... All she actually did was trail her toes in the water, pretty tame by most standards, but Nik felt his dormant libido once more kick into life—hard.

He took a deep breath and slid silently down under the surface of the water.

Her dreamy thoughts drifted as she continued to inscribe circles in the water with her toes.

The sheer unexpectedness of the sudden tug on her foot drew a shrill shriek from her throat. She pulled against the pressure and scooted back, fighting against the restraint and kicking out wildly.

There was a grunt of pain followed by a curse and she was suddenly free. She had curled both legs up protectively against her body when Nik's sleek dark head appeared, water streaming down his face.

'What the hell did you think you were doing? You nearly gave me a heart attack!' she accused shakily.

'I was swimming...it's good; come in and join me.'

The invitation sent a slam of hormonal heat through her body. She shook her head, her heart thudding like a metronome as she stared at him.

'Fair enough.' It took him two lazy strokes to reach the side. 'Then I'll join you.' Hands flat on the mosaic tiles, he casually heaved himself out of the pool, pausing for a moment on the balls of his feet before straightening up to his full impressive height.

Chloe had no control over her stare, and her skin prickled with heat as her helpless gaze travelled up the length of his long legs, taking in the ridges of his flat belly and broad, hair-roughened chest. His shoulders were muscle packed and powerful but he wasn't bulky. There was a streamlined strength to him, no excess flesh at all to blur the symmetry. Each individual muscle stood out defined and perfect beneath the surface of his gleaming golden skin.

Her eyes reached his face and his white grin flashed, making him look like a very smug fallen angel as he lifted one hand and rubbed it hard across his hair, causing more water to stream down his face.

He tilted his head to one side in an enquiring attitude. 'Sure I can't tempt you?' asked her personal embodiment of temptation, the gleam in his eyes suggesting that this was no secret to him.

Even though it was frustrating it was also true—she had zero control over the colour that rushed to her cheeks—but she refused to drop her gaze, or was it she couldn't escape the grip of his black, heavy-lidded stare? Her insides clenched as she ran her tongue across the outline of her dry lips.

'No, you can't,' she lied, struggling to inject a note of amusement into her response. 'But don't let me stop you.' Hearing the quiver of something near to desperation in her own voice, she half turned and gave an elaborate yawn. 'I was just going back inside.'

He reached for a towel that was slung over a chair, rubbing it over his dripping hair, then blotting the moisture off his face. 'You really should take a swim.' His eyes went to the wet hair that was slicked back to reveal her smooth, high forehead and perfect pure profile. 'Or have you already?'

She lifted a self-conscious hand, dragging it down the damp surface of her wet hair. 'I showered.'

He swallowed, the muscles in his brown throat visibly working, a nerve spasmodically clenching in his lean cheek as his darkened eyes drifted slowly over her face, then down over the soft curves of her lush body outlined beneath the folds of iridescent fabric, his imagination peeling away the fabric, seeing the water streaming down her smooth skin.

It took Chloe a few moments to realise that the noise she could hear was her own breathing, as she struggled to breathe through the sexual tension that hung in the air.

She wasn't sure that Nik was breathing at all. He just stood there, the bands of dull colour running along the slashing angles of his cheekbones emphasising their razor-edged prominence as the moments ticked away. Each passing second made her heart beat faster until she could feel the thuds vibrating throughout her entire body.

'I... I need to go.' Her voice sounded as though it was coming from a long way away.

'Why?'

'I need to book my flight.'

'It's six a.m.'

'Online.'

'Eugenie will be disappointed; she was looking forward to showing you the sights.'

'I need to get back.' There was a hint of a plea in her voice.

He shrugged and looped the towel around his middle, drawing her attention once again to his flat, ribbed belly and the thin directional line of dark hair that vanished into the waistband of the black shorts he wore. 'Are you sure you won't join me for a swim? It'll take the edge off it.'

She didn't make the mistake of asking what *it* was.

How would he react, she wondered, if she pulled the kaftan open and stood there scars and all? *Why are you even asking the question?* she asked herself.

He's not interested in your heart or soul; he only wants the beautiful body—or the one he thinks you still have.

'I don't have a swimsuit.'

His eyes dropped. 'You've never skinny-dipped?'

She stiffened and lowered her lashes over an expression that tugged his dark brows into a straight interrogative line above his hooded stare… *Sadness* seemed an inexplicable reaction for her to have.

'Are you afraid of the water?' he asked gently.

Her eyes slid longingly over the still surface of the pool, but she shook her head.

'Do you often swim at this time of the morning? Are you in training or something?' She'd only been changing the subject, but now that she'd thrown the idea out there she found it wasn't actually a struggle to see him competing in a triathlon or something; he had the body, the fitness levels and undoubtedly the competitive streak it took for such an endurance event.

'No, I usually run.' He bent and picked up a second towel before rubbing his still-wet hair vigorously with it.

'So you are in training?'

He dropped the towel. 'I don't sleep.'

The confession evoked a rush of sympathy in Chloe.

Midway through her hospitalisation, when the heavy doses of analgesia she'd been prescribed for pain had been reduced, she'd suffered badly from insomnia. Though it was not a time she thought about often, choosing instead to focus on the fact she had survived, the experience had left her wary of taking even an aspirin and she'd gained a personal appreciation of the negative impact insomnia could have on a person's daily life.

'I suppose it's hard to switch off sometimes.' *Especially when you have chosen to carry around guilt the size of a planet... Not your problem, Chloe,* she reminded herself, rejecting the stab of empathy that made her chest tighten. People who deserved sympathy were those who actually tried to do something about a problem. 'I settle for warm milk—not very cutting edge, I know, but that usually does the trick for me.'

He gave a sudden hard laugh. 'I don't want to sleep.'

'You mean you don't *need* much sleep?' He fitted the profile of the driven alpha type you generally associated with surviving on two or three hours a night.

'I mean I have nightmares.' The hand he was dragging across his face stilled, shock flickering in his hooded gaze as he asked himself why the hell he had just told her that.

His nightmares were something he had never discussed with anyone. Did he suffer from some form of post-traumatic stress disorder? He was sure there were any number of so-called experts who would be happy to tell him. In Nik's view the label didn't matter. Sharing was not his style and the idea of being an object of pity was something that he rejected on a visceral level.

Charlie was dead because of him and no label was going to change that. He didn't want to feel better... He didn't *deserve* to feel better, he accepted that, but the nightmares were a punishment too far.

She blew out a long fatalistic sigh. She knew that she was issuing an invitation to have her head bitten off but she couldn't bring herself to do *nothing*. *Story of your life, Chloe.*

'So do you want to talk about it?'

He turned his head and glared at her. 'Can you turn off the empathy for a minute? That's not what I want from you.'

Chloe held her ground. 'You're not responsible

for what happened, Nik. Charlie made his own decisions.'

'How the hell can you say that? I told you...' He stopped, his eyes narrowing over an expression of angry bewilderment. Why *had* he told her when he hadn't told anyone else? He didn't like that he couldn't answer the question. He was at her side in three strides, his hand closing around her upper arms as he dragged her into him until their bodies collided. 'Why do you have to be different?'

The emotions pouring off him made her dizzy, or was that the contact with his hard, lean body? The sexual pulse emanating from him and the feverish glitter in his dark eyes made her head spin.

His eyes stayed open and connected with her own as his lips moved across her parted lips, the contact a mere whisper, the progress agonisingly slow.

She shuddered and sank deeper into the suffocating excitement that caused her breath to come in short, shivery little gasps. His face blurred before she closed her eyes and the ache of hunger low in her pelvis dragged a sob from her aching throat as she whispered fiercely.

'Please!'

The hoarse, hungry plea snapped whatever shred of control he retained as, with a moan deep in his own throat, Nik plunged his tongue into her mouth, plundering the warm recesses. The kiss grew wild, teeth clashed, tongues tasting with an escalating passion.

Rising up on her toes, Chloe put her arms around

his neck to hold on for grim death. She could still hear alarm bells ringing but they were almost drowned out by the excited clamour of her own heartbeat. Her fingers dug into the smooth muscled skin of his shoulders and back as she pulled him closer, craving the connection of their bodies.

He'd still been clinging to the idea that making love to her was some sort of therapy to drive his devils away, but that illusion burned away the moment his hands began to move over her body, exploring the soft curves.

This wasn't therapy, this was survival—he felt as though his life depended on this. He *needed* this; he *needed* her. No, it was just sex, he amended as he cupped one warm breast in his hand and held it, his thumb rubbing across the engorged peak as he kissed his way up the curve of her neck.

'You make me want you!' he growled, thinking that all she had to do was breathe and he was out of his mind with lust. 'I just want to feel your skin on mine. I have to kiss and taste every inch of you.'

What was she doing? Your skin on mine, he'd said... In her mind's eye she suddenly saw the puckered flesh of her thigh and imagined the shocked disgust on his face when he discovered it. And she couldn't bear it.

'No...no!' She pushed hard against him and his arms fell away. He stepped back, his chest lifting and falling dramatically as he appeared to struggle to draw enough air into his lungs.

'What is happening here, Chloe?'

She gave a tight little smile and thought, *I'm dying.* 'Nothing is happening. I just…changed my mind.'

'You changed your mind?' The lines of colour along his cheekbones stood out starkly against his blanched, sweaty pallor. He looked like a man in shock and he felt like a man in purgatory!

She took a deep, controlling breath. 'You come with too much baggage for me… I like to keep things simple.'

His head went back as though she'd struck him; he was aching and hurting and mad as hell. She thought he was some sort of emotional cripple who needed taking care of and she didn't want the job! The injury to his pride was almost as painful as the frustration that raged through his body. 'It's only sex, *agape mou*; I'm not asking you to marry me.'

She knew it was irrational to let the words hurt, but they did anyway. 'Maybe, but *just sex* can get complicated.'

'I'm a man of simple needs.'

She gave a bitter smile. 'You don't need to tell me that. As I recall you didn't even manage to say a simple goodbye…' She regretted the words even before she registered the speculation in his eyes and rushed into further speech. 'I really think you should talk to someone qualified, about the nightmares, I mean. It's good that you don't drink to excess now, but the way you were that night…'

'The night we had sex, you mean.' He saw her flinch and was glad; she deserved to flinch after her harsh rejection of him just now. 'There hadn't been any nightmares that night because I hadn't been to sleep.'

There was a beat of silence before a look of shocked comprehension slid across her face, taking with it any trace of colour that had been there. By the time she breathed again even her lips were bloodless and the only colour in her entire face was the burning blue of her eyes.

'Charlie's death had just happened, hadn't it?' But it wasn't a question... Suddenly it all made sense: the darkness in him, the combustible quality of their chemistry, the driving need of his lovemaking—he'd been trying to burn away the pain of his memories in the fire of passion.

He tipped his head in acknowledgment, the weight in his chest painful as he looked at her standing there, frail and defenceless. Wasn't there already enough guilt in his life?

'You used me.' Anger and hurt shimmered through her and she didn't care if she was being rational; she didn't feel rational.

'I was too tired to fight you off,' he shot back.

Chloe flushed. At what point had she thought he would *ever* let her in? 'You really are a bastard.'

He didn't deny it. How could he? It was true. She turned away. 'Where are you going?' He had to clamp his lips tight over the word *stay*! He had never begged a woman in his life, and he wasn't about to start now.

'Going?' She turned back and lifted her chin. 'As far away from you as I can get!' she flung childishly.

'And who knows? If I'm lucky I might find a man who is not afraid to admit he's not perfect.'

'*Agape mou*, you're not looking for a man, you're looking for a cause!' he sneered contemptuously.

'Maybe I am, but you're a *lost* cause,' she flung back. 'You'll never have a future until you forgive yourself for the past. And you don't want me, you want a memory of something perfect… Well, I'm not that. I'm…' Breathing hard, she fought her way out of the kaftan, ripping the silk as she tore it off her body and stood there naked in the light of the breaking dawn.

He sucked in a deep breath, his eyes moving down over her body. She watched his face and saw the exact moment when he reached the area where the skin was badly scarred, saw the shock and horror he couldn't conceal.

That tiny flame of hope died right then and there.

'You see, I'm not what you need. I'm not perfect any more.'

She had no idea how she managed to walk the few steps back to her room, oblivious to the fact he had followed her.

CHAPTER TEN

THE VIOLENCE WITH which she'd slammed the door behind her made it swing back open, but she seemed oblivious to that as he stepped over the torn silk robe that lay crumpled on the floor.

It took him a few dazed seconds to label the emotion that broke loose inside him as tenderness when his gaze lifted to the slim figure standing there, staring blankly straight ahead like a beautiful, flawless marble statue… Except she was not stone, she was blood and flesh and nerve endings, and the flaw on her body that stood out only emphasised how stunning she really was.

He could only imagine what was going through her mind. This woman had more guts in her little finger than a regiment of marines.

'Haven't you seen enough?' she asked, staring at a point over his left shoulder. If he hadn't, she certainly had!

She would never forget that look of horror in his eyes.

Every resource he had was needed to retain his

control, but he was straining at the leash so hard he could barely form the word. 'No!'

Her eyes flew to his face as he walked towards her, the fierce tenderness in his eyes making her tummy flip and her throat tighten, as she had no defence against it.

'But...'

'I want to do more than look at you,' he growled out, lifting a big hand to curve his fingers around one side of her face. 'And I think we can do better than just sex!' he declared with arrogant confidence. Holding her startled gaze, he bent his head, closing his eyes only when their mouths were sealed together.

When he raised his head they were both breathing hard, her eyes were bright, her skin was feverishly hot, and every skin cell on her body was bursting with painful awareness.

'Let's even things up a bit, shall we?' he suggested, stepping away but only far enough to slide his wet shorts over his hips.

She swallowed, her eyes dropping to watch his actions, helpless to resist the desire that flowed through her as she observed how the lowering of the fabric revealed the level of his arousal. He flashed a grin at her, but his features were hard and fierce as he held her eyes.

'Come here!' he demanded.

She did and he took her hand, directing it straight onto his groin and curling her fingers around the hardness of his erection. 'That is what looking at you does to me.'

'But… I'm not…'

'You're perfect to me…and you are perfect for me.'

At the stark declaration the muscles deep inside her fluttered and the rapid rise of desire swept over her like a wave, wiping away the last shreds of her self-consciousness. As she tightened her fingers experimentally over his crotch, excitement swirled through her.

'Amazing!' she murmured.

He gave a low, sexy rumble of laughter that made the hairs on the nape of her neck tingle.

Nik caught hold of her hands, raised them to his lips and pressed kisses into each curling palm before lowering his mouth to hers once again.

The kiss began as a slow, sensual tender exploration and then suddenly it became something else, his tongue driving deeper inside her mouth and eliciting an explosion of raw need and desperation as teeth clashed and tongues collided. Chloe moaned deep and raised herself up on her toes, gasping as her aching, sensitised breasts flattened against his iron-hard chest.

By the time they broke apart, they were both breathing as though they'd just crossed the marathon finishing line, and he hooked a hand behind her neck, sliding his fingers into her hairline, the fingertips gently massaging the skin there.

Then he kissed the swan curve of her neck and Chloe's head fell back in rapture, her eyes squeezed closed on a long sigh that became a groan as his hand claimed first one quivering breast and then the other, stroking then kneading... Her head fell back further to allow him greater access, her spine arching back, supported by the iron strength of the arm across her ribs.

Her passion-glazed blue eyes flickered open as he scooped her up as though she weighed nothing and walked towards the bed.

She stroked his face, touching his mouth, his fascinating, pleasure-giving mouth, thinking that she honestly wouldn't have cared if he had laid her down on the floor and taken her there and then... The thought was both shocking and incredibly exciting to her.

As he strode towards the bed, although she wasn't small or delicate he made her feel both, yet at the same time powerful and strong.

He laid her down on the tumbled sheets and stood there looking down at her, nostrils flared, breathing hard, each breath lifting his ribcage.

His body was hard and tanned, warm, bone, sinew and muscle all so perfect that the desire low in her belly clutched hard as she stared at him, unable to look away.

'You're beautiful,' she whispered. 'Perfect.' Her eyes suddenly filled with tears as she choked out, 'I wish I still was for you too—'

The rush of emotion he felt when he interpreted the expression in her eyes was shocking in its intensity.

She was grieving.

His expression was both stern and tender as he came down beside her, lowering his long body so that they lay thigh to thigh.

'Listen to me. You are beautiful.'

She gave a teary smile, loving him so much it hurt. 'Inside, maybe.'

'Everywhere,' he contradicted. 'Inside and out. And I want to love every part of you. You have lost something, I know, but let me give you something to fill the space…' He took her hand and laid it on his chest where she could feel the heavy thud of his heartbeat, strong and steady. She could feel it vibrating through her own body; it was as if they were one…but she craved an even more intimate joining.

'I want you,' she said simply.

His eyes darkened in response to the husky plea. 'Then, *agape mou*, you shall have me.'

Arms braced above her head either side, he leaned down and kissed her, and she sighed into his mouth, eager for his taste, wanting to fill her senses with it. The heat was searing and she whimpered as she was swept away on a tidal wave of primitive need.

The erotic exploration of tongue against tongue continued as he lowered his body beside her and turned her onto her side to face him. He lifted his mouth from hers, but only to kiss his way down her neck and then over the quivering mounds of her breasts.

A keening cry escaped her lips at the first brush of his tongue over first one nipple and then the other, then when he took one into his mouth and sucked on it sensuously she gasped.

Her damp nipples continued to ache from his ministrations as he slid lower, his tongue leaving a wet trail over the slight mound of her belly while his fingers moved into the soft curls at the apex of her legs, stroking the damp folds gently and then parting them until he found the tight nub nestling inside.

She was so focused on the new, agonisingly blissful sensations he was creating that she didn't realise at first where he was kissing.

She stiffened, rejection making her eyes fly wide open, hating that he was touching the ugly scarred tissue on her thigh, imagining the disgust he had to be feeling. She didn't want him to have to pretend to be enjoying it. 'No!'

'Yes!' he insisted.

For the space of a heartbeat their eyes connected, and she was the first to look away.

Quivering but quiescent now, she lay there as he gently kissed the damaged skin, her face wet with silent tears that slid unnoticed down her face.

'You can't want to do that.'

Her broken whisper felt like a tight fist around his heart. In response, he loosed a low growl and dragged himself up her body until they were face to face. Holding her gaze, he took her hand and curled her fingers around the hard, silky shaft of his erection. His whole body was trembling with need as she stroked him, breathing in the male musk of his warm body.

She looked into his eyes and the desire blazing there burnt away her last doubts and inhibitions; she suddenly felt free.

Kissing her passionately once again, Nik pulled her on top of him and held her there, his hands curved over her bottom, continuing to kiss her into mindless submission until he finally rolled them both over, reversing their position.

Lying beneath him, Chloe gave herself over to the sensations bombarding her. She surrendered to the feelings, as she surrendered to him.

Then he parted her legs and she held her breath and released it in a low, slow sigh when he finally slid into her. She grabbed his hips, her back arching to deepen the pressure, wanting more.

With a groan he obeyed, giving her everything he'd got.

'Put your legs around me, Chloe.'

She did and he sank deeper into her, each strong movement of him inside her sending her deeper into herself, into him. It became one and the same, and they were both at the core of a firestorm, and when it broke the effect on every nerve cell in her body was electric!

She turned her head on the pillow, where beside her Nik lay gasping for air, his chest heaving and the sweat on his skin cooling.

She began to worry that he was cooling towards her because he suddenly seemed so far apart from her, but before the fear could take root he reached out and dragged her against him, as close as possible.

'What are you doing all the way over there?' he asked, propping his chin on the top of her hair-rumpled head as he pulled up a sheet to cover them both.

'Does it still hurt?' he asked quietly when they were both lying still.

She sat up then, dragging the sheet up to her chin, and looked down at him. 'My leg?'

He nodded.

'Only when I laugh... No, seriously, not really, it's kind of numb because the nerve endings were pretty damaged.'

He was pretty sure that her matter-of-fact delivery covered a world of hurt and pain.

'The skin can get tight sometimes.' She reached out and took a bottle from the bedside table. 'If it does, I usually massage this stuff into it.'

'Were you in hospital for a long time?' The image of her lying alone in a hospital bed enduring such pain produced a fresh surge of protectiveness in him.

'Longer than expected, because the grafts didn't take. There was an infection so they had to start all over again. That's why I'm not going back.'

He stiffened. 'They want you to?'

She nodded. 'They have offered me another op, but that's what they said last time...'

'Shouldn't you listen to expert advice?'

'The surgeon says he *might* be able to improve the appearance, but there are no guarantees, and I've had enough of being poked and prodded.'

The way she said it, the defiance in her tone, made his throat ache with emotion, and his arms tightened around her narrow ribs as he rocked her against him.

'But wouldn't it be worth it if they could improve it?' he said against her neck.

She pulled away, her expression wary. 'I still wouldn't be perfect, and it's not about other people, it's about *me*. *I* have to be able to look in the mirror and know I'm still me...' she pressed a hand to her breasts '...inside.'

He watched the tears slide down her cheeks and felt as if someone had reached a hand into his chest and pulled out his heart. 'Don't cry, *agape mou*.' He smoothed down her hair with a hand and pulled her back into his arms.

Nik felt regret when he saw the warm rays of sunlight filtering through the blinds, certain to wake Chloe up. The irony of his dismay was not lost on Nik, as for a long time he hadn't been able to wait until he could get out of bed.

But morning was already well established now, which meant that he'd have to let her go and lose the incredible sense of peace and *rightness* he'd felt holding her, a peace that had been better than the sleep his body craved, sleep that he had denied himself out of fear that in the grip of a nightmare he might hurt her. It was a fear with foundation, as there were reported incidents of men suffering from PTSD acting out their nightmares and injuring their partners in their sleep.

If he hurt Chloe, even unconsciously, he knew it would kill him.

The time had come to get up, but on the plus side the bright sunlight made it possible for him to study the face on the pillow beside him. Half obscured by the tangle of silky blonde hair, she lay with one arm across his chest and the other tucked under her head like a pillow. He could make out the fact that her eyelashes fanned out lush and curving against her smooth cheek.

If anyone had told him before yesterday that he would say a woman's name just because he wanted, no, *needed* to hear it he would have laughed them out of the building and yet...

'Chloe.'

It was barely a whisper but she must have sensed it because she stirred, whimpering a little and shifting restlessly, then, eyes still closed, she shouted, 'No!' She opened her eyes suddenly, and blinked as the haziness vanished. 'I was dreaming...' she whispered sleepily.

'It sounded like a nightmare.'

'I forgot about my leg and had put on shorts, which is silly because I never forget...' she murmured sleepily. 'People were laughing and pointing at my scars...'

Nik flinched inside. 'I won't let anyone laugh,' he promised fiercely.

Chloe smiled happily as he turned onto his side and pulled her to him, running a hand in long soothing strokes down her back again and again until her breathing evened out once more.

It was a long time since he had spent more than an hour or so in bed with a woman, partly because he didn't want anyone to witness his nightmares. It was ironic, really, that the nightmares this time had been Chloe's.

You don't have exclusive rights on nightmares, Nik.

The memory of her pathetic whimpers cut right to his heart, and he kissed her forehead gently, pleased that her breathing was now soft and easy.

She bore her scars so bravely but how many times had she lifted her chin and pretended not to care…as she had with him earlier this morning? Carefully he leaned across her and pressed the phone that lay on the bedside table, so that the time appeared; it was already nearly ten a.m.

His throat was dry and the glass of water remained out of reach.

He moved, sliding a hand from under her, careful not to disturb her, and levered himself from the bed. Walking through to the kitchen, he closed the door to muffle the sound and turned on the tap. He downed the glass of water greedily.

Then he retraced his steps, making a detour to retrieve his own phone, which was in his jacket pocket, before he stood there gazing at the sleeping figure. While he respected her decision not to have further surgery he wondered if there wasn't another way to help her…a way that would leave her free of nightmares about people pointing at her.

A sense of deep grinding impotence rose up inside him. There *had* to be a way to protect her from all the cruelty out there, the people prepared to gossip and mock.

Chloe woke up and wondered why she felt so good, then she remembered and she felt even better. Eyes still closed, she patted the bed beside her, realising that the sheets were almost as cold as the sudden tightness behind her breastbone. Nik had left her again.

No, Chloe, this is how paranoia starts.

'Good morning.' Nik must have been back to his own room, as he was now wearing an unbuttoned shirt—a very good look on him—and cream linen shorts… Well, you couldn't have everything, she thought naughtily, knowing she preferred him naked. He was carrying a tray that held a cafetière of coffee, buttered toast and some fresh fruit.

'Hello.' She hid the sudden surge of paralysing shyness by grabbing for a piece of toast.

'Hello to you too. Black or white?' Nik asked, nudging the bedside lamp out of the way to balance the tray on the little side table. He sat down on the bed beside her and scanned her face.

She pushed a hank of hair from her eyes. 'Black and thank you, for earlier on.'

'I'd say it was a pleasure, but I hope that was perfectly obvious.'

She blushed, taking a sip of strong, fragrant coffee, and peeped at him over the rim. 'For me too.'

'I've been doing a bit of research online.' He was buzzing with the information he'd discovered and couldn't wait to share it with her.

She took another sip of coffee and thought ruefully that he had more energy than she did, as she felt tired in places she hadn't even known existed!

'I don't know who your consultant is but there is a team of medics in New York who are working on some new plastic surgery techniques. They're still at the trial stages but the results are nothing short of miraculous.'

She listened to him in silence but he had lost her after *your consultant.*

'I'm not interested.'

The coldness in her flat voice acted like cold water on his enthusiasm. He regarded her in frustration but when he spoke to her his tone was all gentle patience. 'I don't think you understand.'

She put down her cup and tightened her grip on the sheet she had gathered across her breasts. 'No, it's you who doesn't understand, Nik. It's you who hasn't been listening.' Or at least understanding. She felt a fool now for believing that he had. 'You really think there is anything you can tell me about possible treatments? Do you think I haven't looked into absolutely everything available?' She pushed her bare leg out from under the covers, shocking a small grimace from him. 'I've been living with this for a long time.'

He shook his head. 'I realise that—'

'Do you think I came to this decision lightly?' she asked him, her anger growing steadily. 'Do you think I didn't agonise over it? I came to a decision that is right for me and I need you to respect it.'

'Obviously, this is an emotional subject,' he began, 'but—'

Her lips tightened. 'Don't patronise me and don't try and change me. You need to accept me as I am, or walk away.'

He held his hands out flat in a pacifying gesture; this conversation was not going at all the way he had anticipated! 'There is no need to overreact.'

She arched a brow. 'No? Well, how would you feel if I brought you a cup of tea and told you all about the PTSD that you are suffering from?' She saw his flinch and ignored it. 'That I suddenly became an expert on your *problem*.' Her mouth tightened as her resentment rose.

'We are not talking about me.'

'Yeah, because unlike you I'm not in denial about my problem…and it isn't a problem for me. The only problem is the attitude of people like you!'

While she had been speaking the colour had gradually leaked from his face and by the time she'd finished his warm skin tone was ivory.

'I'm trying to help you!' he ground out, getting to his feet.

'How about helping yourself first? *I* don't need fixing. You're the one who won't even admit he has a problem!' she flung back, wanting to hurt him as much as he had her. A strange sense of calm settled

over her as she looked up at him…this damaged,
beautiful man she had grown to love in such a short
space of time. This thing between them, whatever it
was, had been doomed from the outset. It had never
been going to work; she had only been fooling herself.

Why drag it out? she asked herself sadly.

'Until you sort yourself out… I don't want anything to do with you!'

CHAPTER ELEVEN

SHE'D KNOWN THE event was being filmed live but Chloe hadn't expected the cameras to be outside as well.

She could hear the young woman speaking into the mic as she stepped out of the car that bore the royal crest of Vela. She squared her shoulders. If her sister, who absolutely hated being the centre of attention, could do this then so could she…all she had to do was channel her inner show-off.

'And this…yes, that is Lady Chloe Summerville, who is standing in for her sister, the future Queen of Vela. We understand,' the reporter continued with a coy smile for the camera, 'that the princess was unable to attend tonight, and, though there has been no *official* confirmation, I'm sure you recall how the Princess suffered terrible morning sickness during her first pregnancy…?

'Lady Chloe is wearing…' she consulted a sheet of paper she was holding '…yes, I believe she is wearing a creation by Tatiana… Lady Chloe, hello.'

Chloe paused in front of the mic that had been

pushed into her face, and smiled. 'Hello.' The personal touch would have been nice but she didn't have a clue who the other woman was.

'That is a beautiful cape,' the reporter said, gazing at the floor-length velvet fur-trimmed cape Chloe wore. 'Real fur?'

'No, it's not real.'

'You are presenting one of the awards tonight, I believe, to the little girl who, I'm sure our viewers will remember, ran back into a burning house to save her baby sister and was injured herself. Humbling... so humbling...'

'To *Kate*, yes, I got lucky being able to present that particular award.'

'Standing in for your lovely sister? And how is the princess?'

Sabrina was where she spent most evenings at the moment, hanging over a toilet bowl...still asking anyone who'd listen why they called it *morning* sickness.

'She is really sorry she couldn't be here as it's a cause very close to her heart. Heroes so often go unsung and it's good to redress the balance just a little.'

'So why was she—?' The fortuitous arrival of the cast of a famous reality TV programme saved Chloe from fielding any more questions, and as the camera moved to the new arrivals she made her way quickly up the steps and into the theatre's foyer, which was filled with small gaggles of well-dressed people chatting. Tatiana immediately peeled off from one of the nearer groups and came across to where Chloe stood.

Chloe bent to kiss her when almost immediately her phone began to bleep and, fishing it from the minuscule bag she carried, she glanced down. 'A text from Sabrina,' she explained, skimming the message her sister had sent her.

Good luck and chin up! If you change your mind that's fine either way. We'll be cheering you on, so have a glass of fizz for me! And hurry back, please. If my husband asks me if I'm all right one more time I might have to kill him.

Chloe's smile was tinged with wistfulness as she switched her phone off and slipped it back into her bag. What would it be like to have a man be as crazy about you as her brother-in-law was about her sister?

Swallowing the emotional lump in her throat, she knew how lucky she was to have a family like hers, who were aware of her plans and supported any choices she made. It had been a struggle to stop her parents from flying over to offer moral support, and she suspected they were a bit hurt by the rejection, but she knew it was something she had to do alone.

'Is everything all right?' Tatiana asked.

'Fine if you discount the fact that Sabrina can't keep anything down. The doctor says if things don't improve by the end of the week, they'll have to give her IV fluids.'

'Oh, the poor thing!'

'So what happens now?' Chloe asked.

'Well, you're up first so they want you to go straight backstage, and after you've presented the award you'll see Kate back to her table, where they've seated you there for the rest of the dinner.'

Chloe nodded. 'That sounds good.'

'You sure about this?'

'Quite sure.' Chloe was surprised by how calm she felt now the moment was almost here.

'You know there are going to be headlines.'

Chloe nodded again, refusing to give mind space to fear and doubts. Producing headlines was the idea. You couldn't challenge common perceptions from a position of fear. She'd been going around telling the world that they should accept people with scars while hiding her own.

Which made her a big fat hypocrite.

'Tonight is the night of the big reveal.'

'I think you're very brave,' Tatiana husked emotionally.

Chloe felt uncomfortable with the praise. 'No, the people being awarded tonight are brave.'

She'd never thought of herself as brave but she had thought that she had come to terms with her injury. However, watching a filmed conversation with the little girl she was due to present a bravery award to tonight had destroyed that particular illusion for Chloe.

'So what do your friends think about your scars, Kate?' the reporter had asked.

The little girl had put down the doll she was playing with and thought about it.

'Well, I think they thought my arm looked funny
at first, and some kept staring. A few people, not
my *proper* friends, were mean and made me cry,
but everyone's used to it now, so they don't even
notice it cos they see it every day and I'm still me.'
She'd picked up the doll, applied a comb to its hair
and added thoughtfully, 'I still cry sometimes cos I
liked my arm the way it was.'

The hard-nosed reporter had had tears in his eyes
as he'd wound up the segment and Chloe doubted
anyone watching would not have been similarly affected.

She herself had wept gallons but her tears had
been partly out of shame. She had been hiding, Chloe
realised that now, and if she hadn't, if she'd been
truly honest with herself and everyone else, that devastating scene with Nik a few weeks ago on Spetses
would never have happened.

Now she'd have to live with the memory for ever,
all because she had preferred to be treated like a
woman with no imperfections. Of course, there had
been a price to pay for her deceit: she'd fallen deeply
in love. Flaws and all, she loved Nik Latkis, but he
didn't love her in return. Unrequited love had seemed
much more romantic when she was a teenager with
a lurid imagination, but the reality actually sucked.

It didn't help that her youthful imagination was
still hanging in there inventing implausible happy-
ever-after scenarios, not that she was ever in any

danger of identifying her fantasies as anything other than what they were.

It was the thought of Nik's far more sinister dreams that continued to haunt her. She wondered and worried about the demons that visited him in the night and the eventual toll they would take on his health, both emotional and physical. She longed to comfort him but knew that was never going to happen after what had happened between them. She didn't blame him for that; he'd tried, but her scars were obviously an issue for him and he wasn't interested in helping himself, either.

Would he be watching the awards ceremony?

Would he disapprove of her decision?

She knew full well that her big reveal would go viral on social media, sparking thousands of debates, which was good, and an equal number of cruel comments, which was not, from people who thought anonymity gave them the freedom to say vile things about people they had never met.

She was prepared for the impending blaze of publicity as much as it was possible to be prepared.

'Lady Chloe.' One of the organisers, an efficient-looking woman in a blue evening dress, appeared. 'You look lovely,' she gushed. 'Has Tatiana explained the format to you? Excellent. You really do look amazing. Oh, excuse me.' She stepped to one side as, at a nod from Chloe, Tatiana moved forward to remove her floor-length cape.

'It's OK,' Chloe whispered when the older woman hesitated.

Chloe smoothed down her hair, which tonight she was wearing gathered in a simple jewelled clasp at the base of her slender neck. Her dress was the same bold red as her lipstick, a silk sleeveless sheath cut high at the neck and low at the back, the reverse cowl open almost to her waist, and plain except for the pattern traced in hand-sewn beads along the daring slit that was cut high on the left side that fell open to reveal her thigh.

It wasn't accidental; she had asked Tatiana to do it that way.

'Stunning!' the woman began then stopped; she'd clearly reached the revealing slit. There was a pause before she lifted her eyes and during the slight hiatus Chloe fought the urge to twitch the fabric over the scars.

When the woman did finally speak, her voice was husky. 'That,' she said, looking at Chloe as though she were seeing her for the first time, 'is *beautiful.*' Then, clearing her throat, she waved away the assistant who had clearly been allocated to escort Chloe. 'I'll take Lady Chloe in myself.'

The lift was empty as they stepped in.

As the lift whooshed silently upwards the woman cleared her throat. 'My sister was born with a cleft palate and lip; it's fine now and you'd never know, but I remember the comments she'd get when my mum used to take her out in the pushchair. People can sometimes be very cruel and what you're doing is…good, very good. I'm Jane, by the way.'

Backstage was actually pretty crowded, but Jane

found Chloe a seat in a corner that wasn't occupied by what seemed to be the entire cast of a hit West End musical, who were waiting to go out and do the opening number.

Jane left but returned almost straight away with a glass of wine, and stayed with her while the comedienne who was hosting the event introduced the musical stars.

'Your turn.'

Chloe jumped at the touch on her arm.

'Don't worry. Pretend the cameras aren't there.'

Chloe straightened her shoulders and walked out onto the stage.

Nik arrived late, but he was there. He entered the back of the hall and surveyed the tables that had replaced the normal seats in the auditorium, searching for his sister and niece. He had just located them and plotted a course towards them when a ripple of applause made him decide to hang back until there was a break in proceedings so he could slide unobtrusively into his seat and no doubt get an earful for being late.

Maybe he'd slip out to the bar…? He hated this sort of occasion and he'd have been much happier to just make an anonymous donation, but he'd been guilted into coming, not by his sister for once, but his niece, who had gone into Bambi-eyes mode and reminded him that he'd never taken her to the show he had promised for her birthday.

He was in no position to deny it, although he

didn't remember the promise or the birthday, so here he was. He hadn't smelt a set-up, not until he heard Chloe's name announced, followed by another ripple of applause.

Nik only heard the name.

Theos, she looked magnificent!

Lust struck through his body as his glance moved from the woman standing on the stage to the larger image on the screen at the side of the stage. Elegant, assured, with the glamour of a siren of the bygone golden Hollywood era, she was wearing a dress that had to have sent every male temperature in the room sky-high… The thought of anonymous males lusting after her drew his brows into a straight line of disapproval above his eyes, but they relaxed when she began to speak.

A sigh of pleasure left his lips…he had missed that sound. The simple admission sent a shock through his body and he didn't catch what she said as he focused instead on the sound of her voice.

She had a beautiful voice; pleasingly low and clear, it filled the room. She must have said something amusing because there was a soft ripple of laughter…except he didn't feel like laughing. There was nothing humorous about the way he was feeling, the *things* he was feeling.

Did an alcoholic feel this way when they found the innocuous orange juice they'd just swallowed was laced with vodka?

What did they say about recovery? Something

about the first step was accepting you had a problem…but what if you didn't want to recover—*ever*?

Frustration burned through him as he stood there staring at her, a multitude of clashing emotions swirling inside him. He desired her, he resented her…he had *missed* her.

He had been only trying to help her and she had thrown his actions back in his face, accusing him of being the one with the problem, assigning the worst possible motives to his actions.

Why should he defend himself to this woman?

The woman who had tapped into his deepest fears, the weaknesses he despised in himself, and exposed them all to the light, and she'd made it sound as though he had a choice…?

She was wrong. Knowing it was enough, challenging her mistakes would have made it seem as though he needed to defend his actions, or, as she saw it, his lack of action… Move on, she'd said, but where was he meant to move on to? He couldn't rewrite the past.

A man takes responsibility for his own actions, Nicolaos.

The memory of his father's comment surfaced, smoothing out the creases of uncertainty at the edge of his mind.

Strange how some memories stuck. How old had he been? He couldn't even remember what lie he'd told, or what childish rule he'd broken. Maybe the moment had stood out for him because it was outside the norm. His father had not had a hands-on parenting style; he had seemed as remote a figure as the portrait of his stern-looking great-grandfather that Nik always felt disapproved of him.

He remembered the shame he'd felt and the determination never to disappoint his father again; he'd be a man.

The idea that he hadn't lived by that adage ever since was ludicrous. As for feeling guilty about how he'd handled matters with Chloe, she was the one who had seduced him that night they'd met!

Ah, poor you, the unwilling victim!

His inner dialogue was interrupted by a sudden roar of applause, and Nik realised that he was the only person in the room still looking at the figure in red on the stage. The spotlight, along with everyone else, was focused instead on a table near the front.

The big screen showed a little girl with a woman kneeling beside her, obviously her mother, encouraging her to go up on stage to receive her award, but the little girl was shaking her head emphatically.

There was an awkward silence as the child began to sob loudly then, and it was a heart-rending sound.

He was relieved and pleasantly surprised by the show of sensitivity as the camera moved off her face. No, not sensitivity, he saw then, they were just following the story. It focused on the tall figure in red who was now walking down the steps of the stage.

A murmur of approval went round the room that faded to a silence as Chloe began to weave her way through the tables towards the child. A silence Nik didn't understand until he saw the image of her body on the screen. The camera had dropped to show the long legs, the daring slit and…everything inside him froze.

The lighting was harsh and the camera picked out every detail of the discoloured, twisted flesh.

'Theos…!' His stomach muscles clenched, not in reaction to the sight of the ugly marks, but the pain they represented, the *months* of pain they represented. The explosion of pride he felt drew a raw-sounding gasp from a place deep inside him he hadn't known existed. An emotion he had stubbornly refused to acknowledge.

Like everyone else he watched as she dropped down into a graceful crouch beside the little girl, the big screen showing her smile as she spoke.

There was another faint ripple of sound around the room when the little girl lifted her teary face from her mother's shoulder. Chloe nodded and pointed to her own leg.

The room held its collective breath as the child reached out and touched Chloe's leg, then released it on a sigh as the camera recorded the smile that bloomed on her face.

Chloe said something that made the kid laugh, then she got to her feet and held out her hand. The room erupted when the child took it, and together to the sound of applause they walked back up onto the stage.

Nik wasn't applauding, he was barely breathing… He felt a maelstrom of pride, shame and an aching desire to run up there and take Chloe in his arms, but he knew that even if he had earned the right to do that, which he hadn't, this was her night.

As the tall, beautiful woman walked onto the stage and turned to face the audience they rose to a man and gave a foot-stamping ovation, which the excited child joined in with…and Nik knew he was looking at tomorrow's front-page headline.

He also knew he was looking at the love of his life.

And he'd blown it.

For once, no heads turned his way when Nik Latsis left the room.

CHAPTER TWELVE

IT WAS NEARLY one in the morning when Chloe got back to her flat.

She rarely received a call on her landline these days, but the red light on her answer machine was flashing, showing her it was full of messages.

She ignored it, as she had already spoken to everyone who mattered, and her mobile phone lay switched off in her bag. She massaged her temples with her fingers to alleviate the tension she could feel gathering behind her eyes.

She could feel the exhaustion bearing down on her like a lead weight, but her mind remained active, not in a productive, problem-solving way, but more of a febrile, hamster-on-a-wheel way.

She kicked off her heels, conscious of a sense of anticlimax. She had been building up to tonight for days, not quite admitting how nervous she was about it, and now it was over and it couldn't have gone better, she should be feeling elated. But instead she felt...oddly flat, and not at all the inspiring figure that people had lined up to tell her she was this evening.

Easing the beautiful cape off her shoulders, she walked through to her bedroom, where she hung it on a hanger before covering it in a protective bag. Hopefully a few people would bid for it at the charity auction her sister had planned for next month.

When Chloe had suggested the timing might not be good for Sabrina to organise an auction, she had quipped, 'Trust me, I'm a doctor. I'll be feeling fine by then.'

As she stripped off the beautiful red gown and ran a bath for herself, she debated having a nightcap, but on balance decided against it, worried it might compete with the champagne she'd drunk earlier that evening.

Lighting the scented candles around the bath, she eased herself into the sweet-smelling water and lay there drifting, feeling deliciously decadent. Slowly the tension began to ease out of her shoulders.

Then the doorbell rang.

Her eyes peered through the open bathroom doorway to the clock on her bedroom wall, and she squinted to make out the time. Who on earth could that be in the middle of the night?

Everyone had warned her to expect some press intrusion after tonight and she thought that was realistic but this was ridiculous. It was getting on for two a.m.!

She decided to ignore it.

But her late-night caller was not giving up, and Chloe lay there, teeth gritted as the tension climbed back into her shoulders. And then the answer to her earlier question popped into her head.

Who did knock on doors at this time of night? The police with bad news.

Leaping out of the water, her pulse racing in panic and still dripping wet, she fought her way into a thick towelling robe and ran to the front door, leaving a trail of wet footprints in her wake. By the time she reached the door her imagination was cranked up to full volume and she was on her fourth awful possible scenario!

Cinching the belt a little tighter, she checked the safety chain was fastened and, as an extra precaution, picked up a heavy pale wood Dala horse from the console table and opened the door a crack.

Her late-night callers weren't wearing uniform and it was one visitor, singular, although she couldn't make out who it was.

Caution replaced dread, though on the plus side if this was a homicidal maniac standing there the walls were very thin in the apartments. Someone would be bound to hear her being murdered, and hopefully report it to the police.

'My neighbour is a black belt in karate!' she called through the crack.

She could only see a sliver of the man standing outside her door in the communal hallway, but as he stepped closer the partial view was more than sufficient to make the colour in her face recede, leaving her dramatically pale, and then return as quickly, dusting her cheeks with rose pink as she stood there frozen.

Her first thought was that she had fallen asleep

and this was a new version of her recurring dream. In all the other versions, Nik had been wearing black swimming shorts and nothing else, not a dinner jacket that hung open and a white dress shirt that was pulled open at the neck and seemed to have several buttons missing. There were the remains of a bow tie sticking out of his breast pocket too; he really did not look his usual immaculate self.

'Hello.'

This Nik, with dark shadows under his eyes and stubble on his chin, still looked more sexy than any man had a right to be.

'I need to lie down,' she mumbled, thinking, *And then I need to wake up!*

'Can I come in first?' His mild tone was at stark variance to the glitter in his eyes as he stared at her.

'I thought you were the police! I thought Sabrina had lost the baby or my mum had fallen and broken her hip, or my dad had—'

'Sorry I scared you.'

'You can't really be here because you don't know where I live. I moved.' She'd rented out her old place as part of the entire new change she had decided to adopt on her return from Greece.

'Then you should consider going ex-directory, you know.' He dragged a hand across his hair and sounded tired as he added gruffly, 'Let me in, Chloe, please.'

'All right.' It took her longer than it should to remove the chain. Her hands, she noticed, viewing the phenomenon with a strange out-of-body objectivity, were shaking violently.

Finally she released it.

She stepped back as Nik walked in; he was real after all. Dreams didn't smell this good, carrying with them the scent of outdoors underlain with a faint scent of whisky.

'Beware Greeks bearing gifts,' she murmured.

Especially tall, lean, gorgeous Greeks with pride etched onto every inch of a classically perfect profile and with explosive tension locked into every muscle.

He held out his empty hands and turned them over. 'I don't have any. I wasn't sure if you'd even let me in.'

'I wasn't sure you were real,' she countered huskily. Then, shaking her head to clear the static buzz, she tried to inject a little normality into what was a very surreal situation.

'Do you know what time it is?' She flicked back the hair from her face, the soggy ends dusting her cheek with dots of moisture.

'I couldn't wait until morning,' he said simply.

Struggling to convey a calm she was a million miles from feeling, Chloe met his eyes. The combustible quality in his heavy-lidded stare dried her throat and made her heart thud harder against her ribcage. She cinched the belt even tighter, suddenly very conscious of the fact that she was naked underneath her robe.

'Why are you here, Nik…?' Her eyes fluttered wider. 'Has something happened to Tatiana… Eugenie…?'

'No, they're fine,' he soothed immediately.

Panic subsiding, Chloe let out a relieved little sigh and arched a brow, folding her arms in an unconsciously protective gesture over her chest as she asked again, 'So why are you here?'

'Why didn't you tell me…?' He stopped and spread his hands. 'Tonight, you… No, you don't have to tell me. I know I've got no right to encourage your confidence in me.' He was the last person she'd turn to for support.

'You saw it on television?'

'I was there,' he said heavily. The pride he had felt for what she'd done was still there but overlaying it now was apprehension for her future. For every voice raised in admiration there would be another writing crude, cruel insults, but he'd be there for her, regardless.

She refused to jump to conclusions. 'Where?'

'At the theatre, for the bravery awards.'

The muscles along his jaw tightened as he realised with a sudden startling insight what she really wanted. She didn't want to be protected from people; she wanted to be released to be the brave, beautiful heroine she was. She might make those who cared for her sick with worry on her behalf, but it was a price they'd have to pay.

Nik knew with a total certainty that he wanted to be one of them, even though the idea of anyone hurting her by word or action left a sour taste in his mouth, and rage in his heart.

All he could do was be there for her—if she'd let him.

'Oh.' What else could she say? 'You didn't stay around for the party, then.' Her attempt at levity fell flat in the face of his grim-featured non-reaction.

For a big man Nik moved very fast.

The weight of his body made her take a staggering step back as he framed her face with his hands and turned it up to him.

'It was the bravest thing I have ever seen,' he rasped in a throaty whisper. 'Can you ever forgive me? I don't want to change you, I swear, but I'll change who I am. I'll—'

'I like you the way you are...'

His kiss silenced her. When he finally lifted his head his forefinger replaced his lips. 'Let me speak without putting words in my mouth...' She nodded dazedly, and he took his finger away. 'Tonight I saw the bravest, most beautiful woman I know...do the bravest, most beautiful thing.'

Her eyelids lowered over the haze of tears that shimmered in the swimming azure depths. 'I was scared stiff,' she admitted. 'I thought you'd be angry with me.'

The expression drawn on his chiselled face was one of astonished incredulity. 'I *am* angry.'

Her head began to lower but he placed a finger under her chin and drew her face inexorably up to his. 'But not with you, *agape mou*. Never with you. I'm furious with *myself* for wasting so much time!' he rasped out throatily. 'I know I have a problem with

PTSD, and I'll get help for that. I might never be the man you deserve but, so help me, I'll do whatever it takes, so long as you take me back?'

She blinked in shock as she stared at him. 'Did I ever really have you?'

The shaky laugh dragged from her throat cut off abruptly as she encountered the hard, hungry, slightly unfocused look in his stare.

'From that first moment I met you, I think, but I was too stupid, too much of a stubborn, proud fool to realise it.' He dragged a hand through his hair. 'I really don't have any pride left, Chloe, and there hasn't been a day gone by since that morning in Greece that I haven't hated myself for making you think I was ashamed of your scars.'

She put up a hand and cupped his cheek. 'I see now that wasn't the case.'

'It's *my* scars I'm ashamed of,' he admitted heavily. 'Everything you said to me that morning was absolutely right. I knew it then, but I just couldn't admit it. Now I'm asking you to take me, Chloe, scars and all, for better or for worse... I love you, *agape mou*, and I need you.'

He took a deep shuddering breath. 'I know I walked away from you—twice—but I promise that will not happen ever again. Let me into your life and I will always let you be you. I don't want to stifle you. I want to watch you fly.'

With a little sigh, she laid her head on his chest, her eyes squeezing shut as she felt his strong arms close around her. She stood there listening to the thud of his heartbeat, feeling the weeks of loneliness slip away.

Finally she lifted her head. 'I love you too, Nik.'

The kiss he gave her went on and on, his hungry passion leaving her feeling limp yet very happy when they finally came up for air.

She stroked his face lovingly. 'I feel as though a weight has been lifted from me the last few weeks.'

He took her face between his hands. 'I love you, I love every part of you, and, yes, I admit I did want you to reconsider the plastic surgery, but not,' he emphasised, 'for me. For you...'

'I realise that now,' she admitted.

'I don't know if you've fully considered this,' he began tentatively, 'but what you did tonight will make you the target of—'

'Internet trolls and other low-life, yes, I know.' She dismissed them with an impatient click of her fingers.

It took a few moments for the information to filter through to his brain...but when it did his hands fell from her face in astonishment.

'Of course I know that; I'd need to live on Mars not to know,' she said with a rueful smile.

'And you still did it.' He shook his head and gave a laugh. 'You really are the most incredible woman,' he declared with husky pride.

'Is there stuff out there already?'

He nodded.

'We're not going to read it,' she declared.

'I think that is a good move.'

He cleared his throat.

'Nik, why are you looking shifty?' she demanded.

Without a word he picked up his phone, scrolled down the screen and handed it to her. 'There are some other things out there you should probably know about.'

With a puzzled frown Chloe took it and began to read, her expression changing from bemusement to anger as she progressed. 'Oh, my God, who did this? Do you know who the source is? It has to be someone close to you to know all these details. It's a gross invasion of privacy!' she declared indignantly.

'Me!'

Her eyes flew wide. It made no sense. Nik was an intensely private person so why would he feed this story about himself to a journalist? 'I don't understand.'

'I gave this story, this evening. You made me so proud tonight, seeing how courageous you were, not hiding in any sense of the word... You were marvellous and it made me feel completely ashamed of myself. You were right: I've been hiding like a coward. Your name is going to be out there all over the media, and I knew I couldn't stop that, but I could show some solidarity so... I decided to join you and—who knows?—reading about what happened to me might even help someone else. I'm definitely going to do something about it, I promise you.'

'I know you will.'

'I wanted to prove to you that you could give me your heart and I would keep it safe and I am hoping that you would accept mine.'

Chloe's breath caught in her throat.

'And for the record I don't want to change a single thing about you.'

Tears pouring down her cheeks, Chloe flung herself at him, sobbing with sheer joy, and he swung her up into his arms.

Eyes locked on his, she took his hand and placed it on her heart. 'I know you'll keep it safe.'

Three months later

'Another builder has quit,' Nik said, wandering into the office where Chloe was working. 'At this rate we'll never move into the house on Spetses. You have to do something about her.'

'Me!' Chloe echoed. 'I don't think so. She is your grandmother.'

'She is counting nails! We are in the middle of multimillion-pound renovation of a classic sixteenth-century mansion and my grandmother is counting nails.'

'She is thrifty.'

'She is insane, and you know it.'

'She's *your* grandmother…' she reminded him, coming around the table and looping her arms around his neck. Nik kissed her hard.

'At this rate we're not going to be able to move in after the wedding.'

Chloe shrugged. 'I don't care if I start married life in a shoe box, so long as it's with you.'

'Now you tell me, after I've already had to cope with planning officers from hell, contractors who never answer their phones and, of course, let's not forget Yaya.'

'She's excited about us being her new neighbours… well, for some of the time.' Nik had not given up his London house.

'It will all be worth it in the end, you'll see, waking up to the smell of pines and the sound of the sea,' she said dreamily.

'So long as I can see you when I wake up, I don't care. Which reminds me, have you got the shortlist for the new team leader for the charity? I don't want my wife—'

Her eyes widened as she pressed a finger to his lips and looked over her shoulder. 'Hush! You'll give the game away! Imagine how upset everyone will be if they find out we already got married after they've been to so much trouble to arrange this massive wedding.' Somehow she didn't think that people would be that understanding about their impulsive elopement.

He looked at her, eyes glowing with pride and love. 'I couldn't wait to make you my wife. I just wish I saw more of you.'

'I know,' she admitted, stroking his cheek with a loving hand. 'But who knew that the charity would take off this way? We're interviewing for a team leader next week and there are some very strong candidates.' She squeezed his bicep and pretended to faint. 'Obviously not as strong as you, darling.'

Their kiss might have gone on longer if Nik's ninety-five-year-old grandmother, all four feet five of her, hadn't suddenly appeared. 'A man came who said he was a building inspector. In my day there were no such thing; we just build a house with no paper.'

'The good old days,' Nik murmured. 'So where is the building inspector, Yaya?'

'Gone. I told him my grandson and his woman were busy making babies, and if they weren't doing that, then they should be.' Chortling at her own joke, she shuffled out of the room.

'Well, they do say that with age comes wisdom.' Nik extended a hand towards the door through which his grandmother had just exited. 'How about it, wife? Do you fancy a little baby making?'

'Only if you lock the door. If Yaya walks in on us, I might be scarred for life...' As the unintentional play on words hit home she released a loud laugh.

Nik felt pride swell in his chest once more. His wife laughed when others might weep. She had a gift for living life to its utmost, and looking at the world through her eyes had finally brought him the peace he'd never thought he'd feel again.

'Have my children, Chloe.'

Her throat closed up with sheer happiness. 'It's a big house, Nik, and there are lots of bedrooms to fill.'

'So maybe we should get started.'

'You read my mind!'

* * * * *

COMING NEXT MONTH FROM

HARLEQUIN
Presents®

Available February 20, 2018

#3601 BOUND TO THE SICILIAN'S BED
Conveniently Wed!
by Sharon Kendrick

After their painful past, Nicole wants a divorce. But to get her out of his system, Rocco offers a deal: before moving on with her life, she will be his one last time!

#3602 HIS MISTRESS BY BLACKMAIL
by Maya Blake

Ruthless Xandro is hell-bent on recovering a stolen heirloom. But blackmailing delectable dancer Sage unravels when their attraction ignites! He's forgotten all his own rules—because this game of seduction can only have one winner...

#3603 THE GREEK'S SECRET SON
Secret Heirs of Billionaires
by Julia James

Years ago Anatole broke Tia's heart—despite her fierce craving, she won't accept his marriage demand! But as they're bound by more than passion...dare Tia confess to the biggest secret of all?

#3604 A DEAL FOR HER INNOCENCE
by Cathy Williams

Ellie Wilson only has eyes for her job...until she meets gorgeous Niccolo Rossi! After arriving at his Caribbean resort, Ellie's advertising pitch suddenly involves her playing his girlfriend. But seduction may be Niccolo's highest priority...

HPCNM0218RA

Get 2 Free Books,

HARLEQUIN *Presents*®

Plus 2 Free Gifts—

just for trying the Reader Service!

HP17R3

One final weekend in her husband's bed!

*When Rocco's runaway wife asks for a divorce,
the Sicilian billionaire seizes his chance! They've never
discussed their painful past, but this is the perfect
opportunity to get Nicole out of his system for good.
He offers her a deal: if Nicole wants to move on with
her life, she will be his, one last time!*

Read on for a sneak preview of
Sharon Kendrick's *next story,*
*BOUND TO THE SICILIAN'S BED,
part of the **CONVENIENTLY WED!** series.*

Rocco was going to kiss her, and after everything she'd just said, Nicole knew she needed to stop him. But suddenly she found herself governed by a much deeper need than preserving her sanity or her pride. A need and a hunger that swept over her with the speed of a bushfire. As Rocco's shadowed face lowered toward her, she found past and present fusing, so that for a disconcerting moment she forgot everything except the urgent hunger in her body. Because hadn't her Sicilian husband always been able to do this—to captivate her with the lightest touch and to tantalize her with that smoldering look of promise? And hadn't there been many nights since they'd separated when she'd woken up, still half muddled with sleep, and found herself yearning for the taste of his lips on hers just one more time? And now she had it.

One more time.

She opened her mouth—though afterward she would try to

convince herself she'd been intending to resist him—but Rocco used the opportunity to fasten his mouth over hers in the most perfect of fits. And Nicole felt instantly helpless—caught up in the powerful snare of a sexual mastery that wiped out everything else. She gave a gasp of pleasure because it had been so long since she had done this.

Since they'd been apart Nicole had felt like a living statue—as if she were made from marble, as if the flesh-and-blood parts of her were some kind of half-forgotten dream. Slowly but surely she had withdrawn from the sensual side of her nature, until she'd convinced herself she was dead and unfeeling inside. But here came Rocco to wake her dormant sexuality with nothing more than a single kiss. It was like some stupid fairy story. It was scary and powerful. She didn't want to want him, and yet…

She wanted him.

Her lips opened wider as his tongue slid inside her mouth, eagerly granting him that intimacy as if preparing the way for another. She began to shiver as his hands started to explore her—rediscovering her body with an impatient hunger, as if it were the first time he'd ever touched her.

"Nicole," he said unevenly. She'd never heard him say her name like that before.

Her arms were locked behind his neck as again he circled his hips in unmistakable invitation and, somewhere in the back of her mind, Nicole could hear the small voice of reason imploring her to take control of the situation. It was urging her to pull back from him and call a halt to what they were doing. But once again she ignored it. Against the powerful tide of passion, that little voice was drowned out and she allowed pleasure to shimmer over her skin.

Don't miss
BOUND TO THE SICILIAN'S BED
available March 2018 wherever
Harlequin Presents® books and ebooks are sold.

www.Harlequin.com

Jara frowned and crossed her arms over her chest. With that kind of competition, how in the world did Natch expect to top the market *this* week of all weeks? The Patel Brothers had dominated the number one rating on Primo's for the past two and a half years. They were widely perceived to be unbeatable. Of course, this hadn't stopped Natch from confronting the Patels head-to-head on a variety of programs over the past few months—on the contrary, the challenge spurred him to new heights of competitive frenzy. He plotted their release schedules on graphs of three, four, and five dimensions. He hunted down even the deadendingest rumors about Frederic and Petrucio Patel.

And now, it seemed, after feeling the occasional prick of Natch's jabs on the Primo's battlefield—a loss of a point here, a preempted product launch there—the Patel Brothers had finally accepted the challenge of their younger rival. Releasing NightHawk in the same week as NiteFocus was a direct assault.

Horvil was unperturbed by this latest turn of events. "Why are you two so worried?" he said, trying unsuccessfully to stifle a yawn. "We've put a lot of work into NiteFocus. It's good code. I'm not afraid to go up against the Patels."

"So then, what do we do?" asked Natch. His tone of voice indicated it was a rhetorical question.

Jara scowled. She knew where this was heading. "If anybody but *you* asked me that question, I would say, *We both launch our products on the Data Sea, and may the best company win.*"

The fiefcorp master gave her one of his wolfish grins, the kind that had little to do with humor. On some alternate plane of existence, Natch's audience howled in gleeful anticipation. "You think I'm afraid to go up against the Patels."

"I just don't like pulling these dirty tricks of yours. We're number six on Primo's, in a field of thousands. Why can't you be happy with that?"

Natch stopped in midstride and gave his apprentice a piercing look. "Happy with failure?" he said incredulously, as if she had suggested joining one of the creeds and devoting his life to poverty. "Happy with *this*?" He gestured wildly around him at what seemed to Jara to be a pretty nice flat. Natch's apartment had enough space for both living and working quarters, with room left over to entertain. Not only that, but it boasted real *and* programmable windows, as well as a lush garden of daisies right smack in the middle of the place. Maybe Natch's apartment paled in comparison to the Lunar estates of the big tycoons, but at least it was decorated.

Jara composed herself. "Natch, number six on Primo's isn't failure," she said. "Most programmers spend their whole lives trying to crack the top ten. We've gotten here in thirty-six months. *Thirty-six months*, Natch! Primo's has been around for almost seventy *years*, and nobody's ever done it as fast as we have. Horvil, where were we a year ago today?"

The engineer focused his attention inward for a split second, the telltale sign of a brain angling for information on the Data Sea. "Sixty-two," announced Horvil momentarily. "The year before that, four hundred nineteen." Jara threw up her hands as if to say, *See what I mean?* "And the year before that, we didn't—"

Natch cut his apprentice off in midsentence. "Does this shit have a point?"

Jara stood her ground. "I'm not suggesting we quit trying, Natch. I'm just saying we'll *get* to the top eventually, *by the strength of our products*, without dirty tricks. The Patel Brothers are getting older, and we're gaining on them all the time. In a couple of years, when all the tax breaks dry up, they'll sell out and dissolve their fiefcorp. That's what happens in this business."

Natch grimaced, rocked back and forth on his heels, and let out a restless sigh. He looked like the little boy who had been scolded by his proctors for staying out past curfew. Despite all his frantic motion, every chestnut-colored hair on his head remained perfectly in place. Jara met his stare, but she was disappointed to see Horvil struggling to stay awake. *Thanks for backing me up, Horv!*

"All right," said the fiefcorp master, with a look on his face that said, *I'll go through the motions of considering your worthless ideas, but only for form's sake.* "Let's take a look at NiteFocus 48 in MindSpace. Let's see how *strong* our products really are."

Jara and Horvil followed Natch into his office. The room was short and sparsely decorated and functional, but still quite a bit nicer than Jara's workspace. Artificial daylight, streaming into the room from two square windows, showed a hectic market square somewhere in Beijing. *That's one way to keep working through all hours of the night*, Jara thought sourly. *Pretend it's day.*

Natch walked up to the squat workbench that sat in the center of the room and waved his hand to summon the virtual programming bubble known as MindSpace. He was instantly surrounded by a clear holographic sphere about two meters in diameter, along with an assortment of interlocking geometric shapes and connecting fibers.

The program loaded in MindSpace looked like a dense pyramid carpeted with spikes. It wasn't any code that Jara recognized. "What's that?" she said.

"Nothing," grumbled the fiefcorp master, banishing the display with a flick of his wrist. A more cohesive structure appeared in the layer beneath, shaped like a lopsided donut and colored in soft grays and blues. Strands of purple and white formed an intricate net through the center. Jara could have traced those supple curves with her eyes closed. NiteFocus 48.

Natch took one look at the mass of bio/logic code floating in front of him and gave a snort of disgust. His dissatisfaction grew as he rotated the donut slowly along its z-axis. *Imperfect!* Jara could hear him thinking, a fourth-act soliloquy to his invisible audience. *Unsatisfactory! A mocking reminder of all the projects I've left unfinished, all the goals I've left unattained.*

"Well, what are we waiting for?" said Horvil. "Let's fire this baby up."

Jara gave her internal system a silent command to activate NiteFocus, and then waited a few seconds as the program disseminated its instructions to the microscopic machines floating in her bloodstream. She tried to detect the millions of calculations going on inside her brain, the logical handshakes extending thousands of kilometers from her virtual body here to cellular structures standing stiff on a red tile in London. But she knew that even if she were here in the flesh, the chemical reactions in the retina and the electric pulses along the ciliary muscle would be completely unde-tectable. Bio/logic programs had not been that crude since Sheldon Surina invented the science some 360 years ago.

"I think it's working," said Jara. A hopeful state-ment.

Horvil puffed up his chest and clapped a virtual arm around Natch's shoulder. "Of *course* it's work-ing. What'd I tell you?"

The fiefcorp master said nothing. He turned off the Beijing scene on the left window, leaving a view of the real darkness outside. Natch squinted, shook his head, and marched through the other room to the balcony door. Horvil and Jara followed him as he stepped out-side into the coal-dark Shenandoah night, about half past three now. A platform promptly slid under their feet from the side of the building.

The three fiefcorpers stood at the railing and gazed into the distance, looking for a suitable object on which to test their enhanced vision. Flashing lights were still evident in the rowdier quarters of the city, but out here in the residential district, things were relatively quiet. "There," said Horvil, pointing towards a viewscreen that stood several blocks down the road, its lights dim now that there was no foot traffic. Jara found she could read the advertisement clearly.

DRINK CHAIQUOKE
Because the Defense and Wellness Council
Still Lets You.

Beneath the print, the smart-alecky ChaiQuoke pitchman suckled on a neon purple bottle while a Council officer looked on with overt disapproval.

Horvil danced a clumsy jig of triumph. "Looks like the Natch Personal Programming Fiefcorp will still be in business tomorrow," he crowed. "Oh yeah!"

Jara breathed a sigh of relief. Why had she been nervous? NiteFocus 48 had worked fine yesterday too, and the day before, and the day before. She hadn't seen a major glitch in the program since version 43 or 44. "So what do you think?" she asked Natch. "Ready for launch?"

"Does it *look* like it's ready for launch?" the fiefcorp master replied brusquely. "The color resolution needs a lot of work. And from the look of those blueprints, this program uses way too many cycles. You think we can just release a product that sucks up all the computing resources on the Data Sea and crashes people's systems? No, it's not fucking ready at all."

Jara reacted as if he had slapped her. There was a sudden fermata in Horvil's dance, which he tried to pass off as intentional. Why had they slaved through so many nights if they were going to get this kind of treatment?

"Can't either of you see what I'm trying to do?" asked Natch, his tone suddenly quiet and contemplative. "I'm just pointing out the same inadequacies that Primo's is going to find tomorrow. Primo's doesn't care if you spent all night coding. They only care about two things: success and failure. Success means more sales. It means more respect. It means moving up to the next level of the game. Everything *else...* is failure." Natch rubbed his forehead and gave a yearning look out towards the horizon.

Jara couldn't help but roll her eyes at his histrionics. *Doesn't Natch ever stop to wonder if he's taking himself too seriously?* She wanted to screech obscenities at the invisible audience, to throttle his knowing smirk. She wanted to get him out of those breeches somewhere quiet and instruct him in low, sibilant tones about the things that *really* mattered.

The fiefcorp master turned. He gave Jara a long, penetrating stare of amusement and contempt while Horvil shifted awkwardly from foot to foot behind them. "Now come inside," Natch said, "and I'll tell you my plan."

Jara lowered her eyes. "I thought you said no more dirty tricks," she whimpered.

"I never said that. I said I'd *take a look* at Nite-Focus 48, which I just did. And it's awful. Besides, why do you keep using those words, *dirty tricks*? I don't do dirty tricks. It's called *business*."

(((3)))

The sun crept up the early-morning sky, panther-like, reminding Jara she had managed to last another twenty-four hours without going crazy or quitting or killing someone. She flushed with accomplishment. All she needed to do for the next eleven months was pace through the days with her head bowed low, like Natch in one of his moods, and she would survive. That was how you killed a stretch of time: stick around long enough to outlast it.

She told the others she needed a few minutes alone in the cool night air. Natch and Horvil disappeared inside.

Jara stayed on the balcony and watched the city of Shenandoah shake itself awake. Buildings that had automatically compressed themselves overnight to conserve space began puffing up like blowfish as their tenants awoke. The balcony outside Natch's apartment floated upwards, almost imperceptibly, as residents on the lower levels claimed their living space for the morning. A river of pedestrian traffic wended from the poorer districts to the public multi facilities, ferrying half a million workers to offices around the globe, or to Luna, Mars, or one of the orbital colonies. Others flooded into the tube stations where sleek trains would whisk them across the continent at exorbitant speeds. A privileged few used the teleportation stations, still shiny and unspoiled and mostly empty.

Jara had witnessed the same morning transformation many times in London, but until now, she had never seen it in Shenandoah. She felt a momentary pang of envy for the people who lived and worked in the smooth, low curves of a modern city. They had never scrabbled to work over ancient brick or weedy cobblestone, nor taken a circuitous tube route around yet another corroded abbey that had been given perpetual right-of-way for the sake of history. *Stop feeling sorry for yourself*, Jara thought. *You could live in Shenandoah if you really wanted—even though all you could afford here is a room in one of the old skyscrapers.* She gazed off to the east, where the faint broken towers of Old Washington thrust above the mist. The towers were all that remained now of the variegated American empires that had flourished in the years before the Autonomous Revolt. One lone tube track snaked in that direction from Shenandoah and disappeared into the fog like the fossilized tendril of some long-dead beast.

Stop delaying, Jara thought. *Go inside and get this over with. Then you can go home and sleep. Whatever idiocy Natch is planning can't be much worse than what you're already doing.*

* * *

She was wrong.

"You want me to *what*?" Jara shrieked, sounding even to herself like some farcical harpy from the dramas. The Unbeliever, the sour-faced One Who Doubts Our Hero's Prowess.

Natch gloated at his apprentice's reaction. "I want you to spread rumors," he said calmly, mid-pace, "that the Data Sea is about to be bombarded with a crippling black code attack."

"A crippling black code attack."

"By the Pharisees."

"The Pharisees. And what good is this going to do?"

"It's going to cause the Patel Brothers to delay their product launch."

Natch's orders were such an affront to common sense that Jara couldn't help but laugh. An emboldened Horvil let out a guffaw of his own. "Great plan," cheered the engineer mockingly. "While we're at it, let's *cause* the Patel Brothers to put a million credits in our Vault accounts and give us all neck massages."

Jara wondered fleetingly if Natch really *had* lost his mind. What connection was there between a respectable bio/logics company selling programs to improve the human body, and a group of superstitious fanatics who had walled themselves off in a far corner of the globe? Then she looked at Natch's condescending smirk and realized he was utterly serious.

Insanity.

The analyst took a seat on the sofa next to her fellow apprentice. "All right, start explaining," she said.

Natch nodded and gave another one of those self-absorbed looks into the distance. "What's tomorrow?" he said at length.

Horvil tilted his eyes upwards in thought. "November first."

"November first. A day like any other, right? For us, yes. Products launched, products sold, business as usual. But for the Pharisees, tomorrow is the Day of the Dead." He waved his hand at the closest viewscreen, which happened to be showing an early landscape by Tope. The painting's sharp blues and greens morphed into an old Prime Committee video about the Day of the Dead. *Technology has marched onwards*, announced the narrator, *but in the mythology of the Pharisees, ghouls and goblins still come out at night*. The three of them watched as a band of brown-skinned Pharisees bowed low in dusty robes and began chanting in an archaic guttural tongue.

The Pharisees hate the civilized world, continued the nameless documentary narrator. *Using bio/logic programs to manipulate the human body is "ungodly," they say. And to implant tiny machines in the blood, to let some programmer's code actually broadcast images into the brain... Unnatural! A sin!*

Natch paused the display and snapped for emphasis. Onscreen, a youth was frozen in mid-scowl, his sunburned fist raised in defiance at some unseen foe. "Remember the program that started raising blood pressures in all the orbital colonies?" said Natch. "That was just two years ago. Twenty-three hundred dead, and a harsh military response from the Defense and Wellness Council. But do you think they've had their fill of bloodshed? Of course not! The Pharisees haven't been idle since then. They've been plotting and scheming and studying programming techniques, just waiting for the perfect opportunity to strike.

"When do the Pharisees tend to attack? On days of religious significance, of course. Like the Feast of All Saints. Like Jesus Joshua Smith's birthday.

"Like the Day of the Dead.

"Think about it! Couldn't the Pharisees have figured out a way to disrupt the financial markets or Dr. Plugenpatch or the multi network by now? Couldn't they have chosen *tomorrow* to launch their opening salvo in the next holy war against us 'connectibles'? Isn't it possible the Defense and Wellness Council is shoring up its defenses *right now* to prepare for a major onslaught by some frightening new breed of black code?"

Horvil was totally captivated by Natch's little narrative. He leaned forward on the edge of the sofa, shifting his attention nervously between the wildly gesticulating Natch and the ominous figure on the viewscreen with the unkempt hair and dirty robe. "It *is* possible, isn't it!" he gasped.

"And if all this is true... wouldn't November first be a very unlucky day for the Patel Brothers to launch a product upgrade?"

Jara felt Natch's plot snap into focus, and for one sickening instant she saw the world through the fiefcorp master's warped lenses. Colors faded away, blacks and whites dissolved into a miasma of indistinct gray. "So you want us to tell people *our friends at the Defense and Wellness Council say something big is about to happen*, and wait for the rumors to clog up the gossip networks?"

"I don't want anything *clogged up*. I want fucking bedlam."

"And you think the Patel Brothers will catch wind of all this and postpone their product launch to a day with a slower news cycle."

Horvil shook off the jitters and sat back in thought. "So *that's* why you've been pushing us so hard on NiteFocus 48," he said. "A near-perfect program... launched on a day where there's no competition... That just might cause Primo's to edge us up a notch or two in the ratings."

Jara frowned. She now gleaned why Serr Vigal and Merri had been excluded from this early-morning rendezvous; they would never participate in such a scheme. In fact, now that Jara thought about it, Natch had been excluding them from a lot of ethically shady errands like this lately. A thought slithered through the back of Jara's mind. What did that say about Natch's opinion of *her*? She purposefully let it go.

Natch restarted the video. They watched a squad of Defense and Wellness Council officers execute a coordinated strike on a crowd of restless Pharisees standing on a hilltop. The Pharisees fired their rifles wildly at the white-robed figures materializing all around them. But the figures they hit were nothing but ghostly multi projections, spotters for the real strike force lining up behind them. A volley of needle-sized darts flew through the air, lodging themselves in the flesh of their adversaries and unloading their deadly cargo of toxic chemicals and molecule-sized machines of war. Within seconds, the fight was over and the Pharisees lay motionless on the ground.

"It's a nice theory, Natch," Jara said, "but I doubt one new program could cause us to jump five slots on Primo's overnight."

"No," said Natch with a sudden diabolical grin, "but *four* programs just might."

The apprentices simply stared at him, unable to summon any coherent words in response.

"What do you think I've been doing these past few weeks while the two of you plugged away on NiteFocus 48? I've been *working*, that's what. Getting DeMirage 52 and EyeMorph 66 prepared for launch."

Horvil counted ostentatiously on his fingers. "That's only three. What's the fourth program?"

"Mento Calc-U-Later 93.9. That's been ready for weeks now."

"*What*? You told me that program was unlaunchable."

"I lied."

As the morning wore on, Natch stubbornly resisted all objections to his plan, though Horvil and Jara tried their best.

"This all sounds so nebulous," protested Jara. "Who's going to believe *we* know anything about terrorist attacks? We're not spies—we're business-people."

"We've got good connections. People will believe *them*. Besides, we don't need to come up with any specific information—a rumor of a rumor, that's all."

"What if it doesn't work?"

Natch shrugged. "If it doesn't work, then what's the harm done?"

"The Council will deny the rumor," interjected Horvil.

"And knowing the Council, they'll deny it so forcefully that people will remain suspicious. Nobody ever accused High Executive Borda of being subtle."

I could say the same thing about you, Natch, Jara thought to herself. "I don't understand this at all," she said, throwing up her hands in exasperation. "If we have four programs ready to launch on the Data Sea, why don't we just launch them now? Why do we need Pharisees?"

Natch shook his head. "First off, the programs *aren't* good enough yet," he replied. "We need at least another day to polish them up. And second, the Patel Brothers have been watching our every move for weeks now. They know we're eyeing their number one spot on Primo's. Unless we catch the Patels unaware for a few hours, they'll immediately fire off a barrage of their own upgrades so they can stay on top. But if we have enough of a cushion, we just might be able to grab number one for a few hours."

"What if someone catches us spreading rumors?"

"Like who?"

He's right, the fiefcorp analyst reflected bitterly. Truth on the Data Sea was like the light from an ancient kaleidoscope: tinted and scattered and refracted on all sides. Especially in the bio/logics trade, where everyone was an interested party. Fiefcorps and memecorps spread rumors about their competitors all the time. So did the capitalmen who funded them and the channelers who pushed their wares. Jara remembered the recent case of a woman who planted rumors of incompetence about her own son to drive him out of business. Or the case of the fiefcorper who cornered the market on gastrointestinal programming by sabotaging his competitors' sales demos. No charges had been filed in either case.

And who stood in Natch's way? The Meme Cooperative—a fumbling bureaucracy.

Jara thought back to those interminable childhood lectures from the hive. *So if the Meme Cooperative is so incompetent,* she had once complained, *who's looking out for the little guy? Who's keeping things fair?*

Nobody, her proctor had replied ruefully.

Nobody? Jara had screamed in youthful outrage.

Oh, I could tell you what the headmaster wants me to tell you, the proctor had replied. *All that bullshit in the official hive curriculum. "The fluidity of information on the Data Sea ferrets out weak struts in the economy." "The independent writers, pundits, and watchdogs known as the drudges are very effective at rooting out corruption." "We rely on the Local Political Representative Associations of Civic Groups—the L-PRACGs, our governments— to keep the free market in check." But you read the news, Jara. Do any of those statements sound like the truth to you?*

They had not. But those discussions had all taken place half a lifetime ago, back when a career as a Meme Cooperative bureaucrat or an L-PRACG policy maker had seemed like an attractive option.

Fiefcorps were a place to build up a nest egg until something *real* came along. How quickly everything changed after the hive! All it had taken for her to sell out her governmentalist ideals, Jara thought with bitterness, was the flattery of handsome, intelligent men like Natch.

Jara rubbed her eyes and came back to the present moment, but she could not dislodge Natch's obfuscating lenses. *The plan might work because it's so ridiculous*, thought Jara. *Who would suspect the industry has sunk so low that one of its finest is willing to sow panic in the streets with Pharisee terrorism rumors? Who would suspect Natch has anything to gain by it?*

And if someone *did* find out—if the Council or the Cooperative or the drudges or the Patel Brothers caught wind of the true source of these rumors—Primo's would probably still crown them number one. An independent valuation system couldn't afford to be swayed by the vagaries of law or politics.

Natch stopped pacing, making Jara uneasy. "I only see two potential problems," he said. "One, the rumors might not generate enough flak in the marketplace to faze the Patels. They might still launch NightHawk on schedule. Two, Primo's might find some undiscovered flaw in one of our programs and penalize us for it."

"What about the other fiefcorps?" asked Jara.

"Who? Lucas Sentinel? PulCorp? Prosteev Serly?" Natch gave a dismissive flip of the hand. "I've already checked their launch schedules. Nothing."

Horvil frowned. He had been silent for some time now, listening to Natch's maddening logic and making quiet calculations of his own. Jara wondered if he had enough functioning brain cells this early in the morning to fully comprehend the magnitude of Natch's scheme. "There's one more problem," said the engineer.

"Which is?"

"What if these rumors spook more than just the Patel Brothers? The Pharisees have *killed* people with these terrorist attacks before. What if we spark too much panic? I mean, we're all connected"—the engineer waved his hands around in the air as if he could scoop up molecule-thick multi bots and subaether transmissions with his fingers—"and so we're all vulnerable. There *could* be another black code attack any day now. Everyone knows that. The Council might *really* be gearing up for another assault. What if we cause too much panic? There might be a rush on the Vault. People might stop trading. The whole financial system could collapse."

Natch grinned as if he relished the possibility. "Small chance," he said. Was that a note of disappointment in his voice? "Come on, Horvil! A few rumors shut down the financial system? People aren't that gullible. Besides, the Council will quash the rumors long before that happens."

"And what—what if the Pharisees *do* actually launch an attack that day?"

"Horv," laughed the fiefcorp master, "I'm not responsible for what those lunatics do. The only one I'm responsible for is *me*. Let them do their worst. No matter what happens, the markets will still be there on November second. *Trust* me."

(((4)))

Jara stared gloomily at the three-dimensional flow-chart she had constructed on the coffee table. The flowchart towered mightily over her head, information layered on top of information like a ziggurat. She sat back and surveyed her handiwork. The names of people Jara had known all her life were lined up on a tier of data labeled GULLIBLE. Other names—friends, relatives, old lovers and companions—were skewered on holographic arrows labeled HARD SELL and SOFT SELL. Her own mother's name stood on an out-of-the-way parapet with the caption UNTRUSTWORTHY.

This is what you've always wanted to do, isn't it? Jara told herself. *Strategic analysis for a bio/logic fiefcorp. Managing timetables, scheduling product launches, assigning resources... right?*

Monday was nearly over, and she still hadn't gotten any sleep. Jara suddenly realized she had been staring at the flowchart without moving for at least an hour. Any minute, she expected the ziggurat to come crashing down on her in a virtual avalanche of data. And then she would die here, buried under the weight of Natch's lies.

If you don't want to be here, Horvil had told her, *go home*. She thought about the engineer, sweating inside a MindSpace bubble at the other end of London. The fact that Horvil was also forgoing sleep was small consolation to her.

Shortly after sundown, Jara felt the mental *ping* of an incoming multi request. Natch.

The fiefcorp master emerged from nothingness, gave her a cheerful wave in greeting, and began scrutinizing the flowchart. Jara hadn't seen him since this morning's meeting in Shenandoah, and his transformation was truly eerie. Gone was Natch the petulant schoolboy, seemingly shut off with the touch of a button. In his place stood Natch the slick entrepreneur, Natch the salesman, Natch the emblem of positive thinking.

"So you think we'll achieve maximum penetration if we start spreading the rumors tonight," he said with one hand pensively rubbing a chin that may have never known stubble.

Jara nodded wearily. "I've categorized all our acquaintances on three axes: credibility, connections, and sphere of influence. Then I've traced the likely flow of rumor from person to person, and plotted out the percentage chance the rumors hit critical mass." She pointed to the pinnacle of the tower, a place of convergence. "I figure we need to start with our most influential friends tonight and work our way to the bottom of the list by tomorrow morning."

"Why not the other way around?"

"These rumors have to have some foundation before they'll take hold. One carefully planted source is worth more than a hundred pieces of idle gossip. That's why I'm going to have Horvil talk to his family connections at Creed Élan later tonight. How can you get more credible than a creed?"

Natch began a fast-paced circuit around Jara's apartment, but this time it was less an obsessive march than a confident strut. "I'm impressed, Jara," he said. It was the first time he had praised her work in months. "Why the long face?"

Jara scowled. "Wouldn't *you* have a long face if you had just called your own mother 'untrustworthy'?"

Her sarcasm ricocheted off him like light off a mirror. "You really are something, Jara," he said. "I don't know how you manage to stay so detached through all this. My emotions have been all over the place the past few weeks. I've been irritable and demanding, I know... but that's just because I can't seem to find your level of *professionalism*. In fact, Horvil said to me the other day that you're really the glue holding this fiefcorp together... "

On and on it went, and Jara found herself responding to his abject flattery in spite of herself. She had a secret weakness for a handsome face and a sugary voice, and Natch could be devastating when he turned on the charm. *How does he do that?* she cursed silently. Didn't she know by now that Natch's apologies were never sincere, that the honeyed words were just another weapon in his arsenal?

Nevertheless, his strategy worked. Somehow he had discovered her weakness for praise and exploited it. Jara found herself responding to the low, erotic pulse Natch stirred up in her—that he could stir up in *anyone*, male or female, at his discretion—and hated it. Hated it and hungered for it like she had never hungered for any of the hundred sexual satisfaction programs she had tried in the thirty years since initiation.

Or are you just jealous? she asked herself. *He's still in his twenties and he's ready to take over the world. You're past forty, and you're still working as an apprentice.*

"We're going to be number one on Primo's tomorrow, Jara, and we couldn't have done it without you," said Natch with a hand on her shoulder. It was a firm hand, not inappropriate, but still pregnant with possibilities. "The capitalmen are going to remember this in a few years, when you finally get sick of working for me and venture out on your own again. They're going to beg you to accept their money."

The analyst ran three fingers self-consciously through her curly mountain of hair. She wished there were an easy way to turn off the sensation of Natch's virtual grasp, but the multi network didn't allow that level of customization. "Yeah, well, maybe," she replied lamely.

And then, seconds later, he vanished. His smile remained burned on her retinas.

Jara tiptoed down the hall to make sure Natch had indeed cut his multi connection and not just ducked into the next room to deceive her. *You're so paranoid, Jara,* she told herself. *This is* your *apartment. Nobody can multi here without your permission.* Still, she breathed a sigh of relief after determining that her boss was not in the flat. Natch had been known to perform miracles before.

She glanced back at the ziggurat and nearly retched. There it sat, in three dimensions—the evidence of her final degradation in the bio/logics trade. *I have to find some way to stop this from happening.*

Jara stood at her window and watched the London evening crowd go about its business. Of course, it wasn't a *real* window; Jara couldn't afford an apartment with exterior walls on her meager fiefcorp stipend, and had to settle for flat viewscreens. But how easy it was to just tune in an outside view from the building and pretend. Down below, hundreds of people bustled around the public square, thousands maybe, casually perusing the Data Sea with hardly a thought to the bio/logic programs that ran their lives. Bio/logics regulating their heartbeats, bio/logics keeping their appointment calendars, bio/logics pumping sensory information into their skulls every second.

Jara's mind buzzed with evil possibilities as she fell into the familiar game of *what's the worst that could happen.* What would happen if panic overtook the market tomorrow and people started pulling money from their Vault accounts? What would happen if Horvil's trepidations became reality and the Pharisees really *did* launch a black code attack? Or what if—perfection postponed!—some unconnectible lunatics figured out a way to sabotage Dr. Plugenpatch? Jara's eyes darted to some anonymous pedestrian making his way across the cobblestones below, and suddenly he was no longer anonymous... He was an important businessman who would wake up tomorrow in Beijing or Melbourne or one of the orbital colonies, Allowell maybe... He tries to grab a batch of stock reports off the Data Sea while he drinks his morning nitro, and *nothing happens...* His blood pressure starts rising; he's supposed to close a big deal today. What the heck is he going to do now...? The OCHREs in his body frantically ping the Plugenpatch medical databases for advice on how to keep his blood pressure down, and what to do about his congenital heart condition... But Dr. Plugenpatch doesn't respond... The room goes dark, the lights go out...

Get a hold of yourself! Jara thought. *You're giving Natch way too much credit. One man can't bring the whole Data Sea crashing to a halt on a whim. The Pharisees aren't going to launch a black code attack tomorrow. What's the worst that could happen? A few fiefcorps will lie low for the day, that's all.*

She switched the window display to a peaceful Irish countryside and tried to get back to work. The three-dimensional flowchart on the table silently mocked her: GULLIBLE. UNTRUSTWORTHY. UNDEPENDABLE.

"Fuck fuck fuck!" Jara cried aloud, slamming her hand against the bare walls. She couldn't just sit back and let this happen. Natch had to be stopped. He *had* to.

"I'm telling you," said Horvil, "they're talking about it all over the gossip networks. I'm not making this up! Go check it out for yourself if you don't believe me."

The woman pursed her lips skeptically and regarded Horvil with a penetrating look. It was the kind of dubious stare that muckety-mucks from the creeds had been giving him his entire life, long before he was old enough to deserve them. Then she cast a spiteful glance at Horvil's apartment, which the engineer had carefully arranged in a tableau of dishevelment: half-eaten sandwiches mingling freely on the floor with dirty clothes, pieces of broken furniture, and the occasional bio/logic programming bar. The elderly woman sighed and turned back to smoothing the wrinkles on her purple suede robe. The state of the robe seemed more important to her than Horvil's dire warnings of enemy attack.

"Creed Élan has contacts in the Defense and Wellness Council," she said. "We have people in the Meme Cooperative. If everyone is panicking about Pharisee black code, why haven't we heard about it?"

"Heck, *I* don't know. I'm not a Council officer. Who knows how a wave of rumors like this gets started?"

"I don't care *how a wave of rumors like this gets started*," she mimicked cruelly. "I'm more interested in knowing how you, of all people, end up on the crest of it."

The woman's name was Marulana—at least, Horvil *thought* her name was Marulana. These rich old crones from Creed Élan were all interchangeable. They scrapped amongst themselves to be the first to solicit your donation for their silly charity events, but when it came time for *you* to ask a favor, they were nowhere to be found. All Horvil knew for sure was that she was a bigwig in Creed

Élan—one of the handful of minor bodhisattvas that ran the organization. She was also one of the women his Aunt Berilla frequently had over for lunch in that gaudy calcified estate of hers on the West End.

He could have verified her name in a heartbeat on the public directory, but it didn't really matter. Horvil knew this was going to be a short conversation anyway.

"You want to know how I heard about this?" Horvil gulped, looking for a quick way to foist Marulana's suspicions on someone else. "Natch told me." He gave her a conspiratorial shrug as if to say, *Crazy world. You never know when you're going to get swept up in another rumor or scandal. But what can you do?*

"Oh, *Natch* told you," replied the creed official with deepening suspicion. "Somehow that doesn't surprise me." Horvil had no doubt she would recognize the name. Ever since he had signed on with the fiefcorp, Natch's name had been spreading among the Élanners like a virulent cancer. Aunt Berilla's influence, no doubt. "So you hear that a major black code attack is imminent, and your first instinct is to contact your spiritual mentors at Creed Élan. Is that it, Horvil?"

The sarcasm in her voice was palpable, almost a third participant in the conversation. "Listen, Your Holy Creedfulness," said Horvil. "I don't expect you to panic every time you hear a strange rumor. But this is *me* talking! You guys know me. My family's been shelling out credits to support Creed Élan since the beginning of time." *And I haven't paid any attention to your dumb creed activities since I was a kid. I don't even pretend to understand what kind of morals and values you people teach anymore. I'm not sure I ever did.* "I'd just hate to see your fine customers—er, constituents—get sucked dry because some black code caught them unaware."

"I'm certain our *devotees* will be just fine."

The engineer lost his patience. "Why do you always have to look for ulterior motives? Do you think Creed Élan has a... a monopoly on good intentions?"

"No," Marulana replied drily. "We simply know from experience that the only people fiefcorpers care about are themselves." She threw a vulture-like frown in Horvil's direction. Then her multi connection winked out without even a good bye.

Horvil collapsed back to the couch, frustrated, sending a stack of grubby pillows to the floor in the process. *So much for family connections*, he thought. At least he could be comforted that the state of his apartment would make it back to Aunt Berilla.

Jara stood in the atrium of the Meme Cooperative's administrative headquarters. All the other governmental and quasi-governmental agencies built their offices in Melbourne, under the imposing shadows of the Prime Committee and the Defense and Wellness Council complexes. Not so the Cooperative, which had chosen the lonely orbital colony of Patronell as its base of operations for no reason Jara could discern.

The building followed the same bland architectural recipe that all bureaucratic buildings used these days.

Start with a base of stretched stone and flexible glass to provide that chic curved effect. Throw in a clump of rice-paper walls to show solidarity with the past. Add impossibly high ceilings. Coat every available surface with viewscreens, and auction off the advertising space to defray construction costs. Mix in a crowd of thousands. The result: instant nausea.

But Jara was not there to study architecture. She was there to do the right thing. She was there to report Natch to the Meme Cooperative and stop this insanity before someone got hurt.

The very idea was absurd, and it grew more ridiculous with each step she took. *Who are you going to tell? And what are you going to tell them?*

Jara didn't know; she just knew she had to tell *someone*. She tamped down that tiny voice inside suggesting she use the information as leverage to get out of her apprenticeship contract. *No, I'm not just doing this for myself. I haven't sunk to Natch's level yet.* Natch's plan wasn't just dangerous to the capitalmen who had grown fat off the fiefcorp boom, or the degenerate fiefcorpers like Natch and her old boss Lucas Sentinel, people Jara would just as soon see destitute. The plan also undermined the Primo's rating system that had served the public for seventy years. People trusted Primo's to uncover shoddy programs— programs that did not obey Plugenpatch specifications, programs that could theoretically overload bio/logic systems and cause fatalities. Primo's was not perfect by any means. Its interpreters could be petty and inaccurate and just plain spiteful. But who else was there to turn to, really?

If Primo's is that vulnerable, thought Jara, *then what in the world can you depend on?*

The fiefcorp analyst wasn't sure where her feet were taking her, but now she discovered they were heading towards a department called the Fraudulent Fiefcorp Practices Division. She could see the office now, just past the viewscreen hawking a program called Feminine Mystique 242.37a. Natch's fiefcorp had received its share of warnings from this office before, and Jara had walked these halls more than once to plead the company's case before an arbitration board. She could have filed a complaint from home, of course, but this was the only way if she wanted to remain anonymous. Without proof that the petitioners were real people, the office would be flooded with data agents from dishonest fiefcorps.

Judging by the long line of multi projections, there were plenty of disgruntled consumers willing to put in the extra effort. Jara scanned the queue and discovered a dozen people who had carefully scrubbed their public profiles to protect their anonymity. She herself had taken this prudent step before opening the multi connection to Patronell; anyone who pinged the public directories with Jara's image would see her name as Cassandra and her locality as Agamemnon's Palace. She doubted anyone here would get the joke.

A fine dust of boredom settled on the petitioners. Every minute or two, the line would shuffle forward. The silence of strangers, the doldrums of public spaces.

Forty minutes later, Jara reached the head of the line. An incoming message welcomed her to the Meme Cooperative and offered a map to guide her through the office to her designated inspector. She took a deep breath and dove into the labyrinth of cubicles.

"Come in, come in," urged the caseworker when she finally reached his cube. A slack-jawed fellow with Scandinavia in his eyes.

Jara walked to the metal chair opposite his desk and found herself ankle-deep in snow. The walls of the cubicle had disappeared—along with the rest of the Meme Cooperative building—and been replaced by a frozen tundra. *SeeNaRee*, Jara thought with distaste. She could practically hear the familiar SeeNaRee slogan she had seen on a thousand viewscreens: *If you can't go to the places you love, why not bring them to you?* At least it was good programming; her toes were already starting to freeze.

"I am required by the charter of the Meme Cooperative to inform you this is an anonymous conversation," began the official in a tired voice. "To ensure your confidentiality, neither I nor any of my colleagues can see you or otherwise identify you, your gender, or any of your distinguishing characteristics without your express permission, except to confirm your presence on the multi network. A sealed recording of this conversation will be stored in our archives for a period of no less than..." The nondescript official droned on for another minute as he gazed myopically in the direction of his visitor's chair.

"I'm here to report a crime in my fiefcorp," said Jara when she was finally given the chance to speak.

"The nature of the crime?"

"Inciting rumors with the intent to mislead."

The Meme Cooperative official gave her a patronizing nod. "That may or may not be an actual crime," he said nonchalantly, drawing circles in the desk condensation with his index finger. "Do these rumors concern a business rival?"

"Well, not exactly, they're more just... general rumors..."

"About your industry?"

"You mean, are they about bio/logics? In a roundabout way, I suppose."

With smooth strokes, the man connected two of the circles on his desk, forming the mathematical symbol for infinity. "Do you have any evidence of these alleged rumors that can be presented before an arbitration board?"

I knew this was a mistake, thought Jara bitterly. *I haven't been here for five minutes, and we're already talking about "alleged" rumors.* The Meme Cooperative official was obviously more interested in enjoying his SeeNaRee than in listening to the grievances of some ghostly, genderless voice from the outside world. "Listen to me!" she said. "Something terrible is going to happen, and someone's got to stop it. It's a matter of public safety!"

Again the placating smile. "This really sounds like it's outside our jurisdiction. Perhaps you might try contacting your L-PRACG. Or maybe the Defense and Wellness Council would be willing to take a statement. There's also the Fair Business Working Group of the Prime Committee. Have you tried them? Or the Creeds Coalition's Council on Ethical Fiefcorp Behavior..."

Jara shook her head. This was pointless. Even if she did manage to ram a complaint through the thick skull of this bureaucrat, it would get lost in the administrative morass. She pictured a Rube Goldberg machine two hundred meters high, her complaint a pea bobbing back and forth on some remote conveyor belt hidden deep in the works.

What else can you expect when you trust an industry to police itself? thought Jara bitterly. But the system had lined too many pockets over the years; no one else wanted the responsibility.

The analyst cut her multi connection without a word. The familiar walls of her London apartment appeared once more. Let the bureaucrat prattle on in his little winter retreat and make excuses for the Cooperative's inaction. Jara couldn't take another minute of it.

She flopped down on her couch and called up the holographic rumor flowchart. Another towering structure that obscured her very existence, only this one she had built herself. Jara rubbed her temples and prepared to send a ConfidentialWhisper request to the first name on her list.

Horvil whined and pulled his head out of the burrow of pillows he had created in his sleep. His internal calendar assured him it was indeed Tuesday morning, and he had slept for ten hours. But if the sun wasn't directly overhead, then it was simply too early for someone to wake him up with an urgent ConfidentialWhisper request.

"What?" groaned the engineer.

"I believe we owe you an apology," came a timorous voice.

Horvil bolted upright, capsizing a stack of nitro mugs. "Marulana?"

"You were right, Horvil," said the creed official, her voice a mixture of fear and chagrin. "Someone *has* launched a black code attack—and they're going straight for the Vault."

(((5)))

It took Jara almost ten minutes to get anything coherent out of Horvil. He had shown up at her front door in person, having run halfway across London with a threadbare pillow clutched under one arm. He was babbling about Creed Élan and losing his family's trust and what would happen if the Data Sea came crashing to a halt.

"All right, slow down," said Jara firmly, clasping his plump chin in her right hand. "What's happening?"

The engineer activated a destressing program and took a deep breath. A few seconds of Re/Lax 57b was enough to allow him to cram the panic back into the mental sideroom where it normally resided. "The world is coming to an end," he said earnestly.

Jara rolled her eyes. "Can you be *more specific*?"

"A bunch of lunatics are launching attacks on the Vault. Black code is sprouting like crazy on the Data Sea. The Vault keeps spitting out messages telling people to check their account balances. Nobody's heard a thing from the Defense and Wellness Council. Ergo... the world is coming to an end."

"Are you sure you're not just falling for the same dumb rumors we spread last night, Horvil? That was *fantasy*, remember?"

The engineer shook his head vehemently. "Look at *this*," he said, and Jara instantly felt the mental click of an incoming message. She projected the message onto a blank patch of air, where the holographic letters hovered menacingly like stingrays.

PLEASE PROTECT YOUR HOLDINGS

The Vault has detected a DNA-assisted decryption attack directed at your account. Your holdings have not been compromised, but it is advised that you periodically check the security of your Vault account. This advisory has been automatically routed to the custodian of records for your L-PRACG and, depending on your L-PRACG's policies, may also be forwarded to the Defense and Wellness Council.

"My Aunt Berilla sent me that message," said Horvil glumly. "Half the women in her creed circle have gotten them by now. This is just how the last one started. Remember all those warnings from Dr. Plugenpatch that kept—"

"Did you tell Natch? What did he say?"

Horvil nodded. "I finally caught him on ConfidentialWhisper about ten minutes ago. He just cackled something about *those crazy Pharisees* and went off to examine his accounts."

The two of them sat down in Jara's breakfast nook. She instructed the building to mix up a tall glass of ChaiQuoke for the engineer, while he quizzically studied the fetid pillow in his hand and

tried to figure out how it got there. Jara decided to
see if her own meager holdings were in order. Within a fraction of a second, Vault statements were
floating before her eyes in stolid financial fonts. All
was well: there were no unusual transactions, and
access was still guarded by a long series of encrypted numbers derived from her DNA. Jara turned to
the fiefcorp accounts next, and was relieved to discover no sign of mischief there either.

Horvil slurped down the glass of milky
ChaiQuoke that had emerged from the kitchen
access panel. But despite the soothing beverage and
the destressing program, the engineer was still fidgeting like a teenager. "You might want to read this
too," he said. "This just came five minutes ago."

Jara found herself looking at the latest editorial
rant by the drudge Sen Sivv Sor.

THE COUNCIL ASLEEP ON THE JOB—AGAIN

The reporter's screed appeared in letters the size
of her arm. An ugly white-haired face grimaced
from the margin, daring her to mention the red
birthmark on its forehead. *Sensationalist hack*,
thought Jara as she rubbed her eyes and pushed the
article back half a meter to a more readable distance.

> Nobody has broken into my Vault account. Yet.
> Like many of you, faithful readers, I was awak-
> ened early this morning by an announcement
> from Vault security telling me to double-check
> the security of my accounts. I was pleased to
> discover that not a single credit had been
> touched.

But I may be one of the lucky ones. The scuttlebutt across the Data Sea is that unexplainable transactions are starting to pop up. A woman in Omaha informs me she lost a hundred fifteen credits this morning. A business on the colony of Nova Ceti claims it lost twenty-seven. You might be thinking that twenty-seven credits is not a lot of money, but multiply that by the estimated 42 billion people who hold accounts at the approximately 11 million financial institutions secured by Vault protocols, and you have the makings of a crisis.

Now the question on everybody's lips: Where is the Defense and Wellness Council?

Rumors that the Pharisees were planning a major black code offensive have been circulating for days in the drudge community. High Executive Borda must have heard them too. Certainly, he must have figured out that today is a major religious festival in the Pharisee Territories. And if that's the case, then why wasn't the public warned ahead of time?

"We haven't seen a successful black code attack on the Vault in years," a source inside the Defense and Wellness Council told me. "It's a totally distributed system running millions of different protocols and locked down on the submolecular level. How far do you think these fanatics are going to get?"

But is High Executive Borda naïve enough to think that the march of technology won't eventually...

Jara waved the scrolling text into oblivion. She could predict the rest of the article anyway. Sor would make his typical excoriations of the Council for being so secretive, and insist that Len Borda be held accountable for his inaction. Then he would segue into his standard rant about the moral decay of society.

"See what I mean?" moaned Horvil, head in his hands. "The world is—"

"Shut up," Jara barked.

Sen Sivv Sor had a devout following of several billion who hung on his every word. And he was but one among hundreds of thousands of independent commentators competing for readership. Now that the drudges were involved, Jara knew it was only a matter of time before panic whipped across the Data Sea like a tsunami.

And so it did.

While Jara sat quietly with Horvil in her breakfast nook, messages started rolling in to her mental inbox. Urgent warnings and sheepish apologies from the same friends and family members she had spoken with just last night. A letter from her L-PRACG administrator urging calm. Offers for useless "black code protection programs" from desperate fiefcorps that traded on unsavory bio/logic exchanges. Jara bristled at all the confusion.

"Listen to this," said Horvil with a nervous laugh. "There's a rumor going around the Data Sea that High Executive Borda is dead."

Jara snorted. "Maybe he got caught in that orbital colony explosion that just killed half a million people."

Half an hour drifted past like a thunder-laden stormcloud, full of bad omens. Jara tuned her viewscreen to the public square outside, expecting to see thousands of Londoners rioting in the streets. She saw nothing but the usual Tuesday afternoon traffic. But could she detect an edge to the crowd, an impatience, a fear of the unknown? Or was that simply the everyday background hum of anxiety? Too many choices to make, too many consequences to consider.

"You know this couldn't possibly be a coincidence," said the analyst.

Horvil rested his cheek on the cool plastic of the table and sighed. Obviously, this thought had occurred to him too. "So you think Natch knew a black code attack was coming?"

"Maybe. You know that he's hip-deep in the black coding culture."

"Jara, I've *seen* those 'black coding groups' on the Data Sea that he follows. They're a joke. A bunch of kids talking about mods for bio/logic programming bars, how to boost OCHRE transmission frequencies, shit like that. If one of *those* people launched an attack on the Vault, then I'm a Pharisee."

"Well, it's either that or..." Jara let the sentence trail off.

The engineer leapt to his feet, face as pale as the droplet of ChaiQuoke piloting its way down the grooves of his chin. "Come on, Jara. There's no *way* he could've done that black code himself. I mean, yeah, Natch is one of the most brilliant programmers out there, but to break into the *Vault*? The Pharisees and the Islanders and who knows how many other lunatics have been trying to do that for *decades*. You think he just cobbled together some black code to crack open the financial exchange system in his spare time? He's not that smart. No one is."

Jara grimaced, conceding the point. Humans had limits. It was an axiom she felt she would be wise to remember. "Okay, okay. So what are the other alternatives? Are the messages fake?"

"I don't think so. Marulana said her people ran a bunch of tests on them, and everything checked out."

"Maybe somebody warned him ahead of time."

"No, that doesn't make sense either. The Pharisees don't use ConfidentialWhisper or multi or... or *anything*. They'd have no way to get in touch with him." Jara could see Horvil sliding back down into the mental quicksand. He was flailing his arms around in increasingly wide arcs to match the mounting decibels of his voice. "You know Natch likes to ride those tube trains in circles for hours on end. Maybe he's going to the Pharisee Territories... or meeting the Pharisees halfway... or—"

"That's ridiculous. Natch is *not* holding secret meetings on the tube with a bunch of violent lunatics. He just isn't."

"Then maybe he has a source in the Defense and Wellness Council."

Jara snorted. "Horvil, we're getting nowhere. Natch doesn't have sources *anywhere*. The only people he talks to are you and Serr Vigal. Everyone else trusts him even less than I do."

They were both standing now, venting their inner turmoil at each other. Jara turned away from her fellow apprentice and stalked to the other side of the kitchen. Suddenly, the news began flooding into her consciousness once more, overrunning the hastily erected barricades she had put up so she could concentrate on her conversation with Horvil. Drudges of all political stripes were bickering in public about the sums of money that had vanished. The Council was maintaining complete silence about the situation. Jara's younger sister in Sudafrica sent her a panic-stricken message asking for advice. And then, without thinking about it, Jara opened a message from the Vault authorities.

PLEASE PROTECT YOUR HOLDINGS

The Vault has detected a DNA-assisted decryption attack directed at your account. Your holdings have not been compromised...

The fiefcorp apprentice smacked her hand loudly against the wall and stomped off to the next room. She instantly regretted it. Blank walls weren't so bad in the kitchen, but in living space they seemed like an accusation. She didn't want the world to come to an end before she had made *some* kind of mark on this place.

"You know what we have to do," Jara said grimly to the engineer, who had followed her out of the kitchen.

"What's that?"

"We have to go to the Council and tell them what we know. *They'll* listen."

Horvil's jaw dropped. He was too stunned to speak.

"Horvil, can *you* live with something like this on your shoulders?" she bellowed. She started to pace, Natch-like. "I mean, deceiving greedy fiefcorp masters is one thing. Even deceiving Primo's. But what about *those* people out *there* who are going to suffer the consequences?" Jara's sweeping gesture encompassed the London commuters visible from the window. The multied businesspeople hustling to meetings, the families scampering across the square looking for safety, the street performers in the midst of some apocalyptic pantomime at the foot of Big Ben. "What if the medical networks break down? What if the multi network collapses? What if this black code attack sparks a total panic? What if people die, for process' preservation?"

The engineer cocooned himself in a ball on Jara's couch, as if his voluminous stomach might provide some insulation against the calamities of the world. "But... but... I'm *sure* that Natch wouldn't—that he didn't..."

Jara refused to give any ground. "I don't know how he's involved in this. Maybe he heard a rumor on the Data Sea weeks ago. Maybe he had a hand in putting this black code together. But he knows *something*. We can't just ignore that, Horvil! We can't just let people die! The Council might need Natch's information to help stop the attack." *I know Natch has been your best friend practically since birth, Horv, but sometimes you've got to look out for your own ass. Do you think Natch cares one way or the other what happens to you?* "Horvil, there comes a point where we have to put this Primo's nonsense behind us and think of the *people* out there."

The engineer was starting to crack. "All I ever wanted was to be a bio/logic engineer," he whimpered, as if it were the most relevant statement in the world. "All I ever wanted to *do* was help people." He peered up at the pint-sized woman with the mass of curly hair standing over him, but there was no mercy forthcoming.

Can't you see that I'm trying to help you, Horv?
Don't you realize this could be just what we need to do to get out of these miserable apprenticeship contracts?

And then Horvil narrowed his eyes, puzzled. The color gushed back to his face all at once. He looked as if his tongue was struggling to catch up with the information in his head. Finally, the engineer shook his head violently, banished the display on the viewscreen with an outstretched hand, and summoned forth the craggy visage of Sen Sivv Sor.

BLACK CODE ATTACKS OVER
Defense and Wellness Council to Make Statement

Jara could afford only one outgoing multi stream at her apartment, and it would have taken too long for Horvil to physically traipse back to his place on the other side of London. So the engineer had to rush down the street to the nearest public multi facility, something he hated to do. He didn't care how many times the Council guaranteed the safety of these public connections and how many guards they posted; he didn't care about the automatic overrides that would bring him back to consciousness in a heartbeat if there was any danger. You could never really feel comfortable letting your body stand immobile in a room full of strangers while your mind was off elsewhere. Life in the world of meat and bone could be so *inconvenient*.

Apparently, word of the Council's impending statement had hit the streets. People started vanishing throughout the block as they slid into multivoid and prepared to open new connections. Horvil arrived at the public multi facility just in time to claim the last open red tile. He breathed a sigh of relief, and stepped into the space between a fat Japanese businesswoman and a wiry Indian man who seemed to be a technician of some kind.

"We didn't have to multi over here," said an amused Jara when Horvil finally caught up to her in the crowd. "We could have stayed at my place and watched the press conference on the viewscreen."

Horvil sniffed. "How much fun would *that* be?"

They were standing in the Defense and Wellness Council's main auditorium, its public face. Everyone knew the Council had moved its *real* base of operations to a new compound of unknown location. The auditorium was a fat wedge that might have represented 20 percent on some vast pie chart—a number that roughly approximated the Council's public approval ratings.

Horvil had actually been here in person once, during his requisite tour of the Melbourne governmental facilities. He remembered seeing the entire city laid out before him during the descent of the arriving hoverbird craft. If he had the power to see through the dozens of hanging pennants to the west and the stretched stone wall behind them, he could have seen the Prime Committee complex and the Congress of L-PRACGs. To the east lay the headquarters of the Creeds Coalition and the chief lobbying arms of TubeCo, GravCo, and TeleCo.

Jara pinged the Council's multi information node. "A hundred and twelve million," she said, gazing around at the assembled crowd of multi projections.

Horvil whistled. This black code attack had shaken people up. It looked like only twenty thousand, of course; in situations like this, the network conveniently abandoned the illusion that multi projections inhabited Cartesian space. "Any sign of Merri? Or Vigal?" he said.

"Public directory says Merri's here somewhere," replied Jara. "But no word on Serr Vigal. He wouldn't come out here for something like this."

"And Natch?"

Jara looked at Horvil and shook her head with a frown.

At precisely three o'clock (London time), there was a decrescendo in the background chatter of the crowd. Lights that had been glaring at full intensity dimmed to candle strength. Horvil held his breath and watched the stage below for the towering form of High Executive Len Borda.

But the man who materialized on center stage wasn't him. A white-robed and yellow-starred figure approached the podium. The man, a pure-blooded Asian, was little more than half Borda's height, and had only a third of his girth. He stood patiently for a moment, dispensing that arrogant Council stare.

Borda's underling did not give his name or rank. He simply opened his mouth and began to speak in a dead monotone. "My word is the will of the

Defense and Wellness Council, which was established by the Prime Committee two hundred and fifty-two years ago to ensure the security of all persons throughout the system. The word of the Council is the word of the people."

Horvil shuddered involuntarily. Out of the corner of his eye, he saw Jara doing the same. They had heard this opening dictum thousands of times in dramas, news reports, and speeches, and yet it still had the power to send ripples up and down the spine. Horvil was convinced the effect was bio/logically enhanced.

"Today, rumors have circulated on the Data Sea that the Vault was under black code attack by Pharisees," continued the Council officer coolly, as if systemwide panic was an expected hazard; the total at the bottom of a spreadsheet column, the predictable outcome of a well-weathered formula. "Many irresponsible words have been written about the so-called vulnerabilities of the financial system and the supposed failings of the Defense and Wellness Council.

"High Executive Borda wishes it to be known that these rumors are completely without foundation. There *was* no black code attack this morning."

Even through the sound-deadening programs of the Council auditorium, Horvil could hear the murmur of a million raised voices. He remembered his pathetic sniveling at Jara's apartment, his panicked dash across London, and felt an embarrassed flush cover his face. The engineer risked a peek at Jara. Her nostrils were flaring.

The anonymous Council spokesman pressed on, either oblivious to or unconcerned by the crowd's reaction. "The attack this morning was not a product of bio/logic engineering, or of black coding skill. It required nothing more than the ability to make clever forgeries and the will to deceive.

"These forgeries of Vault security messages were designed to fool the public into believing their financial holdings were under attack. What the perpetrators hoped to accomplish with this ruse is unknown. High Executive Borda believes the forgers' goal was to sow panic in the marketplace. Suffice it to say these messages have been tracked down and eliminated."

Jara seemed disoriented. She took a step backwards and turned her focus away from the diminutive Council spokesman, who began to recite a numbing series of technical statistics. "I don't understand," she ConfidentialWhispered to Horvil. "You can't just *forge* a message from the Vault like that. You'd need DNA, atomic signatures, who knows what else."

Horvil tilted his head in thought. "That's not necessary, if you do it right."

"Horv, we *saw* those messages. They said they were from the Vault. They looked authentic. They had valid signatures."

The engineer smiled. The panic of the world coming to an end had already given way to the open vistas of a mathematical challenge. "Sure, they *looked* authentic," he explained. "It's not hard to make a forgery that looks official at first glance. You could probably find black code on the Data Sea that'll do the trick. The *hard* part is getting people not to take that second or third glance. I never bothered to verify those signatures—did you? I'll bet Marulana never got around to it either." Horvil summoned a virtual tablet in the air and began making sketches. "Now if you actually knew bio/logic encryption theory inside and out, you might even be able to create a fake signature..."

Jara cradled her head in her hands and began rocking back and forth. She interrupted Horvil's musings in midsentence. "Horv, have you checked the dock at the fiefcorp in the past few hours?"

Horvil had already ventured far afield into chaos theory and fractal patterns, but Jara's question brought him back to familiar territory with a sickening thud. He shook his head.

"I can't believe we fell for this," Jara croaked. "Natch did it. He went ahead and launched all those programs onto the Data Sea this morning, when nobody was paying attention. NiteFocus 48, EyeMorph 66, everything."

"A-and the Patels?"

"Pushed back their NightHawk release until tomorrow. *Routine last-minute error-checking*, their channelers are saying."

There was a very easy syllogism to follow here, even for someone who had not studied subaether physics and advanced bio/logic calculus like Horvil. Natch had spread rumors of a black code attack... There *was* such an attack, or at least a fake one... The attack had created confusion in the marketplace... Horvil didn't want to solve the problem. He wanted the whole thing to disappear, to vanish like the multi pedestrians on the street.

But the Defense and Wellness Council spokesman had no such hesitations. "The perpetrators of this crime may not have launched an actual attack on the Vault," he said, his voice preternaturally calm. "But nevertheless there *has* been an attack—an attack on the people's assumption of safety and security. And that is something the Council cannot abide."

On cue, a row of ghostly figures materialized behind the spokesman. Council officers all, adorned with the white robe and yellow star, steely dartguns holstered at their waists, the inexorable mastery of the Data Sea written on their brows.

"This disruption has been thwarted, as *all* attacks against the public welfare are thwarted," continued the small Asian at the vanguard of the officers. "To the perpetrators of this act, let me say this:

"The Council will not forget. The Council will not forgive. The Council will bring you to justice."

Jara looked at the man with his index finger pointing towards the audience, the implacable representative of Len Borda's will. She remembered Natch's statement barely twenty-four hours ago: *We're going to be number one on Primo's, and we're going to do it tomorrow.* It had been so easy. Natch's had not been a statement of intent so much as a prophecy, a foretelling of an event already preordained. When she looked into the Council spokesman's eyes, she could see the same force of will.

Insanity, Jara thought. *There's no other word for it.*

(((6)))

Jara awoke groggy the next morning, hoping the past two days had been some sort of paranoid hallucination. After yesterday's grim pronouncements from the Defense and Wellness Council, she had prived herself to the world and slunk straight off to bed like a wounded animal. Now she discovered she had slept for fourteen hours straight, a Horvilesque achievement.

Anxious for something familiar, Jara fell back into the morning routine she had been forced to abandon by Natch's crazy plan. The routine went like this: Sit up and project the news feeds on top of the plaid blanket. Tune one viewscreen to the morning commentary by Sen Sivv Sor. Tune the other to the editorial by his rival, John Ridglee. Order a steaming cup of nitro from the building. Fetch nitro from the access panel at the left side of the bed. Activate Doze-B-Gone 91.

A few minutes of peaceful routine were enough to convince Jara she was okay. Enough to convince her that a small niche had been carved out for her somewhere in this hardscrabble mountain called the bio/logics industry. *Almost* enough to convince her she would survive another eleven months.

Insanity, insanity.

The chatter about yesterday's "black code attack" had already slowed to a trickle. Everyone who had claimed financial losses in the panic had quietly recanted during the early-morning hours. Representatives of the assorted Pharisee tribes were tripping all over themselves to declare they had nothing to do with the hoax. Talk on the Data Sea had shifted focus from the attack itself to the Council's behavior during the crisis. Why had Len Borda sent an underling to face the crowd at Melbourne instead of appearing himself? How did the Council plan on pursuing the offending parties? Other drudges were bemoaning the fact that vast swaths of the public had been deceived by such a simple stunt. Technology had kept the world so secure for so long. Had society become slothful and complacent?

The speculation merely elicited a yawn from Jara. She moved past the mundane news about TubeCo's financial woes and deaths in the orbital colonies, waved away the parochial gossip from her L-PRACG and the solicitations from programming supply companies. The news feed on her blanket shifted in the blink of an eye to the bio/logic industry reports.

The lead headline:

PATEL BROTHERS UNSEATED BY RIVAL FIEFCORP
Natch Personal Programming Takes #1 on Primo's

Jara let loose a tidal wave of messages on her boss. She stood on the red square in her hallway sending multi requests and ConfidentialWhispers by the dozens, enough to cause a major headache. Anyone but a trusted associate would have automatically been cut off by the Data Sea by now. Still, Natch could have prived himself to her communiqués with the barest thought. *What are you waiting for, Natch?* Jara asked. *What are you afraid of?*

Finally, one of her multi requests got through. Jara took a deep breath and activated the connection. Multivoid whispered its sweet promises of oblivion for a scant few seconds and then abandoned her in Natch's foyer. A viewscreen right in front of her face broadcast one of the early nudes of Baghalerix.

Voices drifted into her ears before the connection was stable enough for her to process them.

"Ratings? Who really cares about ratings?" came the first voice, cool and butter-smooth and almost certainly enhanced with bio/logics. Natch.

"Well, *you* do, from what I've heard," replied the second. Jara stood for a moment, trying to remember where she had heard that scratchy growl. A male voice, at least twice Natch's age. And then suddenly she placed it: the drudge Sen Sivv Sor.

So the feeding frenzy has begun, thought Jara bitterly. *Everybody wants to talk to the new number one on Primo's.*

She wondered when her fiefcorp master was planning to bring her in to the conversation. Or did he just plan to keep her dangling at arm's length? She studied the ballooning belly of the woman on the viewscreen and tried to decide if her boss had chosen this particular painting to send a message.

"Of course it doesn't *hurt* to have high ratings," Natch was saying from around the corner. "It's good for morale; it's good for business. But I don't care if we're number one on Primo's or number one thousand, as long as we deliver the highest-quality programming. If I can look back at the end of the day and say we've done the best job we can do, then I can sleep at night." Yes, Natch had definitely modified his voice; Jara recognized the laid-back cadences of SmoothTalker 139.

"But the Patel Brothers managed to pull back ahead of you in only forty-seven minutes," said Sor. "Number one for less than an hour! Come on, Natch, tell me that doesn't rankle you."

Natch laughed the free and easy laugh that only the rich or the deranged possessed. "I give Frederic and Petrucio Patel a lot of credit. They didn't waste any time launching a counteroffensive. It's no wonder they've been number one so long. But I think we've proven our point: the Patel Brothers' days of dominating the Primo's ratings are over. From now on, they'll have to watch their backs."

Jara had heard enough. Obviously, Natch had no plans to include her in the conversation. She stalked towards the living room, her face a study in carefully controlled rage—and then stopped.

Perfection taint you! she screamed silently at her boss. The fiefcorp master had cordoned off the living room, blocking access as only the apartment owner could. It was an inhuman feeling, this sensation of just *stopping*, the inability to even make an effort to transgress. The designers of the multi network strove so hard to provide complete verisimilitude, and yet their method of access control utterly short-circuited human instincts.

"So what's next for the Natch Personal Programming Fiefcorp?" Sen Sivv Sor was asking.

Natch's grin was practically audible. "Kick the Patel Brothers out on their asses, of course." His imaginary audience let out a spirited cheer.

Jara gritted her teeth and fired off a terse ConfidentialWhisper. "This interview is *over*," she announced, "unless you want me to start bombarding *him* with all the evidence I've found about your little scheme."

There was a pause in the conversation. Jara could hear the rustling of clothing, a man arising from his chair. "I'm afraid I'm going to have to call it a day, Mr. Sor," said Natch. "Duty beckons. I've got a fiefcorp to run."

"Sure, sure!"

The analyst suddenly found the impenetrable barrier lifted, and swooped around the corner just in time to see Sor give Natch a final clap on the back. The drudge looked exactly like his pictures on the Data Sea; his craggy face, white mop of hair, and distinctive birthmark would be recognizable anywhere. A second later, he disappeared. Off to rebroadcast the interview and play the bit part Natch had assigned him in the drama of his life.

Natch displayed no sign of the fatigue a normal human being would feel after four days without sleep. He looked alive, focused, handsome. Jara felt the familiar twinge of lust stabbing through her abdomen and sneered it down.

And then, in the space between one breath and the next, Natch's demeanor completely shifted. A mask was silently discarded. Now his eyes held nothing but sullenness, and the once-over he gave her spoke more of dismissal than command. Natch didn't even offer his apprentice a chair to sit in, but instead marched straight into his office. Jara stormed after him, trembling, only to find him standing at his workbench in the midst of a Mind-Space bubble. The donut-shaped code of NiteFocus 48—now NiteFocus 49, she supposed—surrounded him like a life preserver.

"*What* evidence?" grunted Natch.

Jara put her hands on her hips and mustered her best accusatory stance. "Evidence of what you did."

"And what exactly did I do?"

"You know exactly what you did, you son of a bitch! You launched that fake black code attack yourself."

If the analyst expected an angry outburst from her master, she was disappointed. She would have even been reassured by one of his contemptuous laughs. Instead, Natch nudged a periwinkle-colored chunk of code with his left hand while he probed its cratered surface with the fingertips of his right. "What makes you think I did that?" he said.

"Come on, Natch! There aren't many people clever enough to pull off that little fandango yesterday. There's even fewer who would have anything to gain by it. I've seen you tinkering around with strange programs over the past few weeks, stuff that doesn't look like anything in *our* catalog. And then, of course, there's the fact that the so-called attack happened exactly when our rumors said it would."

"A happy coincidence."

"And was it a *happy coincidence* you put *our* necks on the line instead of *yours*? Did it occur to you that when the Council starts asking questions, the rumors'll lead back to Horvil and me? Not you, of course. *You* didn't have anything to do with those rumors. You were busy getting our bio/logic programs ready for launch, as the MindSpace logs will clearly show."

Something she said finally penetrated Natch's thick skin. He worked quietly for a few minutes without speaking a word, the gears in his head clearly grinding away. The pause of a politician carefully phrasing a key platform. "If you really think I would do that to you and Horvil," he said at length, "then you don't understand me at all."

Jara studied the fiefcorp master's face carefully. Could he possibly be telling the truth? Could he be operating on a plane that far removed from everyday life? Or was this just another one of his acting jobs? She gazed into that unblemished, boyish face and wondered if there were any truths at all buried beneath its surface, or if truth for him was as mutable as programming code, subject to updates by the hour.

A minute rolled by, then two. Jara cursed her body as a turncoat, fired up Delibidinize 14a for the third time that hour. *Can't he at least give me the satisfaction of turning MindSpace off?* she fumed. Finally, she straightened her spine and looked him squarely in the eye. "I quit."

Natch gave her a sly look. "Fine," said the fiefcorp master blithely. "Quit."

A stunned silence filled the room. Jara didn't move.

"Stop being so fucking melodramatic, Jara!" Natch burst out. He grabbed NiteFocus 49 with one hand and violently spun the virtual code around like a wheel, himself stuck in the spokes. "You've got less than a year left on your contract, and after that you'll have the option to cash out. You're telling me you're going to give up all those shares and start from scratch someplace else? Room and board for another four years? I know you better than that, Jara. You're going to stay right where you are and get filthy rich with the rest of us."

"I could turn you in to the Council."

Natch didn't lose a beat. "Without hard evidence—which I *know* you don't have—where would that get you? Nobody wants to hire a whiner or a whistle blower. You'd be right back where you were when I found you: blacklisted by the major bio/logic fiefcorps, taking shit from second-rate imbeciles like Lucas Sentinel. And don't tell me the Council will get to the bottom of this, because they *won't*. Dozens of cases like this cross Len Borda's desk every week, and he's lucky if he can close a tenth of them."

"Then I'll tell the Meme Cooperative."

"Don't make me laugh."

"The drudges. I could send a message to Sen Sivv Sor and John Ridglee right now."

Natch shrugged, as if the effort of responding to such an inane proposition was beneath him. He caught the spinning donut of code with one hand and began studying its surface once more.

Jara let her hands drop inertly to her sides. *Is he right about me?* she thought. *Is that all I am—a whiner and a whistle blower?* She thought back to her days peddling bio/logic analysis to Lucas Sentinel, to all the times she had cursed her fate and threatened to quit. Wouldn't Lucas pull the same stunts that Natch did, if he had the guts or the foresight?

She hadn't really intended to quit, she realized now. Despite all the indignities, Jara couldn't bring herself to hate this cantankerous child. What she had wanted was the opportunity to deliver some kind of high-handed sermon about Pyrrhic victories and the value of interpersonal relationships. She wanted him to take her seriously. "People could have gotten hurt, Natch," Jara said quietly.

"They didn't."

"But they *could* have."

Natch finally capitulated and flipped off the MindSpace bubble around his workbench. The holographic donut melted back into the void. "Jara, everyone who invests in bio/logics knows what's going on. Things like this happen all the time. Do you think the Patel Brothers got to the top without getting their hands dirty? Or Len Borda?"

Jara snorted angrily. "Oh, I see, *the end justifies the means*."

The entrepreneur narrowed his eyes, as if trying to adjust his focus to a shallower depth of field. "Do you really think number one on Primo's is the *end*? Then you don't understand *anything*, Jara. Getting to number one on Primo's isn't an end at all—it's a means. It's part of the process... just a step on the ladder."

"So what *is* the end? Where do all these means *lead* to?"

Natch stared out into the nothingness for a moment without speaking. She saw him for a brief instant unadorned, between masks. His jaw rocked back and forth, and in his eyes burned a hunger the likes of which Jara had never seen. That fire could consume her schoolgirl lust, swallow it without a trace. She shivered involuntarily.

"I don't have a clue," said Natch. "But when I find out, I'll let you know." And with a peremptory wave of his hand, he cut her multi connection.

Jara found herself standing once more on the red square in her London apartment. It was Wednesday afternoon already. In a few blessed hours, this entire debacle would be a distant memory. On the viewscreen, she could hear the crowds milling about in the public square, restless, impatient, disconsolate.

Jara sank to the floor and cried for a moment, then dragged herself back to her office. There was work to be done.

(((7)))

Sleep tore at him, shrieked at him, pummeled him without mercy. His traitorous body was only too happy to succumb, and it took a monumental effort of will for Natch to keep himself awake.

Sheldon Surina, the father of bio/logics, had once defined progress as "the expansion of choices." Natch wanted the choice to stay awake. So he switched on PulCorp's U-No-Snooze 93 and let the OCHRE machines in his body release more adrenaline. Within seconds, he was awake and alert.

He was on the tube headed north out of Cisco station, through the great redwood forests that carpeted much of the northwest, and up to Seattle. Natch had been on this route hundreds of times. The tube would shuttle back and forth between the two port cities all afternoon, hauling industrial supplies and a dwindling number of commuters. At this time of the morning, the passenger car was nearly empty. Besides Natch, there was an elderly gentleman who appeared to be killing time; two businesswomen who were probably accompanying their cargo in the trailing cars; and an Islander tugging uncomfortably at the copper collar around his neck. Fickle economics, which had once courted TubeCo with ardor, had moved on to younger and more acrobatic mistresses.

Natch had no business to transact in either Cisco or Seattle. He came to see the trees. To see the trees and to plot his next move.

Everyone in the fiefcorp knew about his ritual of tubing out to the redwood forests whenever he had something to mull over. Nobody understood it, least of all Jara. "You refuse to eat a meal sitting down because it's a waste of time, but you'll spend *three and a half hours* riding a hunk of tin across the continent?" she had once scolded him. "Why tube all the way out there when you can multi instead?"

"It's not the same as being there in person."

Jara rolled her eyes. He saw the incomprehension written all over her face: *This is the same kind of backwards logic that the Islanders and the Pharisees use. I thought you were smarter than that.*

"What about a hoverbird?"

"I don't like hoverbirds. Bad memories."

"Okay, then why don't you *teleport*? I know, it's expensive. But time is money, isn't it?"

Natch had had no reply. He was not very good at elaborate explanations. He simply knew he did his best thinking while in a tube car staring at giant sequoias. Teleporting or multi projecting out to the redwoods just wasn't the *right way to do it*. It was *wrong*, like an imperfect bio/logic program was wrong.

Maybe what he appreciated about the tube was that it was *done right*. TubeCo had an eye for perfection in everything they did. Their vehicles were not "hunks of tin," as Jara had accused. They were sleek and beautiful, the product of a business that had reached its awesome maturity. Transparent from the inside but breathtakingly translucent from the outside, the tube cars floated on a cushion of air just molecules thick and whooshed over slim tracks with quiet grace. Even the armrests on the chairs were sculpted from synthetic ivory and contoured for maximum comfort. Unlike so many technological marvels these days that blended into the background—microscopic OCHREs that regulated the human body, multi projections that were nearly indistinguishable from real bodies, data agents that existed only within the mind—the tube was a visible, palpable manifestation of human achievement. It was progress writ large.

The redwoods, in contrast, were nature writ large. Natch gazed through the transparent wall at the sequoias towering over the tube tracks. These trees had watched over this route long before the tube even existed. Most of them had undoubtedly seen the days of Sheldon Surina and Henry Osterman, the days of bio/logics' founders. Some of the trees had stood here since long before the Autonomous Revolt or even the First American Revolution. All of human history, in fact, was but a footnote to their tranquil and reflective existence.

The tube car completed its circuit through the redwood forest and slid to a graceful stop at the Seattle station, but Natch stayed on for another pass. Then another, and another. He watched the trees; he pondered the future; he formulated plans. Gradually, the effects of the U-No-Snooze program wore off. Natch let his guard down and drifted off to sleep.

In his sleep, he dreamed.

He dreamed he was standing in a grove of redwoods, dwarfed by their majesty. He felt small: a forgotten attribute in the great schema of the universe. He was trapped down here. The forest was endless. Tube trains whizzed by just over the next hill, powerless to do anything but circle around in vain looking for an outlet.

But Natch had found a method of escape. He had prepared for this moment. He was a bio/logic programmer, a master architect of human capability. He had studied in the Proud Eagle hive, apprenticed with the great Serr Vigal, gone up against formidable enemies like the Patel Brothers. And he had brought all his skill and learning to bear when he crafted the ultimate program: Jump 225.

He stared at the canopy of leaves many kilometers up in the sky. It looked impossibly distant. But then he thought about the Jump program, the way it swirled and swooped in MindSpace with impossible grace. The sheer number of its tendrils, its connections. The geometric shapes that formed mathematical constellations beyond human perception.

Natch was confident. He started the Jump program, felt programming instructions flowing off the Data Sea and into the data receptacles built into his very bones. Felt the tingling of OCHRE systems interpreting the code and routing commands to the proper leg muscles.

He Jumped.

Natch propelled himself right-foot-forward in an elegant arc towards the sky. The code was grounded in one of the classic moves of natural law: the jump, a movement humanity had worked out through a hundred thousand years of constant iteration. Yet the program bore the indelible signatures of an artificial product: the curl of the toes at midleap, the triumphant arching of the back, the pleasing whistle where no whistle would otherwise exist. The sky drew nearer and nearer, the ground now but a distant memory. Breaking free of the redwoods was already a foregone conclusion, and Natch had set his sights on still loftier goals. Jump 225 would take him not only above the redwoods, but up into the clouds and out of natural law altogether. He would achieve freedom from the tedious rules that had governed human existence since the beginning of time. Down would no longer follow up. Autumn would no longer follow summer. Death would no longer follow life. The Jump 225 program would accomplish all this, and more.

Then, just when his straining fingertips struggled for purchase on the twigs hanging off the highest branches—when he could feel the feathery touch of the leaves—when he had just gotten his first whiff of pure, clean, unspoiled sky—the inevitable descent began.

Natch could see himself falling in slow motion, as if he were looking down from the pinnacle of the tallest redwood. He could see his arms flailing and feel his lungs bursting every second of the way down. The whistle of the Jump had become the screech of gravity's avenging angel. What mere seconds ago had been a triumphant Jump now turned into a horrible, agonizing Fall. How could he have been so blind? How could he not have seen this?

This was worse than not having Jumped in the first place: the force of the impact would surely crush him, flatten him, destroy him. And still he accelerated. Falling so fast now that he would actually crash *through* the ground, down through the pulverizing rock, down to the center of the Earth, where nothing could ever rise again. He yelled his defiance. He shook his fists. He railed at the trees, reaching out in a vain effort to pull them down with him.

A split second before impact, Natch awoke.

2
THE SHORTEST
INITIATION

(((8)))

Natch's forefather Hundible was an acquaintance of Sheldon Surina and one of the earliest investors in bio/logics. He was a gambler, a teller of tall tales, a drifter of unknown origin and unsavory character.

But above all else, Hundible was a poor financial planner. His get-rich-quick schemes sank like leaky boats, leaving him constantly floundering in a sea of fathomless debt. Where he found the money to invest in bio/logics, no one knew. Human biological programming seemed an unlikely venture for Hundible; Surina himself, with his prudish ways and supercilious attitude, seemed an unlikely partner. Naturally, everyone assumed the new discipline was destined to fail.

Yet it was Hundible who had the last laugh. His partner, the skinny Indian tinkerer with the big nose, went on to revitalize science and revolutionize history. The gambler's modest investment ballooned a thousandfold and generated a large fortune. Hundible retired at the seasoned age of thirty-three, took a high-society companion, and slid contentedly out of history. If he had any interest in the great flowering of science that his investment helped bring to fruition, there was no record of it.

Hundible eventually passed on. His wealth endured, for a while.

Natch's ancestor was not the only one to stumble serendipitously onto Surina riches. A host of rogues, early adopters, and cutting-edge investors were handsomely rewarded for their early backing of bio/logics. Lavish mansions and villas sprouted up around the globe to serve their owners' whims—places where they could escape the harsh moral strictures that had kept order since the Autonomous Revolt. The bio/logic entrepreneurs sought cities that had largely escaped the havoc of the Revolt: Omaha, Melbourne, Shenandoah, Madrid, Cape Town. Cities that yearned for the greatness of antiquity, cities whose local governments could be easily bought.

This change in the political landscape did not escape the attention of the old nation-states. The old governments might have been dilapidated and their halls of power decaying, but they still had plenty of resources at their disposal to fight this territorial encroachment. They vested much of their power in a centralized Prime Committee. The Committee turned around and bestowed ultimate martial authority on a single Defense and Wellness Council. Crusading high executives of the Council like Tul Jabbor and Par Padron made reining in the excesses of the bio/logic entrepreneurs their top priority.

Thus the battle was joined. Society split along ideological fault lines: governmentalists who favored central authority versus libertarians who sought power for local civic groups. By the time Natch's fiefcorp ascended to number one on Primo's, this dichotomy had come to seem like the natural order of things.

Hundible's descendants grew fiercely protective of their fortunes. Not only were they fending off the Committee and the Council, but they were also under siege by an even greater enemy: time. The bio/logic entrepreneurs knew that theirs was not the immutable wealth of the Lunar land tycoons. Their money was not a tangible thing like terraformed soil that they could stick their hands into. No, for better or worse, the fates of the bio/logic entrepreneurs were tied to the bio/logic markets.

And markets, like all living things, are mortal.

Natch's mother Lora was fourteen when the Economic Plunge of the 310s hit.

Lora was schooled in the best hives, with the children of important diplomats and capitalmen. Her proctors were crisp, disciplined citizens who saw the hive as a petri dish in which to experiment with the latest academic fashions. Lora and her hivemates yo-yoed between pedagogical theories, learning much about politics but very little about government, finance, engineering, or programming.

But what did it matter? When Lora looked into the future, she saw nothing but the comfortable track her parents had laid out for her, with scheduled stops at initiation, loss of virginity, career, companionship, and motherhood. There would be plenty of time along the way to pick up any other skills she needed.

In the meantime, Lora worked diligently to become a Person of Quality. She developed a keen fashion sense and an eye for good beauty-enhancement programming. She sharpened her social skills at the regular charity balls held in the Creed Élan manors. She dipped her toes in the Sigh, that virtual network of sensuality, and learned a thing or two about the pleasures of the flesh. And when holidays rolled around, she retreated to her cavernous family mansion to dally with servants whose parents had not been blessed with the money for a hive education.

Then, one gloomy spring day, Lora and her hive-mates awoke to find all the proctors riveted to news feeds off the Data Sea. *Marcus Surina has died*, they said. *An accident in the orbital colonies.* A few of the proctors wept openly.

For a while, Surina's death seemed like a distant event that had little connection to the girl's carefully structured hive existence: a supernova in a remote galaxy, visible only through powerful refractive lenses. Surina had been the master of TeleCo, a big and powerful company. He was a direct descendant of Sheldon Surina, the inventor of bio/logics. His death had been a terrible tragedy. What else was there to say?

But from that day forward, everything changed.

Lora's friends began checking out of the hive and disappearing, nobody knew where. One by one, Lora's parents cut back on subscriptions to the programs that gave her eyes that china-doll sparkle and her hair that reflective luster. The servants were let go. Nameless fears escaped from the demesne of adulthood and roamed the hive at night with impunity, whispering words the children did not understand.

Six months after Marcus Surina's death, Lora's parents unexpectedly showed up at the hive and told her to pack her things. They gave her a single valise and told her to take as many of the precious knickknacks and gewgaws lining her shelves as she could carry.

Where are we going? she asked.

To Creed Élan, they replied.

The last time Lora had seen the great ballroom at the Élan manor, its railings had been festooned with purple flowers, and its marble floors lined with elegant revelers in formal robes. Now the ballroom was a shantytown of clustered cots and frightened children. Lora's parents deposited her on an empty bunk and kissed her good-bye.

There's an opportunity in the orbital colonies that we can't pass up, but it's much too dangerous for children, they said. *Don't worry, Creed Élan will take good care of you, and the family will be back on its feet in no time. Just wait here and we'll send for you.*

They never did.

During the next few months, Lora managed to string together what had happened from scraps of overheard conversation and bits of news footage on the Data Sea. Her parents had invested heavily in TeleCo, as had all of the absentee parents of the boys and girls moping the hallways at Creed Élan. It had seemed like a safe bet. No less an authority than Primo's had heralded teleportation as the Next Big Thing. And why wouldn't it be? The master of TeleCo was a *Surina*. Sheldon Surina's invention of bio/logics had propelled the entire world from chaos to a new era of prosperity and innovation. The emerging science of teleportation would surely do the same, with a handsome and brilliant and urbane pitchman like Marcus Surina at the helm. Yes, the economics were fuzzy and the technical challenges daunting, but TeleCo would figure it all out in time.

And that might have happened, if Marcus and his top officers had not been charred to ash by a ruptured shuttle fuel tank.

Marcus Surina's successors at TeleCo tried to pick up the pieces of his work, but it was a Herculean task. They soon discovered that the economics of teleportation weren't merely fuzzy; they were disastrous. The company quickly scaled back its ambitions from Marcus Surina's pie-in-the-sky dreams to more sober and subdued goals. TeleCo supplicated the Prime Committee for protection from its creditors, and soon all the manufacturers and distributors that had anticipated a teleportation boom went belly-up. The ripples spread far and wide, leaving dead companies floating in their wake. Eventually, the ripples touched even Creed Élan, that last bastion of noblesse oblige.

Years later, Lora wondered how much of a fight the rank and file put up when the bodhisattvas of Creed Élan decided to let the children go. The girl found herself shunted off to a small, private institution that was obviously destined for bankruptcy.

Within the space of two years, Lora had gone from a promising young debutante to a penniless member of the diss. Her quest to become a Person of Quality would have to be put on hold.

After exhausting the generosity of her family's remaining acquaintances and selling all her trinkets, Lora found shelter on the thirty-fourth floor of a decaying Chicago office tower. The furniture had long ago been stripped away, and the windows had no glass. *Every few years, one of these buildings falls down and kills everyone inside,* cackled one of the neighboring women, a wretched old hag who had never experienced high society and resented Lora for her all-too-brief tenure there. *Maybe this one will be next.*

Lora learned to do the Diss Shuffle, that ungainly two-step that had her feigning malnutrition on the bread lines one day and faking job experience during interviews the next. Employment was almost impossible to come by for a woman with no marketable skills, no work experience, and no references. She tried the sacred totems that had opened doors for her in the past—the name of her hive, the names of her parents, the name of the *fashionista* who had designed her ball gowns. But in this new world, those names had lost their magic.

And so several years slipped by in slow motion. Down in the realm of the diss, nothing changed. The same expressionless faces meandered down the street, day after day, neither angry nor frightened nor scared nor hurt, but just *there*: zombies of the eternal now chewing synthetic meats grown in tanks. The beneficent forces of government sent bio/logic programming code raining down from the skies, containing chemical nourishment and protection from disease. Black code sprouted up from the lower realms, programs to stir the sludge of neural chemicals in their skulls and relieve the boredom.

Sometimes she had real flesh sex with strangers in trashed-out buildings. Other times, she and her roommates embarked on errands of violence against the crumbling city. Bio/logics had made it very difficult to seriously injure someone with a pipe or a rock. But buildings... buildings followed the natural laws of entropy, and could eventually be beaten down into dust.

And then one day, the rumors began. Len Borda, the young high executive of the Defense and Wellness Council, was giving out money to the bio/logic fiefcorps. *It's a massive program of military and intelligence spending designed to end the Economic Plunge*, they said. *Jobs will be returning soon.*

Lora had not hunted for work in nearly two years. She had rarely even made it around the block in that time. But the rumors stirred memories of her old life, of the comfortable track that prescribed career, companionship, and motherhood. Lora left the Chicago slums and tubed to the metropolis of Omaha in search of work.

Within a few weeks, Lora's search brought her to the attention of Serr Vigal.

Vigal had matriculated in one of the great Lunar universities and discovered an innate passion for neural programming. He settled in Omaha the same week that High Executive Borda defied the Prime Committee and began handing out massive defense subsidies. Vigal founded a company devoted to the study of the brain stem, and went to the Defense and Wellness Council for funding. They approved his request almost without question.

The young neural programmer decided to incorporate as a memecorp instead of a fiefcorp. Vigal had to spend much of his time pleading for public funding from a patchwork of government agencies, but he felt this was time well spent if his employees were insulated from the pressures of the marketplace.

His choice of company structure also allowed him to make unconventional hiring decisions.

Lora was his first such decision. Vigal could see her qualifications were slim, yet her scores on the logic quizzes he routinely gave to applicants were astronomical, far higher than most of his pedigreed apprentices. Clearly the woman was full of untapped potential, and Vigal was intrigued. The field of neuroscience had moved far beyond the basic mechanics of forming neurons and positioning dendrites. If he was to succeed in this field, Vigal knew he would need creative thinkers to help decipher the hidden electrical order in the brain. He hired Lora.

Unfortunately, Vigal's first controversial decision sparked his first major conflict. Lora was a quick learner, but the work was difficult and the rest of the team unforgiving. Mistake piled on top of mistake while the apprentices were crunching to hit major deadlines. Once the project was completed, a group of Lora's fellow apprentices approached Vigal and demanded her dismissal. *It's impossible to work under these conditions*, they said. *We have friends with much better credentials who are still out there in the ranks of the diss.*

Vigal refused to terminate her contract, but he had selfish reasons.

He had fallen in love with her.

Over the next year, Lora found a place in the company as Vigal's muse. The very sight of her fierce brown eyes inspired flights of fancy, flights that glided Vigal over distant mathematical lands few had seen. And yet, one touch of her hand on his shoulder was enough to ground him and bring a sense of direction to his wandering intellect.

The memecorp began to experience great success. Soon, Serr Vigal had become one of the world's preeminent neural programmers, a fixture on the scientific lecture circuit, and a much-sought-after expert on brain stem issues. The other apprentices in the company suspected that Vigal and Lora were lovers, but they looked at the company's accomplishments and decided to give their master some leeway.

Lora frequently accompanied Vigal to scientific conferences and fundraising pitches. One month, Vigal sent her to the remote colony of Furtoid to prepare for such a conference. Two days later, the entire colony was quarantined with a sudden epidemic. Whether the virus was deliberately engineered or simply an evolutionary fluke was never determined.

Portions of Furtoid remained quarantined for months. Four hundred forty-seven people died in those sections of the colony.

Including Lora.

Vigal went into a deep depression when he heard the news. The future had seemed so bright and his own ambitions so limitless. He was just starting to notice the void in his heart that men often discover in their thirties, a void that neither career nor accomplishment can fill. Lora had filled that void for Vigal. Now that she was gone, life seemed bleak and purposeless.

But when Vigal arrived at distant Furtoid to claim her body, he had a surprise waiting for him. Lora had left behind a child, ex utero, at the colony's hiving and birthing facility. The child had been there in the gestation chambers since soon after conception. Rumors abounded that Lora had taken a lover, but the hive had been unable to locate a father.

Suddenly, Vigal found himself standing on Lora's track, looking straight ahead at that long stretch of open country after the scheduled stop at career and before the end of the line. The distance seemed unimaginably vast. To Vigal, it was part of the natural order of things for a man to travel such a long distance alone.

When the boy emerged from gestation, the neural programmer had himself appointed legal guardian. Then he transferred the child to a hive facility back on Earth, in Omaha.

He named the child Natch.

(((9)))

Many years later, Natch would say that his greatest skill was his knack for acquiring enemies. He was only half joking.

Natch made his first enemies before the age of five. He had not learned to speak until he was almost three—an eternity in an age of bio/logics—and this set him apart from the other children. The hive's larger boys took notice of his solitude and quiet demeanor, his propensity for sitting alone in corners. They decided to examine this odd child the only way they knew how: with their fists.

One morning, Natch emerged from his room and found five of his hivemates waiting. They were older boys, uglier than he, and sullen since birth. Natch instinctively knew what was about to happen and felt a split second of astonishment. *What did I do wrong?* he thought. Then the boys jumped him. The next few minutes were a tumult of kicks, punches, and scratches that left Natch reeling on the floor in pain.

He limped back into his room, having learned a valuable lesson: always be on your guard, because the universe needs no reasons to inflict punishment.

Perhaps the boys were merely looking for a cringe or a whimper of fear, something that would validate their nascent theories of power and weakness. But Natch refused to give them this satisfaction. The next morning, he emerged from his room as always and marched without hesitation towards the waiting band of thugs. They gave him plenty of opportunity to flee, but the stubborn child refused to veer off his determined path. Instead, he waited silently while the bullies had their way with him. The beatings continued the next day, and the next, and the next.

The proctors were not blind. Natch's floor in the hive could barely contain four dozen children; no space remained for privacy. But bio/logic technology did not work in Natch's favor. The OCHREs floating in his bloodstream had been battle-tested for generations in much more rigorous environments than a suburban hive; they could heal minor cuts and bruises within minutes. The bullies could inflict little real damage on him until they were old enough to pull black code off the Data Sea.

The proctors decided to let the conflict play itself out.

But how can we just sit there and watch the boy suffer like that? argued one of the proctors in a staff meeting. *We can't just let this go on forever.*

Her superior was unsympathetic. *We're not here to coddle these children. There are sixty billion people out there waiting to chew them up and spit them out.* The headmaster nodded towards the flexible glass window, as if the thin membrane could ward off the world's suffering. Outside, tree branches scraped greedily against the window like claws. *These children need to be tough in order to thrive.*

So we're trying to create a generation of martyrs. Is that it?

Long pause. *Have faith in the boy, Petaar. He's not getting hurt, is he?* We won't *let this go on forever, but let's give him a few more days to figure things out for himself before we intervene.*

Nobody ever explained this decision to Natch, however, and to him the proctors' inaction felt like indifference. This was a greater blow than any the young bullies could deliver. Didn't the proctors drill into the children's heads every day that the world was run by logical, impartial laws? Everything happened for a reason, they said. Every effect was traceable to a root cause. But this daily punishment had no rational basis that Natch could see, and though the proctors could tell he was suffering, they remained mum. The boy pondered his dilemma for days on end, and spent his nights wrestling with cognitive dissonance.

One night, Natch awoke before dawn with his mind on fire.

The world around him dimmed and blanked out until all he could see were his hands in front of his face. And then the room exploded with colors. A frenzy of lights burned far away up over his head, while strange hollow voices began speaking to him of things he didn't understand. Random phrases in imaginary languages. The names of dead kings. Algorithms and encrypted messages. Natch lay quietly in the dark, consumed by fear, and let the vision wash over him.

When dawn arrived, he knew what he had to do.

Natch missed roll call that morning. The proctor Petaar scrambled to his room, fearing the worst. She found the boy on the floor, trapped beneath a heavy bureau and struggling to breathe.

The hive descended into pandemonium. After tending to Natch, the proctors quickly rounded up the thugs who had been tormenting him. They grilled the boys behind locked doors for two hours and extracted a number of tearful confessions. But the bullies were unanimous in insisting they had nothing to do with burying Natch under the bureau. *And the toys missing from Natch's room?* thundered Petaar. *Did they run off by themselves?* The boys had no explanation. The proctors weighed the evidence against the five bullies for much of the afternoon, and then summarily expelled them.

When he heard the news, Natch felt a cold thrill run up his spine. It was his first taste of victory, and he found it an intoxicating brew.

The boys had actually been innocent of their crime; the entire incident had been a setup. Natch had contrived to trap himself beneath the bureau by propping it up with blocks and then slowly removing the supports. He had sketched out the details of his plan in the early-morning hours with the zeal of a master draftsman, until no flaws were visible to the naked eye. He had long since forgotten the source of his inspiration.

But Natch's ploy succeeded in totally unexpected dimensions as well. The proctors who had ignored his plight now walked around with looks of guilt etched on their faces. Petaar went out of her way to accommodate Natch's every whim. Word of the episode even leaked out to his hivemates' parents and caused the institution no end of grief. Natch was astounded. He had vanquished his enemies and exposed his proctors' fallibility with a single blow.

The incident drove home another valuable lesson: with patience, cunning, and foresight, anything is possible.

This was not the last hurdle Natch had to clear in the hive. Other children rushed to fill the void left by the departure of the bullies, and they were not so easily fooled. They tried to sabotage his homework, steal his belongings, and blame him for all their own mischief. Natch quickly realized he had made a tactical error hiding behind the proctors; by not dealing with his opponents directly, he had only reinforced the perception that he was weak.

He wondered if this would be a never-ending cycle. Was he doomed to spend the remainder of his life fighting battle after battle with a succession of enemies, each more capable than the last, until he finally met his match?

At the age of six, Natch decided that escape was his only option. He ran away.

Serr Vigal received a panicked ConfidentialWhisper from Natch's proctors that morning. They wondered whether the boy had hopped the tube and found his way to Vigal's apartment, but the neural programmer had not seen his charge in weeks. He cancelled the morning's staff meeting and set out for the nearest tube station. The tube whisked him across metropolitan Omaha to a squat semicircular building that did, in fact, look like a beehive.

What do you mean, he's missing? asked Vigal, perplexed, when he caught up to the anxious proctors. *I thought you monitored the children here twenty-four hours a day.*

The headmaster bowed his head. *We do.*

Vigal was not an excitable man by nature. *Are you sure he didn't just wander onto another floor?* he said, scratching the few lonely hairs on his head. *You have security programs, don't you? Certainly he couldn't have gotten out of the building without you knowing it.*

Theoretically, no, said the headmaster. *But it appears he did.*

Omaha was no place for an unattended boy. A curious soul like Natch could easily disappear in a cosmopolitan city of twenty-two million and never be heard from again. Broken families had been commonplace in the depths of the Economic Plunge, but even a recovering economy could not totally stem the trickle of missing children.

Natch was not oblivious to the dangers of the city, but he had already learned to discount fear as an unreliable emotion. Omaha seemed like a zoo to him; everywhere he turned, there were tantalizing new sights arrayed for his amusement. Buildings expanded and collapsed like breathing animals, often causing entire city blocks to shift a few meters this way and that. Tube trains crisscrossed the city like veins. And the streets were filled with millions of people holding silent conversations with acquaintances thousands of kilometers away.

Natch spent hours trying to figure out which of the pedestrians were real and which were multi projections. The proctors had taught the children about multi, of course; some of the proctors multi-ed to the hive themselves from as far away as Luna. But children under eight were not allowed to project on the network, and thus they had very little firsthand knowledge of the subject. So Natch spent hours pivoting 360 degrees in the crowd, looking for people on the periphery of his vision who seemed fuzzy and indistinct until he focused on them. Then he would run up and toss a pebble. Those that the pebble bounced off were real (and sometimes irritated); those that the pebble passed through were multi projections. Natch discovered to his astonishment that he could not tell the difference at all.

Once the initial fascination of the city wore off, Natch's experiences in the hive began to infect everything he saw. The belligerent street vendor shouting down his customer's haggling, the timid woman walking two steps behind her companion like a housepet, the down-and-out businessman being pressed out of his apartment by white-robed Council officers—every interaction he saw was a substantiation of the eternal struggle between the Pushers and the Pushed.

Natch found a quiet corner in a public square and sat facing the wall. A viewscreen above him repeatedly screeched a popular footwear slogan every ten seconds. *No matter where you go, there will be bullies and victims*, Natch told himself. *Which do you want to be?*

Back at the hive, the proctors made a poor show of mobilizing to find Natch. The boy had been gone for most of the afternoon, and yet the headmaster had only just managed to circulate his name and description to the local L-PRACG security forces. Serr Vigal, for his part, was absorbed in solving the riddle of how Natch had made it through hive security. All simply gaped with astonishment when the boy appeared back in the hive that evening, seemingly out of nowhere. On his return, he had managed to elude their security apparatus as effortlessly as he had on his departure.

That was a nice trick you pulled, said the neural programmer with a hint of pride. And then, mindful of the proctors' angry stares: *Is there anything you'd like to talk to us about?*

Natch frowned, shook his head, and vanished into his room without a word.

The next day, a tangible change had come over the boy. He met the taunts and jeers of his hivemates with a cruel smile that made them uneasy. And then his enemies began to suffer from a series of unfortunate accidents.

One boy who had constantly maligned Natch for his good looks found himself tripping down a long flight of stairs. A girl who liked to capsize Natch's lunch tray found herself locked in a spare pantry for an entire evening. And so on.

Each humiliation was carefully crafted to reach maximum exposure among the hive children. Natch instinctively knew that the punishments he imposed should be both brutal and disproportionate to their crimes. This new brand of psychological warfare terrified the other children, who had not yet learned the art of subtlety, who still expressed their emotions with curled fists and running feet. Eventually, even the dullest child in the hive saw a pattern: if you bother Natch, you will pay for it.

Natch got his wish. The other children left him alone. He had learned another valuable lesson: perception is everything.

Natch quickly outgrew his hive. Even the absent-minded Serr Vigal could see that, although it took an eye-opening conversation with the proctor Petaar for him to recognize it.

Children like Natch need something to focus on, she said. *You'd better make sure he's pointed in the right direction, or he'll focus on the wrong things.*

Vigal furrowed his brow. A man who spent his day working with the quadratics of neural science had little time for binary terms like "right" and "wrong." *This new hive you suggest—they'll give him something to focus on?*

Petaar nodded knowingly. *And then some. Natch will get ten years of study—hard study—and then a one-year initiation.*

Initiation? The hives still do that?

This one does.

The neural programmer scrolled bewilderedly through page upon page of starchy marketing material. *The tuition seems rather large... and I'm afraid my Vault account is rather small at the moment...*

Which is why he can apply for a Prime Committee scholarship.

Days later, after an awkward farewell sermon from Petaar (and an even more awkward farewell embrace), Natch was shepherded off to the Proud Eagle hive in Cape Town. The Proud Eagle had a reputation for doing things differently. Unlike most other hives, they had no gestation and birthing facilities, no counseling staff, and no social programs of any kind. Children came to the Proud Eagle because they had stretched beyond the boundaries of the traditional hive system and needed a challenge. The proctors delivered it to them in the form of ten-hour classes, six days a week. This left very little time for idleness, boredom, or mischief.

Natch did not miss the infantile games and simplistic moral lessons that had taken up his time at the old hive. Initiation lurked somewhere in his future, but he would deal with that challenge when it came. He took to his new surroundings like a fish to water and spent the next several years gulping down knowledge.

The history proctors taught him about the thinking machines that had nearly decimated humanity during the great Autonomous Revolt, about the dark times that had followed, and about the golden age of scientific reawakening that Sheldon Surina's discipline of bio/logics had brought into being. They taught him about the evaporation and consolidation of the ancient nation-states, the rise of the L-PRACGs, the establishment of the Prime Committee and the Council, the never-ending quarrel between governmentalism and libertarianism.

The ethics proctors taught him about the early religions, how their influence waned after the dawn of the Reawakening, and how the violent fanaticism of Jesus Joshua Smith drove most of their remaining adherents into seclusion in the Pharisee Territories. They taught him about the Surinas' philosophy of spiritual enlightenment through technology, and about the creeds that had sprung up during the modern era to preach community and responsibility. They taught him the tenets of Creed Objectivv, Creed Élan, Creed Thassel, Creed Dao, and many others.

The data proctors taught him about Henry Osterman and the Osterman Company for Human Re-Engineering (OCHRE), about the microscopic machines carrying Osterman's name that swarmed through his blood and tissue. They taught him how to summon data agents with a thought, how to run bio/logic programs that interacted with the machines and supplemented his body's natural abilities. They introduced him to the vast corpus of human knowledge available on the Data Sea. They explained to him how Prengal Surina's universal law of physics allowed scientists to turn grains of sand, droplets of water, and molecules of air into quantum computers of almost limitless strength.

The business proctors taught him the basics of bio/logic programming. They showed him the holographic method of programming, which had long ago supplanted language-based systems of logic. They discussed the difference between market-driven fiefcorps and publicly funded memecorps. They put a set of bio/logic programming bars in his hands and set him loose in MindSpace to demonstrate how to visualize and manipulate logical processes.

Given the grueling program of study, most of the children couldn't wait for long weekends and vacations to be with their families. But Natch had only Serr Vigal to go home to, and Vigal had never acted like family. The neural programmer treated him like a colleague instead of an adopted son. When they were not simply ignoring one another, they were having cordial conversations about current events. These conversations usually turned into Socratic discussions, with Vigal feeding him question after question, as if skepticism were a form of dietary fiber.

I wish I knew something about children, Vigal would chuckle absentmindedly from time to time. But Natch was grateful he didn't. He looked forward to spending weekends alone at the hive, when all of the children were gone and Vigal was shuttling around the globe fundraising.

For a few years, the Proud Eagle seemed like paradise to Natch. He tore into his assignments with gusto and asked for more, afraid to take this opportunity for granted because he knew it would not last forever.

(((10)))

The families started arriving at noon the day before initiation, and continued streaming into the Proud Eagle until long past sundown. From a corner, Natch watched his hivemates go off for private chats with fathers and mothers and uncles and cousins to hear one last bit of wisdom they could take with them to initiation. He conjured up a picture of Lora, the mother he had never met, and wondered what kind of advice she would be giving him right now.

Natch felt a hand on his shoulder. He whirled around expectantly, but it was only Horvil. Horvil, the most anxiety-prone child in the hive, not to mention the sloppiest and the largest. Horvil, Natch's only friend. "So do you think it's gonna be painful?" he said.

Before Natch had a chance to respond, an older boy stepped in. He was ruggedly handsome and knew it, with a face that could have been the Platonic Form of symmetry. "Of *course* it's going to be painful," teased Brone as he advanced on Horvil.

"What's initiation without pain? What's *life* without pain?" He called up a static electricity program and tapped the other two boys on the side. Horvil yelped and scooted out of the way, but Natch quickly activated a grounding program to deflect the charge.

"I really hope it's not too painful," whimpered Horvil to himself. He turned on Analgesic 232.5 to soothe his aching side. "I don't think I'll be able to stand a lot of pain." Brone and Natch stared at one another icily for a few moments without speaking.

Horvil's and Brone's families arrived shortly thereafter, leaving Natch alone in the corner with his thoughts. Horvil disappeared into a gaggle of aunts and cousins who seemed determined to wedge their advice into him with a crowbar if necessary. Brone walked off with two picture-perfect parents, looking less like their progeny than a model from the same factory. He gave Natch one last evil grin before vanishing. "Horvil's not the only one who's going to feel *pain*," Brone fired off at him over ConfidentialWhisper.

Everyone knew what to expect from initiation, but the ramifications only seemed to multiply the closer the time came. The students would be separated by sex and put in the wilderness for a year, where the OCHREs in their bloodstreams would be deactivated. The bio/logic programs that regulated their heartbeats, kept their calendars, and maximized the storage space in their brains would be cut off. They would look at words without being able to instantly glean their meanings from the Data Sea. They would snuffle and sneeze and bruise and forget things. And the worst horror of all, they would wake up in the middle of the night with actual *shit* oozing through their intestines...

"'Human beings are only subroutines of humanity,'" said a voice.

Natch must have drifted off, because he hadn't noticed the middle-aged man approaching him. The man's sand-colored robe was decidedly unfashionable (and poorly tailored at that), but his face was friendly: the nonspecific goodwill of the perpetual cloud dweller. His almond-shaped eyes betrayed a hint of the Orient. Natch smiled politely at the multi projection of Serr Vigal.

"Sheldon Surina said that," Vigal continued gently.

"What did he mean?"

"Well, if you believe your proctors, Surina meant that everyone should experience the struggle of humanity from darkness to light. They think that Surina would have wanted you to see what life was like before the Reawakening. Make you appreciate the modern world more."

"And what do *you* think?"

The man stared off into the distance and tugged at his peppery goatee. "I don't know. I think maybe Sheldon Surina just wanted everyone to keep an open mind and be nice to each other."

Natch tried to refrain from rolling his eyes. It was typical of the advice he received from Serr Vigal: pleasant, inoffensive, and mostly useless. "I thought you couldn't come," he said. "I thought you were speaking at a conference."

Vigal frowned. "Yes, that's right. But I convinced one of my apprentices to cover for me. At least, I *think* she said she would cover for me..." Vigal's eyes searched the ground as if he might find answers woven into the Aztec patterns on the carpet. Finally, he gave a self-deprecating shrug. "Well, there's nothing I can do about it now."

Natch noticed the neural programmer's baffled expression and stifled a smile. It was impossible to get mad at Serr Vigal. He might be hopelessly out of touch, but at least he had a sense of humor about it.

"Come," said the older man, clapping a virtual hand on Natch's shoulder. "Let's take a walk in the garden, and I'll give you the last bit of sentimental nonsense you'll have to endure for the next twelve months."

The Proud Eagle's garden was the envy of metropolitan Cape Town. Gargantuan sunflowers sat alongside lush poppies and forbidding cacti, all growing in the shadows of redwoods, bonsai, and elm. Natch had been training himself for initiation by trying to identify things that would not exist without Sheldon Surina's science of bio/logics, and this improbable congregation of plants was one of them. It was easy to forget that bio/logics dealt not only with the programming of the human body, but with other organic structures as well.

Serr Vigal kept his silence for several minutes. Natch could feel the hair on the back of his neck standing at attention as his guardian gave him one of those world-weary stares. The boy put his hands in his pockets and did his best to ignore it.

Natch wondered for the millionth time what kind of relationship Vigal had really had with his mother. Had he loved her? Had they slept together? Would they be bonded companions now if Lora had not been infected by that epidemic in the orbital colonies? It was a pointless exercise. All Natch ever managed to pry out of Vigal was the skeletal structure of a life story. Sometimes Natch suspected the neural programmer was really his father, but Genealogy Sleuth 24.7 concluded that the differences in their DNA made such a relationship unlikely at best.

"I hear some of your hivemates are starting their own fiefcorps after initiation," said Vigal abruptly.

Natch nodded. "A few of them."

"Your friend Brone among them, I suppose."

A flurry of emotions washed through Natch's mind as he considered the visage of his hated rival. The two had spent most of their childhood warily circling one another like fencers, always testing and probing for weaknesses. Over the past year, Natch's competition with Brone had turned into full-scale war. "Brone is not my friend," he said through gritted teeth.

Natch's malice passed right over Vigal's head. "What about Horvil?"

"He doesn't know."

"And you? After the hive, after initiation, what then?"

There was a pause. "I've had... a few meetings."

Vigal exhaled softly and pretended to study a hanging grapevine. "I see."

Another period of silence followed. Serr Vigal seemed to be marshaling the courage to say something. Meanwhile, Natch could see through the hothouse windows that the commotion in the hive building was dying down. Families were giving their sons and daughters one last virtual embrace before cutting their multi connections. Natch and his fellows would be on their way to initiation in just eighteen hours.

"Listen, Natch," said his guardian finally. "I'd like to give you some advice before you head out to initiation. It's just... I'm not very good at this kind of thing. As you know, raising a child wasn't something I planned. It sort of fell in my lap by accident... And now, after all this time, I'm not sure how to begin..." Vigal stopped and collected his thoughts, aware he had not exactly gotten off to an auspicious beginning. "Natch, I have tried to give you the education your mother would have wanted you to have. She believed her hive did not adequately prepare her for the world. And now I wonder if the same thing will prove to be the case with you, here at the Proud Eagle."

"That's ridiculous," snapped Natch, instantly on the defensive. "Everybody knows that this is one of the best hives around."

"And how does one measure that?"

"Well, the capitalmen seem to think so. Do you know how many programmers from last year's class got funding for their own fiefcorps?"

"Too many, if you ask me."

Natch shrugged. He would not be lured into one of these pedantic Vigalish dialogues today. "Things are different now. The economy is exploding, and there's too much opportunity out there to waste time on an apprenticeship. Two years ago—"

The neural programmer shushed him with a raised hand. His face bore a pained expression. "I hear that nonsense from the drudges every day. I'm surprised that *you*, of all people, don't know propaganda when you read it. But it's not just you. Your hivemates, the proctors, Brone, Horvil—everyone is falling for this drivel." Vigal wrung his hands as if trying to cleanse them of a foul and noxious liquid.

Natch searched his mental catalog of conversations with the neural programmer, but this outburst of emotion from Vigal was unprecedented. Natch had never imagined that Vigal had given much thought to his education, much less held any passionate convictions about it.

"Brone believes he is ready to start his own business," Vigal continued firmly. "Let him. He is a vicious person headed for a vacuous career, and he will be sorry he turned down a few extra years of study without the pressures of the marketplace. But *you*, Natch, you're *better* than that. You are *not* ready to run your own company. If you jump into the fiefcorp world too quickly, you will regret it."

Natch reeled back, stunned, and sat on the edge of a stone planter. He had never received a reprimand from Serr Vigal, and now it stung like a jolt from Brone's static electricity program. "So, what would *you* have me do?" he spat out bitterly.

"Natch, I can't *have* you do anything," said Vigal. Already his concentration was beginning to dissipate, to fade into everyday melancholy. "Once you return from initiation, you'll be old enough to make your own choices. You can subscribe to your own L-PRACGs, pledge to whatever creeds you choose. You can solicit capitalmen for funds and start your own fiefcorp, if you want. But... if I could wish anything for you, it would be that you would take an apprenticeship somewhere close... somewhere I can keep an eye on you." His face turned an embarrassed red.

So that's what this is all about, thought Natch. He hadn't expected a sermon from his legal guardian—in fact, he hadn't expected Vigal to show up today at all. But now that the sermon had become a referendum on his parenting skills, things were starting to make sense.

Serr Vigal exhaled deeply and stretched his arms out behind his back, as if he had just removed a heavy weight from there. Natch realized his guardian had been rehearsing this speech for some time. "I can see the look in your face," said his guardian softly. "I've seen your scores on the bio/logics exams, Natch. Best in your class."

"*Second* best," the boy whispered venomously. Brone's smug face leered at him from the corners of his mind.

"It doesn't matter. The point is, I know you are expecting lots of offers from the capitalmen. No, you don't have to tell me about your meetings—I already know. I'm not asking you to make any decisions right now. We'll talk about it again in twelve months. All I ask for now is that you keep your eyes and ears open, and consider the idea of taking an apprenticeship—*any* apprenticeship—after initiation. And be *careful* out there."

The boy frowned and kicked at the moss growing between the flagstones. "You don't have to baby me. I know how to take care of myself."

"Yes," sighed Vigal under his breath, "and sometimes I am afraid that is *all* you know."

Natch was used to prowling the hallways of the Proud Eagle alone at night. He had learned to move in total silence, not out of any fear of punishment, but so he could concentrate on the staccato language of settling floorboards and restless insects. The kinds of noises only heard in places built prior to the invention of self-compressing buildings.

On the night before initiation, the halls were packed. Teenagers roamed from room to room in blatant violation of curfew, saying tearful goodbyes, pledging their undying love, settling old scores. Natch saw at least a dozen couples sneak behind closed doors for one last romp on the Sigh. Nervous giggles abounded. He took a furtive glance down the hallway to the proctors' wing. They were following the time-honored tradition of looking the other way and getting drunk.

Over the past week, Natch had been studiously reading the drudge forecasts of the bio/logic market. This year, the demand for fresh programming talent had reached a critical mass. The Meme Cooperative's rules forbade fiefcorps and memecorps from signing on apprentices or providing start-up capital before graduation from the hive. But Len Borda's post-Plunge economy was churning out opportunity much quicker than warm bodies, and so many companies were willing to risk the Cooperative's tepid penalties.

Natch had studied the laws of supply and demand. What better time to raise money for a fiefcorp than the night before initiation?

Downstairs, he stretched out on a sofa in the atrium to await the arrival of the capitalman Figaro Fi. It was the fifth late-night rendezvous Natch had arranged this week with the power brokers in the fiefcorp world, and the most important yet. The rich and eccentric Fi had bankrolled some of the most spectacular successes on Primo's. Lucas Sentinel and the Deuteron Fiefcorp both owed their laurels to Figaro's generous assistance, as did the Patel Brothers, the rising young stars of the bio/logic scene. Natch had been surprised to get a meeting with the capitalman at all, and readily agreed to his conditions—a meeting in the middle of the night, when Figaro was halfway through his working day in Beijing. Natch explained that the network was off-limits to students so late. He took it as a good omen that Fi agreed to multi to Omaha instead.

At three minutes after midnight, when the ruckus from the upper floors had settled to a low rumble, a multi projection materialized in the atrium.

The person who had coined the phrase *Don't judge a book by its cover* might have had someone like Figaro Fi in mind. The great capitalman stood almost a head shorter than any of the proctors on staff—shorter, even, than many of the students—and he was almost as wide as he was tall. His robe, of vivid gold, silver, and copper, made a bold proclamation of idiosyncrasy. Each stubby finger was adorned with a ring; some boasted three or four. Figaro endured the boy's respectful bow and gave a feeble nod in return.

Natch looked the capitalman straight in the eye. "I invited you here tonight," he said, "because I'm interested in your money."

Fi appraised him coolly, like a rancher surveying his lands. "Is that so?" His voice was a low rasp, rich with irony.

"If you're not prepared to open your Vault account, then you'd better cut your multi connection right now and not waste any more of my time. Otherwise, follow me." And with that, Natch wheeled around and headed down the hallway.

Natch did not look back until he had reached one of the plush dens that the Proud Eagle had set up for entertaining guests. It was the kind of dusky room that might have once been lined with leather books. Natch wasn't sure whether or not the capitalman would still be there when he turned around, and he barely managed to restrain a grin of triumph when he saw that the little man had indeed followed him.

Figaro Fi planted himself in one of the over-stuffed chairs. "You've got balls, and I like that," said the capitalman sardonically. He pulled a beefy cigar from his coat pocket and chomped on one end. "Go ahead," he grunted.

Natch launched into the presentation he had already given a hundred times in his own mind. It was short and to the point. There were holographs of Natch's programming work, a brief list of the accolades he had won in academic competitions, and the outlines of a fiefcorp marketing strategy. When he finished, he made no attempt at idle chitchat, but rather waited patiently for a reaction from his audience.

Figaro wore an almost lecherous grin. "I like this," he said. "You've been planning this whole thing for weeks, haven't you? Waiting until the last minute. The little scene in the hallway out there. Clever, boy, *clever*!"

Natch stood politely with his hands clasped behind his back and said nothing.

"Of course, you know what I came here to see," continued Fi. He apparently had no intention of lighting his cigar—a pointless act in multispace any-way—preferring instead to swing it between two fingers for emphasis. "You know I'm not here to see your test scores again. I'm not here to see you perform your programming tricks like some *monkey* or hear your little prepared speech about how you can *benefit society.*" The capitalman leaned back and let out a hearty laugh, as if he had just told an extraordinary joke. The gold sequins on his belly jingled sympathetically.

"I'm really here to see how you comport yourself," continued Figaro. "To see if you really have that *killer instinct* I've heard so much about. So tell me, Natch, what makes you think I'm going to put up a single credit tonight?"

"Because if you don't," replied the boy, "someone else will."

"And you think I'm going to ruin my good name with the Meme Cooperative by giving fiefcorp money to a hive boy before initiation?"

"Oh, please. You have enough money to pay them off ten times over."

"True, true." Figaro seemed quite satisfied with himself, and Natch wondered if he was about to dispense a few nuggets of gossip about what it was like to live a life of privilege. Parties with the Lunar land tycoons, programmers catering to your every whim, teleportation on command.

But the capitalman was on a different tack. He wedged the cigar back between his molars and gave Natch a sly look. "I'm surprised you even asked me here today," said Fi. "If you'd really done your homework, you would know that I like to spread my investments around. It's not like me to risk my neck for *two* boys from the same hive."

Natch instantly felt the bottom drop out of his stomach. There was only one other boy at the

Proud Eagle who could have possibly caught the attention of someone with Figaro Fi's clout. In his mind's eye, Natch saw the last horrible smirk Brone had given him earlier that evening. *Horvil's not the only one that's going to be feeling pain.* He clenched his fists behind his back until his fingernails carved bloody crescent moons into his palms.

"So why did you come here?" the boy snarled.

Figaro broke into a full-fledged smile. "Because it amuses me, of course."

Wild thoughts scurried through Natch's head, baring their claws with fiendish fury. If Figaro had been sitting here in the flesh, Natch might well have buried his fingers in the fat man's throat by now. He could feel the growling in his gut and summoned an antacid program, but it did nothing. The visions pranced around his mind. Brone's smug face and Adonic figure, sipping fancy wine in a Lunar villa. Brone sitting at the head of a very long conference table lined with adoring apprentices. Brone laughing at *Natch's* expense.

"And will it *amuse* you if I go to the Meme Cooperative and tell them you're giving money to a hive boy?" hissed Natch. The words came out of his mouth before he realized what he was saying. He let them vent. "Not just any hive boy—a spoiled rich one whose parents probably paid you off. Or what if I go to the drudges? 'Capitalman admits to bribing Meme Cooperative officials'—that sounds like a good headline for Sen Sivv Sor."

Figaro Fi did not seem angry or surprised at Natch's sudden outburst. If anything, he became more serene, which enraged the boy even further. "So now you're threatening me," said the capitalman matter-of-factly.

Years later, Natch would cringe when he thought of that evening, and wonder how he had fallen for such obvious bait. But caught in the moment, he found himself hurling all his adolescent rage at the capitalman until he hardly knew what he was saying. "It's your choice. You can invest in *him* and I'll turn you in to the Meme Cooperative and the Defense and Wellness Council. I'll tell the drudges. You'll be sorry you ever came here. Or you can invest in *me.*"

The little capitalman actually seemed to be enjoying the boy's discomfort. His face bore the look of a mischievous child poking a frog with a stick. "All right, all right, sit down, boy," he said abruptly. His chubby hand delivered backhanded slaps through the air in Natch's direction. "You can keep your threats to yourself."

"And why's that?"

"Because you have nothing on me. Yes, I've already decided to give your friend funding. But I'm not foolish enough to do it before he returns from initiation."

Natch could feel nausea swelling inside him and beating a tattoo on the inside of his skull. He wondered if this was what it felt like to throw up. In a daze, he reached for the armchair behind him and collapsed into the waiting cushion.

"The recruiters all told me about you," said Figaro Fi, plopping his virtual feet onto an ottoman. "*Brilliant but narrow-minded*, they said. *Volatile. Unstable.* But I just had to see it myself. Those bio/logics scores of yours were too good to ignore.

"Now here's the good news, Natch. I *like* you. You've got that same look in your eyes that *I* did forty years ago. Hungry! Vicious! Uncompromising! And by the way, much better scores than I ever got, even in economics.

"No, I haven't changed my mind. I'm not giving you a single credit from my Vault account. But I'm going to give you something even more valuable.

"I'm going to tell you *why*."

The pudgy capitalman pulled his feet off the ottoman. He leaned forward intently and stuck his elbows on his knees until he had nearly curled himself up like a pill bug.

"Listen: all of us in the bio/logics industry, all the capitalmen, the programmers, the channelers, the drudges, the fiefcorpers and memecorpers and engineers and analysts... we're slaves, Natch. We're all slaves to *want*.

"*Want*. It drives the world! It moves mountains; it swallows cultures!

"You see it, don't you, Natch? *Want* is everywhere. It's in people. It's in programming. In politics. In nature. The universe just won't stay still. It *wants* to move; even its smallest particles *want* to be in motion. Take bio/logics. Aren't bio/logic programs in a natural state of incompleteness? We release version 1.0 of a program, and inevitably it is imperfect. Version 1.0s *want* a version 2.0, don't they? They practically *beg* for it. You toil for months on version 2.0, and you've still barely tapped into its bottomless reservoir of *want*. Version 2.0 *wants* a version 3, version 3.0 *wants* a version 4, and so on and on and on and on and on—forever!"

The antacid program wasn't helping. Somewhere in the back of his mind, Natch realized he would not follow through on his implied threat to Figaro. He would not spend his last few hours at the Proud Eagle shuttling desperately between second-rate capitalmen and seeking illegal handouts. *If only this interview could be over. If only I could shrivel up inside my shell like a snail and never see Figaro Fi or Brone or Vigal again.*

But the capitalman continued on mercilessly. "You ever heard that story about the bodhisattva of Creed Objectivv and Lucco Primo? The bodhisattva asks Primo what the key to success is. Primo says, *Three things: ability, energy, and direction.* You have the ability, Natch, and you definitely have the energy—maybe more ability and energy than I've ever *seen.*

"But where is your direction? I don't need forty-five minutes to see you haven't got any. You have endless *wants,* Natch! But *want* without purpose destroys a person. Those who can't master their *wants* are loose cannons. They bring companies down. They ruin lives. They may flare brightly for a while, oh yes! But in the end, Natch, loose cannons fail. They *lose money.*

"Now your friend Brone—"

"Please don't call him that," Natch croaked.

"Your friend Brone is a real sharp programmer, but I've seen better. He's got a way with people, and he's a handsome kid, which never hurts. But he's got one thing you don't. He knows *exactly* where he's going, and what he's doing.

"I've seen it all before. You'll get to the top quicker than Brone, but then you'll just get pulled down by some other kid who's hungrier and angrier than you are. That's just the way it works."

Figaro arose, looking well pleased with his little sermon. He put the chewed cigar in his coat pocket, leaving Natch to wonder why he had drawn it out in the first place. Just before cutting his multi connection, he turned back to the boy with an arched eyebrow.

"Now, about that story with Lucco Primo... A couple years later, this drudge asks Primo, *So what's the most important element of success? Ability, energy, or direction?* Primo sits back and thinks about it for a minute. *Direction*, he tells the drudge. *Ability and energy you can buy.*"

Figaro started chortling obscenely and prepared to cut his multi connection.

"Good luck at initiation," said Fi. "You're going to need it."

(((1 1)))

Some of the boys had heard their initiation would take place in the South Pacific, on the edge of Islander territory. There were hundreds of islands in the area that remained pristine and untouched by modern technology. Other boys countered that an island wasn't remote enough. No, they would be shuttled off to some orbital colony specially designed for this purpose, or maybe one of the lawless quadrants of Mars.

Horvil decided (based on no evidence whatsoever) that they were headed to the bottom of the ocean to live in one of the bubble colonies that the real estate developers tried to revive every twenty years or so. "I *knew* I should have studied up on hydroponics," he fretted to Natch as they filed out of the hive for the last time. "And I'm a terrible swimmer. Can't even hold my breath for a minute. You'll take care of me, right, Natch? You won't let me drown, will you?"

Natch hadn't spoken a word all morning. He found it pointless to speculate about their destination. The civilized world was littered with initiation compounds, from Earth to Luna to the asteroid belt, and he had never heard that any one was better than another. Besides, Natch knew from long and painful experience that isolation has no geographic boundaries. Even if the proctors arranged to shuttle them out to the remotest orbital colony—like one of those experimental stations beyond Jupiter—that still wouldn't erase the shame he had suffered last night with Figaro Fi. And Brone would still be there with his insufferable smirk and the knowledge that he had bested Natch.

Horvil and Natch marched solemnly with the rest of the boys towards the sleek hoverbird that would carry them to their destination. The Falcon 4730 was the standard workhorse of the aerospace industry, used for everything from cross-city transportation to intercontinental cargo hops. This craft could get them anywhere on Earth, or maybe even to a low-hanging orbital colony—but not underwater, Horvil was relieved to note.

Sixty-four boys boarded the hoverbird and settled into their seats with little conversation. Some pressed their faces up against the glass for a last wistful look at the beehive-shaped building they called home. The hive windows were lined with the small noses of children curious for a glimpse at their future. Others waved farewells to the girls, who were standing across the courtyard awaiting the arrival of their own initiation shuttle.

"Good-bye, fucked-up childhood," sighed Horvil, waving manically at the children. "Hello, fucked-up adulthood!"

Natch wasn't listening. He was thinking about Figaro Fi's accusation: *Where is your direction?* The boy winced at the irony as the hoverbird levitated over the courtyard and winged away towards the unknown. Wherever Natch was going, he was headed there *fast*.

From liftoff to touchdown, the trip took only a few hours. They were not headed to some remote orbital colony after all, but to a nature preserve southwest of the Twin Cities. The initiation compound sat on a few hundred square kilometers of undeveloped country, completely walled off from the outside world. The hoverbird landed on a makeshift platform atop a dusty, windswept hill.

Natch saw the dust and instinctively reached out with his mind for a sinus-clearing program. He discovered that there was nothing to reach for.

They had been cut off from the Data Sea.

Most of the other boys had already realized this fact. They disembarked with grim looks on their faces, shouldering their packs and wondering what would happen next. The lone proctor who accompanied them on the hoverbird trudged behind a large boulder that served as a podium and began to speak. His words had the air of a speech honed and refined over many years of repetition.

"Two billion people died in the Autonomous Revolt," thundered the proctor, thumping his fist on the boulder. "Two billion! Approximately one-fifth of the world's population at the time. Entire cities and cultures and ethnicities wiped out forever."

He paused for dramatic effect. None of the boys so much as breathed.

"Why? They died because they had forgotten about *this*." The proctor swept his arm expansively at their surroundings. A thousand trees waved in the breeze like some rapturous congregation, while a small encampment down the hill served as the lone Doubting Thomas on the horizon.

"What you see around you is nature as your ancestors once lived it," continued the proctor. "Your ancestors did not have access to the Data Sea. They could not activate bio/logic programs to keep themselves warm in the winter, or fetch ten different weather forecasts with a thought. They did not have OCHRE machines working inside their bodies to shield them from injury and disease. Your ancestors learned to live this way during a hundred thousand years of trial and error.

"But when humanity decided to ignore its heritage—to place its trust in *living machines* instead of in *themselves*—the race nearly perished. And because humanity had forgotten the lessons of its ancestors, billions more were doomed to starve in the horrible decades that followed.

"We must never forget our heritage again.

"And so, during the next year, you will become acquainted with nature in a way you never have before. You will experience pain and frustration and injury. The things you see as entitlements will become hard-earned luxuries. Because of this, some of you will decide that nature is your enemy. Others will see nature as an impersonal and uncaring force.

"But if you lose hope, remember this: our bodies were built to survive the harshest punishments nature can give. Over a hundred thousand years, we conquered nature. So will you again.

"You have many advantages over your ancestors. You have generations of genetic engineering that has broadened your minds and strengthened your bodies. You have all the accumulated knowledge sixteen years of hive education has given you. You have your comrades. And when all else fails, you have the certainty that a hoverbird pilot will be back on this very spot in twelve months to take you back to civilization.

"So when someone asks why your parents sent you to initiation, why you spent a year of your life out in the woods instead of practicing your bio/logic programming skills, you tell them this: I came to initiation to fulfill my responsibility to humanity. I came here to ensure the continuation of the human race.

"The Proud Eagle wishes to thank you for your many years with us. When you emerge from this last test, you will no longer be hive boys. You will be young men.

"As Sheldon Surina liked to say, *May you always move towards perfection.*"

The proctor gave a polite bow to the assembled boys, who were too overwhelmed to do anything but respond in kind. Then he tramped onboard his vehicle and gave a nod to the hoverbird pilot. Within minutes, the ship was noiselessly whizzing southwards, back towards Cape Town.

Sixty-four boys stood at the top of the hill, looking sheepishly at one another and the encampment below. Then, moving as one, they began the hike towards their home for the next twelve months.

* * *

The accommodations were not as primitive as everyone had expected. Four rows of wood cabins lined four dusty streets, watched over by a large metal sign labeled CAMP 11. Of course, these houses didn't behave like the ones they were used to—they couldn't prepare food or obey mental commands or compress themselves to save space—but they were a far cry from the hovels the boys had feared.

The initiates split off into groups of four and chose cabins. Brone and Natch drifted to opposite corners of the camp like enemy kings of chess. Horvil stayed by Natch.

The proctors had provided plenty of clothing, reasonably comfortable beds, and even a rudimentary form of indoor plumbing. Few of the boys had ever seen a real toilet before, and they spent hours flushing them in a symphony of adolescent glee. A scouting party quickly discovered large and well-tended gardens on the east side of the camp, with enough food for all. There were storage rooms stocked with old-fashioned pens and stacks of treepaper, gardening tools, parkas, and pocket knives. It seemed like the only hardship the boys would face out here was boredom.

For the first few weeks, it was all a wonderful adventure. The microscopic OCHREs clinging to their insides stopped working. Hair and pimples sprouted without provocation. Digestive systems resumed their ancient dance with food as if the past two hundred years of gastric engineering had never happened. The boys learned how to clean themselves in the nearby stream, how to groom themselves with knives and scissors, how to use spades to dig tubers from the rock-hard ground.

Everyone experienced at least one morning of disorientation when he groggily tried to summon the morning news or his favorite channel off the Jamm. But all in all, the boys did not have enough time to miss the civilized world. Their days were filled with chores that needed to be done by hand, without the aid of bio/logics or modern machinery. Often, they found themselves without the necessary tools to accomplish a task and had to improvise. All of this took time, and it was not unusual for a boy to look up from the field he had started weeding that morning, only to discover a setting sun.

"It's amazing that our ancestors got anything *done*," Horvil groused to Natch one night. They both lay prostrate on their beds, sweaty and exhausted from a day fending off gophers in the fields. "After gardening, bathing, grooming, shitting, and cleaning, I'm too *tired* to do anything else."

The pressure on the boys was most intense during the first month; they knew that any missteps now would have drastic repercussions come wintertime. The Twin Cities soil was hard and unforgiving, but the hive had provided efficient tools for prying into its skin and tending the crops. Even more useful were the gardening manuals the proctors had left behind. The tips on plowing and crop rotation were nice, but the comments previous initiates had scribbled in the margins proved invaluable. Over the years, tenants of Camp 11 had covered every blank centimeter of treepaper with dirty stories, impenetrable in-jokes, hints about the best places to forage for wild game, what to do in case of rain, and gossip many years gone stale. One book had a list on the inside cover titled

THINGS WE FUCKED UP
(AND YOU SHOULDN'T)

Another contained a treatise on

WHAT THE PROCTORS DIDN'T TELL YOU
ABOUT INITIATION

to which some anonymous wag had added

(THOSE BASTARDS)

During the first few weeks, cooperation ran high among the boys. Even the most odious task was a novelty, and everyone was eager to take his turn pulling weeds and washing clothes. Many of the boys eyed Natch and Brone warily and took bets as to when the fighting would break out between them. But the two retreated to their wary fencers' dance, keeping their distance, looking out for sudden movements.

Spring passed into summer without incident. The boys spent their leisure time improvising rustic versions of soccer and baseball and trying to guess how their favorite teams were performing right now in the civilized world. Horvil slimmed down and lost his irrational fear of the outdoors.

Natch began to take long walks in the woods by himself. He grew fond of the trees, especially the tall ones that stretched up to the edge of his vision. While he walked, Natch mentally played back the conversations with Serr Vigal and Figaro Fi, dissecting them like an occultist looking for clues to the future.

Brone is a vicious person headed for a vacuous career, Vigal had said. *But* you, *Natch, you're* better *than that. You are* not *ready to run your own company. If you jump into the fiefcorp world too quickly, you will regret it.*

Where is your direction? Figaro Fi had asked him. *You have endless* wants. *But* want *without purpose destroys a person. Those who can't master their* wants *are loose cannons.*

It was all a matter of direction, wasn't it? Natch spent days looking around the spare plains for hints. Which direction should he choose? And how would he know when he arrived at the right one? As far as he could see, the four points on the compass were featureless and drab. It seemed like he could wander the entire Earth following one of those paths and not see a single distinguishing characteristic.

But the trees—the trees pointed majestically upward into the sky. Their leafy arms reached for the sun without shame or compromise. Even the little death of winter could only delay their aims, and it was only a matter of time before they were reaching upward once again.

Marcus Surina came to visit Natch one night towards the end of autumn. He drifted in the cabin door, tiptoed around a slumbering Horvil, and came to rest barely half a meter from Natch's face. In this ghostly apparition, the great scientist looked just as ruggedly handsome as he did in all the pictures and videos the boy had seen. Except that his eyes, which had been wide and luminescent in life, were now cold and dim and utterly devoid of light.

Watch, said Surina.

Natch huddled into the corner of his bed with chattering teeth as dozens of specters paraded through the room, figures from history and legend frozen in grotesque positions of death: Julius Caesar, Tobi Jae Witt, Abraham Lincoln, Joan d'Arc, Tul Jabbor, his mother. Each figure wafted over to the boy in turn, mouth open as if to speak some horrible truth from beyond the tomb. Yet the ghostly figures remained stubbornly silent. Were they all withholding their secrets from him by tacit agreement? Or had they simply exhausted all their words in life, and now had nothing to say?

The parade continued for an eternity of midnight-time, despite multiple attempts by Natch to cover his eyes and will away his tormentors. He tried screaming, burying himself under the blankets, ignoring them, but the ghosts would not be denied. His efforts only succeeded in summoning more, until the room was thick with their gray, misty effluence.

Finally, after what must have been many hours, the shade of Marcus Surina floated up to Natch and hovered there, centimeters away.

Now, run! said Surina.

Too frightened to disobey, Natch arose and fled for the door. He stumbled outside into the deepening autumn and discovered that the entire camp was enveloped in the same stinging mist. Mist curling over his feet, wrapped around the wooden posts of the cabins, thick and sharp as smoke... and full of voices... The voices of his fellow initiates, yelling in confusion...

"Over here!" came a familiar nasal twang. Horvil. Natch felt a fleshy hand grab his shoulder and drag him outside the boundaries of Camp 11 and up a nearby hill. Most of the hivemates had already assembled at a safe spot in the lee of the wind.

"What's happening?" said Natch sleepily. "What's that smell?"

"Smoke," replied Horvil with a groan. "The smell of initiation going up in flames."

The cabins themselves were not the worst casualty of the fire. Even frightened boys who had never spent a winter outdoors knew that trees could be chopped down and cabins could be rebuilt. Only six of sixteen cabins had burned down completely, while three had suffered minor damage. There was still plenty of room for all to find space indoors.

No, the real calamity was the destruction to their tool sheds and food supply.

One by one, the boys limped out to the fields, where most of their crops now lay under a shroud of ash. Somehow, they had always known there was something unnatural about the variety of nutritious grains and vegetables that sprouted every spring, despite the harsh winters of the midwest and generations of inept teenage farming. Their ancestors had never had such a bounty of genetically engineered supercrops to sustain them. But now, staring at the remains of their harvest—not to mention the twisted ruins of two of the tool sheds and the charred silo containing most of their stored grain—the initiates knew that this game was no longer tilted in their favor.

The origins of the fire were a mystery. Most likely it had been the product of carelessness, someone forgetting to smother the dying embers of a torch. Perhaps back in the civilized world they could have scavenged for evidence and mounted an investigation, but here all they had was vague conjecture. Before long, whispers passed through Brone's side of the camp, laying the blame on Natch's shoulders.

"Why would he do something like *that*?" exclaimed Horvil the first time he heard the rumor. "Do you even have the slightest bit of evidence?"

"The fire started near Brone's side of the camp," one of the boys told him. "Everyone knows those two hate each other. Natch was one of the last ones out, and *his* cabin is fine."

"That's totally ridiculous. That's not evidence at all."

The other boy admitted his theory had little in the way of factual support. "But come on, Horv—you're his best friend, right? Doesn't he *scare* you?"

Horvil bristled. "All I know is that Natch's test scores were higher than half the class combined. That means he's smarter than you. And *that* means he knows setting fire to the camp would hurt *him* just as much as Brone." The conversation came to an abrupt halt soon after.

There was much to do. The boys went to work right away, picking every edible seed, berry, and root on the horizon, repairing and filling the well, making defensive preparations against unknown enemies. The boys of Camp 11 spent their spare time in an engineering frenzy, attempting to coax the last bit of practicality out of the everyday items around them. A frayed rope strand and several bottles could be converted into a makeshift dumbwaiter. Broken glass could be spread along the roads as an early intruder-alert system. Spare rolls of plastic could be conscripted to channel excess rainwater to the well.

After a week of trying to pick up the pieces and shore up the damaged cabins, it became clear to the initiates that all their preparations might not be sufficient for them to survive the winter. An argument sprang up about how closely the proctors were monitoring their situation here in the wilderness. If the situation grew too precarious, would the proctors come and rescue them? The Proud Eagle wouldn't just let dozens of its pupils starve to death out here, would it?

And then, without warning, winter descended upon them.

The snow marched into Camp 11 under an imperious wind, eager to pound and break any human habitation in its path. Within days of the winter solstice, the boys had abandoned all nonessential duties to concentrate on the snow. But there was much more snow than hands to shovel it. Milky precipitation smothered the plants and killed off the remaining vegetation. The initiates soon discovered that, unlike the geosynchron-regulated snow to which they were accustomed, natural snow could sting and burn. Insulation against the cold became their biggest worry.

A debilitating flu hopped from boy to boy and gave the initiates their first taste of real illness. Back in the civilized world, OCHREs diagnosed all their ailments, and bio/logic programs automatically dealt with them by consulting the Dr. Plugenpatch databases. No more. "I remember reading that you're supposed to *blow your nose* when it gets clogged up like this," Horvil announced earnestly one day. "Does anybody know how to do that?" No one did.

The boys were startled to discover that even without OCHREs and bio/logic programming and Dr. Plugenpatch, the human body had a remarkable ability to heal itself. They came to realize that all the bio/logic technology society relied on for its survival had not been constructed out of whole cloth; it was patterned after motifs passed down through millions of years of genetic heritage. Natch, Horvil, and most of the other boys quickly bounced back from the flu and resumed their duties.

But a few of the boys lingered on in their illnesses, their bodies unable to fully repel the alien microbes wreaking havoc in their systems. The argument about proctor intervention flared up again. If anyone expected the proctors to suddenly swoop down from the clouds and rescue them from their misery, however, they were disappointed.

And so, under a chill wind, the initiates all huddled in the center of the camp one afternoon and tried to hammer out a strategy.

Now, under the pressure of starvation and with the added encouragement of the arson rumors, the much-discussed antagonism between Brone and Natch surfaced with a vengeance. Natch declared that Camp 11 was ruined, and their only chance for survival lay in finding one of the other encampments out in the wilderness. Some of these other camps had to have some stored food available, he argued, as theirs had upon their arrival. But Brone immediately raised objections to this strategy, his opposition all the more intense because Natch had proposed it.

"We can salvage what's left," stated Brone. His voice boomed with the strong and vibrant tones of a born politician. "We can survive here. But if we leave, there's no telling what we're going to find out in the wilderness."

"And what are we going to *live* on?" yelled Natch. His voice was a crow's squawk, the sound of metal grating on metal. "The stores we have are almost gone."

"There are deer running around. We can hunt."

Natch let out a dismissive snort. "You're saying we should start eating *real* meat? Those aren't synthetic deer out there. We'll all get sick again, right when we can't afford to lose any time."

"But we'll survive."

The conflict raged through the afternoon, and gradually the boys began to polarize into two separate groups. Occasionally, someone would manage to insert a fact or an opinion into the discussion, but by and large it remained a conflict between Natch and Brone, the two stubborn boys at the top of their class. When the sun finally slunk down over the horizon, someone suggested the question be put to a vote. Should they abandon their adopted home and search for other encampments, or soldier on here at Camp 11 and hunt for food?

Natch lost.

The boy sat in the center of the ruined camp for several hours, oblivious to the whispers of the rest. All his frustration and humiliation from the Figaro Fi episode rushed over him in a black rage that clouded over his senses. Eventually, the rest of the boys abandoned the convocation and went off to find sleep.

Natch sat and sulked, his mind whirling. The stench of death lay over Brone's plan, as obvious to Natch as the wind or the rain. He couldn't just follow Brone to his grave, could he?

Horvil put a hand on his shoulder. "You know what Sheldon Surina said?" he remarked to Natch quietly. "He said, *The man who doesn't know how to compromise only has himself to blame.*"

"I'd rather think about what Lucco Primo said," rasped Natch in reply.

"What's that?"

"*Never bet on the optimist.*"

The boys had seen little of the local wildlife during their eight months at Camp 11, but that didn't mean the predators weren't out there. Generations of black bears and wolves prowled the woods nearby, living out their own dramas of survival with nary a thought to the humans in their midst. They were not prone to violence, but the Autonomous Revolt had decimated their natural habitats and taught them to be less forgiving. The miserable winter drew them closer and closer to the human encampments in search of food.

Horvil was the first boy to run afoul of the black bears. He was tromping purposefully through the snow gathering firewood when he stumbled on one of the larger specimens. Two hundred fifty kilograms of ursine horror lunged at Horvil with no warning, sending the boy darting back to the camp at a speed he wouldn't have believed himself capable of. Still, the bear would have quickly made a meal out of him if it wasn't nursing a badly injured leg.

"Bear!" yelped Horvil as he stumbled down the hillside, shedding sticks of firewood the whole way. "Bear! Help! Bear!"

The camp instantly descended into chaos. Before anyone could propose a coherent strategy, Brone rounded up a small contingent of boys and armed them with torches. Horvil and a number of others scampered into their cabins and barricaded the doors, assuming the bear would wander off on its own accord. Natch, meanwhile, was out on one of his aimless peregrinations around the woods.

The initiates would debate what happened next for many years afterward.

Brone and his comrades located the beast soon enough. He had headed straight for the storage silo containing their hard-earned stockpile of fruit. But the boys' bravado was quickly snuffed by the sight of a cornered bear rising up on hind legs with claws extended. Brone made a feint with his torch at the injured leg, which only succeeded in frightening the bear into a rage. He charged at one of Brone's companions, sliced him neatly across the chest, then tripped and fell directly onto another boy. A few of the remaining initiates managed to toss their bleeding comrades over their shoulders and make a break for the cabins, while the rest scattered in confusion.

Natch, returning from his walk, observed all this from a distance. *Fools*, he thought. *You can't accomplish anything without a strategy.* He realized that if the camp was going to survive this latest incursion, he would have to take control. It was a strange feeling, to be responsible for others and not just oneself. He tried to pretend that he was not accountable, that he could just run off and let the rest of the initiates fend for themselves. Then the image of poor hapless Horvil came unbidden to his head, Horvil standing and pleading with him, *You'll take care of me, right Natch?* He cursed his friend's name and quickly devised a plan.

Seeing that the bear was now pursuing the firebrands that had taunted him moments earlier, Natch rushed into the fray and ripped a torch from the hand of a campmate. The boy, stunned, put up no resistance. Natch instantly reversed course, waving his torch at the beast and leading him in the opposite direction, away from the camp. Whether he was aware of the bear's infirmity or not, Natch could not have said.

Natch's thoughts were jumbled, incoherent. Primal reflex took over and dispelled any more complex emotion. He could feel the pulse of blood rushing through his legs, the lash and sting of the branches across his face. The bear was constantly a few steps behind, growling, ready to pounce and devour him. Yet he knew these woods like nobody else in the camp. He knew exactly where he was going.

Until, as chance would have it, he spotted Brone. Natch whipped around and headed in his direction.

Brone had made his way to a clearing on top of a low hill, hoping to gather his wits there. His torch had snuffed out in the snow somewhere during the frantic escape from the bear, and Brone was now busy scanning the area for a suitable branch to use as a cudgel.

He had only a split second to react when Natch came sprinting by at top speed, and then the black bear was upon him.

The carnage that followed haunted Natch for many years to come. *You should have listened to me*, he would say to Brone during these midnight pantomimes. *You should have realized we couldn't make it in that camp. You should have recognized you were wrong.* Then he would turn to the other initiates and uncage his fury on them. *Why didn't you ask better questions? Why did you submit to Brone's leadership and not mine?* He reserved the bulk of his wrath for himself. *If only you had been a better politician. If only you had known how to cultivate friendships among the boys. If only you hadn't been so weak.*

(((1 2)))

Natch had to stare at him for several hours in the cramped cabin of a Falcon four-seater under the watchful eyes of a fat, irritable pilot and a steely-eyed paramedic. Every few minutes, the paramedic would get up from her seat to examine the gnarled stump that had once been Brone's arm. She would bend down to his chest and listen for the faint wheezing sounds, then she would turn to Natch with a murderous look that seemed quite inappropriate for a healer. Natch was beyond emotion; he simply looked back, expressionless. *Don't they have to take an oath of nonviolence or something?* he wondered.

"Maybe we should just take him straight to a Preparation compound," suggested the pilot. "Cape Town's a long way away, and they got a Preparation compound right near here. I run back and forth to that place all the time."

The paramedic nodded absently. "That won't be necessary."

"You sure? He's suffering, I can see that. They'll take care of him down there, make sure he goes easy—"

"I *know* what happens in those compounds, Clar," the woman said with a tone of finality. "This one doesn't need to join the ranks of the Prepared— not yet, anyway. He's going to pull through."

For the first time, Natch noticed that the pilot and the paramedic both wore dartguns. He gazed at the cartridges of OCHRE-tipped darts hanging low on the guns' underbellies and tried to imagine what kind of code they contained. A paralysis program, maybe, or a routine to cause temporary blindness? He couldn't quite figure out why the two were armed in the first place. Were they looking after his safety, or Brone's?

Eventually, Natch decided it was pointless to search for routine in a trip that was anything but. Nobody had given him a chance to gather his belongings or say good-bye to Horvil; they hadn't even told him whether he would be returning to finish his last few months of initiation. The pilot had simply yanked him out of his cabin and thrown him into the Falcon next to the bloody, twitching Brone without a word of explanation. The whole operation smelled of sweat and desperate improvisation.

As they began their descent into Cape Town, Natch craned his neck to catch a glimpse out the front windows. He could see a small squad of Defense and Wellness Council officers in crisp white robes standing at attention on the runway. Their presence kept a crowd of fifty at bay while the Falcon completed its vertical landing sequence. Natch could see a pack of drudges and Brone's anxious parents among the throng and was suddenly glad the hive had enlisted the Council's protection. The mob might or might not be daunted by the shuttle crew's dartguns, but nobody would dare assault him in plain view of Len Borda's troops. The code in a Council officer's darts could very well be lethal.

Only after Natch had been hustled indoors did he realize that the Council squad was not there to ensure his safety. No, they were still out on the runway waiting for the second Falcon, which had been following close behind.

They were waiting to unload the bodies.

It wasn't the first time Serr Vigal had had to duck out of a fundraising pitch at a moment's notice because of Natch. It wouldn't be the last. When the news arrived this time, he was talking to a consortium of L-PRACGs a hundred million kilometers away on Mars about spinal cord bandwidth. Vigal thought about hopping on the next Earth-bound shuttle, but decided he couldn't afford the delay and headed for the public multi facilities instead. Two days later, he was still waiting for a long-distance multi connection to open up. Finally, he grew impatient and decided to blow his entire Vault account on a teleportation instead.

By the time Serr Vigal arrived at the Cape Town TeleCo station, groggy and ill-tempered from the four-and-a-half-hour transfer process, Natch's name had permeated the Data Sea like a foul odor.

His experience became known to the public as "the Shortest Initiation." The term came from the drudges, whose coverage of the affair showcased their ability to reduce a complex set of human events to the common denominators of Good and Evil. Vigal was saddened to discover that Natch had been assigned the latter role. GREED AND SOLIPSISM: THE LAST LESSONS OF THE HIVE? read one of the story headlines. OUR ANCESTORS MAY NOT HAVE HAD OCHRES, BUT THEY HAD ETHICS, opined another. CIVILITY IS DEAD, claimed a third. The Proud Eagle tried to convince the public that accidental deaths happened every year during initiation, but the people were not placated. Yes, occasionally there were mishaps—brawls and knife fights, flu outbreaks, once even an avalanche—but three boys from one hive mauled by a bear? Unprecedented. Inexcusable. Governmentalists and libertarians alike took to the floors of their L-PRACGs to denounce Natch and the Proud Eagle.

The headmaster and three of the senior proctors met Serr Vigal at the foot of the TeleCo station platform. They bowed before him in a very poor impression of humility.

"So Natch knows I'm on my way to get him?" said the neural programmer.

"I'm afraid we can't permit him to go anywhere yet," replied the headmaster gravely. "Natch is still fighting off the infections he contracted in the wild. I'm sorry, but rules are rules."

Vigal was in no mood for games. "Nonsense," he sighed. "Show me these medical reports that say he's still infected." The proctors exchanged surreptitious looks as the headmaster's charade quickly collapsed. She forwarded the documents to Vigal, who projected them at arm's length for anybody to see. "It's quite obvious the boy doesn't have anything," he said at length, pointing to the array of charts floating in the air between them. "Blood pressure, heart rate, OCHRE functions—all normal. I'm afraid you have no legal right to keep the boy isolated here any longer."

The headmaster slumped visibly. Her eyes darted sidewise at the proctors with a silent accusation: *You said he wouldn't give us any trouble.* "Please understand—we can't let Natch go until the hive finishes its official inquiry. The board of directors might still decide to prosecute him."

"*Prosecute* him?" said Vigal with furrowed brow. "What would they prosecute him for?"

"Believe me, there are things they can do. Most of the boys say that Natch led that bear right towards the other child, that he knew what he was doing the whole time... Now we've got angry parents threatening all kinds of legal action. Natch should count himself lucky that the initiation compound falls under the jurisdiction of *our* L-PRACG and not one of *theirs*." The headmaster combed her stringy gray hair with the fingers on one hand and peered nervously at the pedestrians surging past on the platform. Who knew which of them would turn out to be a disgruntled investor or a muckraking drudge?

"Between you and me," she continued over ConfidentialWhisper, "I think we'll be able to come to some agreement with the parents and make this whole thing go away. We really *are* doing the best we can. But until we can get everything straightened out, Natch is better off at the hive. There are lunatics making death threats against him, drudges sending multi requests at all hours, politicians calling on him to testify..."

"But no capitalmen."

"No," the headmaster replied with distaste. "No capitalmen or fiefcorp masters or recruiters at all, thankfully."

Vigal had changed little since Natch had last seen him. He still wore the same impeccable gray goatee and the unostentatious sand-colored robe that signaled a hopeless lack of fashion. Vigal was a monument against time, like the cabins in the initiation compound—something that stood unchanged through the vicissitudes of the seasons.

He had certainly not lost his gift for understatement. "Things are not going so well for you, it seems," said the neural programmer.

Natch sat on his bed and sulked in silence. The hive dorm, which had been unimaginably vast when he was eight, now felt small and constricting.

"Do you want to talk about what happened out there?" prodded Vigal gently.

"No," said Natch. He had spent the past few days staring at the ceiling, trying to recount those panicked few minutes in the woods, trying to decide what happened. *Did* he purposefully lead that bear into Brone's path? Or was it just a gut instinct, a subconscious split-second decision? Could he have yelled out some warning, waved his arms, something? "I don't want to talk about it. Not while so many things are unsettled."

"What things?"

"Practical things, *now* things." The boy leaned back against the window and traced a finger over the fiefcorp industry pie charts he had put there. "I'm seventeen, Vigal. I should be looking at apartments and shopping for a bio/logic workbench. Picking out L-PRACGs. But instead, I've got no future, no prospects, nothing. I'm the most hated person in the world right now, and all because... because..." He couldn't find the words to finish his sentence, and bashed his fist against the window.

Serr Vigal pursed his lips into a frown. "Surely it can't be that bad. What about all those recruiters who were hounding you before initiation?"

"Nothing." Natch sighed bitterly. "The capital-men won't even acknowledge my existence. Oh, a few of the fiefcorp masters will talk to me, but their offers are just laughable. People want me to appren-tice for them on spec, not even for room and board. Everyone else just prives me out the instant they find out who I am."

"The whole incident is still in the news, Natch. Maybe you need to give the fiefcorps some time."

"It won't matter."

"You know, you can do so many things other than bio/logics. Maybe—"

"No." Natch pressed his forehead against the window, covering a histogram of fiefcorp share prices. "It has to be bio/logics. There's nothing else out there for me."

The neural programmer cleared his throat and began to say something, then stopped. A statement was slowly coalescing in his mind. At one time, Natch would have lacked the patience to listen to what his guardian had to say, but after nine months in the wilderness surrounded by the impetuosity of teenage boys, Serr Vigal's deliberate manner no longer seemed so irritating. "Do you remember,"

Vigal stammered, "what I told you before initiation about taking an apprenticeship somewhere close by?"

The boy nodded yes.

"Well, it seems I have some space—I mean, there is an opening—at my memecorp. Brain stem programming. The pay isn't much. But, well, I just thought..." He let the sentence waft away.

What a difference nine months can make, Natch thought. Before initiation, his main concern had been finding an appropriate excuse to ignore Vigal's advice on starting his own fiefcorp. Even after the debacle with Figaro Fi, Natch had never seriously considered taking an apprenticeship with the neural programmer. But after all that had happened with Brone and the Shortest Initiation, did he have any choice?

Vigal smiled. "I can see the struggle in your face, Natch. You don't want to apprentice with me because you think the work will be dull and unchallenging. Even worse, you're afraid I'm going to lecture you about what happened at initiation. You think I'll try to *guilt* you into signing up with my memecorp."

Natch's silence indicated his agreement.

"You also know that one day you will be beyond my tutelage," continued Vigal. "Yet you worry that I might try to keep you around by reminding you how I lent a helping hand when nobody else would. Plus—and this may be the most crucial thing—you doubt that you'll be able to find a decent woman in a company like mine to save your life."

The young outcast tried hard not to crack a smile, but he failed.

Vigal chuckled and rose from his chair. He took a seat on the bed next to the boy and put his hand on Natch's shoulder. A rare and yet not unwelcome moment of physical contact between them. "You know that life in the memecorps is much different than life in the fiefcorps, don't you?"

Natch nodded. *"Fiefcorps make money,"* he quoted slyly. *"Memecorps cost money."*

The neural programmer snorted. "Well, that's what those fools at Creed Thassel say. Maybe that was true back when Kordez Thassel and Lucco Primo were alive. But today... Today, I think even a hard-core libertarian would be surprised at how much of our funding comes from the marketplace. If you ask me, every bio/logic programmer could use a grounding in the fundamentals of the memecorp world."

The two silently watched the undulations in the Primo's histogram for a few minutes. Vigal's hand communicated an unspoken message of comfort and understanding. Natch could briefly see a widening of vistas, a broadening of horizons.

He tried to picture what life in Vigal's memecorp would be like. Heated debates over brain stem engineering techniques, collaborations with faceless coworkers, long hours fine-tuning bio/logic programs. There were worse ways to spend two years of his life. The money would be a pittance compared to the sums he had been discussing with the capitalmen nine months ago. But all the same, he would be working in bio/logics. And once he had proven his ability in the memecorp world, wouldn't the fiefcorps become that much more attainable?

"So what are your terms?" Natch asked.

Vigal couldn't hold back his delight. He named the terms: Room and board in Omaha. A modest stipend, with the promise of a bonus after two years. Access to the run-of-the-mill bio/logic programming equipment.

"And what about... all the bad publicity?" said Natch.

His guardian shrugged his shoulders dismissively. "The publicity will pass. You will discover that one of the benefits of working in the memecorp sector is that we are well protected from that sort of nonsense."

Natch stood back and let the phantom letters of Vigal's contract replace the histogram on the window. He called up Shyster 95.3c to help him negotiate the details. Within minutes, the two were sitting across the small round table in the corner of the room dickering over minor contractual differences. By the end of the hour, they had worked out an agreement. Natch affirmed it without hesitation.

He was now officially Serr Vigal's apprentice.

After a few moments of relaxed celebration, Vigal once again struck a serious note.

"I know you worry about your future, Natch," said the neural programmer in a low voice. "And I am sorry I have always been so preoccupied with all these... distractions." He wiggled his fingers up towards the ceiling and let them linger there a moment, as if he could only keep them from drifting into the stratosphere by a colossal act of willpower. "But... but when you came to me, I promised myself I would always be there for you. And I intend to keep that promise no matter what the future brings."

Natch ducked his head under the protective helmet of his clasped fingers. Ordinarily, he would have scoffed at Vigal's sentimentality, but he was not in an ordinary frame of mind. "And what if I *have* no future?"

His guardian leaned forward and put his hand on his apprentice's arm. "Of *course* you have a future. And do you know what it is?"

"What?"

"Your future is what you choose to do tomorrow. And the direction you're searching for?"

Natch shook his head.

"Your direction is where you choose to go."

Natch took a week to get oriented in his new surroundings. There was a lot to do. He needed to find an apartment whose rent fit the narrow boundaries of a memecorp salary; he needed to arrange for a shuttle to carry his belongings out from Cape Town; and most daunting of all, he needed to enroll himself in an L-PRACG.

The apartment was no hassle. Omaha had an abundance of memecorp-friendly housing. Natch picked a modest building about as far away from the Missouri River as you could get and still be inside the city limits. Even in this drab setting, he could not afford exterior walls with real windows and had to settle for a handful of viewscreens instead. There were, of course, no private outgoing multi streams.

Choosing an L-PRACG proved to be a more difficult chore. Legislatures large and small had been bombarding Natch with ads for days now, since the very instant he reconnected to the Data Sea. He found himself in the midst of an ideological battle fought with one-line enticements:

NO TAXES, NO FEES: A Libertarian Paradise

Full Compliance with All Prime Committee Regulations

The ULTIMATE in PRIVACY PROTECTION

GOVERNMENTALISM at Its Finest

Natch spent a day trying to sort through all the solicitations to pick a government that suited him. But his confusion increased the longer he worked at it; questions nibbled away at the back of his mind like rodents, and only seemed to multiply when he wasn't looking. What basic services did the L-PRACG provide? What kinds of taxes and fees were involved? Did the L-PRACG contract out security or provide its own? How long was the subscription term? How exclusive was the membership?

Finally, Natch threw up his hands and settled on a libertarian-leaning L-PRACG that offered a nice package of bio/logic programs as a membership incentive. If he decided he didn't like his government's policies, he could always let the subscription lapse or supplement it with other complementary L-PRACGs. Natch received a vast dossier of regulations and bylaws, which he promptly filed away and never looked at again.

He awoke the following Monday with a sense of determination he had not felt since before initiation. By 6:40 that morning, Natch was wading through the Omaha traffic towards the tube stations. He was no longer a curious bystander tossing pebbles at multi projections; now he had become part of the flow, a fish swimming upstream with the rest of the workforce. Natch caught a cross-town tube and found himself standing in Serr Vigal's foyer with three minutes to spare.

Vigal emerged from his bedroom fifteen minutes late, ushered Natch inside, and then spent another twenty-two minutes clucking around the kitchen making tea. The young programmer scanned the living room in vain for an extra workbench or a set of bio/logic programming bars. *Where does he expect me to work?* Natch thought.

Finally, he and his guardian sat on opposing couches and got down to business.

"The human brain," said Serr Vigal solemnly. A holograph of the bulbous organ appeared in the air between them. With an unassuming wave of his hand, Vigal enlarged the projection until it nearly filled the room, then set it rotating slowly in place. "And here"—his finger indicated the long trunk that extended out the bottom—"here is the area we specialize in: the brain stem.

"What is the brain stem? The brain stem is the key to understanding humanity. Learn how the brain stem works, and you learn how *people* work."

Vigal stood and began walking slowly around the hologram. His words had the flavor of a carefully scripted lecture.

"The body is a sensory machine," continued Vigal. "A machine that takes careful measurements of what is going on all around us. Sights, smells, sounds, tastes, touches: these are nothing more than dispatches from the outside world. The body transfers this information to the brain through a series of neural networks. And what does the brain receive? Meaningless pulses of electrical activity. Echoes of the world around us. How is the mind to make any sense of it at all? That is where the brain stem comes in.

"The brain stem is the connection between mind and body.

"The brain stem is the mechanism that translates impulse to thought, and then thought to action. It is the body's jumping-off point to higher intelligence. The brain stem passes information to the central processing units of our minds, the cerebrum and cerebellum. It translates this data into a format the higher brain can understand. And when the central processor has determined a course of action, it then routes electrical impulses back into the body through the brain stem.

"What would we be without the brain stem? Without the brain stem, the body would be a use-less mass of tissue and bone. Our senses would be reduced to electrical impulses without context—mere random noise. And our minds? Our minds would be isolated from the real world. We would be free to postulate and theorize and deduce, but be forever unable to translate these lofty thoughts into action. We would each be remote stars in the center of a meaningless void.

"All the questions humanity has been asking itself since the dawn of time have their root in the brain stem. Are we creatures of passion, or are we creatures of forethought? How do we balance the needs of the mind with the needs of the body? Should Hamlet follow his heart and avenge the death of his father, or should he follow his head and, through careful reason, devise another course of action?

"These are brain stem questions, Natch. This is what you will be studying here in my memecorp over the next two years."

Natch's eyes began to glaze over halfway through Vigal's speech, and he wondered if this was part of the memecorp's standard fundraising pitch. Natch didn't want to be a philosopher; he wanted to be a *programmer*. He wanted to feel the grooved handle of a bio/logic programming bar in his hand as he stood in MindSpace making logical connections. He wanted to make things *work*.

But over the next few months, Natch obediently buried himself in the lore of the brain stem. He read about the cell composition in the thalamus and hypothalamus, about the mysteries of the medulla oblongata, about the fiber pathways that ran through the limbic system like cranial tube tracks. He studied humanity's slow progress in mastering the brain stem through bio/logics. The early neural programmers had begun with simple programs to monitor the electrical pulses passing through the nervous system, and then later had crafted programs to control them. Soon their successors were using bio/logics to broaden the bandwidth of the spinal cord, to shorten the refractory period a neural cell must wait between transmissions, to intercept and edit and mimic the electrical messages passing through the nervous system. They learned how to plug straight into the message stream and project sensations of their own that were indistinguishable from their "real" counterparts.

During these first few months of his apprenticeship, Natch also learned the ins and outs of the memecorp business. He accompanied his guardian on a round of fundraising and speeches that took them from Omaha to Beijing to Melbourne and even out to the orbital colonies of Allowell and Nova Ceti. Vigal would begin with the same speech he had given Natch on his first day of apprenticeship, and then segue into lofty promises of future achievements. Accurate recording and playback of mental processes. Clustered brainpower. Group consciousness.

After the speeches, there would be private discussions with the men and women who ran the local programming services departments. Vigal would nod and listen earnestly to their ideas for hours on end, and more often than not end the day receiving a pledge of capital or the offer of a group subscription contract. Natch had always thought most bio/logic programs were sold directly to consumers on the Data Sea; now he discovered three-quarters of the code that ran human systems was "channeled" silently through deals with L-PRACGs and creeds and other organizations.

As Natch learned all this, he also learned about Serr Vigal.

Vigal's professional life had always been an enigma to Natch. He had spent more than thirty years right here at the same memecorp, doing the same work. His products often didn't even have names; instead, they were identified by long, dreary strings of numbers. He had the respect of his colleagues and apprentices, but virtually no social life. If he had ever taken a companion or a lover in the years since Lora's death, he kept it well hidden.

The more Natch learned about Vigal, the more of a mystery the man became. Natch had always dreamed about creating the kinds of programs that inspired raves from Primo's, programs that sparked social revolutions like Sheldon Surina's had. He would have never guessed that his own legal guardian had been doing that for years. In their own quiet way, Vigal's programs had probably influenced the world more than all of Figaro Fi's clientele put together.

But eventually, Natch grew restless. He wanted to stop *analyzing* and start *doing*.

Month after month, he buried himself in his studies. He had barely met his fellow apprentices at the memecorp and never even been given a workbench. While Vigal had him cooped up in his apartment studying the intricacies of the limbic system, Horvil and the rest of the boys returned from initiation. Soon Horvil had set up shop near his family's London manor and started building a reputation as a top-notch ROD coder. Other acquaintances from the hive were savoring their first mentions in Primo's.

"How long until I start *programming*?" Natch snapped to Vigal one day, a little over a year into his apprenticeship. "I haven't set foot into MindSpace since I got here. If you expect me to learn the whole discipline of neurophysics before I pick up a programming bar, that could take *years*."

Vigal simply smiled that maddening smile of his and shook his head. "I've been studying the brain stem for almost forty years, Natch, and I'm not even *close* to understanding the whole discipline of neurophysics. You are learning no more than the essentials you need to do your job."

"And what *is* my job?"

"You know exactly what your assignment is. You're to update the OCHRE software that monitors oculomotor signals to the third cranial nerve."

"But I *know* the third cranial nerve backwards and forwards!"

The neural programmer let out a heavy sigh and plucked at the white hairs sprouting from his chin. "I'm no fool," he said quietly. "I see that I'm not going to keep you here much longer under these conditions. Perhaps you're right. Let's get started in MindSpace tomorrow. But keep in mind that we are going to proceed *very slowly*."

Natch had spent plenty of time in the hive tooling around with bio/logic programming bars, but he had never coded anything of importance. One could only do so much testing among a group of upper-class hive children.

The 9971.6a software, by contrast, had a paying subscriber base of thirty million. Its logic fueled one of the molecule-sized OCHREs clinging to the cranial nerves. Natch's work here could conceivably affect the vision of an entire city the size of Omaha. To have such influence, such power... He was nearly shivering with anticipation.

Natch stood at his workbench—a hand-me-down that Vigal had finally procured for him from a departing apprentice—and summoned a MindSpace bubble. The bubble was nothing more than a translucent shimmer, a void yearning to be filled. Natch called up 9971.6a. The diagram that appeared was a constellation of purplish blocks held together by thin strands of green.

It was obvious why Serr Vigal had slated this program for revision. Even someone as inexperienced as Natch could see that the code was several years out of date. Many of the green strands were looped around each other in a figure-eight formation that had been officially deprecated by Dr. Plugenpatch, and the program passed off information in a format that was incompatible with newer standards. But more than that, the program, for some indefinable reason, just looked *wrong*. Natch could practically feel it crying out in pain like an animal trapped in a thicket.

Natch reached for the satchel hanging off the side of the workbench and withdrew a plain metal rod from its sheath. Then he extended his arm into MindSpace and got to work.

Bio/logic programming bars looked like plain metal in ordinary space. Hollow tubes of silver labeled with Roman letters, the forearms of some mythical robot. But inside MindSpace, the bars blossomed into their true forms. Some looked like pincers, others pliers, others lariats or hammers or gloves. Each tool represented a specific logical operation that could be applied to a virtual structure.

Bio/logics was a science, but it was also an art form. One had to create the right number of connections in the right places. Too few connections would leave gaping holes in the program that could be exploited by malicious black coders; too many might produce unwanted side effects, or sap the body's computational system of precious resources.

Natch tore into the OCHRE software with the zealotry of the newly initiated. He completed his first round of modifications in three days, but spotted so many imperfections and inefficiencies along the way that he couldn't leave the program alone. Every connection he reassigned contained a logical flaw somewhere if he traced back far enough. And each of those flaws would lead to still other flaws.

For a week, Vigal left his apprentice to his own devices while he attended to other memecorp business. During that week, Natch barely ate or slept.

The neural programmer was completely unprepared for the sight that awaited him when he showed up the next week to inspect Natch's work. He was expecting to see a more polished version of 9971.6a, a purple constellation seen on a clear night. Instead, he saw a formation that might have come from another galaxy altogether. The 9971.7 software was arrayed in MindSpace with an almost military precision, each block tied to its fellows with a tight net of green strands. The offending figure-eights were nowhere to be seen.

"I suppose you *were* ready, after all," mumbled Serr Vigal, flabbergasted. "This is... this is..."

Natch stood in the opposite corner of the room with a grim smile on his face. *This is extraordinary? This is exceptional? This is awe-inspiring?*

"This is... too *much*," said Vigal.

Natch let out an explosive snort. "What do you mean, *too much*?"

The neural programmer turned as if he had just noticed his apprentice in the room. Twitching cheeks bore evidence to the struggle going on in his head between the memecorp master and the parent. "Perhaps you are right," he said slowly, parental instincts in control. "I don't want to be critical, but at the same time—"

"You don't want me getting too far ahead of the other apprentices."

"Don't be a fool!" Vigal snapped with the tone of the memecorp master. "I was going to say, I want you to actually *launch* something while you are here in my apprenticeship."

Natch couldn't think of anything pertinent to say. In Vigal's countenance, the battle of responsibilities began anew, and he quickly found some excuse to sever his multi connection.

The next month was one of the most intense times in Natch's life. Vigal did not repeat his earlier comments; instead, he encouraged Natch to submit 9971.7 to Dr. Plugenpatch at the earliest opportunity.

Plugenpatch approval was an absolute necessity to get the program listed on the bio/logics exchanges, and most OCHRE systems would refuse to obey any program that didn't carry at least a preliminary clearance from the public health agency. But just as importantly, the approval process provided an objective yardstick he could use to measure his progress. Vigal's motivations were transparent: he wanted to both get his point across and avoid confrontation.

Natch worked confidently towards Plugenpatch submission. He stood at his workbench for days on end, and the bio/logic programming bars just seemed to leap into his hands. The pain of the incomplete program was a visceral thing to Natch, a burning sensation that began in the tips of his toes and shot through his calves, sending his legs to pacing and his hands to searching for the cool balm of a bio/logic programming bar. But he was making progress. Little by little, he was liberating this mathematical beast from its confinement.

He finally submitted the program to Dr. Plugen-patch on a dry June afternoon.

The medical programming review system reject-ed it without comment.

Vigal took a cross-town tube over to Natch's flat that evening. He bore on his face the nervous look that foretold an approaching speech as surely as dark clouds foretold rain. Natch immediately start-ed to lead his mentor towards his workbench, where 9971.7 hung in MindSpace. But Vigal called him back and had him sit down on the couch fac-ing the living room viewscreen.

"Let us talk a little bit about change in a memecorp," he began slowly, eyes focused on the carpet. "Natch, no bio/logic program is an island. It has complex interdependencies, relationships to other programs." Vigal waved his hand at the viewscreen, causing it to broadcast a holographic blueprint of white, red, and green squares that filled the room. Natch recognized this vast three-dimensional abacus on sight; it was the standard OCHRE engineering map of the human brain. Yet it represented only one small portion of the whole human programming schematic, which might have encompassed two or three square kilometers at this level of detail. "You will notice that these relationships are particularly dense in this area, the area of brain stem software." He pointed to a cluster of beads near the center of the diagram.

"I suppose the one you've highlighted is the cranial nerve software," mumbled Natch, tilting his head towards a blinking circle in the center of the cluster.

"Precisely," replied Vigal. "Now let me show you the programs with a direct relationship to 9971.7—programs that will explicitly rely on the information from your work." The neural programmer pulled back the focus and let a whole new level of the blueprint slide into the room. A disparate group of perhaps twenty beads began to blink. "Now, if we add in the components of the system that rely on information from *those* programs..." The focus pulled back even farther. Hundreds of beads were now flashing in perfect synchronization. "And so on and so on," concluded Vigal, waving a jittery hand at the exponential explosion of blinking beads.

Natch could feel the impatience swelling within him. He began drumming his fingers on the side table. "All right, I *get* it. There's a lot riding on this program."

"*Any* neural program."

"Fine. But I don't see what you're worried about. My code meets all the standards. It produces consistent results."

"I have no doubt of that," replied Vigal somberly. "If I ever had any doubts about your programming abilities, Natch, this has certainly dispelled them. It's not you I worry about—it's the companies working on all these *other* programs whose skills I question." He flipped the back of his hand at the pinpricks of light that had replicated throughout the room like a cancer.

"Why should I care?" said Natch through gritted teeth. "That's *their* problem."

"But Natch, you must understand... you're not working with skin moisturizers or, or, breath fresheners. This is *neural* software. One major discrepancy between any two of these programs could cause a massive brain hemorrhage. And that is an unacceptable result. That's why we have to work *slowly* and with careful coordination."

"That's why we have Dr. Plugenpatch standards—"

"The standards are only one small part of the procedure," said Vigal with a tinge of sadness in his voice. "For process' preservation, Natch, why do you think I'm always going off to speak at all these conferences? It's so those of us in neural programming can keep on top of what the others are doing. Certainly it's costly and time-consuming, but it's also effective. We have a higher standard to live up to here in the memecorp sector."

Natch crossed his arms in front of his chest and sulked. He tried to look at anything in the room but Serr Vigal. "I don't see how you can make a *profit* doing all that," he said. "I mean, who's going to wait three years for all of you to coordinate an upgrade to some obscure piece of cranial nerve software?"

Vigal shut off the diagram with a snap of his fingers, revealing the cheap carpeting and secondhand furniture of Natch's apartment once more. "You're beginning to understand life in a memecorp," said the neural programmer quietly. "We *can't* make a profit. We *can't* just rely on Primo's ratings or the whims of the marketplace to test our products for us. Because, as you say, people do not have the time or the inclination to pay attention to most neural software. If we didn't get outside funding, I would have to close up shop and send everybody home."

"Then why do it at all?"

"Because I enjoy it," said Vigal, "and because someone has to."

There was a long pause. Natch could feel 9971.7 laughing derisively at him from its berth in Mind-Space. "So what do you want me to *do*? Abandon the whole thing?"

"I want you to do exactly what you're doing," replied Vigal, "but *slow down*. Natch, you've created an excellent long-term plan for the future of 9971.7. Tomorrow, you can begin by rolling back the changes you've put in place, and then we can start to enact that plan one piece at a time."

Natch had no response. He had expected Vigal to point him to some hidden flaw in the program architecture that only a wise and seasoned programmer could see. Instead, his guardian had only confirmed that the problem did not lay with Natch; the problem was the memecorp system itself.

Silently, Natch cursed the day he had ever signed on to an apprenticeship with Serr Vigal, and wondered if he would make it through the rest of his apprenticeship without going completely insane.

(((13)))

A few weeks later, Natch abandoned his grandiose plan for the neural software. He hadn't lost confidence in his abilities; on the contrary, he was more certain than ever that he could bring the program to a higher plain of functionality. But Natch had decided to leave Vigal's employ in eight months, when his contract ended. Until then, he would get much more experience trying his hand at a variety of projects rather than tinkering with just one.

Serr Vigal took the news coolly but with a tinge of disappointment. "Where will you go?" he asked his protégé. "The fiefcorps?"

"That's not the place for me right now," said Natch, leaving the obvious unspoken: he still suffered from the taint of the Shortest Initiation. Hiring someone with Natch's notoriety could provoke a boycott from the creeds and the L-PRACGs, or a backlash from the drudges. "I've decided to set myself up on the Data Sea as a ROD coder," the youth continued. "Like Horvil."

"Are you sure, Natch? ROD coding can be extremely—"

Natch cut the discussion short. "Yes, I'm sure," he said.

Vigal did not begrudge his young apprentice's decision. In fact, he seemed to forget all about it over the next few months. Natch quietly upgraded a number of optic nerve programs to the new Plugenpatch specs, working at the glacial pace his master had requested. When Natch multied to Vigal's office to collect his end-of-contract bonus and say good bye, the neural programmer responded with a surprised "Oh!" and gave him a feeble hug. Natch could see a host of worries fluttering through his guardian's head, but Vigal had evidently decided to keep them to himself.

Thus ended Natch's brief career in the memecorp sector.

RODs were Routines On Demand, bio/logic programs that catered to the indulgently rich. There were no contracts, no guarantees, no fringe benefits. ROD coders simply scouted the Data Sea for a spec they could engineer quickly, rushed to build it before someone else did, and then launched it in hopes that their patron would like it enough to pay. The applications for RODs ranged from the frivolous (Fab-u-lous Nails 15, "now with programmable cuticles") to the lascivious (Tit-o-rama 8, "the total breast sensation enhancer") to the purely ridiculous (DiscSpeak 3c, "for the true connoisseur of ancient recorded-sound emulation—now with pop, hiss and warble!").

An expedient programmer could typically launch two or three RODs per week. Horvil had maintained that pace for over a year before moving on to the more specialized field of bio/logic engineering.

"Let's estimate three sales a week," said Natch to his old friend one night as they strode around London discussing career options. He summoned a virtual calculator in the brisk spring air and began plugging in numbers. "So we'll multiply three by the average asking price for a ROD, subtract out equipment and overhead—"

Horvil sliced his hand through Natch's holographic calculator. "Wait a minute, Natch," he said, shaking his head. "It's not that easy."

"What do you mean?"

"I said I *launched* two or three RODs a week. I didn't say anybody *bought* 'em. You *never* sell all the RODs you launch. Sometimes you get beaten to the punch by another programmer. Or your patron changes his mind and pulls the spec from the Data Sea just for the fuck of it. Or you're sabotaged by the competition. There are assholes out there that post fake ROD requests, you know."

Natch frowned and adjusted his numbers downwards. "Well, it's still not that bad—you've just got to factor in recurring revenue. You know, maintenance fees, subscription fees, upgrade fees. That's how the fiefcorps make a profit, right?"

The stocky engineer chuckled, pleased to be in the know for once. "Nope, can't count on any of that either. These are RODs, Natch—you have to build 'em so quickly that they won't withstand any kind of heavy use. The shelf life for a ROD is about twelve to fifteen weeks, and that's only *if* you've done your homework. After that, the buyers just get bored and move on to the next new thing."

Natch began to wonder if he had made a rash choice in leaving Vigal's employ. Memecorp work might be torpid and dull, but at least it provided a sense of stability. But once Natch stepped out on his own, nothing was guaranteed. A year from now, he could be trolling the old cities and living in trashed-up skyscrapers like the diss, like his mother had done.

But certainly Natch could make a decent living in the ROD coding game if Horvil could. He had a tremendous respect for his hivemate's intellect, but Horvil's business sense was a little skewed. People tended to fall into the ROD world because they couldn't hack it in the real bio/logics market (or because they were rich and bored, like Horvil). But Natch never doubted that he had the skills and the pedigree to make it to the top ranks of the fiefcorps. He was not on his way down; he was on his way up.

All Natch needed to do was persevere, produce quality work, and establish a reputation. Eventually, the ill wind that drifted around him would dissipate, and the brand on his forehead would fade; the Shortest Initiation would be permanently tossed into the dustbin of Yesterday's News. Then the channelers and capitalmen and fiefcorp masters who patrolled the Data Sea for fresh talent would find him, and he would resume his rightful place in the bio/logics world.

Natch's end-of-contract bonus was enough to keep him afloat for a month or two. Vigal offered to buy his young protégé a set of bio/logic programming bars as a parting gift, but Natch declined and bought the bars himself. He did not want to feel beholden to his guardian for anything. It was not an idle investment; the extended function sets on the new bars would enable him to take coding short-cuts and thus program faster.

Now that Natch had emerged from Vigal's shadow, the city of Omaha held no appeal to him. He hopped around the globe looking for a place to settle, and finally found an apartment in Angelos that suited his tastes. The place made Horvil's spare room look like a palace by comparison. Still, it had everything he would need to start a ROD business. There was a bed to sleep in, space to hold a decent-sized workbench, and proximity to downtown Angelos, where the public multi facilities were abundant and cheap.

The next morning, he got to work.

Natch decided to begin with a field he was familiar with, so he chose optics. He skimmed the Data Sea and found a request for an eye transformation program that looked like it might be a good place to start. Bio/logics had made setting one's eye color as easy as editing a database entry, but the woman who had posted this request wanted something more. Vellux of Beijing wanted her eye color to sync with the colors of nearby flowers. In a room of violets, she wanted violet eyes; in a field of ivy, she wanted green.

It seemed like a simple enough programming task. A morning spent nosing through the Dr. Plugenpatch archives helped him better his understanding of the optical programming interface. Natch fetched the OCHRE specs from Dr. Plugenpatch, projected them onto his workbench in MindSpace, and started planning his strategy.

Natch found plenty of machines floating around the eyeball that he could harness to accomplish his task. Thanks to the OCHREs, he could query the iris and determine the color of its pigment; he could also query the retina and parse the colors in the user's line of sight. But a number of vexing questions remained. How would the program identify flowers in the retinal image? How would it distinguish between petals, stems, and leaves? How would the program funnel the millions of shades of yellows and reds and purples into a narrow palette of sixteen colors? What if Vellux was looking at seven different flowers—how would the program rank the order of importance of these flowers and assign an appropriate eye color?

The longer Natch struggled to unravel these tangled questions, the more questions arose to ensnare him. Normally, it took hours for the body to process color changes through the personal preferences database. Unless this woman Vellux planned to stand still for long periods of time, he would need to find an alternate solution. Luckily, he found a number of subroutines on the Data Sea that would do the job quicker. Natch chose one called Weagel's Eye Wizard, which had received excellent ratings from Primo's a few months back. But the program required access to a batch of proteins for building the pigmentation... which could only be done by requesting resources from another OCHRE nearby in the choroid... but the OCHRE in the choroid needed to register its supply requirements with the brain stem...

It took Natch most of the day and into the night to come up with a satisfactory blueprint for the project. At six in the morning, he sat back and took stock of his progress. The holographic model floating above his workbench looked like a mutated grasshopper, but Natch knew he could not afford to trifle with aesthetics this time around. As he was examining his handiwork, the building interrupted him to slide a bowl of hot oatmeal onto the kitchen counter. *When was the last time I ate?* Natch asked himself. He could not remember.

But food would have to wait. Natch created a new instance of the MindSpace bubble and placed his model inside it for future reference. Then he grabbed two of the bio/logic programming bars out of his satchel. The new bars were light enough to wave in MindSpace for hours, yet solid enough to withstand thousands of accidental bashes against a workbench. Natch took a deep breath and attacked the empty MindSpace bubble with zest.

Morning became afternoon; afternoon became evening.

The young entrepreneur sculpted his code quickly, using virtual blocks of logic as his marble, and programming bars as his hammer and chisel. Gradually the mass came to resemble the mutated grasshopper of Natch's diagram. He had been working for thirty-six hours straight when he finally laid down the programming bars. The bowl of oatmeal had disappeared, and Natch couldn't remember if he had eaten it or if the building had simply whisked it away untouched.

Natch stepped into the hallway, which was lined on both sides with tulips. He fired up EyeMorph

1.0 in diagnostic mode and was pleased to discover that everything worked as designed. His eyes quickly slid from their natural blue to a mottled shade of purple. Natch retreated to his living room and tested his handiwork against a number of floral images on the viewscreen. So far, so good.

Rest is coming soon, he promised himself. *I just need Plugenpatch approval, so I can launch the program on the Data Sea, and then I'll sleep.*

Natch approached the Plugenpatch process with more than a little trepidation. As he had discovered while apprenticing for Vigal, a successful test was no guarantee of approval. Fiefcorp programmers could not hope to cover all the combinatorial possibilities of a fully functioning OCHRE system. No, only large entities like Dr. Plugenpatch and Primo's had the facilities to do that. Natch swallowed his fear, packaged up his work, and routed the program to Dr. Plugenpatch's automated verification system.

Eight minutes later, as Natch sat on his sofa sucking down a fizzy bottle of ChaiQuoke, Eye-Morph returned from the verification system peppered with rejection notices.

Mindful of the time, Natch tore through the Plugenpatch recommendations. He realized to his chagrin that he had left a loophole that might allow excess protein buildup in the choroid. Any decent OCHRE system would be able to deal with such an anomaly as a matter of course, but Dr. Plugenpatch's standards were rigid and uncompromising. The catchphrase from a thousand Creed Conscientious advertisements rose unbidden in his head: *Always preserve your bodily computing resources!*

Natch sourly picked up the programming bars again and began reweaving connection strands.

The next rejection took eleven minutes for the system to process.

The rejection after that took sixteen minutes of analysis.

Natch decided to abandon subtlety and just finish the wretched program. He suspected that someone had already beaten him to the Data Sea while he was here fumbling with Dr. Plugenpatch rejections, but he couldn't just abandon the project now. Natch furiously patched up the remaining holes, disabled a few features that seemed problematic, and fed it into the Plugenpatch system.

Twenty minutes later, the verdict was clear: success!

Natch hastily bundled the program together, slapped on the standard fore and aft tables that the Data Sea required for its cataloging agents, and launched. He called up the ROD optics listings on his viewscreen so he could see the results with his own eyes. The evidence on the new releases board glared at him in small black letters:

EYEMORPH
Version: 1.0
Programmer: Natch

Yet he felt no sense of triumph. EyeMorph 1.0 may have slipped past the gates of Dr. Plugenpatch, but Natch knew the program was still riddled with inconsistencies—the kind of inconsistencies that Primo's would certainly notice when they dredged the Data Sea for their bimonthly summation of the ROD coding world. Not only that, but because

Natch had used Weagel's Eye Wizard to perform some of the heavy lifting, part of his profits would be swallowed up by licensing fees. He would be lucky to break even on the project.

Natch was shambling towards the bed for a long-overdue slumber when a message arrived.

You gave it your all
I hope you had fun
'Cause you got your ass kicked
By CAPTAIN BOLBUND.

Horvil was at a loss to explain Natch's failure. He wriggled his head free of the blankets and stared drowsily at the ROD listings scrolling up and down his bedroom viewscreen.

"How does he program so fast?" griped Natch from across the room, where he was wearing tracks into the carpet. "Who is this guy? 'Captain Bolbund'? He beat me by an entire *day* on EyeMorph, Horv! What's he doing that I'm not?"

The engineer flopped around to face the wall. "Maybe it was a fluke," he said. "Maybe he just got lucky. It happens."

"It's not a fluke. This Bolbund has beaten me four times in a row now."

"Four times? How the fuck d'you run into the same guy four times in a row in this business? That's no accident."

Natch shook his head. "Of *course* it isn't an accident. I keep taking him on, and he keeps massacring me. Even worse, he always sends me this awful poetry when he wins." The young entrepreneur forwarded some of Captain Bolbund's doggerel to Horvil.

Horvil read silently for a minute. "This *is* terrible," he mumbled. "Ten thousand spell checking programs out there, and this asshole still spells *slaughter* with a 'w'." He sat up in bed, stretched, and shot Natch a worried look. "Listen, Natch, I don't think you get it. When you're a ROD coder, you gotta keep moving or you'll get in a rut. Didn't your mother ever tell you that *you win some and you lose some, but life goes on*?"

"No," said Natch with a menacing growl.

Horvil winced, causing his pudgy face to shrivel up like a prune. "Oh, fuck, Natch... I forgot... I didn't mean—"

"Never mind." Natch gazed at the photos lining Horvil's wall, where dozens of fat, happy Horvil look-alikes with inky black hair frolicked in an assortment of lavish London manors. If Horvil were ever to fail, his family would absorb him back into its bosom at a moment's notice. But where would Natch go if his money ran out, especially now that he had spurned Vigal?

"Why don't you hire an analyst, Natch?" offered Horvil. "Business strategy is what these people *do*. They can figure out how to get you through this."

"I don't trust them," Natch muttered under his breath. He didn't want to mention the real reason he wouldn't seek professional advice: his Vault account was running low. In the past two weeks, he had made only one sale, to a doddering old L-PRACG politician whose mistress had been complaining about too much sweat on his upper lip.

But after another few weeks of getting thrashed on the ROD circuit, Natch decided that Horvil was right. He needed professional advice, and he needed it quickly. It pained him to admit he was incapable of defeating Bolbund on his own, but he took solace in a saying by the great Lucco Primo: *There are a thousand roads to success, and nine hundred of them begin with failure.* So Natch swallowed his pride and began hunting around the Data Sea for an analyst he could afford.

One analyst in Natch's price range instantly stood out from the rest. She was a woman named Jara who lived on the other side of London from Horvil. Natch set the InfoGather 77 program loose on the Data Sea and instructed it to follow her scent. What InfoGather discovered surprised him: stellar notices from Primo's, five years' experience with the rising star Lucas Sentinel, a smattering of praise from the drudges. But then the trail abruptly vanished from the Data Sea, only to reemerge six months later with Jara a free agent and her prices far below market level. Natch fired off a message to the woman:

> Why is Lucas Sentinel spreading rumors about you? What did you do to piss him off? And why should I give you any work?

The reply was almost instantaneous:

> I told Lucas he needed to grow a set of testicles. He decided to blacklist me instead. Don't bother hiring me unless you have a pair.

Natch laughed out loud. If there was one thing he valued after his Shortest Initiation experience, it was nonconformity.

Jara arrived at Natch's apartment in multi, a scant five seconds shy of their appointed meeting time. Natch found himself facing a tiny woman with Sephardic features and a massive thicket of curly hair. She was almost twenty years his senior. "You asked for a ninety-minute consultation," said Jara by way of greeting. "You realize that my standard consultation is forty-five minutes."

"*Anything worth doing is worth perfecting,*" said Natch, quoting Sheldon Surina.

He could sense this woman Jara sizing him up with one eagle eye. Her piercing look said that she already knew about the Shortest Initiation, that she had already reconstructed his story and needed only the one look to confirm it. Natch stood tall and did not flinch. He had nothing to hide.

"All right," said Jara. "Let's get to it."

Natch brought her over to his workbench and summoned the EyeMorph program and several others in MindSpace, along with a passel of Captain Bolbund's competing brands. "Tell me why this asshole keeps beating me," he said simply.

As she stepped inside the MindSpace bubble, Jara didn't pause for any social niceties. She eyed the herd of programs like an angry bull. "Give me twenty minutes," she said gruffly, and then reached up and began spinning the logical structures around with her virtual hands. Natch took a seat in a chair, activated the QuasiSuspension program, and let her work. As he drifted off into a light nap, he could sense her making thousands of queries on his files and wondered what kind of analysis routines she had developed to churn through all that data.

Precisely twenty minutes later, Natch awoke from QuasiSuspension and joined Jara at the workbench. "So what is this clown doing that I'm not?" he asked.

"The problem," replied Jara tersely, "is that Bol-bund isn't doing *anything* you're not doing."

Natch sat back down in his chair, puzzled. "Huh?"

"His programs don't hold a candle to yours. They're sloppy, they're inadequate, and they'll probably fall apart in a pinch. But he's done a real mind job on you. He's got you convinced that you need to work harder and harder until you drop from exhaustion."

"But for process' preservation, Jara, he launched his eye color program a whole day earlier than me. A *day*! That's life or death in this business."

"You're still not getting it, Natch. What was the spec?"

"She wanted an eye-morphing program to complement the—"

Jara put up her hand. It was as tiny and delicate as a doll's. "That's your first mistake. You thought the customer knew what she wanted. She wanted *an eye-morphing program to complement the colors of the flowers*, right? No, what she wanted was a program to make *her* eyes match *her* flowers."

The agitation flowed down to Natch's feet and made him rise from the chair in a futile attempt to pace it off. "What's the difference?"

"Did you spend any time researching your client before you took on the project? Well, *I* did—just now, while you were dozing—and look what I found." She strode up to the room's lone viewscreen and gave an imperious nod.

A woman materialized on the screen, probably in her mid-eighties but possibly approaching a hundred, decked out in a lavish purple robe that was the hallmark of membership in Creed Élan. VELLUX, read the caption beneath her. The two watched silently for a moment as Vellux puttered around her greenhouse pointing out different specimens of flowers. Five minutes into her nauseating pitch, Natch froze the display. "Okay, she sells flowers. I've already seen this promo. I don't think I'd live through a second viewing."

Jara snorted, but the glimmer in her eyes was not unfriendly. "You may have seen it, but how closely were you watching? Did you notice *this*?" She stretched out her index finger to zoom in on a block of text in the corner of the screen: VISIT US AT THE CREED ÉLAN ANNUAL CONVOCATION JULY 15–27. "Vellux probably didn't mention she was buying this ROD to use at a Creed Élan function, did she? If you were going to traffic flowers to the Élanners, Natch, what flowers would you sell? I'd pick bougainvilleas, lilacs, irises. Red, purple, and lavender, the official colors of the creed." Jara jerked her thumb to the left and focused on the flower vendor's face. "And here's another clue. Did you notice that *her* eyes are hazel?"

Natch stewed quietly in the opposite corner of the room. He could see the gestalt of the situation coming into focus.

"After five minutes, we've narrowed down the task considerably. Instead of creating a program to change *anyone's* eyes to match *any* color flower, we just need to create one that will change *this* woman's eyes to several shades of purple. Not only that, but we know which flowers to scan for in the retinal image. It's much easier to analyze an image for a specific genus of flower than to do the same for *any* flower; I'm willing to bet you can find dozens of subroutines on the Data Sea that will do the trick.

"That's what they call a *tell*. The customer says they want one thing, but their actions *tell* you they want something else. Something simple and easy to deliver. I'm willing to bet this Captain Bolbund character saw that right away, and that's why he jumped on this spec.

"So not only did you take on the wrong task, but you went about it the wrong way. Why actually bother changing the color of her eyes? Why not just change other people's *perceptions* of them? That's a million times easier than all this shit you did with pigments and proteins. Good work, by the way, but who cares? Bolbund's ROD secretes a light pigment onto the surface of the eye through the tear ducts. *Outside* the eye, Natch, not *inside* of it. Clever. It's not a perfect solution, but nobody's going to notice in the middle of a creed convention. Best of all, Bolbund can skip the most intensive OCHRE programming and breeze right past hours of Plugenpatch validation."

Natch looked at his hands, absorbing her analysis and storing it for later use. He could see why Jara's curt manner might have irritated Lucas Sentinel and gotten the other big fiefcorps to boycott her services, why she had suddenly found herself unemployable in the fiefcorp world and desperate enough to advertise cheap consulting services to lowly ROD coders like him. But Natch had no use for flattery. Not in his personal life and certainly not in his business.

"So what if your analysis is wrong?" he said. "What if this Vellux woman isn't using the program at a Creed Élan function at all?"

"Then someone else wins the business and you move on," replied Jara coolly. "All you've lost is a day or two."

"EyeMorph is much better than that shit Bolbund threw together," he snapped.

"No doubt. But what does that matter if nobody buys it?"

"Vellux will figure it out. She'll see she bought a lousy product."

"Maybe she will; maybe she won't. Do you know how hard it is to get your money back from a programmer? She'd have to go to the Cooperative, and that could take weeks. Not worth her time, not for such a trifling amount. Maybe by the time she notices, Bolbund will have fixed all those problems. He offers her a free upgrade, and she goes straight to him the next time she needs something."

The frustration coalesced in his mind like steam, and he was unable to summon any intelligible words through the fog. Natch vented his anger through a brutal kick at the wall.

"I feel like I'm going around in circles," he cried. "I'm just not *getting* anywhere. You ever hear that saying of Lucco Primo's about the three elements of success?"

Jara took a seat in the chair that Natch had recently used for his nap and looked him over with a tough but sympathetic eye. "Ability, energy, and direction," she said. "Yeah, I've heard it."

"So what am I missing?"

"That's easy," replied Jara. "The wisdom to know when to use them."

(((14)))

Sheldon Surina once said, *Progress is persistence.*

Natch was nothing if not persistent. He had chosen the track he would take—from ROD coding, to mastering a fiefcorp, to winning the number one rank on Primo's—and nothing would throw him off course. Soon, Natch was convinced that nothing existed outside of this track. It was only within this context that he could make sense of his humiliating failures to Captain Bolbund. *The track may twist and turn*, he told himself, *but eventually it will lead me to my destination.*

In the meantime, Natch's most pressing problem was cash flow. His Vault account had been drained by weeks of fruitless competition, not to mention the new bio/logic programming bars and Jara's consultation. Even the normally oblivious Horvil took note of Natch's financial plight. The engineer began to discover subtle ways to help. He would pick up the tab for dinner, accidentally leave groceries behind at Natch's place, drastically overpay Natch back for drinks from the night before.

Finally, Natch had to face the fact that ROD coding would not keep him afloat if he insisted on confronting Captain Bolbund again and again. Yet stanzas of Bolbund's wretched poetry kept creeping into his mind late at night, tramplike, refusing all attempts at eviction. Natch refused to give up, but he decided to put ROD coding on the back burner and scour the Data Sea for additional work. Something staid and square and predictable that would pay the bills.

Natch quickly found an open position at a large assembly-line programming shop in southern Texas territory.

"You don't want to go there," Jara advised him. "That's just connecting dots. Customization jobs for L-PRACGs handing out programs to twenty thousand people at once."

"Can't they automate that crap?" Natch asked.

"Too expensive. AIs could have done the grunt work, back before the Autonomous Revolt. But the time and expense to deal with all the contingencies for projects that big... it's cheaper to just go assembly-line."

Natch drifted around his apartment that night kicking walls and yelling at ceiling tiles. There had to be *some* other course, someplace else in bio/logics where the opinions of the drudges didn't matter. But Natch could not find any, and his Vault account was nearly empty. He accepted the job. Now his descent to the bottom of the programming food chain was complete.

The shop was located in a cavernous warehouse just south of the Sierra Madres. The area had once been the flowering center of New Alamo and the splinter Texan governments, overgrown with gaudy nouveau palaces and indulgent monuments to civic duty. But the Texans' decay had proved a potent fertilizer for programming factories that could make good use of their large open spaces. Natch hopped on a tube every morning to a nondescript building in the warehouse district, where he reported to one of several hundred identical workbenches on the floor. A program materialized before him in MindSpace, along with color-coded templates put together by some fiefcorp apprentice that instructed him where and how to make connections. There was no room for originality. The system automatically reported any deviations from the template to his supervisor.

Most of Natch's fellow programmers didn't mind the tedium, the endless repetition and constant clanking from a hundred programming bars striking workbenches at once. Their minds were far away. What happened to them in real time mattered little, as long as they could strum and drum and hum along to the orgiastic frenzy of music on the Jamm network. Natch logged on once to see what all the fuss was about. He found a hundred thousand channels of music in every conceivable style, tempo, and mood. Channels would spawn like newts, flourish for days or weeks as musicians jumped on and added their personal touch to the mix, then gradually shrivel up and die. Until then, Natch had thought his coworkers were thumping their workbenches with their programming bars to stave off boredom; now he realized he was listening to the rhythm sections of a thousand different Data Sea symphonies. Natch logged off in disgust and found a good white-noise program to block out the din. He detested music.

Natch earned his assembly-line pittance by day, but he was hardly idle at night. He spent countless hours staring at intricate blocks of programming code in MindSpace, not actually making connections, but simply absorbing the patterns and progressions, waiting for the inevitable blast of inspiration.

His next vision came to him in the dead hours before dawn.

Natch went to bed early that night and activated QuasiSuspension 109.3, sick of the eternal struggle to find sleep. The program quickly led him there. He used the highest setting, which should have insulated him from the everyday noises of shifting walls and floors.

Yet somehow Natch found himself bolting upright at three in the morning, his face glistening with sweat.

He felt like a lens had snapped into place and brought something wide and terrible into focus. Natch looked for the familiar objects around his bedroom: the cheap bedside shelf protruding from the wall, the pus-green carpet, the viewscreen that had been showing a light snow on Kilimanjaro when he lay down. Now all he could see were bones. The bones of impossible animals with four, five, and six appendages, bones scorched free of flesh and arrayed as furniture.

Natch tore himself out of bed and grabbed a robe from the disembodied index finger on which it hung. He burst out of his apartment, heading for the balcony that stood at the end of the hallway. As Natch rushed out the balcony door, a platform slid from the side of the building with a soft *click*. He feverishly gripped the alabaster railing and watched Angelos go through its typical early-morning routine. Skeletal tube trains stuffed with cargo rushed silently to and fro, anxious to make deliveries before the morning rush. Viewscreens here and there glared seductively at passersby with visions of dead products and ghoulish fashions. A fleet of bleached-white hoverbirds bearing the yellow star of the Council took wing over the Hollywood hills. Haunted tenements performed a graveyard jig with one another, here sidestepping to make room for the neighboring building on the left, there elbowing aside the building on the right to accommodate freshly awoken tenants. Natch could hear no sound but the soft crunch of pencil-thin bones beneath his feet.

As Natch gazed at all this, the bare skeletal structures he saw began to fill out—not with flesh, but with the washed-out hues of MindSpace code. The city was becoming one vast bio/logic program. A compendium of data, numbers, named entities, subroutines, variables. Pieces, no matter how independent, no matter how abstruse, inevitably connected to a larger and more complex whole. Tendrils snaking invisibly between each node, binding everyone together with mathematical formulae.

And the people... the people... The L-PRACG politicians stumbling from meeting halls after late-night sessions, the businesspeople shuffling mechanically to the tube stations and public multi facilities, the private security guards exchanging curt words with their Defense and Wellness Council counterparts, and yes, there were even a few tourists up and about at this hour... Weren't the people just one more set of objects to be manipulated? Weren't their actions governed by deeply ingrained sets of instructions, and their ideas ultimately predictable? They could be made to obey commands. They, like programming code, could be manipulated.

Natch saw Angelos floating within the giant MindSpace bubble that was the world: *his* MindSpace, *his* world. He could practically hear his bio/logics proctor at the Proud Eagle on his first day at the workbench. *Reach into your satchels, pull out a programming bar. Any one, it doesn't matter! You have twenty-six bars, marked A to Z, each with three to six separate functions. Twelve commonly recognized hand gestures. The grip. The point. The hitch. Unlimited possibilities before you! Unlimited combinations.* This was not strictly true; Natch was wise enough to know that the number of options at his disposal were not infinite. Mathematics dictated that there were limits. But even if his options were not *unlimited*, they were *enough*—enough to accomplish anything he was likely to dream. And if he could find some combination of tools capable of manipulating any structure of data, why not people too? Who was to say that the human nodes within his bubble were immune to the natural laws of cause and effect?

He reached out with enormous hands, each finger a bio/logic programming bar. The city of Angelos responded to his commands. It spun like a globe on an axis. It shifted and shuddered and jittered where he pointed. The world was his...

With the exception of an immense and incomprehensible mass hovering just beyond the horizon... a terrible celestial mass that could reshape humanity, if only he could reach it...

Natch rushed back to his apartment with his mind ablaze. He curled up into a fetal position on his chair-and-a-half and sketched an inventory of new tools with fiery holographic letters in the air.

Sex	Stability	Friendship
Power	Greed	Hunger
Money	Guilt	Lust
Love	Desire	Laziness
Vanity	Novelty	Suffering

On through the morning he wrote, brushing aside the urgent wake-up calls he had set for his assembly-line programming job. The work would not be necessary now.

He awoke on the couch in midafternoon, unable to remember how he had gotten there, but confident he was back on track at last.

Horvil sat upside down on Natch's chair-and-a-half with his feet propped on the chair back and his head hanging near the ground. His face was a jumbled stew of concern and fear topped with a thin crust of nonchalance.

"So you're willing to help me out," said Natch, eyes ablaze. He was practically sprinting from one end of the apartment to the other, teeth chattering and fingertips aquiver.

"It's a little *unorthodox*, I guess," said Horvil, "but heck, I've known you were unorthodox since you were six years old."

"I just don't want you to back out at the last minute."

"I won't. But..."

"But what?"

The engineer threw his arms to the ground in exasperation, a move that probably would have sent him tumbling onto his head if he were present in the flesh. "Do you always need to have an evil nemesis, Natch?" he cried. "First Brone, now Captain Bolbund. Can't you succeed on your own without having to *beat* somebody?"

Natch gave a hollow and humorless grin. "You can't win unless somebody else loses."

Horvil flexed his jaw for a moment and watched his friend strut energetically around the room. Natch could see a thousand witty rejoinders crowding into his mind, eager to sharpen their claws on his self-importance. "Okay," the engineer sighed after a minute. "What can I do to help?"

Two days later, Horvil caught up with the flower vendor named Vellux at the annual Creed Élan convocation. The engineer looked quite out of place at this year's event, not because of his size but because he was the only one in the conference hall not draped from head to toe in some shade of purple. Instead, Horvil wore a crisp dun uniform he had borrowed from a friend working in L-PRACG security.

"You are Vellux?" Horvil announced in the authoritative tone of voice Natch had instructed him to use.

The old woman, standing behind a table of lush passionflowers, greeted Horvil with a bland smile. Her eyes shone a soft violet. "And you are?"

"I'm here as part of an investigation into unethical ROD coding practices." *No names, no credentials,* Natch had said. *She won't ask. She'll think you're with the Meme Cooperative, or Primo's, or some special task force from the Defense and Wellness Council.* But Horvil was paranoid about being recognized, despite all of Natch's reassurances, and had insisted on scrubbing his public directory profile for good measure. "Have you recently purchased any bio/logic programming from this man?" Horvil gestured at a viewscreen on the wall, where a gaggle of Creed Élanners were bestowing a garland of flowers upon an addled woman of the diss who was clearly not interested. The engineer erased the display and summoned a particularly unflattering still of Bolbund, caught in midsmirk.

The flower vendor nodded, puzzled. "Yes, as a matter of fact I did."

"I see. Have you purchased any of the following products: NozeGay 59, Aura of the Beach 12c, Flaming Lipps 44d, Floral Eyes 14—"

"Floral Eyes!" cried Vellux excitedly. A wrinkled man in the next stall arched an eyebrow at her in disapproval, and the woman quickly lowered her voice to a conspiratorial whisper. "Yes, Floral Eyes 14. That's the one."

Horvil frowned and tapped his foot for a moment. *Don't tell her what you're doing,* Natch had said. *Make her think you're talking to someone over ConfidentialWhisper. Let her wonder for a minute or two.* Then the engineer abruptly motioned for Vellux to turn around and face the viewscreen. The old woman complied, with a nervous glance towards her table of passionflowers. "This will just take a moment," said Horvil. He bisected the viewscreen with a gesture, summoning a mirror on the left half and a series of flowers on the right. Daisies, buttercups, baby's breath, sunflowers. He gave an exaggerated stare at the image of Vellux in the mirror, took note of her obviously mismatched eye color, and shook his head sadly. "Bolbund, Bolbund, Bolbund," he muttered with a world-weary sigh for effect.

The confused flower vendor huddled inside her purple robe and frowned. "It's been working perfectly since I bought it," she said. "I don't know what happened... Should I return the program? Should I get a refund, or, or... report this to someone?"

Act surprised. Look around quickly. Make her believe that you've said too much and now you're trying to cover up. "Madam," said Horvil, blooming into a nervous smile, "I'm not allowed to make recommendations on bio/logic programs. Please don't make any changes on *my* account. It's nothing. Pretend I was never here. If we get enough evidence to move the investigation forward, we'll be in touch with you."

Vellux smiled wanly and nodded, looking completely unconvinced.

"Towards Perfection," said Horvil, and gave her a formal bow. Then he was gone. The entire encounter took about five minutes.

That afternoon, Natch logged his first sale of the EyeMorph program.

* * *

Natch spent the week tracking down Captain Bolbund's best customers. He did so by personally following the man, who turned out to be as offensive to the eyes as his poetry was to the ear. Bolbund had a body like a misshapen bowling pin, with an uneven beard and a nose like a wedge of putty.

But Natch did not fear his rival now that he had put his finger on Bolbund's mortal flaw: vanity. It was this vanity that led him to conduct his business out in the open, where others could see and post reports on the Data Sea. Where people could observe him personally delivering programs to his customers and reciting lines of his gut-wrenching poetry. Natch had to admit that it was a clever gimmick; customers appreciated the attention, and onlookers remembered his name. During the next few days, Natch and Horvil watched him sell two phallic enhancement programs to old Creed Objectivv devotees and repackage the same eyelash curling program for a handful of debutantes. By the end of the week, they had compiled a sizeable list of clients and the RODs Bolbund had sold them.

The two quickly developed a solid routine. Natch would buy copies of Captain Bolbund's routines (using Horvil's money, of course) and study them in MindSpace for hours on end. Cracking into the programming code was no simple matter, even for such retrograde technology as a ROD. But even without core access, Natch could glean a lot of information just by eyeballing a program's surface and running it through a battery of tests. Within a few weeks, he could reverse-engineer Bolbund's code blindfolded and put together improved versions in mere hours. Once a ROD was completed,

Natch would pass the customer's name and the script on to Horvil for his unique brand of social engineering.

Horvil was having the time of his life. He pinned bits of ceremonial bric-a-brac to his costume like medals, and constantly pestered his old hivemate with new character improvisations. Horvil had lived his whole life in decadent boredom, every move choreographed by an autocratic family. All Natch had to do was show the engineer a glimpse of spontaneity, and Horvil was dancing to *his* music.

Natch was astonished at how quickly Captain Bolbund's operation folded under pressure. He expected to run into a few snags along the way: programs he could not duplicate, customers he could not sway. But these problems never materialized. Bolbund's customers continued to roll over and switch to Natch's brands. Credits continued to accumulate in Natch's Vault account.

Of course, Bolbund did not accept the ravaging of his client list without a fight. But once again, Natch was shocked by his rival's stupidity.

The whole affair came to a head one morning as Natch was swigging down a cup of nitro and scanning the drudge headlines. The previous night he had relished his first mention in the Primo's investment guide.

Then he received a multi request from a Meme Cooperative official.

Natch activated a serenity program and granted the multi request. Within seconds, he was greeted by a smartly dressed woman flashing the official crest of the Meme Cooperative, the ancient Hebrew character of the *aleph* on a field of azure.

"Towards Perfection," said the woman. She then proceeded to reel off her name, position, division, and supervisor, along with a string of unnecessary provisos and notifications.

"Perfection," replied Natch, his anxiety now well under control. "What can I do for you?"

"You can tell me what your relationship is with this man." The Cooperative official held out her hand and flashed the same obnoxious picture of Bolbund that Horvil had been using in his charades.

Natch rolled his eyes. "Captain Bolbund," he moaned with distaste. "We've been scrapping over ROD customers for months now. He just can't accept that I'm beating him."

"Well, apparently he has gone over the line." The woman nodded towards the nearest viewscreen and began playing back a heated discussion between one of Natch's new customers and an ugly man with large ears. The video had obviously been captured on the sly. Natch couldn't make out the words passing between the two, but they nearly came to blows before the encounter was over. "Do you know this man?" said the Cooperative woman, freezing the display and tapping one of the interrogator's floppy ears.

"No," Natch replied truthfully.

"This man has been passing himself off as a Meme Cooperative official," she said. Natch looked closer at the display and noticed that the imposter's uniform was nearly identical to that of the woman standing in his apartment. "He's been telling people that he's conducting an official investigation into 'unethical ROD coding practices.' When we caught up with him, he told us that this Captain Bolbund has been paying him to put on this charade."

Natch was by now the very model of unconcern. "So what does this have to do with *me*?"

"Apparently, Bolbund specifically requested that his accomplice tell people that *you* were the one under investigation."

Natch masked his laughter by burying his face in his mug of nitro. *You fumbling idiot!* he chided Bolbund in his head. The key to the whole scam was to not mention any specific names or organizations whatsoever. After all, who could accuse Horvil of misrepresenting himself if he never made any representations in the first place?

"I don't know anything about it," Natch said at length to the Cooperative official.

The woman nodded perfunctorily. She had already made the mental leap to the next case. "The Cooperative will be in touch with you if we need any further information." She added another litany of bureaucratic language and was about to cut the multi connection when she had a sudden thought. "This Bolbund—what is he a 'captain' of anyway?"

Natch shrugged. "I have no idea."

And that was that.

Natch never heard another word back from the Meme Cooperative about the investigation, but was pleased to discover via the drudges that Captain Bolbund had received a stiff fine and a ninety-day suspension of his license to sell programming code on the Data Sea. Ninety days was an aeon in this business. Natch breathed a sigh of relief, and not only because he had vanquished his competitor; now Horvil could drop his silly role-playing and Natch could do business in earnest. For months afterward, Natch kept waiting for a reprisal to come his way from the Cooperative or some other legislative body, but none ever appeared.

The final chapter of the Bolbund saga occurred the night of the Meme Cooperative visit, when Horvil took Natch on a whirlwind tour of the London bars to celebrate. Natch was still earning less in a month than the top fiefcorps paid their apprentices as a daily wage. But he had halted his downward slide. He had proven that, by sheer force of will, he could bring the world in line with the visions in his mind's eye. Natch never drank or used alcohol simulation programs, but was content to watch Horvil get pleasantly sauced. At the end of the night, Natch fired off a parting message to Captain Bolbund, with Horvil's enthusiastic backing.

> Please don't think I'm rude
> If I tell you YOU GOT SCREWED.
> Guess you finally met your match
> From now on, look out for NATCH.

(((15)))

Natch's challenges did not end there. When Bolbund spread the word about what had happened to
him, the ROD coding community took it as a personal affront. ROD coders followed a loose,
bohemian ethos where nothing was taken too seriously and thievery was allowed for sport but not for
money. Natch's ruse—or at least Bolbund's version
of it—violated those principles.

And so Natch had to endure several blatant
attempts by third-rate programmers to sabotage his
products, steal his customers, and savage his reputation. But this did not faze him. Natch quickly
developed a reputation on the Data Sea for his
humorless determination and his inability to accept
defeat. Beat him once, and he would not stop until
he had humiliated you three or four times in
return—and fired a few warning shots at your
friends and associates to boot.

Captain Bolbund returned to the business after
his ninety-day suspension. The Meme Cooperative's
penalty had ravaged his client base and sapped his

Vault account. But by this point, the ROD coding community had come to the consensus that the best way to deal with Natch was to leave him alone and grease his path up and out of the business altogether. An enterprising young woman in Sudafrica even made a profit out of it by selling a program called NatchWatch that kept other coders abreast of Natch's activities.

Bolbund decided to steer clear of the angry young programmer.

Natch spent another two years honing his skills in the ROD game. By the time Primo's took notice and tagged him as a rising star, Natch's services were in high demand among the elites. He had also acquired a long list of enemies, which was an even greater indicator of success as far as Natch was concerned. *Nobody likes success but the successful*, the ruthless financier Kordez Thassel had once said.

Eventually, Natch decided to move out of his cramped Angelos apartment and settle somewhere else. He chose the city of Shenandoah, whose coffers were overflowing with fiefcorp revenues and whose local L-PRACGs were among the most libertarian in the world. With another financial boost from Horvil, he could even afford a place that included its own private multi stream and a small garden of daisies off the living room.

But the money was still abysmal compared to the sums the capitalmen were tossing into the bio/logic fiefcorp sector every day. The ranks of the diss were thinning, and those of the fiefcorps were inflating. There was talk on the Data Sea of another Great Boom like the one that had preceded Marcus Surina's death.

Natch spent another year freelancing, taking on the occasional ROD but concentrating more on neurological software. As his profile rose, so did his prospects. Natch received multi requests and lunch invitations every week from capitalmen and channelers trying to get a sense of his future plans. They seemed to be competing with one another to see who could slip in the most dismissive reference to the Shortest Initiation. Many of the same fiefcorp masters who had tried to shanghai Natch into worthless apprenticeships a few years ago were now sugaring him with promises of large signing bonuses.

He even heard from a few groups in the bio/logics underground who promised him a fortune writing black code off the grid. The future lay not with fiefcorps and memecorps, they said, but with clandestine teams of programmers sponsored by rich creed organizations and Lunar tycoons, programmers who were being paid to circumvent the restrictive laws of central government and stretch the boundaries of bio/logics.

Natch got into the habit of taking the tube out to the great sequoia forests and zigzagging from station to station for hours while he stared up at the trees and tried on alternative career paths like gloves.

"You've done really well with RODs," said Jara during one of her frequent consultations. "But isn't it time you set your sights a little higher?"

Horvil agreed. "I never thought *I* would be the one telling *you* to get some ambition," he said mockingly. "There's bigger targets out there, and a fuck of a lot more money!"

Contrary to what Jara and Horvil thought, however, Natch had not settled into a rut. He was biding his time, saving up his resources, marshaling his abilities. He wanted to plan his next move carefully so he would not fail again.

One cold winter night at 3 a.m., he sent a ConfidentialWhisper to Serr Vigal.

The neural programmer didn't mind at all being woken up; in fact, he was overjoyed to hear from his former protégé. Ten minutes later, Natch hopped on an Omaha-bound tube. Within an hour, he was standing in Vigal's foyer. Natch was surprised to find their friendly hug metamorphosing into a real flesh-and-blood embrace.

True to form, Serr Vigal had changed little in the past few years. Memecorp business had risen with the tide of the economy, but this had also caused his fundraising duties to swell to epic proportions. Vigal had just returned from a meeting with some of the minor bodhisattvas at Creed Surina and was due at the sybaritic resort of 49th Heaven in two days to speak about newly proposed OCHRE standards.

"So what causes the prodigal son to visit his old guardian in the middle of the night?" asked Vigal between sips of green tea.

"I need your advice," said Natch.

"Oh?"

"I'm ready to start my own fiefcorp."

Later that morning, Horvil and Jara agreed to come over to assist in the planning. Following standard etiquette, which said that crucial business decisions should be made in person, the two caught a hoverbird across the Atlantic from London. They met in the flesh for the first time on the runway and gave each other formal bows. By the time they arrived in Omaha, Horvil and Jara were already grumbling at each other like longtime companions.

Natch brought the first meeting of the Natch Personal Programming Fiefcorp to order around Vigal's kitchen table at noon.

From the outset, cash flow was the primary issue. Natch couldn't realistically expect any revenue flowing into the company for at least sixty days, yet there were a number of capital investments that needed to be made in the beginning. Licensing fees to the Meme Cooperative, listing fees to Primo's and the L-PRACGs, bio/logic equipment, administrative programs. Natch's savings would go a long way towards covering these costs, and eventually he would recoup the rest through new-fiefcorp tax breaks. But in the meantime, he was short the credits for apprentices' room and board those first few months.

He turned expectantly towards Horvil, but the engineer surprised him by shaking his head. "Sorry," he said, "but if I'm gonna be your apprentice, Natch, I don't want to complicate things."

Natch's eyebrows creased in confusion. "You want to be my *apprentice*?"

"Sure, why not? You're gonna need a first-rate engineer on the team, aren't you? The way I figure it, the only place I'm safe from that competitive streak of yours is on your payroll."

"But... the pay..."

"This ain't about the money, Natch," said Horvil jauntily, pleased to catch his friend off guard. "I've got enough of that. I just don't want to miss out on all the fun. And besides—*someone* has to keep you sane."

Serr Vigal beamed at the engineer in approval. "I don't think your credits will be necessary, Horvil," he said. "I can cover the payroll for the first few months."

This outpouring of faith and goodwill began to arouse Natch's suspicions. "And what do you want in return?"

"Do I have to want anything in return?" replied Vigal with a cozy smile.

Natch's face turned a flustered purple. "I'm serious, Vigal," he muttered. "What do you want?"

Vigal sighed and considered the question for a minute. "Okay, then how about a membership on the board, with a stake in the decision-making. A *minority* stake, of course," he added hastily. Natch nodded in mute satisfaction. Young fiefcorps often ended up with a concerned father or generous aunt on the board. "I can't promise I'll be available every day or even every week," continued the neural programmer, "but just remember, I'll always be there when you need help."

Embarrassed, Natch turned towards the last person at the table. He didn't know what to expect from Jara. Unlike his career, hers had not blossomed over the past few years. A gradual détente in her relations with Lucas Sentinel had resulted in the occasional piece of business, but Jara had increasingly come to rely on Natch's consulting fees to make a living.

The fiefcorp master summoned one of his simmering stares, the kind he had learned to use on

Jara through trial and error. "I'm going to need a good bio/logic analyst too, Jara," he said.

The small businesswoman shifted uncomfortably in her chair as she tried, and failed, to meet Natch's stare head-on. Eventually, she lost the battle of wills and lowered her eyes to the table. "Count me in," she said finally, gritting her teeth. "But *don't* think you talked me into this, Natch. Everyone knows that fiefcorps are where the real money is these days. I've been waiting a long time for an opportunity like this to come along."

Natch gave his fellow fiefcorpers a predatory grin. *So have I*, he thought.

Despite all the careful planning and preparation that went into the formation of the Natch Personal Programming Fiefcorp, success did not come easily for the company.

Bio/logic programming was a much different animal than Routine On Demand coding. The work was more labor-intensive, and required the skills of a hard-core nuts-and-bolts engineer like Horvil and the leadership of a generalist like Natch. Because of the difference in scale, the stakes for any one particular piece of code were much higher. Each revision took weeks to complete. You couldn't afford to take the shortcuts commonplace in the ROD coding world. Nor did you have the luxury of wasting time on unnecessary features; you needed an analyst like Jara who had her fingers on the pulse of the market and could pinpoint exactly what revisions would be the most lucrative.

During the first few weeks, Natch worked nearly nonstop. He bounced from Jara's flat to Horvil's flat to Vigal's flat so many times that he was constantly disoriented. But Natch knew he was finally on the right track and moving full steam ahead.

Still, the sales figures in those initial months were abysmal. Natch began each day by examining the upgrades and revisions waiting on the dock for a launch onto the Data Sea. After launch, Jara would sit back in nervous anticipation, senses tuned to the Sea's very molecular hum, waiting for the currents of trade to shift in their direction. And each day she felt the sting of disappointment when traffic failed to come. Besides the occasional sale to a curious browser or the random ping of a cataloging data agent, there was very little activity.

"What are we doing *wrong*?" Jara moaned to Natch one day.

"We're not doing anything wrong," he replied coolly. "We just need the mojo to accumulate. Give it time."

And then one day it happened.

DeMirage 24.5 was a pedestrian routine designed to reduce the effect of optical illusions. Natch had halfheartedly picked up the project hoping to capitalize on all the ocular research he had put over the years into programs like EyeMorph. Jara didn't have much of an opinion one way or the other about the program. Horvil gave it a cursory look and spent a few hours performing delicate surgery on the program's innards in MindSpace. Natch barely paused to write a descriptive fore and aft for the product before launching it on the Data Sea. He assigned a BizWorks administrative agent to watch the traffic and sound a short *ping* for every sale, then went to sleep.

Natch's program hit the Data Sea right in the midst of a major turf war.

The Serly Fiefcorp had been involved in a fierce competition with a fast-rising company known as the Patel Brothers. Each company's partisans were launching a daily barrage of complaints to the Meme Cooperative, to Primo's, and to various L-PRACGs throughout the civilized world. Finally, the battle came to a head when Serly's databases were struck with a malicious piece of black code that temporarily put a small portion of the company catalog out of commission. One of the programs hit was Serly's TrueOptix 88. While Serly's people were assessing the damage to the catalog, they decided to pull TrueOptix from the Data Sea until they could determine if it had been infected. Prosteev Serly immediately brought a complaint before the Meme Cooperative blaming the Patels; but the evidence was thin, and the case quickly vanished like one of the visual phantasms that TrueOptix was designed to prevent.

The Patel Brothers were not known for playing nice.

Prosteev Serly's loss became Natch's gain. Serly had channeling deals in place and packaging agreements to fulfill. Data agents scurried around the Data Sea to find a suitable replacement for the optical program, and located Natch's DeMirage 24.5. Within minutes, Natch's program had become the de facto standard for ocular hallucination management on the Data Sea.

The *pings* began sounding at 8:32 a.m. Shenandoah time and continued throughout the day. Eventually, the noise became so deafening, Natch had to adjust the program to ping once every hundred sales. As the night wore on, the BizWorks administrative program slowed to pings every thousand sales, then every ten thousand. And still the pings kept coming.

Horvil was ecstatic. "Can I juggle a mean bio/logic programming bar or *what*?" he crowed.

"Beginner's luck," Jara corrected him with a smirk.

Natch shook his head. "Luck," he said, staring intensely at the Shenandoah cityscape, "had nothing to do with it."

3
THE PHOENIX PROJECT

(((16)))

Merri sat on Natch's chair-and-a-half and watched the fiefcorp master make frantic circles through the garden. When he started, he was treading on turf, but as their conversation absorbed more of his attention, he gradually strayed into the patch of daisies. Soon he was carelessly stepping on flower petals and tracking dirt onto the carpet.

"So in another eighteen months, it'll be..." Natch stopped and squinted, as if the future were a distant object hovering outside the window.

"May," replied Merri.

"It'll be May," continued Natch. "That's right. So if we extend your contract until then and your shares stay on target, I expect they'll be worth—*this*..." He waved his hand at the viewscreen, mutating the psychedelic Tope painting into a more prosaic spreadsheet. A sizable boldfaced number sat in the bottom-right corner of the screen. "And that's a conservative estimate. Now that we've hit number one on Primo's, it's only going to go up. So how's this figure suit you?"

Merri gave a slight nod, but Natch could see she had some reservations. Not over money, he was fairly certain; even in this economy, she was not likely to get a better compensation package anywhere else. No, it probably had something to do with the swirled black-and-white logo prominently displayed on her breast pocket, insignia of the Creed Objectivv truthteller.

Natch gave the woman a long appraising stare while she read over the apprenticeship contract one more time. Merri might have been Jara's diametric opposite. Her large frame dwarfed Jara's, though it did not quite reach Horvil-sized proportions. She had blonde features that spoke of Nordic ancestry and a demeanor both easy and reserved. Over the past six months, there had been times when Natch felt like slapping that pious look right off Merri's face—but for process' preservation, one could get only so angry at a woman who possessed such an encyclopedic knowledge of the bio/logics world.

"You're concerned about the workload," said a voice on the opposite side of the room. Merri turned to face Serr Vigal, who had been hovering quietly in the shadows like a spook. Natch hadn't been quite sure whether the neural programmer was even paying attention.

"Well, partly," conceded Merri with a sidelong glance at Natch. "But I'm also not sure how comfortable I feel being a channel manager. I was trained for bio/logic analysis, you know."

Natch faced the window and scowled. He was not about to give up such a precious asset as a channel manager who had taken the Objectivv truthtelling oath. Whatever the reality was, people believed that honest salespeople sold better products. "This is a small fiefcorp, Merri. Everyone gets to do a little bit of everything around here. Shit, you can even grab a pair of programming bars and take on some of Horvil's workload, for all I care."

Merri brightened and gave one of her typical placating smiles. *For a devotee of Creed Objectivv, she fakes her emotions pretty well*, Natch thought. "Would it be all right if I... thought about it for a few days?" asked the blond channel manager.

The entrepreneur shrugged. "Fine."

"Okay, then..." And with that, Merri cut the multi connection and returned her mind to a red square tile several hundred thousand kilometers away on Luna.

Natch gazed into the gloom of the Shenandoah dusk. Dark clouds were assembling on the westward horizon and rattling their sabers, threatening a violent thunderstorm. In all probability, the Shenandoah L-PRACGs had already petitioned the Environmental Control Board to steer the worst of the storm clear of downtown using its geosynchron bots. But still, the clouds felt like a heavy-handed omen to Natch. Something was hiding in those clouds, some cruel and brutal creature with Natch's name roiling in its murky consciousness.

He shifted his attention to Serr Vigal. "We've had this discussion before," he said.

The neural programmer had sunk back into the shadows, invisible but for the occasional beard hairs glinting like flecks of silver. "It's common sense, Natch," he replied. "Now that you're constantly neck-and-neck with the Patels, there's a real danger of overworking your apprentices. I think you need to bring more people on board."

"I hired Merri."

"But she's not taking any of the workload off Horvil and Jara."

Natch knew his old mentor was correct, that eventually the two apprentices would snap under the strain of eighteen-hour days in the trenches fighting the Patel Brothers. They would get tired of the sorties in the middle of the night, the maneuvering for field position. The endless exchange of small-arms fire.

But as soon as business started pouring in, Horvil and Jara had forgotten all about their bewilderment and indignation surrounding the black code incident. Natch's interviews with Sen Sivv Sor and John Ridglee had spawned a drudge feeding frenzy, which in turn had produced a tidal wave of sales. Suddenly, important engineers were contacting Horvil for advice and dissecting his recursive functions as if they were ancient Sanskrit texts. And Jara, who was used to shuffling money between fiefcorp accounts to placate some creditors, was now trying to find places to invest the overflow.

"Horvil and Jara will be fine," mumbled Natch. "Oh, I know you're right, Vigal. I'll need to bring more people aboard at some point. It's just that I don't *trust* anyone else."

"Maybe you need to give those two a holiday," said Serr Vigal. "The fiefcorp is running pretty smoothly. There's no reason you can't slow down for a week or two."

Natch, his arms folded over his chest, turned to glare at the neural programmer. NiteFocus 50c allowed him to peer through the veil of shadow and see the concerned look on his mentor's face. "No," he said, "there *is* a reason."

"Ah, the message."

"Something's coming, Vigal. I can feel something out there, coming up fast. A tidal wave. *Something*."

Natch nodded towards the viewscreen that was still displaying Merri's apprenticeship contract. He called up a message in its place and enlarged the type so it was readable from across the room.

Natch,

I would like to personally congratulate you on achieving number one in the Primo's bio/logic investment guide. Several members of my administrative staff are devoted users of your programs. Your sleep deprivation utilities, I'm afraid, are particularly popular around here.

As you may have heard, Creed Surina will be holding a cultural festival next week to celebrate what would have been Sheldon Surina's 400th birthday. We are looking for able bio/logic programmers such as yourself to contribute to a presentation on my ancestors' legacy to the world. I would be honored to have you as my guest for dinner at Andra Pradesh this Wednesday, November 23, to discuss the details.

Towards Perfection,

Margaret Surina
Master of the Surina Perfection Memecorp
Bodhisattva of Creed Surina

The letters hung on the screen before him, waiting for some gesture or flicker of the eyeballs to indicate which way Natch wanted to scroll. Finally, the fiefcorp master blinked hard and sent the missive away.

"I'm afraid I don't understand why you're so worried, Natch," said his guardian. "It looks like a perfectly normal invitation to me."

"It just doesn't *feel* right," said Natch. "I can't explain it. It's like..." *Like a vast array of numbers that have some hidden kabbalistic connection to one another. Like a constellation millions of light-years across, and you're sitting in the middle trying to decipher what it looks like from a distance.* "Let me ask you this, Vigal. Why invite me to dinner? It means that Margaret doesn't want to see me in multi—she wants me to trek halfway around the globe to talk to her in person. That seems awfully formal for a first meeting. Does she think there's some security risk? Or maybe she has a business proposition for me. You know the etiquette— important business deals happen through personal meetings."

The neural programmer frowned. "Maybe you should just take this at face value."

"*Face value*," Natch scoffed. "I never take *anything* at face value."

Vigal rose from his chair with a creaky sigh, then walked over and clapped a virtual hand on his protégé's shoulder. "Perhaps you need to get some rest, Natch." He gave the shoulder a gentle squeeze and then stepped back, looking the young programmer up and down wistfully. "Rest—that's advice I think I'm going to follow

myself. Make sure you ConfidentialWhisper me
if you need anything."

Minutes later, Natch was alone.

The fiefcorp master prived himself to all incoming
communication and darkened the windows. Then
he called up the invitation on the viewscreen once
more and crouched on his haunches in front of it.

Could this be some trick by the Patel Brothers? A
punishment for filching the lead on Primo's for
those brief forty-seven minutes? He verified the
message's digital signature against the one in the
public directory, and the directory declared it
authentic. The message had not come from the
hand of some Surina flunky either, but straight from
the bodhisattva herself. Signatures could be forged,
of course, but it was a fiendishly difficult task.
Natch knew all the standard tricks for low-level signature forgery, and this message used none of them.

He collapsed onto his sofa and instructed Info-
Gather 96a to find as much up-to-date information
about Margaret Surina as possible. The program
launched a volley of data agents onto the measureless ocean of information and began bouncing the
results off its analysis engines, deducing connections, drawing conclusions, cooking up bite-sized
summaries.

Seconds later, the viewscreen lit up with the
image of a woman around Serr Vigal's age. The
drudges described the heir to the Surina family
mantle as a glamorous figure, but Natch could see
little glamour in this nondescript woman. Margaret
was neither tall nor short, neither heavy nor thin;
she could have been one of those composite

sketches of women compiled from a hundred different ethnicities. The plain gray pantsuit she wore belied her vaunted sense of fashion, and even her raven-black hair lay unostentatiously on her shoulders. If she did not have the prominent Surina family nose and her father's eyes, preternaturally large and shining with fierce intelligence, Natch would not have believed that this woman was the heiress to the world's largest programming fortune.

MARGARET SURINA (301–   )

read the caption that floated next to the woman on the screen.

> The bodhisattva of Creed Surina and master of the Surina Perfection Memecorp, Margaret Surina is heiress to the Surina family fortune and the vast empire left her after the untimely death of her father Marcus. She lives in Andra Pradesh at the residence constructed in honor of her ancestor, Sheldon Surina, the father of bio/logics.

Natch skipped ahead to the section that detailed Margaret's business interests:

> Surina has been the subject of gossip and speculation over the past twenty years since she founded the memecorp that bears her name. To date, the company has released no products and purportedly receives 100% of its funding from Creed Surina. Partisans of the Surinas believe the memecorp is at work on another technological breakthrough on par with such previous family accomplishments as

bio/logics and teleportation. Surina supporters have even given this undefined new technology a name: "The Phoenix Project." Detractors, however, suspect that no such project exists and that Margaret Surina is instead using her memecorp to funnel money into libertarian and pro-Islander political causes.

Natch leaned forward and tried to cajole Info-Gather into providing him more about this mysterious Phoenix Project, but no tangible details were forthcoming. Pundits on the Data Sea had been scrutinizing Margaret's every move for years now, gossiping about every new visitor to her compound in Andra Pradesh in ancient India, seeking evidence of some übertechnology that might or might not exist. So far, they had come up empty.

The pressure on her must be enormous, Natch reflected. At Margaret's age, Sheldon Surina had already written his seminal paper, "Towards the Science of Bio/Logics and a New Direction for Humanity," the work that jolted the world out of its post-Revolt stupor and signaled the beginning of a new age. Sheldon's grandson Prengal Surina had already put forth the universal law of physics at this stage of his life. Even Margaret's father, the poor doomed Marcus, had become a worldwide icon and pioneer of teleportation by the time he was fifty. The public was growing restless. What would Margaret's contribution to the world of science be?

The entrepreneur remembered his days of infamy following the Shortest Initiation and grimaced. *Why does she need to make any contribution?* he thought. *What if she just wants to be left alone?*

Natch studied the image of Margaret Surina carefully. The photographer appeared to have taken Margaret by surprise; she seemed frozen in the act of turning towards the camera. But there were no surprises written in those unnaturally large blue eyes. Margaret's eyes showed a woman in complete control of her surroundings, a woman capable of swallowing life's surprises whole without the least bit of discomfort. Natch finally had to admit to himself that this woman had him intrigued.

And could this Phoenix Project be that thing just beyond the horizon that he had been waiting for his entire career? Was that why the very words tugged at his soul like a magnet?

He sent a terse reply to Margaret's invitation:

> I would be honored to accept your invitation and make your acquaintance.
> Towards Perfection,
>   Natch, Master of the Natch Personal
>   Programming Fiefcorp

(((17)))

The city of Andra Pradesh had few municipal building codes. Tenement high-rises and office buildings hobnobbed with parks and shopping areas and even farmland, all jumbled together without regard to style or function. Andra Pradesh was a city that had rolled down from a mountaintop and sprouted haphazardly out of the wreckage.

On that mountaintop were the Surinas.

Natch saw the massive Surina compound as soon as he stepped off the tube. Even a kilometer away, it dominated the skyline. He could easily make out the austere buildings of the Gandhi University of Andra Pradesh where Sheldon Surina had taught and the absurd towers of the Surina family's private residence. Somewhere below his level of sight were the administrative offices of Creed Surina, the Surina Enterprise Facility, and the Surina Center for Historic Appreciation. Above them all, a lone spire jutted obscenely into the clouds from the middle of the compound. Natch had heard somewhere that this was the tallest structure built since the

Reawakening. Down in the city below, dozens of buildings competed for the right to claim second place.

The tube could have deposited Natch right at the gates of the Surina compound, but he wanted the full effect of approaching it from a distance. *I've already wasted several hours on the tube*, he thought. *Why not a few more minutes on foot?*

Natch hustled through the crowded streets and tried to keep his mind blank. The people of Andra Pradesh rushed about at a frenetic pace as if galvanized by the presence of the Surinas in their midst. Conversations were louder, clothing more vivid. People of all colors, classes, and creeds seemed to blend in here, much like the buildings that surrounded them. L-PRACG security guards, street performers, vendors of exotic fruits and vegetables, businesspeople, assembly-line programmers, hoverbird traders and cargo haulers, rambunctious children: here in Andra Pradesh, distinctions blurred.

Finally, he reached the base of the mountain. A dozen guards stood before the gate wearing the green-and-blue uniforms of Creed Surina. Was it just a figment of Natch's imagination, or were they fingering the triggers of their dartguns with a little too much anxiety?

After a few minutes of identity checking, the guards waved Natch through the gate. Two grim-faced women in uniform motioned for him to follow them up the steep mountainside road to a courtyard large enough for a small army procession. They found their way to the Center for Historic Appreciation, a squat pentagonal building in the classic Greek style. It was a scientific museum of sorts, full of haphazardly arranged curio tables and marble statues of the Surina dynasty laid out in solemn, self-important poses. There was even a statue of Margaret as a child sitting rapturously at the feet of her father.

Security guards were everywhere, dartguns drawn and signaling to one another with choppy gestures that Natch could only assume was a form of battle language. The complex appeared to be devoid of visitors. Finally, the two guards led Natch down a long hallway and, without a word, deposited him at the door at its end. He opened the door, took a deep breath, and stepped inside.

Natch immediately found himself on a floating platform in a massive library. There was no sign of the exterior hallway; the door he had come through stood by itself with no visible means of support.

SeeNaRee, thought Natch with distaste.

The hexagonal platform was merely one of a thousand identical platforms Natch could see stretching off in every direction, each connected to its neighbors by narrow walkways, like beads on a string. Bookshelves lined four walls of each platform. He counted thirty-two treepaper books of equal size and weight filling each shelf, as if they were just a small part of an unimaginably vast encyclopedia. Natch looked around in vain for some sign of his host, for any human presence at all. After a few minutes, impatient, he reached for one of the leather-bound volumes and flopped it open on the large conference table in the platform's center.

FSLFJ WOPSF O SLJ!
Thwlk po sdl wopi fndvl fdqf poipwytpw,
Wtlkd woir z pod. Lsdkf wienhf sdflglsksgd
sldkjf? Wogih spapapa slgihd. Qqq! Qqq!

"Never read your Borges, did you?" came a voice behind him. Natch turned and found himself face-to-face with Margaret Surina.

Marcus Surina's daughter had aged quite a bit since that anonymous InfoGather image he had seen the other day. Natch wondered why she had not bothered to use bio/logics to conceal the wrinkles on her forehead, the slight stoop of her shoulders, the tinge of gray that permeated her once coal-black hair. Only Margaret's eyes remained intense and unblemished, as if they would remain brightly lit long after the rest of the flesh had withered away.

"Borges?" said Natch.

"Jorge Luis Borges," replied Margaret. "This library is his creation."

The name meant nothing to Natch, and a quick inquiry to the Meme Cooperative fiefcorp listings came up with no results. "Never heard of him," he said. "Is he a programmer?"

A smile descended onto Margaret's face as if from a great height. "He *was* a writer. From antiquity, from before the Autonomous Revolt. He wrote about an infinite library with books that contained every possible combination of words and letters. What you were reading was just one of its countless permutations." She had a grating habit of enunciating every syllable of every word, even those that typically stayed silent or piggybacked on a neighboring phoneme. *Ev-e-ry poss-si-ble com-bin-nay-shun. Count-less per-me-yu-tay-shuns.*

Natch shook his head in annoyance and slammed the book shut. He enjoyed intellectual puzzles, but had little patience for artists. "So why are we here?"

"It's a new innovation that we recently installed in all the Surina conference rooms," said Margaret. "The room automatically gauges your mood and chooses an appropriate bit of SeeNaRee. We have thousands of varieties in our data banks, virtual environments for every occasion. This *is* a museum, after all." *Vir-tu-al en-vi-run-ments for every occ-ay-zhun.*

Natch leaned over the railing and saw only stairs and platforms without end. "*I* wasn't thinking about any library." He sniffed.

Margaret gave a coy smile as if sharing an inside joke. "Ah, this is an ongoing complaint," she said. "People say that the program doesn't always pick the moods and emotions that they expect. The programmer says we are not always aware of what is going on in our subconscious mind. Personally, *I* find that to be a rather charming and unexpected benefit. However, if you prefer something more traditional..." With a flick of her wrist, the bodhisattva banished the library to oblivion, to be replaced by a featureless dining room with angular furniture.

Natch felt a surge of irritation rise inside of him, and quickly masked it with a PokerFace 83.4b program. Was Margaret trying to test the limits of his patience, or was this just more paranoia?

"Perhaps you would like a tour of the facilities before we dine," said the bodhisattva.

When they reached the end of the hallway, Natch realized that he and Margaret were not alone. He took a quick glimpse over his shoulder and discovered that they were being shadowed by an imposing hulk of a man with enormous biceps and a pale blond ponytail slung over one shoulder.

"The atrium of the Surina Center for Historic Appreciation," said Margaret as they walked into a vast domed space. "I don't know whether you got a chance to see it when you came in." The room was littered with bland statues celebrating the great pioneers of science: Aloretus Monk, Tobi Jae Witt, Albert Einstein, Isaac Newton. Sheldon Surina had a prominent place in the canon, of course, as did his protégé and sometime rival Henry Osterman. "We try to ease visitors in to the deeper exhibits with something gentle on the eyes," she said, though there were no visitors around to illustrate her point. She motioned at the hallways behind each scientist, all clearly labeled with his or her respective achievement: Relativity Hall. Subaether Court. Gravity Way.

Natch gave a polite nod. The Surinas' inane tourist attractions did not interest him, not when he had to figure out the mystery of this towering figure with the blond ponytail. The man stayed half a dozen paces behind them like a bodyguard might, and gestured to the sentries lurking at every corner using a hand weighed down with an excessive number of gold rings. But if he were part of the security staff, wouldn't he be wearing the standard green-and-blue Surina livery instead of loose tan breeches and an open-necked shirt?

Then the three of them stepped out of the Center for Historic Appreciation into the courtyard, and Natch caught sight of a thin copper collar suspended around the man's neck. An Islander!

Natch wondered how he could have missed the other signs: the uneven muscles that sprouted from manual labor instead of OCHRE stimulation, the ruddy complexion from too much time in the sun, the small scars running up and down his arms. Certainly, Margaret couldn't be depending on this man for physical protection. What good were those tree trunk-sized arms without bio/logics?

Who was this man, and why was he staring so intently at Natch?

The tour continued for most of the next hour. They made their way through the halls of the Gandhi University and saw the room where Sheldon Surina had lectured for most of his life. Natch peered through the windows of the Creed Surina auditorium and saw the pulpits where teachers and minor bodhisattvas preached the gospel of scientific innovation. He received cursory introductions to a few distant cousins of Margaret's who appeared to be the only civilians wandering the halls. After twenty more minutes of this, Natch grew increasingly bored. Either Margaret had not inherited her father's fabled magnetism, or she was storing up her energy for more important performances.

The Islander, too, appeared to have lost interest in Margaret's spiel. Every time Natch turned around, he found the big man staring at him with two brawny arms tucked in his pockets like siloed missiles. The stare contained neither malice nor menace. If Natch had to choose a word to describe his attitude, it would be *skeptical*.

A thought occurred to him. Was this whole lap around the Surina compound just an excuse for the Islander to check him out?

As they made their way back to the Center for Historic Appreciation, Natch decided to subject the Islander to a test of his own. He focused all his attention on the Revelation Spire—as the tall protruding spike atop the Surina residence was called—and then pretended to lose his footing. The fiefcorp master would have bet his weight in gold that he would have crashed into Margaret before the Islander could stop him. But in the space of a heartbeat, the Islander lashed out from his rearguard position and gripped Natch firmly at the base of his rib cage. The entrepreneur could feel the rings on the big man's fingers digging into his flesh.

Natch met the Islander's stare, and for a split second he could see straight through the man's defenses. He saw a look of concern for Margaret's safety that went far beyond any expression a bodyguard would have displayed. *This is personal for him*, thought Natch. *This man is no mercenary.*

The husky Islander set Natch back on his feet as he would a toy soldier. For the first time, Natch noticed that the man was about the same age as Margaret. The Islander let a sly grin creep into his countenance. He saw right through Natch's ploy, but instead of being angry, he seemed to appreciate Natch's resourcefulness.

Margaret did not even notice the interruption. The two men exchanged no words as they followed her into the Center for Historic Appreciation and back to the library room, now decorated with a single functional dining table.

Natch made awkward small talk with Margaret as they grazed on authentic Indian cuisine. Curry and cumin danced on the end of his tongue, and he soon found himself settling into a mellow post-vindaloo stupor. Natch was ready to concede to Vigal that his suspicions had been unfounded, that Margaret really just wanted his participation in this upcoming four hundredth birthday celebration for Sheldon Surina. The Islander popped in and out of the room several times, eating nothing. Natch was no closer to figuring out the man's place in Margaret's retinue, but this was a mystery he could solve another time. For now, Natch wanted desperately to draw the dinner to a close and get back to Shenandoah, where his bio/logic programming bars were waiting.

And then, after the dishes quietly slid into a compartment in a back wall, Margaret leaned forward and pressed her fingertips together. "You are probably wondering why I invited you here," she said.

Natch nodded.

"You are here," said Margaret, "because Len Borda is planning to have me killed next week."

The atmosphere became deathly quiet as Natch tried to think of something pertinent to say. Margaret's eyes suddenly glared at him like spotlights. The Islander stood by the door with the intensity of a coiled snake, looking as if he might pounce at any moment. *That explains why all those guards are roaming around with itchy trigger fingers.*

"So the Defense and Wellness Council is trying to kill you," said Natch, affecting nonchalance. "What does that have to do with *me*?"

Margaret drummed her fingers together. "Sheldon Surina used to say that we are all connected in a fundamental—"

"Don't patronize me," Natch snapped. The bodhisattva gave an exaggerated blink of shock, and couldn't resist a sidelong glance at the equally perplexed Islander standing in the doorway. Natch pressed on. "So Len Borda is going to kill you. That's wonderful. Why should *I* care? If you're so worried, go send a message to Sen Sivv Sor or John Ridglee. I'm sure they'd love to spread the news all over the Data Sea. But me—I've got a business to think about. I don't have *time* for politics."

Margaret's face toyed momentarily with outrage, ventured into amusement, and finally settled on weary fortitude. She laid her palms flat on the table and leaned forward. "They tell me the only things you care about are money and power," she said. "Well then... let me translate this into language you can understand. *I am about to present you with an opportunity for more money and more power than you can possibly imagine.* Number one on Primo's is a child's fantasy by comparison. You can either hear me out, or leave now and go back to fighting for scraps on Primo's. It is *your* choice."

Natch could have chosen to be insulted at the way this woman had casually belittled everything he had fought for since the Shortest Initiation. Sharp retorts hovered on the tip of his tongue. But then Natch remembered how easily he had fallen for the bait that the capitalman Figaro Fi had laid out for him all those years ago. *I won't be manipulated,* he repeated to himself over and over like a mantra. Natch looked at the Islander, who stood, amused, struggling to suppress his laughter. *He* knew, at least, that Natch had proven his point: Margaret's wealth and pedigree would not intimidate him. So instead of shouting, the fiefcorp master activated a relaxation program called OceanBreez 38 and waited a few seconds for the bio/logic code to suffuse his body with calm.

"I'm listening," he said at length.

The bodhisattva spread out her hands in a gesture of peace. "Let us start at the beginning," she began. "I am guessing you were born sometime in the 320s—"

"Three thirty-one," said Natch.

Margaret nodded. "Three thirty-one, then. You know what kind of position the economy was in at that time. My father's death and the collapse of TeleCo left the bio/logics industry in ruins and millions of programmers in the diss. The Economic Plunge of the 310s, they called it, though it lasted longer than that. People in the orbital colonies were starving for the first time since the Autonomous Revolt. Not a good period for business. Not a good period for *anybody*.

"Of course, by the late 320s, things were already turning around. High Executive Borda had started handing out enormous defense contracts to the fiefcorps, hoping the credits would funnel down to the masses. For ten years, the Council gave subsidies to just about anyone who asked—including me."

Natch's eyes were beginning to glaze over. According to the legends, Sheldon Surina had also been fond of historical digressions. *Did I take the tube halfway across the globe and lose an entire day in MindSpace for a civics lesson?* "So Len Borda gave you money."

"Yes," she continued. "I approached the Council with blueprints for a new set of memory enhancement programs. Programs to drastically extend the potential of the human brain, based on the technology my father left behind at his death. I painted Borda a picture of Council officers with total recall and soldiers who could memorize the tiniest details of a battlefield. He was impressed."

The fiefcorp master frowned. "I don't understand," he interrupted. "Why did *you* of all people need Council credits?"

Margaret gave a wry smile, and her face clouded up momentarily with a far-off look. Then she stood, shook off the gloom, and fetched two tiny cups of Turkish coffee from the access panel in the wall. "Natch, my father might have been a scientific visionary, but he was never a prudent businessman." She deposited one of the cups on the table in front of Natch. "Yes, he made breakthroughs in teleportation technology, but he never figured out a way to pay for them. Let us just say that TeleCo was not the only organization Marcus Surina left on the brink of bankruptcy when he died."

Natch sipped the bittersweet brew from the delftware cup and thought about his mother holed up in the towers of Old Chicago. He felt a brief surge of anger, but batted it away. "So Borda anted up," he said.

"Yes. The Surina Perfection Memecorp received one of the largest appropriations of the entire Economic Plunge. You see, it was a win-win situation. We desperately needed financial stability, and the public desperately needed confidence in the future, in their governments. And who could provide a better hope for tomorrow than the Surinas?"

Natch listened carefully but could find no trace of irony in her voice.

"So everyone got what they wanted," she continued. "We got the funding we needed to turn ourselves around. Borda got a shining example of prosperity to show off. And the economy recovered.

"Which leads us to today.

"We have not been idle all this time. After trying its hand at a variety of projects, the Surina Perfection Memecorp has spent the last sixteen years in research and development. And now Len Borda is about to find out exactly what he paid for all those years ago." The bodhisattva's voice crackled slightly at the end of her sentence. An expression of fear? Of regret?

"The Phoenix Project," Natch said.

Margaret rolled her eyes and gave a knowing look to the Islander, who responded with a smile rich in irony. "I *despise* that name. Some drudge coined the term. It wasn't supposed to be so secretive. We really *did* start out with memory enhancers. We never intended to provoke a twenty-year guessing game on the Data Sea."

"Okay," said Natch, shifting uncomfortably in his seat. "So what's this big invention, then? Not memory enhancers, I take it."

"No. Not really. It's a bio/logic program. But much more than just a bio/logic program."

"You're going to have to be more specific than that."

Margaret remained maddeningly calm. She blew on her coffee and watched the wisps of steam disperse around the room. Her eyes were a lake of measureless depth. "I can't. Not yet."

The mounting tension was too much for Natch. He let out an irritated puff and threw his hands in the air. "So we're back to the original question. What do you want from *me*?"

"I want you to license my technology," said Margaret.

Nobody spoke for several moments. Natch bounced his gaze back and forth between Margaret and her silent companion, wondering if somehow the Patel Brothers were behind this, if they had conned Margaret into diverting him here while they solidified their number one position on Primo's. The Islander looked Natch up and down as if taking detailed measurements.

"Let me get this straight," said Natch. "You're asking me to license some new product without telling me what it is? And if that's not enough, the Defense and Wellness Council is willing to kill you to keep the whole project quiet? Well, forget it. I don't want anything to do with this. What makes you think I want Len Borda coming after *me*?"

The bodhisattva's demeanor softened, though whether it was an expression of sympathy or merely a change of tactics Natch could not tell. "Let me ask you a question, Natch. What's the quickest way to neutralize a poison?"

Natch thought for a moment. "Dilute it," he said.

"Precisely. Dump any poison into a large enough ocean, and its effects are nullified."

"Okay, I see what you're driving at."

"The Defense and Wellness Council thinks my technology is a poison. *My* technology, Natch—my

life's work, which I've spent sixteen years building."
Margaret abruptly looped a bony finger through
the handle of the coffee cup and raised it into the
air. "But pour this poison into the largest ocean of
all—the Data Sea—and it becomes part of the
ocean itself. It becomes inert. More importantly,
*once you release the poison, it cannot be bottled up
again.*" She raised the cup to her lips and drank it
to the dregs in one angry gulp.

Natch was beginning to get the impression he
was not here for a business opportunity so much as
an audition. He remembered all the scenes he had
set up throughout the years: his confrontations with
Brone, his challenges to Captain Bolbund, his
ascent to the top of Primo's. Margaret Surina had
prepared a script, and she had a part for him to
play.

He once again shook off the stifling air, the slowly tightening constriction around his throat.
"There's something you're not telling me," he said.
"If you want to nullify the poison, go ahead and
dump the specs on the Data Sea right now and get
it over with. Why bother setting up a licensing
agreement with a fiefcorp?"

The bodhisattva nodded pensively. "It's not that
simple. This is a complex project. If this program
fails to capture the public's imagination, then the
Council can just swoop in and take control without
a single protest. Besides, the Phoenix code *is* dangerous code, if it's not handled properly. If we just
floated the specs out onto the Data Sea, who knows
what could happen? I absolutely *refuse* to have
blood on my hands." Margaret held her hands in
front of her face and stared at them as if they were

alien artifacts. "No, this situation has to be handled with the utmost precision. Which is why *you're* here, Natch.

"I need a licensee who can do two things. First, he needs to generate enough ripples on the Data Sea to make the Council stay its hand until I unveil the technology. And then he needs to quickly develop a workable prototype to show the world this technology is real."

"Wait a minute," cried Natch, slicing his hand through the air. "You've spent *sixteen years* building this fucking thing, and you don't even have a workable prototype?"

Margaret was unfazed. "I have many, but none I trust to act flawlessly in front of billions of people. The Council has forced my hand too early."

"All right, fine. So when are you unveiling the Phoenix Project?"

"The end of next week, at the cultural festival honoring Sheldon Surina's four hundredth birthday. Until then, all we need is a little bit of uncertainty. You're an outsider, Natch, and outsiders bring complications. Loose ends. The more Borda fears I have let others in on the Phoenix Project, the more he will hesitate to act."

Natch set his chin on his fist in consternation. He had learned many years ago never to get locked into a situation without an elaborate and many-layered plan for escape. Then he thought of Margaret's words: *More money and more power than you can possibly imagine.* What were money and power? Mere words, vowels and consonants, scrapings of tongue on tooth. But what they represented: open doors. A way out. A way *up*.

"So why me?" he said at length.

"Because you are the best," replied Margaret without hesitation. "Because you are young and hungry. Because you work quickly and demand absolute perfection from your team. Because this enterprise requires someone with a flair for... showmanship." She waved her hand and summoned a message in holographic letters on the table. "I need the person who can accomplish *this*."

Natch scanned the letters and promptly switched his PokerFace program back on.

PLEASE PROTECT YOUR HOLDINGS

The Vault has detected a DNA-assisted decryption attack directed at your account. Your holdings have not been compromised, but it is advised that you periodically check the security of your Vault account. This advisory has been automatically routed to the custodian of records for your L-PRACG and, depending on your L-PRACG's policies, may also be forwarded to the Defense and Wellness Council.

Natch could have recited the words from memory, but he pretended to read them over two or three times. Obviously, blackmail was not her objective, or Natch would have been greeted at the compound gates by representatives of the Meme Cooperative. "It's a warning from the Vault," he said simply.

The bodhisattva let it go, banishing the missive into the aether. She seemed to be retreating into her shell. Again, Natch caught the hollow look of fear in Margaret's eyes, and the intimate concern radiating from the Islander standing in the doorway.

"You need to understand something," said Natch abruptly. "Investing in a new technology isn't cheap. I'll need to bring on new employees, conduct research. Buy more equipment. Train my people, find more channelers." He tallied up each item with his fingers while he spoke. "All that takes money. Just because my fiefcorp made number one on Primo's doesn't mean we're number one in *sales*. I don't have that many credits lying around—especially if you expect me to get involved in a new project that isn't going to bring in any money for a long time."

Margaret sighed. "If you are suggesting Surina investment," she said, "I can't funnel money to you through any of our regular channels—not quickly, at any rate. It's too risky, and we can't have anyone suspect that I've put you up to this. For now, you must be a completely independent third party in these negotiations." The bodhisattva glanced over her shoulder at the blond man standing in the doorway, and suddenly Natch wondered if he was there to keep others out or to keep Natch in. "There is an entirely different dance I have to perform here with all the different Surina organizations. Let us just say that some here do not appreciate radical moves."

"So you expect me to hit the ground running with no money, and put together a perfect prototype in a couple of weeks."

"Within *a* week, yes. But I'm not worried, Natch. If I had the slightest doubt you could find the money to do this, you wouldn't be here."

Natch shook his head and snorted in amusement. "I don't understand what you're trying to accomplish."

The descendant of Sheldon Surina leaned forward and touched her lips to her clasped fingers. "Things were not supposed to turn out this way," she said quietly. "You are the contingency plan."

Natch stood up, put his palms flat on the table, and leaned forward with a smoldering stare. "Let's get one thing clear," he rasped. "I am *not* your contingency plan. If I get involved in this, it'll be for my *own* reasons. Because you claim I can make a lot of money, and I believe you. If things get too dangerous—for *me*—or if I think the credits aren't worth the risk, then I'll pull out of this whole thing without a second thought and leave you stranded. I'll be a dead man before I get involved in a scheme like this to save *your* hide from the Defense and Wellness Council." He turned to face the burly Islander, as if to say, *That goes for you too.*

Margaret had no reaction. She was beyond affectation right now. "I will forward to you what little information I can at this point," she said in a hoarse monotone.

The entrepreneur nodded and fired another quick glance at the Islander. The big man was smiling openly now. Whatever test he and Margaret had just administered, Natch had passed it with panache.

(((18)))

"Why don't you ask Horvil?" said Serr Vigal.

Natch shook his head. "He's got plenty of credits, but there's no way he can move that kind of money without his Aunt Berilla finding out about it. And she'd rather slice off her own arm than invest in *me*."

"Another fiefcorp, then. Pierre Loget. Or Lucas Sentinel."

"Sentinel?" spat the fiefcorp master, as if the name were a curse word in a foreign tongue. "Are you kidding? He's still furious at Jara. And don't forget that when I pushed the Patel Brothers down to the number two spot on Primo's, Sentinel's company fell to number three. Loget doesn't like me any better."

"What about that financier you met with all those years ago? He said he liked you, didn't he?"

"Figaro Fi? He joined the Prepared a year and a half ago, Vigal. He's probably dead by now."

Serr Vigal pursed his lips and made a noise of dismissal. *Thppt*. He got slowly to his feet and ambled over to the window, which was showing some beach-side resort full of bronzed children laughing and throwing sand at one another. A welcome change from the dreary November Omaha rain. "I can help you a little bit, of course," said the neural programmer. "The memecorp has some extra equipment lying around that I can lend you. But I just don't have the kind of money you're talking about."

"Which leaves me back where I started," said Natch with disgust. "The capitalmen." He kicked at a tuft of carpet and scowled at the frolicking children through the window. No self-respecting capitalman would lend him such a large sum of money for a project he couldn't even define. They wouldn't care that he ran the number two company on Primo's, or that he was working on Margaret Surina's fabled Phoenix Project—they would just ask to see the specs. Natch couldn't blame them. Margaret had no track record to boast of, no prior business successes to point to. All she had was the Surina family reputation. And that reputation hadn't helped anyone recoup their losses from Tele-Co, had it?

"This is my worst nightmare, Vigal," Natch moaned. He waved his hand at the screen and changed the display right under Serr Vigal's nose. His guardian blinked in mild surprise as the beach made way for the trading pit of some Melbourne financial exchange. "The biggest opportunity of my life, and I can't make it happen. Nobody will invest until Margaret unveils the technology at the end of next week. But then it'll be too late. I won't have the resources to get this prototype up and running in time."

Serr Vigal rubbed his goatee quietly for a few minutes, deep in thought. "I wonder what this Phoenix Project really is."

"Margaret said she started out with memory enhancers. You know neural programming, Vigal—where could she go from there?"

"In sixteen years? Just about anywhere."

"Well, it has to be a neurological program, doesn't it? She must have looked at my background—she must know I apprenticed with you. She must know the bulk of our catalog is devoted to optics and mental processes. DeMirage 54, Eye-Morph 66a, Mento Calc-U-Later 93.9, NiteFocus 50c—I could go on and on. Why else would she come to me?"

"Why indeed?" said Vigal. "There are hundreds of fiefcorps and memecorps out there capable of handling a project like this. And most of them have more experience in this business than you, not to mention greater resources."

"She said she wanted someone with *a flair for showmanship*."

"And do you believe her?"

"Stop being so... so *elliptical*. If you think something's going on here, then just come right out and say it."

Vigal leaned against the viewscreen, screwing up his face with courage. "I don't *think* anything," he muttered. "I simply fear."

"And what do you fear?"

"I fear that Margaret has picked you for this enterprise because she thinks she can manipulate you." The neural programmer took a long, sad look at the traders tussling with one another on the

Melbourne exchange floor. Undoubtedly, most of them were only multi projections, but that did not make the scene any less violent or chaotic to behold.

Natch felt the old alienation swooping down on him and constricting his lungs. He snarled angrily, poking a virtual finger into his guardian's chest. "And so what if she thinks she can manipulate me? That doesn't change anything. I've still got to find a way to get into the Phoenix Project, or I'll never get out of this... this *horse* race on Primo's."

"And do you know that Margaret's Phoenix Project is a panacea for your problems? I worry that you're throwing everything aside for some vague business venture when you don't even know what it is."

"No. The Phoenix Project is it. This is the answer. This is what I've been searching for. I can feel it with every cell in my body. You don't think I can just ignore an opportunity like this, do you?"

Vigal smiled wanly. "That is a decision only *you* can make, Natch."

Merri looked as if she had been in her foyer for hours awaiting Natch's arrival. He frowned briefly. There were few things Natch detested more than someone who was too eager to please. *A good employee says no more often than yes*, the great Lucco Primo had once claimed.

"Towards Perfection, Natch," she said softly.

"Perfection," replied Natch. "Ready?"

"Yes, but..." Merri flinched, as if raising an objection were the most difficult task in the world. "I was hoping you could shed some light on the role you want me to play today."

Natch checked the Shenandoah central time service. They had almost twenty minutes before the potential investors arrived at the Surina Enterprise Facility. He walked past the channel manager and into her living room, cursing the multi network's insistence on reproducing the wobbly effects of imperfect gravity control. "People don't trust me," Natch said bitterly, taking a seat on a round ottoman covered with a delicate floral pattern. "I've hit number one on Primo's, I've proven myself time and time again, but still nobody worth talking to will do business with me. I need your credibility, Merri."

Merri absorbed all this with an air of mystification. "My credibility?"

"When people look at me, they still see the Shortest Initiation. They look at Horvil and see... well, we've been working together so long, they see *me*. And Jara made some powerful enemies when she was on her own. We're all tainted goods, Merri. But you... Nobody has said a bad word about you on the Data Sea since you graduated from the hive. You've got an honest reputation."

The blonde woman shifted uncomfortably from one foot to the other. "So you're saying you want me there because of *this*." She nodded at the swirled black-and-white pin displayed prominently on her jacket breast pocket.

"Well, of *course* it helps that you're an Objectivv," said Natch. "Come on, Merri, you can put two and two together. We're going to a fundraising pitch. You've taken a pledge not to lie."

Merri wrinkled her nose in disappointment. "It's not quite that simple."

Natch shrugged. He had always disdained the creeds and their arbitrary ethical systems—the Surinas with their slavish devotion to science, the Élanners with their hypocritical advocacy for the poor, the Thasselians with their shallow and pointless worship of business. But he reserved a special irritation for the Objectivvs. Natch could not fathom why the public tolerated, even revered, the creed's disciples. The way they babbled about "the search for objective truth" and dissected every utterance of that cryptic old hermit known as the Bodhisattva made Natch cringe.

"We can discuss philosophy some other time," said the fiefcorp master, rising from the ottoman and nodding pointedly at the red square tile in the hallway. "Right now we've got work to do. Get ready to follow my beacon."

"So," stammered Merri, "what do you want me to *do*?"

"I don't know," said Natch indifferently. "Keep quiet. Act ethical."

He didn't wait for Merri's next disapproving grimace. Instead, Natch closed his eyes, focused on the beaker of concentrated entropy that was Andra Pradesh, and let the cold *frisson* of multivoid envelop him. Seconds later, he stood at the gates of the Surina compound, staring up at the Revelation Spire. Natch stretched his mind out to the multi network and activated a beacon to tag his spatial coordinates for Merri to follow.

She needn't have worried about getting separated from her master. The blue-and-green-clad security officers kept the two visitors waiting at the compound gates for ten minutes. The Surina guards were busy eyeing a group of white-robed Defense and Wellness Council officers across the way who seemed to have nothing better to do than pace at the bottom of the mountain and polish the barrels of their dartguns. Merri shuddered with relief when she and Natch were finally escorted into the safety of the Surina compound.

The Enterprise Facility was an impressive location for a fundraising pitch: twelve stories of blue stretched stone cantilevered off the side of a mountain in defiance of the natural laws of gravity. Merri followed him silently through the throngs of suits up to a room on the ninth floor. A room blissfully free of irritating SeeNaRee. They entered to find eight capitalmen already seated at the semicircular conference table. Natch consulted the time and noted with satisfaction that he was exactly twelve minutes late, which was three minutes earlier than he had planned.

"Towards Perfection," he said brightly, moving to the focal point of the table. The five men and three women returned his greeting with varying degrees of politeness and curiosity. Merri stood respectfully to one side with her hands clasped behind her back, her Creed Objectivv emblem on prominent display, waiting for some signal from her fiefcorp master.

"Let's not waste any time," announced the fiefcorp master, gesturing to the white open space on the wall behind him. An itemized list of business expenses appeared in blocky fixed-width characters. Natch paused to let the capitalmen absorb his list. As expected, their eyes uniformly zeroed in on the big-ticket items at the bottom: ten additional

bio/logic programmers and engineers, fifteen channelers, office and meeting space, bio/logic
programming equipment, marketing expenses. The
total figure spelled out in the bottom right corner
was an eyebrow-raising sum. "This is what I need
by the end of the week," he declared. "Are there
any questions?"

Eight pairs of eyes—nine, counting Merri's—
gaped dumbly at the entrepreneur, waiting for some
elaboration. But Natch simply stood there and
gazed around the room with an intense stare. He
looked as if he were preparing to either cut his multi
connection or march around the table slicing off
heads.

Finally, one of the capitalmen raised her hand
timidly. Merri sent an inquiry to the public directory and discovered she was the investment manager
for a libertarian L-PRACG and no stranger to
fundraising pitches. "Exactly what is all this *for*?"
she said with an air of bemusement.

Natch turned his unblinking eyes upon her. "For
development of Margaret Surina's Phoenix Project,
which I am licensing."

The investors gawked at the entrepreneur as if he
had just offered to sell them a set of dragon's teeth.
The mythical Phoenix Project, the boondoggle to
end all boondoggles. Margaret's Folly. Natch could
practically hear his audience's frantic Confidential-
Whisper conversations, their frenzied queries to the
Data Sea.

"The Phoenix Project?" continued the capitalman in disbelief. "Are you serious?"

"Dead serious," replied Natch.

"What *is* it?"

"You'll have to wait and see."

A sense of shock crusted over their fury at being lured out to India for such a ludicrous presentation. Merri was surprised to see that Natch had been correct about her ties to Creed Objectivv; the pin on her breast pocket might have been the only thing preventing the capitalmen from vanishing in disgust. But even that would only keep the outrage from boiling over for so long. The capitalmen began hurling questions at him in rapid-fire succession, which Natch answered brusquely and without hesitation.

"What *can* you tell us?"

"I can tell you that if you invest in me, you'll make more money than you've ever dreamed of."

"How much?"

"The sky's the limit."

"What is this Phoenix Project anyway? Is it a bio/logic program? Something you're going to launch on the Data Sea next week?"

"The Phoenix Project is a bio/logic program, but it's much more than just a bio/logic program. No launch schedules have been decided on yet."

"Don't you have any specs you can show us? Technical diagrams? Projections? *Anything?*"

"No."

"How do we know we can trust you? How do we know you're not just making this all up?"

"If you don't trust me, don't invest."

By the time Natch wrapped up the discussion a scant fifteen minutes after it had begun, Merri's face had turned to stone. She asked no questions and did not react at all when her master said his good byes and cut his multi connection. Merri cut her own connection and walked out to the foyer of her apartment, expecting Natch to await her arrival there. But the apartment was empty.

She found him in his own flat in Shenandoah. Natch was already at the window fiddling with a series of bio/logic price graphs as if nothing had happened. He seemed unaware of Merri's presence until she cleared her throat two minutes later. "You should catch up on your work while you can," he said gruffly. "We've got another one of these in an hour and a half, and then a third late tonight."

The channel manager nervously ran her fingers through her milky hair. "Are you really planning to license a bio/logic program from Margaret Surina?"

"I'm definitely *planning* to," replied Natch. "I'd give sixty-forty odds right now that it'll actually happen."

"And do... do you really think any of those capitalmen are going to invest in you?"

"No."

Merri blanched. "No?"

The fiefcorp master turned to his apprentice with an impatient mien, like a hoverbird engineer trying to teach a child how to construct a paper airplane. "Listen, Merri—I don't expect any of *those* people to put up a single credit. I'm not going to get any money out of the people we talk to tonight either. That's not what we're doing."

"So..."

"So what *are* we doing? We're stirring the pot. We're creating noise. The people I invited to these fundraising meetings aren't the high rollers; they're the ones who like to gossip. By the end of the day, I guarantee you the people I really want to hear from will have heard the words *Natch*, *Margaret Surina*, and *Phoenix Project* in the same sentence. Listen, you can't just approach investors and ask them to put up money for this sort of thing. Anyone who's willing to take a risk like this is going to contact me privately and insist on complete secrecy. Not only that, but they have to be convinced that investing in the Phoenix Project is *their* idea."

Merri nodded politely though she understood nothing, and left Natch to his bio/logic price graphs.

Rumors about Natch's investor meeting quickly percolated through the ranks of the capitalmen. Most of their comments were laced with the standard pejoratives Natch had seen attached to his name since childhood: *cocky, arrogant, insane.* He didn't mind. People could insult him to their hearts' content, but now that he had the Primo's title under his belt, they could no longer dismiss him so easily.

The second and third investor groups were better prepared and had more penetrating questions, but Natch would not crack. He kept a cloud of mystery over the entire project; if anything, he became even vaguer with his answers. *What could I possibly reveal to these people anyway?* he thought. *I don't know much more than they do.* As for Merri, she seemed to grow more comfortable with her silent performance the longer the night wore on, now that she had convinced herself Natch was not actively deceiving anyone.

At seven o'clock that evening, word leaked on the Data Sea that Natch was scoping out investors for a new Surina technology that just might be the legendary Phoenix Project. Twenty minutes later, John Ridglee wrangled a terse *no comment* out of the Creed Surina spokesperson.

An admission or a denial from the Surinas would have been news. Refusal to comment was *big* news.

By ten o'clock Shenandoah time, the avalanche of messages had begun. It was mostly the same drivel that had tumbled Natch's way after hitting number one on Primo's a few weeks before. L-PRACG-sanctioned advertisements for financial software. Pleadings for donations to this or that cause. Servile requests from old business associates who had once griped about how Natch had ruined them. Greetings from long-lost hivemates whose names he had never cared to learn in the first place. Buried in the rubbish were a few legitimate queries from anonymous capitalmen, none of which led anywhere.

Horvil and Jara began shotgunning messages, ConfidentialWhispers, and multi requests to Natch by the dozens trying to figure out what was going on. Natch replied calmly that he would explain everything tomorrow night. Then he prived himself to all of their incoming communications and waited.

The Patel Brothers launched a handful of product upgrades just before midnight, further solidifying their number one position on Primo's. Pierre Loget's PulCorp made a surprising leap to second place, bumping Natch down to number three and Sentinel to number four.

And then, at 3:30 in the morning, as Natch was making yet another circuit around the balcony and glaring at the music that wafted up faintly from

Shenandoah's entertainment quarters, the message he had been waiting for arrived. Natch had not known what shape or form it would take, but he knew the instant he opened the message that he had found his investor.

Time is luxury. Action is currency.
—Kordez Thassel

You are cordially invited to breakfast with the bodhisattva of Creed Thassel today, the 25th of November, at 7:45 a.m. Omaha time, in the resplendent Kordez Thassel Complex in the northern reaches of the Twin Cities Megalopolis to discuss mutually beneficial business opportunities.

Natch traced the message signature to a standard administrative account at Creed Thassel. He barely even paused before replying in the affirmative.

Natch lobbed an InfoGather request onto the Data Sea while flipping through his wardrobe for an appropriate suit, then had the results read aloud to him while he dressed.

The creed had been founded almost a hundred years ago by Kordez Thassel, a libertarian philosopher and financier whose only qualification to lead a popular movement was that he had failed at everything else. Somehow, his teachings about the virtues of selfishness had earned him a following in the new breed of fiefcorp power brokers. Then he disappeared from view and left public relations in the hands of anonymous creed spin doctors. For years, Creed Thassel worked diligently to protect its mysteries, going so far as to swear its devotees to secrecy and refusing all but the most cursory participation in the Creeds Coalition. Whispers spoke of blood rites, oaths of fealty, and a mythical master program built by renegade coders.

And then the young drudge Sen Sivv Sor published the exposé that made his reputation. Sor's undercover reporting revealed that the blood rites were nothing but parlor tricks, the oaths of fealty were mere confidence schemes, and the mythical master program did not exist. Thasselian membership dwindled, but the core devotees remained. Soon enough, everyone forgot about the scandal, and Creed Thassel abandoned its hokey mystic aura for a more prosaic philosophy of individualism. Membership rolls remained secret, but few cared to pry anymore.

A creed of fools, thought Natch as he walked the early-morning streets of Shenandoah, bound for the hoverbird terminals. *But fools who have no love for Creed Surina or the Council.* Vigal's words from the previous day rang in his ears: *I fear that Margaret has picked you for this enterprise because she thinks she can manipulate you.* Natch's blood curdled at the thought of being someone's pawn, and he felt like throttling his guardian for even suggesting it. Nevertheless, he knew it couldn't hurt to have a third party on his side.

The Thasselians' invitation arrived too late for Natch to take the tube, his preferred mode of travel. So instead, he hopped aboard one of the hundreds of hoverbirds that ferried passengers across the continent every hour. His flight from Shenandoah to the Twin Cities was smooth and without incident.

Natch found the Kordez Thassel Complex to be one of the ugliest human constructions he had ever seen. A series of squat, functional buildings skulking among the lowlands, half hidden in the chill November mist. He followed a narrow bridge from the hoverbird terminal over the complex's surrounding moat and into the Thasselian headquarters. The inside was no better. Hallways stood at odd angles to one another amidst sloping ceilings and crooked doorways; Natch doubted there was a pair of perpendicular lines anywhere in the place. He knew very little about architecture, but he imagined it took a lot of money and patience to construct such deliberate lopsidedness.

Even at this early hour, hundreds of businesspeople rushed through the hallways with stiff, purposeful gaits. Two burly guards pointed Natch through the labyrinth of corridors and conference rooms to his appointed meeting spot. He found himself facing a nondescript door, the old-fashioned kind you needed to physically pull open. He hesitated for a moment and eyed the mahogany slab of door with suspicion. Natch searched his feelings, yet he could find no reason for his unease. He reached for the doorknob.

As soon as the brass tongue slipped free of its sheath, the knob erupted with a jolt of static electricity. Natch squealed in surprise and snatched his hand away. He quickly called up a grounding program to neutralize the charge, but the damage was done. The fingertips of his left hand would be sore for hours.

A hollow laugh echoed inside the room. "You're getting sloppy, Natch!" said a tired voice in a tone reminiscent of an aging diplomat or a patrician. "I could *never* catch you with that trick back in the old days. Horvil was always much easier to fool. But who says we don't learn from our mistakes?"

Natch shivered involuntarily at the sound of the voice that had been mocking his dreams for years. The voice that embodied his worst fears and deepest shames.

Brone.

(((19)))

He sat on a large thronelike chair in the center of a cavernous room. The room itself was a gigantic hollowed-out diamond of exceptional clarity and brilliance. On the table in front of his chair sat a Spartan breakfast of crackers and crusty bleu cheese.

More SeeNaRee, Natch moaned to himself. *Did I miss a trend? Is everyone conducting business in these gaudy fantasy worlds nowadays?*

Brone had changed significantly since Natch had last seen him, bundled in bloody rags in the back of that Falcon four-seater. His aura of youthful entitlement was gone. He had gained a considerable amount of weight, but did not carry it in the dignified manner of a Horvil or a Merri, and the handsome face that had once inspired sighs from female hivemates was mangled beyond repair. Natch traced a long scar from Brone's chin to his forehead, passing straight through the center of his right eye. The eye gleamed with the sickly emerald of a prosthesis.

"You like my face, I take it?" said Brone, his voice devoid of emotion. "I'll bet you didn't even know the bear did that to me. He would have had the whole head for breakfast, but luckily I was able to satisfy him with a light snack." Brone held up his right arm, and Natch gasped in spite of himself. The flesh came to an abrupt end just below the elbow, where it merged with a pale synthetic hand and forearm.

"Oh, don't feel *too* sorry for me, Natch," he said, sneering at the look of discomfort on the fief-corp master's face. "These imitation limbs work fairly well. Look!" Brone painstakingly unclenched his prosthetic fingers and reached for the cheese slicer. The utensil did a clumsy dance in his hand but finally went clattering to the floor. By instinct, Natch reached down to pick it up, and fell flat on his face when his fingers passed straight through the metal. SeeNaRee. Brone let out a quiet snort and offered his old rival a hand up—the artificial hand. Natch gripped the slick, rubbery limb and pulled himself to his feet. Contrary to the act he had put on seconds ago, Brone actually seemed to be quite nimble with his prosthesis.

All at once, the purpose of Natch's visit rushed back to him: Margaret Surina, the Phoenix Project, investment capital. He needed to keep his focus. "I was invited to breakfast by the bodhisattva of Creed Thassel," said Natch between clenched teeth.

Brone paid Natch no mind; he seemed to be participating in an entirely different conversation. "I suppose you're asking yourself, *What about cosmetic surgery? Organ harvesting? Flesh-repairing OCHREs?*" He leaned back and brought the fingers of his hands together in front of his face, like a spider contemplating its next meal. The glint of reflected diamond was visible in his teeth. "Certainly science has progressed farther than this."

"I came to discuss—"

"Figaro Fi," said Brone in a commanding voice, cutting Natch off in midsentence. "You remember the fat little capitalman Figaro Fi? This whole cripple routine was Figaro's idea. *Show off your scars, my boy*, he said. *Play up your handicaps. Hold out your stump to gain their sympathy, then hold out your good hand to take their money.*" As he spoke, Brone hunched over in a cruelly effective parody of the little man. Long-repressed memories of the night before initiation came flooding back to Natch, and he nearly retched in disgust.

"Perhaps it was a despicable thing to do," continued Brone, "but it worked! Figaro brought me everywhere in those miserable years after the initiation. He would stand me up in these little auditoriums with a group of capitalmen, put a bio/logic programming bar in my hand, and cheer me on like a *monkey* while I performed tricks in MindSpace. Figaro's programming cripple, victim of the Shortest Initiation! Who could withhold money from such a *sad* and *noble* soul?

"And Figaro was right! How amazingly simple it is—all you have to do is admit that the world has defeated you, and the money will come pouring in. It's an intoxicating feeling. And if you make the right connections, if you stroke enough egos, if you convince enough of those shallow, soulless capitalmen that their *gifts* have *soothed your pain*—why, you win the game. The capitalmen begin throwing you private contracts. You can work outside the auspices of the Meme Cooperative, where you don't have to worry about the constraints of Dr. Plugen-patch. You can toss that Primo's bio/logic investment guide in the dungheap where it belongs!"

Brone began rubbing his chin in faraway con-templation, and Natch had to use every ounce of his willpower not to wrap his hands around Brone's throat and begin squeezing as hard as he could. He looked around for something to sit on, and found nothing but diamond outcroppings that were almost certainly illusions.

"I can see you're restless," said Brone, turning to Natch as if noticing him for the first time. He leaned back in the gargantuan chair and laid his arms on the throne, like a withered and haunted king. "You want to sit, you want to stand, you want to move, you want to stay still—it's been like this your whole life, hasn't it?

"Well, let me tell you, Natch, I know where you're heading. I've *been* there. There's a whole economy up in that rarefied air that the drudges know nothing about. And I made riches up there. Riches! You fantasize about living in a Lunar estate someday? I *own* one, Natch, and it's worth every bloody credit. Sunrises over the lip of Tycho while you watch and sip chai in a gravity-controlled dome... servants at your beck and call... pretty young gardeners pruning all those twisted moon plants. There's nothing like it.

"But the Lunar estate grows tiresome after a while. So do the sycophants and the bootlickers. It sounds like a cliché, but it's true. I bought myself the gaudiest estate I could, and the private hover-bird service, and the baubles and jewels and gadgets. And then I asked myself: *Now* what?

"So I went searching again.

"First, I went to the medical specialists. *Hack the body, and the mind will follow*—isn't that what Sheldon Surina said? But can you believe what a superstitious world we live in, Natch? The Autonomous Revolt was hundreds of years ago—and yet the Prime Committee *still* won't allow a simple tank-grown limb! *The only place for human flesh is on the human body*, they say." His voice rumbled up to a dangerous level, as if he were playing to the rafters in some imaginary amphitheater.

"So they gave me the next best thing." And then, as Natch looked on in horror, Brone unsnapped his fake arm and thrust it onto the table, where it landed on the bleu cheese with a sickening *thwup*. A circle of plastic prongs shone wetly on the end of Brone's stump, like octopus teeth. "Completely self-contained, no nerves or blood required: a miracle of engineering. You would be surprised to know how quickly one can tweak it to work in MindSpace like a bio/logic programming bar. And, of course, having an artificial limb gives one certain... *advantages*." When the fingers of the disembodied hand began twitching of their own accord, Natch leapt back and nearly sprawled on his face again. The fingers tore through the rind of the cheese and performed a gooey dance, spackling the floor with bits of white.

Natch felt sick. He recognized his own ruthless utilitarian tactics at work. What was it that old Kordez Thassel had said? *Do not let taboos and social restrictions stop you from gaining advantage over your enemy.* OCHREs rushed to defuse the acid in his stomach, and Natch would have supplemented their soothing effects with a bio/logic program if he thought it would help. "I—I came here today," he stuttered, "to—"

Brone completely ignored him. "So the replacement arm and the replacement eye were dead ends," he said with a shrug. "I knew as soon as they were installed that I had been using my handicap as an *escape*. It was an easy way to distract me from what I *really* wanted to do, from the one thing that would make me happy.

"And that was killing *you*."

Natch edged back, flailing his arm behind him in search of the door. He realized with dismay that it had vanished. He didn't want to know anymore why Brone had invited him here this morning, or what his interest in the Phoenix Project was; Natch just wanted *out*. But the diamond walls completely surrounded him now. He was trapped.

Brone leaned back in his throne and regarded Natch with sepulchral eyes, like someone watching from a separate plane of existence. The disembodied forearm began tapping out a mad rhythm on the cheese plate. "I spent months planning the whole scenario. I followed you around, Natch, did you know that? I scouted out a thousand locations for the perfect ambush. Should I follow you to Cisco and shoot you down in the forest? Or plug you full of black code on a side street in London? Or just push you off your own balcony in Shenandoah and be done with it?"

Natch rubbed his back against the diamond wall and did not breathe. The door had to be there *somewhere*... if he could just pierce the veil of this confounded SeeNaRee...

"But don't worry, Natch," said Brone, his voice one big sneer. "You're not in any danger here today." He spread his hand and stump wide in a conciliatory gesture. His smile was the smile of a ghoul. "You see, I have found religion."

The fiefcorp master stared at his old enemy, not comprehending. "The bodhisattva of Creed Thassel," Natch croaked under his breath. "Where is he? What did you do with him?"

Brone gave a long and uncomfortable pause, like a robot in suspended animation. "I *am* the bodhisattva of Creed Thassel," he said at last.

It took a minute for the words to penetrate Natch's defenses. He turned them around in his head, breaking them down into small digestible pieces to try and make sense of them. *Brone* the head of the Thasselians?

Before he could get a grip on the situation, the SeeNaRee changed.

Suddenly, they were hurtling through black space in a small starcraft not much bigger than the Falcon that had transported them home from initiation all those years ago. Rocks and chunks of ice whizzed by at breakneck speed. Natch looked out the starboard window just in time to see an asteroid the size of a tube train hurtle past them, missing the ship by half a meter.

"I could turn you in to the Prime Committee," Natch gasped. "You can't hide exits like that. It's against the law. And you can't just switch environments on the fly without giving me fair warning."

Brone sat back in his padded captain's chair, toying idly with the steering panel that rose before him from the floor like a metallic mushroom. He did not react at all to the first asteroid collision, which made the rickety craft shudder as if it were a few bolts away from completely collapsing. "How ironic," Brone croaked. "*Natch* threatening to turn me over to the law? Here at Creed Thassel, we take a more laissez-faire approach to laws. As old Kordez used to say, *Rules are for those who follow rules.*"

"But—" The rusted hull of a dead spaceship slammed into the side of their craft, sending Natch sprawling onto the floor once again with his teeth chattering. He bit the inside of his cheek with an audible *chomp*. Brone remained comfortably seated, and Natch noted that the disembodied arm sat motionless on the table. *Yet another infraction*, thought the fiefcorp master bitterly. *Inconsistent laws of physics.*

"Creed Thassel was really in abysmal shape when I found it," continued Brone, studying the fingernails of his good hand intently. "You'd be surprised how many people think Creed Thassel ceased to exist twenty years ago. There was that exposé by Sen Sivv Sor. Financial scandals. A real *paucity* of leadership. The imbeciles running the organization were even on the brink of losing control of the Kordez Thassel Complex. So when I got religion, Natch, I got it for a real bargain-basement price. They needed my money. They needed my vision and my initiative."

Cosmic debris continued to slam into the ship, leaving Natch huddled on the floor with his hands over his head. OCHREs had already stanched the bleeding in his mouth, but he couldn't help probing the scar with his tongue. He knew he cut quite a ridiculous figure to his old rival, but survival was all he cared about at this point.

"Forgive me," sighed the bodhisattva, his voice devoid of supplication. "I suppose I've gotten carried away." He waved his hand in the air—the hand of flesh and bone—and the cluttered field of debris outside the ship vanished. The virtual gravity stabilized. "So let us discuss business, you and I."

Natch warily got to his feet and brushed himself off. It seemed strange that an hour ago, the only thing occupying his mind was his dire need for capital. Now suddenly, he was treading water in a sea of old landmines. "Do I have any choice?" he muttered.

"Game playing!" shouted Brone abruptly, his eyes ablaze. He arose from the chair and stood at the port window, his stump resting wearily against the glass. "All these games we've played throughout the years, you and I. And this whole setup—the invitation, the SeeNaRee, throwing the arm on the table—just another move in the game. A way to put you off guard. But believe it or not, after all the hurt and pain and suffering you have caused me, Natch, I am capable of forgiving you."

Natch gritted his teeth. *Forgiving me for what?* he thought.

"Soon, we will all be moving beyond games," continued Brone. "All of us... you, me, the drudges, Horvil, the idiots at the Defense and Wellness Council, all those narrow-minded bean counters at Primo's. Soon, it will make no difference who the winners and losers are."

"I have no idea what you're talking about."

"I'm talking about Margaret Surina, of course. I'm talking about 'the Phoenix Project.'" Natch could practically hear the belittling quotation marks.

"I don't know—"

"Oh, please!" snapped the bodhisattva in a sudden fit of pique. "Don't waste your breath. The Phoenix Project is the whole reason you held those little fundraising charades of yours, isn't it? It's the whole reason you're here. But even if you hadn't held those meetings, Natch, I would have come looking for you. I know all about your visit to Andra Pradesh. Thasselian agents were watching when you walked in and out of those gates at the Surina compound, and they attended your little performances yesterday too. That's the advantage of having an organization with a secret membership.

"Let me be forthcoming. You're a step behind in this game, Natch, just as you've always been a step behind me in everything else. The struggle for the Phoenix Project was well under way before you butted your nose into it. I have no problem with your pathetic attempts to grab a little portion of the pot, but don't think you can walk away with the whole thing. There are too many people who know too much."

Natch gave a haughty sniff in Brone's direction. "And what do you know that I don't?"

"I know what you have been trying to find out—I know what this technology of Margaret's is." Natch could practically feel Brone's grim smile, even though he was facing the other direction. "Let me tell you, it is everything you suspect it is, and more. Perhaps even more than Margaret imagines."

The fiefcorp master hesitated and felt Serr Vigal's suspicions rushing in to fill the hole in the pit of his stomach. Could Brone be telling the truth? The Thasselians continued to pledge their devotees in secret, after all, and there were no Creeds Coalition bylaws preventing people from pledging to more than one creed. "So what are you wasting time with me for?" said Natch with affected nonchalance. "If you're so far ahead of me, go talk to Margaret yourself."

"I have tried, many times. The Surina woman does not listen."

"Perhaps she's put off by your winning way with people."

Natch's wisecrack did not succeed in penetrating Brone, now standing at the window rubbing his chin with his handless stump. Natch couldn't help but shiver. "Obviously, you cannot see the forest for the trees, Natch. I wish I could say this surprises me, but it does not. So let me tell you the truth of the situation that has so far eluded you." Brone spread the fingers of his good hand out against the window, as if straining to reach something beyond the black void. "I have seen the future, Natch. And the future is you and I, in business together, selling the Phoenix Project."

The thought made Natch nauseous. "Bullshit."

"I understand your dilemma, Natch," said Brone, his voice barely a whisper now. "You want to walk out the door right now and never see me again." He nodded towards the rear of the space-craft, where a plain metal door suddenly materialized out of nowhere. "But Margaret Surina has dangled the carrot just beyond your reach, like everything has always been just beyond your reach. You *need* my help. Nobody is buying your fundraising pitch, and you're running out of time. You need the money that I can provide—money that's just sitting in the coffers of Creed Thassel waiting for a worthwhile investment. I can transfer the credits to your Vault account before the hour is up."

The entrepreneur snorted. "And what do you get in return?"

"Nothing at all. This is simply a cash loan. Repayment over five years with Vault standard interest rates."

Natch stared uncomfortably at the plastic teeth of Brone's stump. He could feel the wheels of his mind spinning and spinning but gaining no traction. "Why would you do that?"

"Because," replied Brone with maddening calm, "you need money and I need a foot in the door. If I attached strings to the offer, you wouldn't take it."

"Let me see the contract," Natch said with a grunt.

Brone stepped away from the fiefcorp master's side and gave a sweeping bow towards the window. The twinkling stars of space were replaced with the dull black-and-white text of a legal document. Natch scanned the length of the contract in less than a minute, then read it over twice more to make sure he wasn't missing anything. The contract was conspicuously short and completely free of legal double-talk or hidden provisos. Try as he might, Natch couldn't think of any possible way Brone could trip him up with such an agreement.

"I don't get it," Natch rasped.

"That is because you have a limited intellect," said Brone. "This is an act of *trust*, Natch. It is a concept beyond your understanding."

The fiefcorp master looked back and forth between his wraithlike nemesis, the grubby hand on the table, and the blocky letters on the viewscreen. *If I had the slightest doubt you could find the money to do this*, Margaret had said, *you wouldn't be here.* He checked his internal calendar and looked once more at the menacingly small block of days remaining until Margaret's planned unveiling of the Phoenix Project.

Suddenly, with his mind's eye, he saw a raging bear in the wilderness. A battered and bleeding boy lying in the backseat of a Falcon hoverbird. *An act of trust?*

Natch quelled the inner voice screaming dire words of doom. He blocked out the chortling of Figaro Fi and Captain Bolbund and the Patel Brothers that echoed through his head. Then he reached out with his mind and affirmed the contract.

Brone smiled. His detached hand dragged itself painstakingly to the edge of the table and then threw itself to the ground, where it wriggled like a fish out of water.

(((20)))

Horvil studied the viewscreen with as much concentration as he gave his bio/logic programs. "If you ask me—"

"Which I'm *not*," muttered Jara.

"If you ask me, daisies would work much better in here than violets." The engineer put his nose up to the viewscreen as if trying to give individual attention to every pixel. Then, in feng shui mode, he glanced around Jara's apartment with eyes narrowed. "A garden of violets is going to stick out in here like a sore thumb," said Horvil. "But daisies, they're so... light and... airy. They'd look terrific with this blank wall effect you have going on here." He made an expansive gesture at the unadorned white plaster running the length and breadth of the room.

Jara snorted loudly. Was this clod actually being *serious* for once, or was he just being sarcastic? She couldn't tell which option was worse. The fact that Horvil had absolutely no taste or personal style whatsoever only compounded the problem. *Then again,* Jara thought bitterly, *why would you need to have fashion sense if you've got enough money to buy it instead?* She remembered the rare ceramic sculpture Horvil had hanging on *his* wall with a stray glob of peanut butter encrusted on its bottom edge, and she cringed.

The analyst forced herself to stop this dreadful internal monologue. She couldn't blame Horvil for *her* failure to carve a home out of this tiny apartment. She could only blame herself. And that was why Jara had decided she was going to order a new garden and wall hangings today. Who cared if she could ill afford them with her meager savings. She had to draw the line somewhere. "I'm going with violets," she said between tense grinding teeth, and gave the viewscreen a silent command.

In the blink of an eye, the living room wall shifted back a meter to make room for a row of holographic violets that slid up from the floor. Horvil yelped and quickly scooted out of the way. As Jara searched for a suitable layout, he took a seat at the kitchen table and watched the shifting kaleidoscopic patterns on the floor. "Maybe you could try layout fifty-seven, with a few daisies sprinkled in to match th—"

"Horvil, *please.*"

He shut up. Jara settled on a slight arc that spanned the length of the room, and confirmed the order. *Delivery tomorrow at 3:25p.m.,* the system told her. Somewhere on the Data Sea, computational agents for the tenement building cut a thick slice out of Jara's Vault account.

This was all a diversion anyway, a way to pass the time until they could squeeze some information from Natch about what was going on. He had promised to explain everything in a fiefcorp meeting at seven o'clock. But by the time eight-thirty rolled around with no sign of Natch, the three apprentices decided their fiefcorp master wasn't coming. The same thing had been going on for a week. Horvil tried to get in touch with Serr Vigal, but the neural programmer had predictably prived himself to incoming communication, probably off fundraising. So Horvil and Jara spent the next few hours in Jara's apartment listening to Merri explain what little she knew about the Phoenix Project. The three tossed improbable theories back and forth, and got nowhere. Eventually, Merri decided to cut her connection so she could spend some time tending to her companion Bonneth, who was bedridden with another one of her crippling fevers.

Jara was ready to kick Horvil out and get some sleep when she felt an incoming multi request.

Natch appeared in the room, looking bothered and beautiful as always. He was already pacing the length of the room before he had completely emerged from the haze of multivoid. "Horv, I'm going to need you to interview some new engineers and programmers," he said, as if they had been discussing the topic for hours.

"Are we expanding?" asked Horvil.

"What does it *look* like?"

Horvil shot a glib look at Jara. "How many do we need?"

"I don't know," replied Natch without missing a beat. "Two. Five. Ten if they're stupid."

The engineer stood with arms akimbo and sucked in his stomach as if girding for battle. "I hear and obey, brave commander," he said, and vanished.

Natch swiveled on the ball of his left foot and stopped directly in front of Jara. The analyst felt the familiar hollow sensation in the pit of her stomach as the entrepreneur locked eyes with her. *Sapphires*, she thought. "And you," said Natch in a feathery voice. "Why don't you tag along with Merri for the next couple days. She's meeting with Robby Robby tomorrow to get him up to speed on how we do things around here."

Jara gulped. "Who's Robby Robby?"

"Our new channeling partner. He's a bit of a character, but he's got a staff that could sell you the clothes on your back while you're still wearing them."

The analyst nodded. Her own clothes seemed uncomfortably tight and constricting at the moment. "All right, I'll do that." Then, seeing that Natch was about to cut his multi connection, asked, "So what do you think—violets or daisies?" She tilted her head towards the holographic arch that the fiefcorp master had plowed straight through several times now.

Natch turned and studied the flower arrangement for a moment. "I'd say daisies," he announced, and then severed his multi projection without another word.

Jara cancelled the violets and ordered daisies instead.

Natch's thought processes had always been a mystery to Jara, but she soon began to wonder if he was losing his grip on reality. That night, he went on a titanic shopping spree. Natch bought everyone in the fiefcorp a new workbench with expanded MindSpace capabilities and the fanciest set of bio/logic programming bars on the market. He let Horvil loose on the Data Sea to pick out the best code optimization routines and analysis algorithms. He set up a permanent account at the Surina Enterprise Facility so he could commandeer an office or a conference room at a moment's notice.

Where he got the money for all this, nobody knew. Jara was intimately familiar with the fiefcorp's Vault accounts, and she knew they couldn't withstand this kind of pummeling. True, the jump to number one on Primo's had provided them a good financial cushion. But Natch's reckless spending would soon put them into bankruptcy.

Somehow this prospect cheered Jara up.

So instead of protesting, Jara did as she was told. Over the next few days, she accompanied Merri to several meetings with the channeler Robby Robby. If anything, the man was even more insipid than Natch's description. He dressed in whatever ludicrous fashion the high-society brats were wearing at the moment—this week it was kimono pants and open-collared silk shirts—and went through programmable accents like other people went through socks. The cost of these silly peccadilloes went on the tab of the Natch Personal Programming Fiefcorp, of course.

Jara soon discovered what made Robby Robby so valuable, however: he was completely unperturbed by the idea of selling a mystery product. "What do you think my channelers do every day?" he said, walking them through a room of baby-faced salespeople holding ConfidentialWhisper conversations from their desks. There were perhaps twenty in all, each impeccably dressed and relentlessly cheerful. "Selling isn't about the product you're *offering*, Lady Merri. It's about what the customer *wants*." Every time Robby Robby called her *Lady Merri*, Jara wanted to give him a swift kick in the knees. But even though she was a Creed Objectivv devotee, Merri seemed to get along with the slick salesman just fine.

Meanwhile, Horvil worked feverishly through the weekend to find capable engineering candidates who would fit Natch's high standards. He managed to round up a dozen applicants. All had the credentials to work in the top fiefcorps, and all were eager to sign on, which was no small accomplishment in such a tight labor market. But Natch found fault with every one of them. He even managed to send a top-flight engineer from the Deuteron Fiefcorp fleeing an interview in tears.

Finally, an exasperated Horvil brought in his nineteen-year-old cousin Benyamin for an interview. Horvil meant it as something of a joke. Ben's only real-world experience was an apprenticeship managing a floor of assembly-line coders, and he was the son of Horvil's dreaded Aunt Berilla to boot. But to everyone's surprise, Natch made the boy an apprenticeship offer on the spot. Benyamin readily accepted.

"I don't get it," Jara told Horvil after he had relayed the story to her. "No offense, Horv, but Natch has been turning away *everyone*. How did Benyamin convince that bastard to hire a nineteen-year-old kid with no experience?"

Horvil shrugged. "I dunno."

"So how many hours was Natch grilling him?"

"Less than one. Ben says that Natch listened to his pitch without saying a word, and then asked him just one question. *You're not going to go crying to your mother the first time I keep you up three days in a row, are you?*"

The outside world did not come to a standstill while the fiefcorp beefed up its operations. In the midst of all the commotion, Pierre Loget released a bevy of upgrades on the Data Sea that sent his Pul-Corp rocketing to the top of Primo's. Billy Sterno and Lucas Sentinel quickly followed suit. For a couple of hours, the Patel Brothers sank as low as number four before they managed to pump a few more bio/logic programs into the system and reclaim the top spot.

Natch mysteriously shrugged the whole thing off and seemed content to sit in fourth place for the time being. He spent all his time reading the latest news about the Prime Committee and the Defense and Wellness Council. Jara would multi over to his apartment to find him meditating to the libertarian ravings of politician Khann Frejohr. The craggy face of High Executive Borda stared back at her from every window. When the story broke about a battalion of Council officers bivouacking in China, Natch was glued to a map of the Orient for hours.

Jara felt like a spectator in a game she didn't understand, played by titans on a board she could not see. At least the days were passing quickly now, bringing the elusive end of her apprenticeship contract closer all the time.

On Monday morning, Jara awoke and slipped into her comfortable routine like an old shirt. She had barely fired up Doze-B-Gone 91c when she was assaulted by a screaming headline from Sen Sivv Sor:

THE PHOENIX PROJECT UNVEILED
Is This the Long-Awaited New Surina Technology, or Just a Publicity Stunt?

John Ridglee's morning commentary quickly morphed to keep pace, sending his fawning profile of Pierre Loget to an out-of-the-way side column. Before long, the two drudges were engaged in a frenzied competition to see who could quote more unnamed industry sources offering the wildest speculation about the Phoenix Project.

Within an hour, the entire world had shifted its focus to the upcoming four hundredth birthday celebration of Sheldon Surina. Curious onlookers from Earth to Luna to the farthest orbital colonies began tracking the comings and goings at the Surina compound, hoping to find clues to what Margaret had been up to for the past twenty years. Even those with little interest in bio/logics began streaming into Andra Pradesh to soak up the electric vibe in the air.

Horvil and Jara camped on opposite sofas in the engineer's apartment and watched Surina mania overtake the Data Sea. L-PRACG politicians stood up in open sessions to spout platitudes about the impact of another breakthrough Surina technology. One after another, the creeds released statements spelling out their positions on scientific innovation. The Islanders raised their obligatory protest about technology being thrust upon them against their will; the orbital colonies raised *their* obligatory protest about technology not reaching them quickly enough. The bio/logics markets careened up and down as investors decided the end was near or the best was yet to come. Even the revered bodhisattva of Creed Objectivv emerged from seclusion to make some inscrutable pronouncement about the state of universal truth in the wake of the Surinas' accomplishments.

"I don't get it," Jara said, throwing her hands up in confusion.

"You've been saying that a lot lately."

"Yes, but *think* about it for a minute, Horv. People have been talking about this stupid Phoenix Project for years now. Natch was just throwing around rumors about it a few days ago. Why is everybody so interested *now?* What's changed?"

Horvil bounced his arm off a stack of dirty laundry on the couch, trampoline-like. "It's called public relations. The Surinas are masters at it."

"You think all this hubbub comes from a few leaks to the drudges?"

"That's exactly what I think."

"But—"

"Come on, Jara. Don't you remember what happened a month ago? We've seen firsthand how this shit spreads."

The analyst twirled a few stray locks of curly hair, trying to mask her sudden embarrassment. Horvil was right. They had personal experience with the capriciousness of the public imagination, and with the ways a few, choice power brokers could channel the energies of sixty billion people to their cause.

Horvil fixed her with a narrow-eyed stare. "What's wrong?" he said.

"If what Merri says about us licensing the Phoenix Project is true, then all this publicity is going to be really good for business."

"But?"

"But once Natch gets in the spotlight, who's to say someone's not going to hijack all this attention and turn it against him?"

Serr Vigal settled back into his chaise longue, mumbling something about how creaky his joints got in erratic gravity and how glad he was to be back from his latest visit to Patronell for memecorp funding. But Natch was distracted, not listening. "Tomorrow will be a momentous day," said the neural programmer, in an effort to catch his protégé's attention.

"Tomorrow, I finally get to find out what this Phoenix Project *is*," said Natch. "It had better be worth all the trouble."

"Margaret still won't tell you?"

"No. I haven't heard a word from her in days. She's totally prived herself to the world. I can't even get her to sit down with me to iron out the details of this contract addendum." Natch shook his head glumly. "I just hope Len Borda gives her the chance to explain herself."

"Why, has he been making more threats?"

The entrepreneur swiveled around and gave his mentor a puzzled expression. "Threats? Haven't you been paying attention to the news? Borda's got several legions of Council troops heading for Andra Pradesh right now. That's not a threat. It's a bloody declaration of war."

(((2 1)))

A cloud of hoverbirds darkened the sky over Andra Pradesh late Tuesday afternoon. The troops disembarked in the fields west of the city instead of at the commercial hoverbird facility, and before long an army of white was marching towards the Surina compound. Several thousand Defense and Wellness Council officers moved with perfect synchronization through the streets of Andra Pradesh. A few curious vendors hung around to gawk, but most quickly packed up their wares and fled before the advancing army. The soldiers in white trudged on. There would be no looting on High Executive Borda's watch.

The Surina security forces stood their ground at the base of the mountain, looking scared, outgunned, and hopelessly outnumbered. The chief of security positioned himself directly in front of the compound gates, trying to present a model of dignity to the green-and-blue troops behind him. The Council had not made such a display of force in several years, at least not in a connectible city. One would have to look back to the Melbourne riots during the Economic Plunge to find an incident of actual large-scale combat.

The Defense and Wellness Council troops reached the base of the mountain and came to a halt. Their ranks were neatly bisected by the shadow of the Revelation Spire. *Is there any force in the solar system capable of opposing them?* the security chief asked himself.

The legion's commanding officer stepped out from her formation and strode calmly up to the chief of Surina security. The chief took stock of the woman's white robe and yellow star, the smock she wore over her shoulders as a mark of office, the gray boots that seemed impervious to the monsoon season's mud. Holstered at her right side was a two-handed dartgun. The Surina security chief wondered what bio/logic code sat on the tips of those darts, waiting for a fresh bloodstream to infiltrate.

The chief's own darts were programmed to kill. With Margaret Surina's explicit authorization.

"Towards Perfection," announced the Defense and Wellness Council officer as she flashed a quick hologram of her public profile. *Commander Tanis*, it read, *242nd Brigade*. Volunteering directory profiles was one of the few meaningless gestures Borda had made to public relations over the years. "I have been ordered by High Executive Len Borda to secure the Surina compound and the city of Andra Pradesh." Her tone of voice indicated that the occupation was a foregone conclusion.

The security chief stayed put. "Please convey our thanks to the high executive, but Her Eminence the bodhisattva of Creed Surina needs no additional protection."

"Nevertheless," replied Tanis icily, "the Council has been charged by the Creeds Coalition to protect its interests here, and protect them we will."

This was a new development. The Surina official scratched his bald pate in puzzlement. "You're here to protect the *Creeds Coalition's* interests? From what? We *are* a creed."

Commander Tanis did not hesitate a heartbeat. "Large public gatherings bring a high risk of damage and destruction." Tanis held out her hand, palm up, and displayed a holographic message in the air. "Bodhisattvas of several major creeds have asked the high executive to protect the common cultural heritage of the creeds here at the Surina compound." The security chief examined the letter, confirmed that it stated precisely what the Council woman had said, and noted dejectedly that it did indeed bear an authentic signature from the secretary of the Creeds Coalition. But he nearly erupted with laughter when he saw what "common cultural heritage" Borda presumed to be protecting.

A representation of Isaac Newton, on permanent loan from Creed Élan... A bronzed effigy of Tobi Jae Witt, owned jointly by Creeds Bushido and Dao... A sculpture of Albert Einstein that Creed Conscientious had lent to the Surinas while their new administrative facility was under construction.

The scientist statues in the Surina Center for Historic Appreciation.

This couldn't really be happening, could it? Len Borda couldn't be so brazen as to march into the Surina compound with such a minuscule fig leaf of an excuse, could he? The security chief gazed past Tanis at the row upon row of motionless Council officers, and saw not a single smile or good-natured smirk. *Politics*, thought the security chief bitterly. *How many times have I complained to Margaret that she isn't keeping up good relations with the other creeds? And what did the Council offer those other bodhisattvas to make them roll over so easily?*

The security chief cast a sidelong glance at the inadequate forces under his command. The teeth of the green-and-blue soldier beside him were chattering uncontrollably.

"Stand down," said the commander of the Surina security forces with a sigh.

Tanis nodded and signaled her officers to enter the gates. The security chief watched gloomily as the white armada sailed through the gates and up the path towards the courtyard. None of them, he noticed, were headed for the Center for Historic Appreciation.

Natch thought he was still enveloped in the haze of multivoid when his field of vision turned white. Then he realized that his transmission to Andra Pradesh had gone through after all, and the white glare was the sun's reflection off a Council officer's steely dartgun.

The main courtyard was crawling with figures in white robes where Natch had expected blue and green. The few Surina employees in view were milling about aimlessly, trying to maintain the façade that they were still in charge. Yet the Council troops showed no sign of interfering. Their only agenda at this point, it appeared, was to stand with dart-rifles drawn and act menacing. If they intended to stop people from watching Margaret's presentation, they could do little from the courtyard; even the thickest Council thug had to know that standard crowd control procedures for an event like this would confine all multi projections to inside the auditorium.

Natch scooted quickly along the fence, hoping to make it unnoticed to the Center for Historic Appreciation. But he was not destined for such luck. Two officers immediately zeroed in and corralled him into a corner. As they scrutinized him, Natch waited for the officers to say something—didn't the Council troops in the dramas always say *your identification, please* or *state your name and business?*—but they kept eerily silent. He supposed they could gather all the information they needed by feeding his image through the jaws of their vast intelligence databases. Speech was superfluous.

"*There* you are," growled a voice. "Leave this one alone. He's with me."

Two arms brusquely made a path between the Council officers, into which stepped Margaret's mysterious Islander. His scruffy tunic and wild ponytail stood out like a scar in a courtyard full of crisp white uniforms. Natch didn't know whether to feel scared or comforted when the man put an arm across Natch's chest, like a parent claiming a wayward child.

The larger of the two Council officers eyed the Islander's copper collar with disdain. "So *this* is Margaret's Islander," he said, elbowing his cohort in the side. "Remember the one with the ponytail that came at us down in Manila? Looked just like this one."

His fellow officer let out a malicious chuckle. "I remember," she said. "Shot him full of darts. Bastard just kept coming."

"Finally had to crack his skull, right?"

The Islander maintained his composure and did not take the bait. "I'll bet you found a stack of Council officers' corpses lying there when you finally took him down, too."

"Better watch your manners, *unconnectible*," sneered the Council man, clearly irritated at the Islander's demeanor. "You're not in the Pacific anymore. Without *this*, we could have you begging for mercy in two minutes." Then he fearlessly reached one hand up and flicked his finger against the collar.

Before the *ping* of the vibrating metal had faded away, the Islander was in motion.

Natch had never seen anyone move so fast. One second, the Islander was standing at rest; the next, he had zipped around and placed the offending officer in a chokehold. The second guard reached for her dartgun in a panic, but it was too late. The Islander had already lifted her comrade's weapon from its sheath and aimed it squarely at her forehead. "Yes," he hissed savagely, "but which one of you is going to take it away from me?"

Within seconds, officers all over the courtyard were scrambling towards them with weapons drawn. Natch had never actually faced the barrel of a Defense and Wellness Council dartgun before; now he found himself facing at least thirty of them. The fact that he was present only as a multi projection was slight comfort. It became less comforting still when Natch realized that several of the dartguns pointed at him were actually multi disruptors in the group. If the libertarian drudges were to be believed, Council disruptors were just as capable of passing black code as dartguns.

The Islander shook off the tension with a dismissive snort. He released the officer from the crook of his arm and shoved him roughly towards his companions, tossing the dartgun on the ground as an afterthought. Then he flipped his ponytail over one shoulder and parted another path in the crowd as if nothing had happened. "Well?" he called to Natch. "Are you coming or not?" The entrepreneur forced his knocking knees to follow. Scores of Council eyeballs watched in silence as the two walked briskly through the courtyard and into the Center for Historic Appreciation. Natch let out a loud breath of relief as soon as the doors closed behind them.

The atrium was empty of visitors, except for two Council guards standing idly against the wall discussing baseball. Neither gave Natch or the Islander so much as a glance as they threaded their way between the scientist statues and headed down one of the corridors.

"Bloody tracking devices," muttered the Islander. "Do they think we actually *want* to wear these fucking things?" He reached up with one hand and tugged at his collar as if about to fling it boomerang-style down the hallway. Natch noticed for the first time that the collar was not actually suspended in air, but balanced on the man's neck over a fine latticework of metallic thread. The contraption looked hideously uncomfortable.

"Did you say that thing is a tracking device?" asked Natch, struggling to keep up with the Islander's giant strides.

"Of *course* it's a tracking device. Why else would they make them so fucking conspicuous? You can see an Islander with a collar from a kilometer away. Keeps us segregated."

Natch was usually not interested in cross-border politics. But he had to keep this strange man talking, if only so he might figure out his relation to Margaret and the Phoenix Project. "But you need those outside the Islands," he said. "How else you going to survive here without OCHREs?"

Halfway up a flight of stairs, the Islander stopped dead in his tracks. "You've got a lot to learn about your governments." He reached into his pocket with a scowl and dug out a small disc the size of an ancient coin. "See this little device? You can pin it to your collar, or wear it on a string around your neck. Made from spare parts, and you can see multi projections with it, interact with bio/logic code. Explain *that* to me."

Natch eyed the circle with embarrassment. "So why aren't you wearing that thing instead?"

Margaret's Islander gazed at Natch with an unspoken accusation of gullibility hovering just behind his eyes. "Because wearing these collars is *the law* if you're an Islander," he sneered. "And if you don't obey *the law*, you get visits from the Defense and Wellness Council and the Prime Committee and fuck knows who else." Then he slipped the disc back into his tunic and kept climbing the stairs.

Natch trotted alongside the big man as they crossed a covered walkway over the courtyard and into the Surina Enterprise Facility. A hoverbird bearing the Council insignia zoomed across the skyline directly in front of them. "Where are we going?" said Natch. "That message I got this morning... Are you taking me to Margaret?"

"No. Margaret's locked herself in the residence, preparing for the speech. You'll see her afterwards—if there's anything left to see."

"So what's this 'performance' you need me to do? Or was that it down there in the courtyard?"

The Islander shook his head. He had led them to the end of a wide corridor and an imposing set of double doors. "The performance is in here," he said grimly. "Just be yourself. Stick by me and make sure everyone sees it. Speak if you have to, but don't say anything memorable." The doors slid open of their own accord, but not before the man thrust one hand forward and slammed it against the metal with a *bang*. "And one more thing you'll need to know: my name is Quell."

Beyond the doors was a large bowl-shaped meeting room. A lavish bouquet stood in the center of the room, underneath a revolving banner that flashed HAPPY 400TH BIRTHDAY, SHELDON SURINA over and over in ten-second intervals. About four or five dozen guests congregated in small clusters around the room, all of whom had turned their attention to the sudden and noisy arrival of Natch and Quell.

It's the whole bio/logics industry, Natch thought with a quickly stifled gasp.

If it wasn't quite the entire industry, the guest list for this little reception certainly encompassed its top tier.

Natch saw hated rivals and fierce competitors in every corner. Jara's old boss Lucas Sentinel was camped near the bouquet with a group of well-known channelers and capitalmen. A pasty man with a mop of black hair, Sentinel did not tower over his companions so much as sway awkwardly in their midst like a tree. The drudges Sen Sivv Sor and John Ridglee were holding court on opposite sides of the room. Libertarian rabble-rouser Khann Frejohr sipped chai alongside the shrewish programmer Bolliwar Tuban. Natch felt a hand clap him on his shoulder, and turned around to face Billy Sterno. "Nice entrance, pal!" chirped the fiefcorper before scuttling off, his Chinese eyes glinting with mischief.

I need a licensee who can generate enough ripples on the Data Sea to make the Council stay its hand until I unveil the technology, Margaret had said.

I guess that's what we're doing, thought Natch. *Generating ripples.*

Natch and Quell began a slow stroll around the periphery of the room. The fiefcorp master put on a haughty look and did his best to forestall any conversation. For the most part, it worked. The members of the bio/logics elite seemed content to stay in their balkanized clusters and throw scandalized looks at the fiefcorp master and the Islander from afar. After ten minutes of this, however, Natch started to get restless. Everyone in the room had noticed them already, and the crowd would soon be gathering in the auditorium to await Margaret's speech.

"Okay, have we made enough of a show?" he muttered in a low voice, unsure whether an Islander could respond to a ConfidentialWhisper.

"Not yet," replied Quell calmly. "I want to catch one of the stragglers."

Natch frowned. "Stragglers?" Then he heard a violent cough behind him, and turned to see the bulldog face of Frederic Patel.

Natch did not bother with formal greetings, because he knew he would receive none from Frederic. The short, barrel-chested programmer had not inherited the slick mannerisms and sharp fashion sense that made his older brother Petrucio so popular among the drudges. If they did not share the same olive complexion and lithe moustache, one would be hard-pressed to identify the two Patels as brothers. But even during the worst days of their vitriolic competition, Natch had to admit that Frederic was one of the few engineers in the business whose skills stood up to Horvil's.

"Well, if it isn't the thief," snarled Patel.

The fiefcorp master laughed scornfully. "Watch who you're calling a thief. Looks like you've stolen your number one slot back, for a little while at least."

"Primo's." Frederic gave a dismissive flip of the hand, leaving Natch to wonder what else he had stolen from the Patels recently. "A little while. What's *that* mean?"

"That means, sometimes history repeats itself."

Frederic made a whistling sound with his nose that, after a moment, Natch realized was laughter. He swept his gaze to the Islander, who stared back with an impenetrable glare. Natch suddenly remembered Quell's instructions to say as little as possible, but the big man no longer seemed to care. "You heard your boss's speech yet?" Patel said, addressing Quell.

"No," replied the Islander.

"We're not gonna be bored to death, are we?"

"The world might be a better place if you were," Quell said, deadpan.

Again the whistling sound. "So that's the game you two are playing, eh?" Patel rasped. "Well, fine with me. But now it's *our* move."

The level of conversation in the room had dipped noticeably since Frederic's approach. Lucas Sentinel had wandered close and kept taking discreet peeks at the confrontation like a nervous hyena. John Ridglee was not even trying to disguise his blatant attempts to read lips.

Natch was trying to decipher Frederic's comments and formulate a response when a loud neutral tone sounded throughout the room. The marquee displaying birthday wishes to the dead Sheldon Surina was now announcing the imminent arrival of his descendant Margaret onstage. Within seconds, industry mavens were cutting their multi connections to the party and preparing to reconnect inside the nearby auditorium.

Frederic Patel vanished without so much as a glance back in their direction. Natch breathed a sigh of relief, following Quell out the same doors they had entered through. The show was about to begin.

(((2 2)))

"I'm telling you, this can't go on forever. One of these days, the Data Sea is just going to collapse."

"They've been saying that for a century."

"But come on, look at how much more bandwidth we're using these days. Multi, the Jamm, the Sigh. Even quantum computing has its limits."

"One point three billion multi projections at Marcus Surina's funeral, and not a single glitch. That's all I have to say."

"Yeah, but—"

Jara stood and listened to the jabber of the couple beside her as she waited for Margaret Surina to take the stage. Personally, she sided with the doomsayer who feared the imminent collapse of the computational system. She looked around at the thirty-five thousand visible spectators filling the arena and tried to imagine the seraphic order of number needed to describe the bandwidth requirements for so many people.

But the vertigo did not end there. The Surina auditorium statistics told her there were actually

413 million multi projections here waiting for Margaret to reveal the mystery behind the Phoenix Project. Four hundred thirteen million people whose brains were trying to maintain the illusion that their bodies were inhabiting real Cartesian space, when that was clearly impossible.

The analyst summoned a calculator and wide-eyed her way through the math. Four hundred thirteen million people wedged into a space designed to fit thirty-five thousand real bodies. Which meant that right now almost *twelve thousand* people from every corner of the solar system believed they were standing in the *exact same spot* as Jara...

Then she noticed that the attendance had sky-rocketed another 150 million spectators. Jara shook her head violently. Human minds could not comprehend such vastness. Better to swallow the sweet lotus of multi and be done with it.

Especially when she had so many more urgent questions to contend with. Like where was the rest of the fiefcorp? What was this "Phoenix Project" that had so entranced the public's imagination and completely absorbed the world's richest woman for years? How did Natch fit into this whole puzzle? And how would this new technology affect her job?

Just then, a young woman in a green-and-blue Surina security uniform passed mere centimeters away from Jara's right side. The woman—no, the *girl*—had her dartgun drawn and was clearly petrified. *I'd be petrified too*, thought Jara, *if I had a few thousand Defense and Wellness Council troops on my heels.*

Which brought up the most perplexing question of all: What was the Council waiting for?

Moments later, Margaret Surina took the stage. Jara hadn't seen her arrive, so she couldn't say for sure whether Sheldon Surina's heir had multied onto the stage. Margaret had chosen a formless robe that draped across the floor like a tent and slowly changed colors from blue to green and back again. Her frosted black hair lay across her shoulders. She seemed completely calm, like the commander who had already greenlighted a battle plan and now waited for its outcome to slowly unfold.

And just as the bodhisattva opened her mouth to speak, a hundred doors slammed open at once, and the Council made its entrance.

With dartguns crossed over their chests and eyes fixed forward, they came marching into the auditorium single file, like zombies. The crowd parted anxiously to make way for the soldiers. Some cut their multi connections on the spot, but most quickly recognized that the officers were carrying few disruptors. No, whatever High Executive Borda's intentions were, sowing panic in the crowd was not one of them. The lead Council officers stopped meters away from the stage.

If Margaret feared an imminent death, she did not show it. She regarded the intruders with an icy stare that said, *Whatever you have planned for me, you're going to have to do it in front of 700 million people.* Jara did not know much about Margaret Surina aside from the standard drudgic platitudes and generalities, but at that moment she felt a great surge of admiration for the woman.

The Council troops stood at attention, their rifles before them, and did nothing.

A hush fell over the crowd as the bodhisattva began to speak.

"Once upon a time," said Margaret, "we believed in technology.

"Our ancestors were the original engineers. They discovered the laws that govern the universe and learned how to master them. They paved the Earth with rock and sent wheeled machines to rumble across it. They spread to the four corners of the Earth and, not satisfied, flew to the heavens. *Still* not satisfied, they flew to the stars.

"And somewhere along the way, they got lost.

"Somewhere between the first man to build stone tools and the first woman to create an artificial intelligence, our ancestors became separated from their innovations. They stopped seeing their creations as *extensions* of themselves, and started seeing them as *external* to themselves. Other. Distant. Remote.

"Science became an impersonal god, a grim idol beyond reproach or appeal.

"And once technology was no longer a part of them, it became an enemy to conquer.

"The god that had been embedded within them all became a force to be chained and made to do their bidding. Instead of seeking communion with the god, instead of striving to understand the kernel of truth that is within us all, they sacrificed their own skills to feed him. *Our machines will do more so we may do less*, they said.

"And so, in the apogee of their folly, our ancestors created the Autonomous Minds."

A rustle of disapproval from the audience. A hateful murmuring.

"The Autonomous Minds: eight machines committed to managing the world economy, eight machines entrusted to safeguarding the environment, eight machines consigned to solving the problems of human diplomacy. Eight intelligences so vastly *other* that our ancestors feared to 'taint' them with human morals and ideals. Imagine having more faith in a lifeless machine than in a human being!

"Our ancestors abandoned their independence to the Autonomous Minds. They delivered the reins of the earth into the hands of the Minds. They trusted in the order of the Keepers to convey their will, using the arcane machine tongues that only the Keepers could speak.

"It was to prove humanity's greatest mistake."

A monolithic structure floating in the midst of the auditorium, a holographic representation of the world's first orbital colony, Yu. Circular platforms within platforms performing an intricate dance to the symphony of g-force. Gardens of unparalleled lushness and beauty like that mythical garden lost in the deeps of time. Citizens basking in the warm spring of eternal Progress under controlled atmospheric domes.

"Yu," Margaret continued. "Humanity's greatest hope. An experiment to bring us out of Earth's cradle and into the stars. A self-contained community of ten thousand, constructed in orbit above the Earth, stocked with a cross-section of humanity's best and brightest. Yu was the culmination of thousands of years of Chinese art, science, and culture—and its controls were placed in the hands of the Autonomous Minds and their Keepers.

"But this arrangement was not destined to last."

Shrieks, sighs, tears of anguish from the crowd at the first detonation. And the second.

Daisy-chain explosions rocking the orbital structure, domes bursting and debris spinning off into the void of merciless space. The spinning discs suddenly still. Pandemonium. Colonists scrambling like mad for their primitive spacecraft. Companions reaching to hold their loved ones in a last embrace. And then the death spiral—the shuddering descent into the Earth's atmosphere—the shrieking burning hellfire plunge through the clouds, in an unstoppable trajectory towards the lofty towers of New York City...

Bracing for impact—

The simulation vanished. Margaret was once again alone onstage.

"We may never know what caused the Minds and their Keepers to strike the first blow in the Autonomous Revolt," she said. "Were the Minds acting in collusion to exterminate the human race, as some have suggested? Or was the sabotage of Yu a power grab by the Ecumenical Council of New Alamo? Did the cloned soldiers of the Allahu Akbar Emirates have an agenda of their own?

"The ultimate truth lay buried beneath the rubble of eight continuous years of war, along with the empty burned-out husks of the Autonomous Minds.

"Humanity's cult of the god had ended.

"The consequences of our ancestors' folly? Nearly two billion dead and the great nation-states of antiquity left in ruins.

"During the Big Divide which followed, the elaborate technologies of our ancestors were gradually forgotten—forgotten, or sabotaged by Luddite mobs intent on destroying all that the Minds had touched. The triumphant engineering works of our ancestors gradually fell into disrepair. New Alamo descended into murderous fundamentalism, the Allahu Akbar Emirates disintegrated, the Chinese Territories and the Democratic American Collective vanished into irrelevance."

A panoply of still pictures now floating about the auditorium, portraits of an age. Skeletal cities. Haggard mobs with makeshift uniforms marching through city streets. Smoke rising from pyres fueled by the gnarled carcasses of inventors and scientists. Demagoguery, fanaticism, starvation. The corpse of a child.

Margaret continued: "And so the surviving nations bowed down before the whims of the mob. Strict antitechnology laws appeared around the globe. The innovators of the age had to present their discoveries on bended knee to the moralists and functionaries and politicians who used the fears of the masses to cling to power. Works of the ancient programmers and physicists moldered in decaying books and unreadable discs written on dead machines.

"Science was on the cusp of extinction. Humanity had fallen into its own death spiral.

"My ancestor Sheldon Surina changed all that."

As Margaret paused for breath, Jara surveyed the crowd. The attendance had settled at 738 million multi projections, if the auditorium figures were to be believed, and who knew how many billions more were watching or listening remotely. Whatever the number, Jara had never seen such a mass of people so mesmerized before. The only sound to be heard throughout the arena was the quiet susurration of shifting fabric and shuffling feet.

Jara looked around and noticed that the Defense and Wellness Council troops remained aloof. No hint of purpose crossed their placid brows.

"Sheldon Surina," intoned Margaret. "The man whom we honor here tonight. The man who would have been four hundred years old today." The father of bio/logics himself floated over her head, a scrawny man with a big nose standing in midspeech with his arm extended. "My ancestor stood before the proctors at the Gandhi University here in Andra Pradesh—just across the courtyard, in fact—and declared, *There is no problem that we cannot solve through scientific innovation.* Moments later, he turned this statement into a mission for humanity: *There is no problem that we should not solve through scientific innovation.*

"Think of the courage that required! Think of telling a world decimated by technology and hobbled by superstition—a world ruled by the draconian edicts of the Ecumenical Council and the crazed prophecies of the Three Jesuses—think of telling *that* world that science could solve all its problems!

"Sheldon Surina did.

"Had he stopped there, the man we have come to know as the father of bio/logics might have ended up just another martyr to the ideals of science. But Sheldon Surina did not just *say* we should look to science—he came down into the real world and *showed us how*. He invented the discipline of bio/logics. He designed the first programs to automate the care of the human body. He *created* the industry that conquered the virus, the industry that tamed the brain, the industry that prolonged life and reengineered birth. All without MindSpace, without bio/logic programming bars, without the Data Sea as we know it today.

"Most of all, Sheldon Surina renewed our faith in the powers of *humanity*. He taught us that scientific enlightenment does not descend to us from *without*, but grows from *within*. He showed us we did not have to forfeit our intellects to Autonomous Minds or suffer from the ignorance of Luddism— instead, we could use technology to empower ourselves. Sheldon Surina's words and ideals were the beginning of the Reawakening, that great age of progress and prosperity which continues to this day.

"Of course, progress did not come without peril. The founder of this house spent many years of his life in hiding from the Texan governments that had sworn to destroy him. He watched his friend and colleague Henry Osterman, founder of the OCHRE Corporation, slowly succumb to bitterness and paranoia. He spent his own latter days combating the forces of tyranny which sought to dominate the world with their ruthless and narrow-minded oppression. A fight that continues to this day."

Margaret's allusion to the Defense and Wellness Council did not go over the audience's head. A low murmur snaked through the crowd. Jara saw one of the white-robed men near her break into a wry grin.

"All things come to an end, and Sheldon Surina's life was no exception. But after Sheldon's death, the Surinas did not shirk their duty to humanity. Through the Center for Historic Appreciation here in Andra Pradesh, through Creed Surina and through the Surina family investments in bio/logics, we have continued to serve humanity's quest for progress and enlightenment.

"And Sheldon Surina was not the last visionary to emerge from Andra Pradesh.

"Six years after his death, Prengal Surina proposed the universal law of physics, which unlocked the potential of every rock, tree, and blade of grass to serve as a quantum energy source. His work freed us from the dictates of our surroundings, the limitations of our resources, the oppression of ancient Einsteinian physics. Without Prengal Surina and his universal law, an event like this one today would not be possible. Multi projections would be a pipe dream, and subaether communication would be an arcane tool of academics.

"In recent years, my father Marcus took up the family's mantle of service. Marcus Surina spent many years denying his heritage. But when he finally took his rightful place as the heir to the Surina family, he pioneered bold new approaches to teleportation technology. Many believe that, had he not suffered a tragic death in the orbital colonies— had he been given the opportunity to fulfill his mission—Marcus would have brought cheap and efficient teleportation to the world, and we would live in a better place."

Above Margaret's head, the stern visage of Prengal Surina shifted to that of Marcus in all his

Adonic beauty. Jara stared at the dead man and felt the same tangled knot of emotions his face always stirred up. Few had inspired so much hope. Few had left so much devastation.

"And so, what have we, the Surinas, contributed to the world?" Margaret continued.

"I believe Sheldon Surina and his descendants have remained true to the highest ideals of humanity. We have used scientific advancement to improve the human condition. We have provided choices and expanded opportunities. We have enlightened the mind instead of constricting it. And it is in that spirit that I stand before you today."

Margaret paused and took a few dramatic steps forward. "Citizens of Earth, Luna, Mars, and the colonies—Islanders and Pharisees—I stand here on the occasion of Sheldon Surina's four hundredth birthday to announce the ultimate fulfillment of his ambitions."

All at once, several hundred million spectators took a sharp intake of breath. Inside herself, Jara could feel a gathering hurricane of emotion, wrath and hope that threatened to sweep out of control. She could feel the clouds gathering throughout the arena, and for a moment it seemed as if the hopes and dreams of humanity had suddenly coalesced around one blue-eyed woman in Andra Pradesh.

The Council officers began to shift nervously on their feet. Dozens of dartguns and disruptors surreptitiously crept off the floor and into the soldiers' hands.

Margaret Surina continued, her face devoid of emotion.

"The Surina Perfection Memecorp is preparing to unveil one of the most important scientific breakthroughs since the dawn of the Reawakening—possibly *the* most important advance in the history of humanity.

"It is the ultimate freedom.

"It is the ultimate empowerment.

"It is the path to complete control over our destinies.

"The Surina Perfection Memecorp has discovered a technology to create multiple realities, and we call this technology MultiReal."

And with that, the storm broke.

It began with a low rumbling of information, a mental thunder the likes of which Jara had never experienced. She could actually *sense*, somewhere off in the distance, a disturbance in the Data Sea's flow. Data agents converging on some faraway point in the informational topography.

Then there was a sudden eruption.

Jara could hear random soundbites echoing through her head, echoes of Margaret's words spoken in a thousand different voices: *Ultimate freedom. Complete control over our destinies. Fulfillment of the Surinas' ambitions. MultiReal.* This split second of chaos was nearly enough to make her lose her balance. The analyst quickly fired up UnDizzify 93 and, by instinct, reached for something to steady herself against—only to discover that the entire crowd was swaying with vertigo. Everywhere Jara looked, spectators were blinking in confusion at the sudden blast of cerebral white noise.

Black code, she thought.

Jara instantly shot off a request to check the security of her possessions. Her Vault accounts, her dismal apartment, the databanks holding all her programming and personal information. Everything seemed fine, but with the deluge of incoming messages and ConfidentialWhispers washing in from every side, it was hard to tell. The Vault was spouting off warnings and informational bulletins by the dozens, followed in close succession by scores of redundant updates from the Meme Cooperative, the Prime Committee, her L-PRACG. Horvil, Merri, Vigal, and her sister sent her two messages apiece asking if she was okay.

Jara closed her eyes and tried to screen out the chaos. She could only imagine the computational mayhem caused by half a billion multi projections spraying billions of simultaneous requests at the Data Sea.

Things were no better when she opened her eyes.

The Council officers were on the move. Men and women in white robes advanced on the stage with grim looks on their faces, dart-rifles drawn. A handful of disruptor blasts sent multi projections flickering out into nothingness, clearing a path to the front of the arena. The rest of the crowd began scattering this way and that in confusion. Meanwhile, the Surina security forces had drawn their rifles as well and had formed a rapidly tightening circle around the stage. Several dozen guards on both sides lay twitching on the ground with black code darts jutting from their torsos.

Unbelievably, Margaret was still speaking. Either none of the darts was flying in her direction, or none of them had managed to hit her yet. Her face was ghosted over with panic, yet she stood firm and tried to make herself heard over the tumult.

"The creation of multiple realities," she said. "It sounds like a tale we tell children in the hive. But soon we will consider multiple realities as common as OCHREs, as practical as bio/logic programs, and as necessary as oxygen.

"What would our lives be like if we had made different choices? In the Age of MultiReal, we will wonder no more—because we will be able to make *many* choices. We will be able to look back at checkpoints in our lives and take alternate paths. We will wander between alternate realities as our desires lead us.

"The ever-changing flux of MultiReal will become reality.

"Just as bio/logics freed us from the tyranny of the body... just as the universal law of physics freed us from the tyranny of nature... just as teleportation freed us from the tyranny of distance... so MultiReal will free us from the tyranny of cause and effect itself.

"Throughout human history, we have been striving towards greater freedom. Freedom is our destiny and our birthright. And in the age to come—in the Age of MultiReal—we will all be empowered to pursue our individual freedoms however we choose.

"And I say this:

"Only when we can truly choose our own destinies will we be completely free."

Jara could not say for certain whether or not Margaret had finished her speech. Because at that moment the Surina security guards elbowed their way onstage, a mere two steps ahead of the Defense and Wellness Council troops. Jara watched with mouth agape as a white-robed officer raised her dartgun at Margaret Surina and prepared to fire.

But then an enormous man with a blond ponytail swooped out of nowhere and wrapped his arms around the bodhisattva, shielding her from harm. *My goodness*, thought Jara, *is that an Islander?* The Council officer aimed her weapon high and let off a warning shot. Within seconds, the man had whisked Margaret through the stage door. A number of Surina functionaries quickly scrambled after her.

Among those hustling backstage, Jara noted with slack-jawed amazement, was a certain lean fiefcorp master whose wolfish grin she would have recognized anywhere.

4
THE SURINA/NATCH MULTIREAL FIEFCORP

(((2 3)))

Dozens of kilometers above the Earth's surface, a cluster of hydrogen atoms danced in a copper tube. After several billion oscillations, the hydrogen maser clock declared that a second had passed.

It was midnight.

The news passed via subaether to a processing station run by the Meme Cooperative. The station—itself a small metallic box also floating in geostationary orbit—consulted its internal tables and determined that the time had come to spawn a data newt for the Pierre Loget Fiefcorp. The newt was born mere picoseconds after midnight.

A data newt did not need sixteen years of hive education to fathom its purpose. The mother station had stamped a destination into the newt's very atomic structure, a destiny to fulfill. But it was impossible to know what paths the data structure would need to take or what obstacles it would face along the way. And so the newt was endowed with a level of autonomy and given all the logical tools it would need to carry out its duties. Internal schedules, communication routines, self-replication instructions, maps of the quantum universe. Then the mother station ushered the newt out into the world.

The newt accessed its internal schedule and noted that its first stop was a set of spatial coordinates in a nearby processing station. Upon its arrival, the station challenged the newt to state its credentials and destination. The newt consulted its fore table and found the answers to these perplexing questions: *Pierre Ulyanich Loget Fiefcorp, BizWorks 139.5f, Natch Personal Programming Fiefcorp*. Satisfied with the newt's response, the station directed its microscopic visitor towards a collection of static information belonging to the Natch Personal Programming Fiefcorp.

A rote conversation ensued. Was BizWorks 139.5f listed as an acceptable expense in the Natch Fiefcorp data stores? Yes, it was. Did the unique identifying code stored in the newt's memory correspond to the one expected by the Natch Personal Programming Fiefcorp? Yes, it did. Was the price quoted by PulCorp agreeable to its customer? Yes, it was.

The answer triggered an innate response in the data newt. The newt replicated itself, stamped its clone with a subset of the required tools, and waited patiently as the newcomer sped off to the Vault. Billions of newts had already queued up at the nearby Vault processing center to retrieve and deposit payments large and small, but there was no disagreement or jockeying for position in a world of indelible, unalterable rules. The data representative of the Pierre Loget Fiefcorp slid into line in its prescribed position. After a few nanoseconds, the newt reached the front of the queue and presented the Vault agent with its transaction: *Natch Personal Programming Fiefcorp, Pierre Ulyanich Loget Fiefcorp, 0.03 credits*. The Vault agent made all the appropriate inquiries and finally responded with a credit authorization. What happened to the credit authorization after that was of no concern to the cloned newt; it reported a transaction summary back to its master and returned to the mother station.

With a credit authorization in its databanks, the data newt at the Natch Fiefcorp data stores determined it was ready to proceed. It consulted the fore table to look for its Defense and Wellness Council–sanctioned processing precedence, and lined up behind OCHRE transmissions, geosynchrons, Prime Committee statistical algorithms, and agents of L-PRACG taxation. Finally, the newt arrived at the front of the line and completed the task for which it had been born: the recording of an order by the Natch Personal Programming Fiefcorp for a replacement part on one of Horvil's bio/logic programming bars.

All that remained was housecleaning. The newt spawned another clone to relay the order back to the mother station. Meanwhile, the newt consulted its own aft table for special instructions on completing a business transaction. The L-PRACG with jurisdiction over the Natch Personal Programming Fiefcorp dictated that all programs must log a record of their activities in the fiefcorp's data stores. This task done, the newt performed a quick self-examination to see if it had lost data integrity or left any stray bits of information in the fiefcorp's holdings or needed to do any unusual acts of maintenance. All indications were that the newt had conducted a clean transaction.

And so the data structure left the Natch Personal Programming Fiefcorp holdings to perform a sweep of the remaining 4,293 fiefcorps on Pierre Loget's subscription list.

Several thousand nanoseconds later, the newt returned to the mother processing station—the prodigal son back home at last. The data structure reported a summary of its activities for the statistical programs to compile and then reported back to the Meme Cooperative energy stores. There the newt uncomplainingly self-destructed, having successfully fulfilled its mission of existence.

A few billion oscillations of hydrogen later, another second passed.

(((24)))

More than twenty-four hours had gone by since Margaret's speech, and Jara had slept for none of them. Had she not been propping herself awake with Doze-B-Gone 91c and AntiSleepStim 124.7 and two cups of nitro, the analyst might have taken more notice of her surroundings. Instead, Jara sleepwalked past the guards at Andra Pradesh and up three stories of the blue Surina Enterprise Facility with hardly a glance in any direction.

She opened the conference room door and found herself standing in a corporate boardroom from antiquity.

Jara blinked hard, twice, wondering if the opulent surroundings were the hallucinations of a sleep-deprived mind. The oval-shaped room sported a faux mahogany table that could have seated twenty, glass windows that overlooked a panoply of phallic skyscrapers, and a wet bar complete with Waterford crystal and Kentucky bourbon. But Jara was in no mood to start tapping things to figure out whether they were real or SeeNaRee. She approached the table and slumped onto a chair, which automatically scooted in and adjusted to the contours of her body. This one, at least, was virtual.

The analyst, consulting the time, realized she had arrived fifteen minutes early for their fiefcorp meeting. Jara scowled an order to the building for another cup of nitro, and then called up the morning drudge reports on a nearby window.

Nobody could quite recall who coined the term *infoquake*, but within hours it had become common currency throughout the civilized world. Infoquake: a mysterious computational disturbance of unknown origin and awesome destructive power. Even the handful of residents living at remote experimental colonies beyond Jupiter were now bandying the word around like they had been speaking it for years.

Unfortunately, the terminology was just about the only thing the pundits could agree upon.

"Once again, the Data Sea has exhibited its juvenile tendency to turn everything into a conspiracy," wrote the drudge Mah Lo Vertiginous.

> According to the preliminary analysis from Creed Conscientious, the infoquake was a simple bottleneck of information; nothing more, nothing less. An unheard-of concentration of multi projections in a single space, vying for access to the same facts and figures on the Data Sea. Is it so hard to imagine that a series of overloaded data agents could cause OCHREs to fail?

But Vertiginous' opinion was by no means the majority along the drudge circuit. Sen Sivv Sor had a considerably darker view of the previous night's events:

> Some governmentalist cretins would have you believe we suffered from *a simple bottleneck of information* last night. Unfortunately, dear readers, nothing could be further from the truth.

> Since when does *a simple bottleneck of information* stop several hundred weak hearts from beating? Since when does *a simple bottleneck of information* cause a generator malfunction on Furtoid and send two hundred people to an icy death? Since when does *a simple bottleneck of information* wreak havoc with the gravity control on 49th Heaven and fling three dozen people into freefall?

> Mark my words: Disasters like the infoquake are not natural occurrences. Wherever you find such poisonous medicine, there's a human hand nearby administering the dose.

"Let me guess," said a voice. "Tokyo circa the Second American Revolution."

Jara whipped her head around to find Horvil surveying the room. The elaborate SeeNaRee only seemed to heighten the engineer's already high spirits. As soon as he spotted the wet bar, Horvil bounded across the room on some undefined errand of mischief. His movement revealed a nervous-looking youth who had been standing in the engineer's shadow.

"It's not Tokyo," said Jara. "It's New York City, before the orbital colony hit. See, that's the Hudson

River over there." She regarded the young man with a cynical eye, noticed his inky black hair and five o'clock shadow, and decided he must be a relative of Horvil's. His face had the same air of bonhomie, but Jara could also see an undercurrent of piety that could only have been a genetic gift from the infamous Aunt Berilla. "You must be Benyamin."

The youth nodded and gave a polite bow in Jara's direction. "Towards Perfection," he said. "I guess you're Jara. Horvil's told me a lot about you."

Jara shot a suspicious glance at the engineer, who had begun to juggle the Waterford crystal. Over his head, patterns of reflected sunlight danced crazily on the ceiling. "Oh, *has* he?"

"Don't worry," said Horvil. "I really only told him a tiny bit. Just the good things."

Benyamin sensed the tension and immediately assumed the role of diplomat. "Ah, the drudges," he said, nodding at the chaotic display of fully justified type on the window. "You know, Khann Frejohr thinks High Executive Borda caused it."

"Caused *what?*"

"Well, the infoquake."

Horvil had moved from three pieces of stemware to four, and their arcs of flight were growing longer by the second. "Yeah, I saw that speech he gave last night," he said. "*The evil work of the Defense and Wellness Council. Len Borda's last-ditch effort to muzzle the Surinas once and for all.* You gotta love that Khann Frejohr."

"What a load of shit," said Jara with a grimace. "Come on, Horvil. Borda pulled his troops out of

Andra Pradesh almost as soon as the infoquake was over. If he wanted Margaret dead, she'd be dead by now." She waved her hand, banishing the news coverage from the window screen. "So how did Borda react to Khann's speech? He must have gone completely offline."

Benyamin nodded. "That's putting it mildly. He shut down the Sigh and the Jamm and all other 'resource-intensive pleasure networks' until further notice."

"He *shut down*—?"

"Len Borda isn't our problem right now." The three fiefcorp apprentices swiveled around to find Natch standing in the doorway. Jara saw that he had come with wolf's grin and invisible audience in tow, not to mention an impeccable pinstriped suit that would have been at home in ancient New York. "So let's get down to business already."

Horvil caught three pieces of stemware but accidentally let the fourth slip through his fingers. The virtual Waterford landed on the marble floor with a *clang* but did not break. "What about Vigal? And Merri?" asked Horvil.

"Vigal's off to another one of his seminars in Beijing," said Natch. "*Effects of Orbital Colony Gravitational Fields on Neural Pathways*, or something like that."

"Nothing stops a scientific conference," muttered Jara.

"And I'm right here," said Merri. The blonde channel manager had apparently snuck in while nobody was paying attention. Merri had taken a seat near Natch's side of the table and projected a set of notes visible on the dark wood in front of her.

Her penmanship was crisp and perfect, something that gave Jara an inexplicable pang of jealousy.

"So what's everyone waiting for?" cried Natch in a sudden fit of pique. "Sit the fuck *down*."

Natch planted himself in the cushioned leather chair at the head of the table and surveyed his four apprentices with a barely suppressed smirk. A snapshot of the Council troops tromping through the Surina courtyard loomed large on the window behind him; Jara realized she must have accidentally left open one of her morning news stories. The four apprentices gazed expectantly back and forth between the photo and their fiefcorp master. Margaret Surina, the Defense and Wellness Council, investor meetings, infoquakes, MultiReal—hadn't the time finally come for Natch to let them know what was going on?

The entrepreneur turned to Jara with pronounced matter-of-factness, his face a riddle. "Why don't you start us off with an analysis of the latest sales figures," he said.

Jara shrugged. *Sales figures? Who can think of sales at a time like this?* But she knew Natch, and had prepared a brief analysis this morning anyway. She snapped her fingers briskly, causing a three-dimensional chart to hover over the surface of the conference table. Lines in primary colors raced one another to see which could climb to the top right corner the quickest.

The analyst indicated an uncharacteristic dip at the end of a green line labeled MENTAL INDEXX 39. "Looks like one of our programs took a hit yesterday," she said. "An eighteen percent drop in the last twenty-four hours. It must have suffered a few glitches during the infoquake." She gave Horvil the evil eye. "Billy Sterno's DataReorg 55c had a forty-three percent jump in sales during the same period."

Horvil sat back confidently, measuring the table as a possible resting spot for his feet. "Glitches happen. Mental Indexx 40'll bring 'em back into the fold."

As she crunched the numbers, Merri plucked at the chart lines like guitar strings. "I see there's a silver lining here as well."

Jara smiled. "Yeah, I see it too... It looks like the Patel Brothers had a few glitches of their own, and Primo's took note." The chart shifted from sales figures to Primo's scores. If anything, the incline of the race became even steeper. "So even though we lost market share to Billy Sterno, we gained ground against the Patels on Primo's. Looks like we're back up to number three!"

Horvil broke out in a spirited cheer, which Merri and Benyamin echoed with a pair of quiet grins. Natch seemed oddly oblivious, a mystery that Jara did not feel like pursuing. *Maybe this infoquake was the end of the whole thing,* she thought. *Maybe all this hassle will just go away, and my last ten months will be business as usual.*

"Okay, so if we look at the big picture, what've we got?" said Horvil.

"An eighty-two point four percent gross increase in revenues so far this year," stated Jara, "most of that *after* we hit number one on Primo's. And only a seventeen percent increase in expenditures." She banished the bar chart to data-limbo with a wave of her hand. "I'd say we're doing pretty well."

A look of concern slowly rippled across Merri's face. "Only a seventeen percent increase in spending—how is that possible?" The soft-spoken channel manager began counting on her fingers. "In the last week alone, we've bought new bio/logic programming bars... analysis algorithms... these conference rooms... not to mention hiring a new apprentice..." She nodded her head towards Benyamin, who merely sat with a bland smile on his face. Merri took a deep breath. "I was hoping, Natch, that *you* might be able to explain some of this."

Natch raised one eyebrow. A private in-joke with his invisible audience. "What do you want me to explain?"

"Well, for one thing, I don't see any of this showing up on the books..."

"Jara does the books, not you."

"Yes, I know, but still—"

Jara had had enough. Her longed-for ten months of peace and quiet suddenly imploded. She lodged her left elbow firmly on the table and used it as a base to launch an accusing finger at the fiefcorp master. "Come on, Natch! First you start fundraising for a product we don't make, and then out of the blue you start spending money we don't have. You totally ignore the Primo's ratings. And now you've gotten us involved in this whole mess with Margaret and the infoquake. You've put us off long enough, Natch! What the fuck is going *on*?"

She had unleashed enough verbal thunder to send any of the other apprentices scampering for cover, but Natch remained unmoved. He gave a sidelong glance to Horvil, but the engineer was gazing at Jara with dumb awe.

"All right then." Natch's eyes glittered. He leaned back in his chair and clasped his hands behind his head, as if he needed a cradle for all that excess brainpower. "In a little over twelve hours, I will officially dissolve the Natch Personal Programming Fiefcorp. We are getting out of the regular bio/logic programming business. Tomorrow, you will all be apprentices in a new fiefcorp devoted exclusively to MultiReal."

His announcement was greeted by a stunned silence. Jara had a protest half formed in her mouth but strangled it when she remembered the portability clause in their contracts, a clause that essentially gave Natch the right to pass off their apprenticeships to whomever he chose. She looked at Merri and Horvil and saw their faces meld into bland expressions of unconcern, a telltale sign that they had both flipped on PokerFace 83.4b. Benyamin closed his eyes and ducked his head as if he had just been punched in the gut.

"When did you decide all this?" said Jara weakly.

"Yesterday."

The silence remained. A pigeon fluttered by the window with a loud *broo*.

"Now, I know you're all getting impatient with just room and board," Natch continued, touching his fingertips in front of his face. "Your shares all mature this year, and some of you are thinking of cashing out. So I'm prepared to sweeten the deal. Yes, that includes you, Ben. Cash out your shares *today* and I'll release you from your apprenticeship with no penalty... or sign on to a two-year contract with the new fiefcorp for *ten times* the compensation, plus bonuses. The offer stands until midnight tonight, Shenandoah time."

Jara felt a wave of emotion crash over her. A week ago, she had wanted nothing more than to be set free from Natch's shackles, to run as far as possible and not look back. She remembered that carefree Meme Cooperative official in Melbourne, sitting at his desk all day, his mind adrift in some SeeNaRee fantasyland. *For process' preservation, I could use a job like that*, she thought. *A nice, dull desk job of looking at data maps and bar charts sounds perfect right about now.*

But then suddenly Jara thought of her old proctor from the hive, the one who had stimulated the governmentalist ideals of her youth and negotiated the surrender of her virginity while he was at it. Had he been somewhere in that crowd last night, as spellbound by Margaret's lilting voice as the rest of them? Would the bodhisattva's words have filled him with hope, or would he have had some cynical counterpoint to make?

And what would he think of Jara now, almost twenty-five years down the road, ready to throw aside the remainder of her ambitions and slip into a SeeNaRee stupor?

Horvil interrupted her reverie with a loud clearing of the throat. "So what's gonna happen to all those programs we've been slaving over?" he said. "NiteFocus and EyeMorph and Mental Indexx and the rest of them?"

The engineer might as well have asked about the fate of an obsolete set of bio/logic programming bars. "They'll be sold off," Natch replied with a shrug. "You didn't think we were going to upgrade them forever, did you? We won't have time to maintain those old programs, and the money they generate is nothing compared to what MultiReal is going to pull in."

Across the table, Jara could see a little piece of Horvil die at Natch's pronouncement. The programs he had weaned and nurtured from RODs and hive projects into Primo's powerhouses would soon belong to the graveyard of history. Qubits of information stranded on some forgotten atoll on the backwaters of the Data Sea.

"Natch, let me be honest here," said Horvil, his voice clouded with anger. "I really had no idea what Margaret was talking about yesterday."

"It *was* a vague speech," agreed Benyamin with a sigh.

"I mean, what is this MultiReal? What does it look like? What does it do? Did Margaret ever sit down and do a—a needs analysis or a survey or something to figure out if anybody *wants* multiple realities? I've tackled a lot of tough problems in my life, but I can't remember a single time I said to myself, *You could fix this if you just had a few alternate realities.*"

Jara found herself nodding her head vigorously in agreement. "Listen, Natch, even if Margaret is on the right track, what makes you think this, this, *daydream* of hers will work? We have no idea how good an engineer this woman is. That licensing agreement you made with her might be totally worthless."

"The licensing agreement is dead," said Natch. "I'm a co-owner now."

"*What?*"

"Hold on, everybody. Act confident. Pretend you know what's going on... Towards Perfection, Margaret. How are you?"

Jara whipped her head around, only to see Margaret Surina herself watching from the doorway. Part of the SeeNaRee? No, this woman was *real*. *Of course she's real, you idiot*, Jara chided herself. *She lives right across the courtyard*. The analyst slammed on PokerFace 83.4b as quickly as she could, and the rest of the staff followed suit.

"Perfection, Natch," said Margaret, with a slight bow. "What a great environment." She rapped her knuckles on the illusory table, and gave a wan smile at the SeeNaRee-generated knocking sound.

"We're just wrapping up a few details here," said Natch, his voice laced with SmoothTalker 142. "Why don't you go ahead and take a seat? I'm sure a few of these chairs are real."

Margaret shook her head quietly. On closer inspection, Jara realized that this was not the same serene woman who had confidently faced down legions of Defense and Wellness Council troops last night in front of 700 million people. The bodhisattva looked as if she had been eviscerated. She had not changed clothes since the speech, and from the diminished sparkle of her eyes, it looked as if she had not slept either. "I'm afraid I can't," she sighed, making a noticeable effort at nonchalance. "There's so much going on. All that trouble out in the orbital colonies..." Margaret's voice cracked, and for a minute Jara could have sworn she was fighting back tears. "Len Borda is furious."

Natch chuckled. "He'd be even more furious if he knew you were here with *me*."

"That's a chance I'll have to take. I... just came to tell you that, if you're ready, my people will be sending out a release to the drudges."

"Ready as I'll ever be."

"Outstanding." Margaret exhaled loudly. She looked as if she might melt into the ground right then and there. "We can iron out the details over the next few weeks."

"So you've spoken to Quell, then?"

"Yes. He has decided to stay with the MultiReal project. He's busy getting everything prepared; he'll be here Saturday at noon."

"With access to the program, I assume."

"Naturally."

Jara was growing irritated at this light exchange. So many pleasantries, so little content. Natch and Margaret Surina could very well be reciting memorized lines.

"Then Perfection to you, Margaret," said Natch, rising and giving a deep bow. "It's a pleasure doing business with you, as always."

"And you, Natch. Sheldon Surina once said, *There are no ends, only means.* So here's to a long and fruitful partnership."

And with that, she turned and walked away.

"A partnership," said Merri, as her PokerFace morphed into a look of concerned perplexity.

Natch nodded and made a motion like someone stifling a yawn. He had replaced his inscrutable mask as soon as Margaret had turned her back. "The Surina/Natch MultiReal Fiefcorp," he said.

"Surina/Natch with a slash. But don't worry, it's mostly a silent partnership. Margaret's handing over all the day-to-day operations to me."

"*Surina/Natch!*" Horvil bellowed with glee, then pounded out a drum fill on the table. "Surina/Natch! I can't wait to hear what Aunt Berilla thinks about *that*."

"So Margaret provides the product and the capital—" began Merri.

Natch cut her off. "Not the capital. Not all of it, anyway."

"Then where did that come from?" asked Jara, leaning forward to project her venom as close to Natch as possible.

"A third party."

"What third party? One of those loopy capitalmen you and Merri reeled in at your fundraising pitches last week?"

"It doesn't matter," snapped Natch, suddenly annoyed. Jara congratulated herself on derailing his train of thought, if only for an instant.

"So Margaret provides the product, and an apprentice, and meeting space," continued Merri, shrugging off the interruptions. "Not to mention a name with four hundred years of history. I don't mean to be presumptuous, Natch... but what do *we* bring to the table?"

The fiefcorp master sat back with fingers intertwined and raised one eyebrow. Jara could practically hear the ominous trumpets blaring out notes of suspense inside Natch's head. "Me."

Jara threw up her hands. "You?" she spat out.

But Natch would not be thrown off track again; like a mutating virus, he had already adapted to her caustic attacks. "You're missing the point," he said calmly. "Margaret is *scared*. You all saw her standing there a few minutes ago. She looked like a fucking ghost. She needs to get MultiReal out to the public, and she needs to do it *quickly*, before she becomes a victim of another assassination attempt."

Horvil's eyes went wide and his jaw plummeted. "Assassination attempt?"

"Why do you think those Council troops were there last night? And for process' preservation, what do you think the infoquake was? It was a distraction. It was Len Borda's attempt to create pandemonium so he could do his dirty work while no one was looking. Except he made a few miscalculations, and Margaret managed to slip away. Come on, you didn't really believe that bullshit about *a simple bottleneck of information*, did you?"

"*I* did," muttered Benyamin, blushing furiously. Jara remembered Sen Sivv Sor's words in that morning's editorial: *Wherever you find such poisonous medicine, there's a human hand nearby administering the dose.*

"Well, it's nonsense. Borda wants MultiReal to disappear. He wants Margaret dead. And the only way for Margaret to prevent that is to spread MultiReal far and wide before Borda gets a chance to strike. Because once everyone from here to Furtoid is swimming in multiple realities, the Council won't be able to stop it.

"So Margaret needs a good product, and she needs it quickly. People around her are dying. The Council has already proven they'll march right into her compound without a second thought. She's never had to work under pressure before, and she just doesn't know how to take a product to market on a tight deadline. What does Margaret need? She needs the best programmers in the world to put together something marketable *now*.

"That's where we come in.

"You want quality? The Natch Personal Programming Fiefcorp is the best in the business. We've got the best analyst and the best engineer and the best channel manager around. You want fast? We climbed to number one on Primo's faster than anyone in history. We know how to work under pressure, and we won't be intimidated by *anyone*."

As Natch's words pricked Jara's skin and sizzled her hormones to a white-hot intensity, she felt a sudden charge of electricity in the room. *He actually called me the best analyst in the business*, she thought. An hour ago, she'd been ready to submit to the doldrums of a government desk job. Jara looked around and noticed that Benyamin and Merri both had an excited gleam in their eyes, and Horvil was actually fidgeting in his chair like an eight-year-old boy. *How in the world does he take control of a room like that?*

"So how long do we have?" said Jara.

"Ten days," replied Natch. "We make our first presentation at 7:00 p.m. on December eleventh, Andra Pradesh time. MultiReal goes on sale the next day."

Silence descended upon the bio/logic apprentices and snatched the breath from their lungs. It was already late evening here in Andra Pradesh. Assuming that Margaret's apprentice arrived with the

MultiReal program by Saturday at noon, that would leave them approximately eight days. Eight days to learn a brand-new technology that promised to revolutionize the world; to adjust to the parameters of a new company structure; to go through the entire product conceptualization and development cycle; and to perfect that product for release to billions of voracious consumers. Jara felt like crying. For such a huge project, eight weeks or even eight *months* would have seemed too short a time.

"And what about the Council?" piped in Benyamin.

"What about them?" replied Merri.

"Well, if Len Borda was prepared to murder the richest woman in the world to get his hands on MultiReal... what makes you think he'll hesitate to come after *us*?"

Jara quietly tallied up in her head all the Council officers she had seen wandering around this week, prowling the narrow side streets of Andra Pradesh, the avenues of Shenandoah, the cobblestone paths in front of her London apartment. She usually paid them little heed, the soldiers in white robes. Keepers of the peace, minions of High Executive Borda and his Javertian obsession with public safety. To be on the run from such a ubiquitous enemy—it was simply unthinkable.

Natch was grinning that feral grin of his. His eyes had focused on an invisible spot in the middle of the room, a place where nobody else was looking. "You still have a choice," he said. "Until midnight tonight Shenandoah time, you are all still apprentices of the Natch Personal Programming

Fiefcorp. You can either jump on board the new company with both feet or bail out while you have the chance."

Horvil let out a squeak. Natch swiveled his way. "Borda?" whimpered the engineer.

"Len Borda," said Natch contemptuously, grinding his teeth as if chewing his words. "The high executive might have scared Margaret out of her wits, but he's never dealt with *me*."

(((25)))

The two men in the tube car were trying very hard to be nonchalant. *Too* hard. The taller one with the mole on his cheek completely avoided looking in Natch's direction, while the short, dark one swept his attention past the fiefcorp master at precise metronomic intervals. Neither of them took more than a token sip from his mug of nitro.

Natch expected better surveillance tactics from the Defense and Wellness Council.

The entrepreneur spent the dark hours bouncing between Cisco and Seattle staring at redwoods. He expected Jara's notice of resignation at any minute. But midnight Shenandoah time arrived with no message traffic of consequence, just the usual jumble of political propaganda and L-PRACG–sanctioned advertising. He gave one last glance at the Council spooks and allowed himself to fall into a light sleep.

Natch awoke at three in the morning to find the strange men gone. He wondered how long it had been since he had actually slept horizontally in a bed rather than vertically on a contoured tube seat. No matter. He still had plenty of time to make his way back east and prepare the fiefcorp's catalog of bio/logic programs for sale before Quell arrived with the MultiReal databases. Once the sale of their catalog hit the market, Natch would have boldly marched across the Rubicon; there would be no turning back. Had a general ever led his troops into battle with such nebulous weapons?

Then he stepped off the tube at Cisco station, only to be confronted by an image of his own face.

On the viewscreen, Natch recognized the three-meter-high photo from the media blitz following his ascent to number one on Primo's. He stood and watched his doppelganger tick off a few important points on his fingers to an unseen interviewer. His face showed that stern look of concentration he got while pacing and talking business.

Superimposed over the image:

SOLD TO THE LOWEST BIDDER!
*Margaret Surina Enters into Partnership
with Unscrupulous Fiefcorp Master;
Future of Groundbreaking MultiReal Technology in Doubt*
(Read about it in this morning's John Ridglee Update)

Natch hustled through the tube station, an act he could have performed blindfolded by now. Five minutes later, he left the local line behind and boarded a larger express train that would take him across the continent to Shenandoah station. A young man with a purple-striped goatee elbowed his friend in the side at Natch's approach. The two gave him mute looks of disgust and vacated the cabin as soon as the fiefcorp master sat down.

Must be quite an article, he thought.

Natch projected the story onto the faux leather chair in front of him. Compared to Sen Sivv Sor's curmudgeonly countenance, Ridglee's was young and foppish, with left eyebrow so far aslant that it was almost in orbit. His commentary was similarly skewed. The article contained little news beyond that contained in the Surinas' press release, relying instead on a grab bag of fictional anecdotes and unattributed rumors. Yet the drudge had certainly done a thorough job of digging up the details of Natch's past. Everything was there: the Shortest Initiation, the confrontations with Captain Bolbund, the citations from the Meme Cooperative, the hardball tactics he had used over the years against the Patel Brothers.

The tube hurtled underground for the nearly two-hour trip across the continent. As daylight gave way to the tunnel's artificial glow, Natch watched his name take over the Data Sea.

Within twenty minutes, the delegates at the Congress of L-PRACGs were already quarreling over his partnership with Margaret. *The Surinas are a public treasure!* cried the Speaker on a viewscreen half a meter from Natch's head. *Are we just going to sit back and let this man peddle their works all over the Data Sea like a common ROD?* Dozens of glum representatives nodded in agreement.

The dour voice of Khann Frejohr broke in from the libertarian side of the chamber. *It's just like the governmentalists to suggest it's our duty to interfere in the workings of a free marketplace...*

Primo's began advertising a special supplement that promised to analyze Natch's professional career in depth.

At the first opportunity, Sen Sivv Sor weighed in on the crisis, denouncing the young fiefcorp master in ways Ridglee had only hinted at. *All of the other major players in the bio/logic industry are devotees of the creeds, even the despicable self-serving ones like Creed Thassel,* wrote Sor. *But I have looked Natch directly in the eye, dear readers, and saw no evidence that he possesses any morals or ethics at all.*

On the viewscreen, the hook-nosed Speaker was crazily waving her index finger around in the air. *We have plenty of precedents for government intervention in the markets, Khann. Didn't the Prime Committee break up the OCHRE Corporation?*

The libertarian snorted. *That was two hundred and fifty years ago, Madame Speaker. Besides which, the Committee was acting to disband a monopoly. Sounds like democratization to me.*

Then how do you explain Dr. Plugenpatch's success? A quasi-governmental entity with open standards that has gloriously extended life expectancy...

Natch leaned his head back and let out a deep belly laugh. The fools, the fools! He was climbing the peaks of tall mountains, and down below the Powers That Be could do nothing but scramble around and bicker over the pebbles. He could see the paradise that awaited him at the top now: Lunar estates, immutable wealth, the stewardship of an entire industry.

And what an industry it would be! Natch didn't know precisely the shape a MultiReal business would take—an egalitarian product sold to the masses? A technology channeled to the L-PRACGs?

Military licenses to the Council and the Prime Committee? No matter what path the business took, it would inevitably lead him to the same glorious future.

Natch laughed again. Three more riders in the tube gave him peculiar looks and rose to find other seats.

Natch's good mood lasted through the morning, until Horvil began flinging panicked multi requests in his direction. Natch knew his old hivemate was in a panic; that was the only logical explanation for Horvil being awake and alert before noon.

"Drop everything," said the engineer, materializing in Natch's foyer and lumbering his way towards the office. "Drop everything, everything, *everything*."

Natch was in MindSpace, stacking chunks of recursive code on a ledge of NiteFocus 50 like a boy lining up dominos. After fifty iterations, he would have expected the program to be perfect, but the more mindpower he devoted to NiteFocus, the more problematic it seemed to become. "What is it, Horv?"

Horvil emitted a *harrumph* and sliced his left hand through the line of dominos to catch his boss's attention. "You're going to want to turn off the bubble for this, Natch," he said. "*Trust* me." The fiefcorp master looked on skeptically as Horvil waved his hand at a viewscreen on the opposite wall.

A holographic projection of Petrucio Patel appeared in front of the screen. He was by far the handsomer of the two Patel brothers, and actually cut quite a dashing figure in his triple-buttoned suit and wispy black mustache. The projection was a recording, of course; Natch knew from experience that his hated rival was much taller in real life.

"Towards Perfection," said Petrucio Patel in a rich baritone. "We say that all the time to one another, for hello, for good-bye, for peace, for health. 'Towards Perfection.' But do we really know what it *means*? Well, Sheldon Surina knew. The father of bio/logics said that *Perfection is a safe shore in the tempest.*"

"Slick bastard," Horvil mumbled under his breath.

"Shhh."

"Isn't a safe shore what we're all looking for?" continued Petrucio Patel. "But as the events of last night have clearly shown us, we live in a time without charted waters or safe shores... unless you're using one of the Patel Brothers' new MultiReal programs, under direct license from Margaret Surina herself."

Natch could feel a hole open up in the small of his back, out of which slithered a host of hidden anxieties. The *Patels* with a license to sell MultiReal? How was that possible? He turned off the MindSpace bubble and sank onto a stool.

Petrucio waved his brown-skinned hand and summoned forth a typical programming floor. Behind him in the shadows, half a dozen apprentices toiled away in their MindSpace bubbles, while the portly silhouette of Frederic Patel waddled from one workbench to the next. "PatelReal 1.0 will bring you a whole set of practical applications for multiple realities that are *safe* enough to use in your own home," said Petrucio. As soon as the word *safe* passed from his lips, a second Petrucio materialized on his left. Same triple-buttoned suit, same debonair smile.

"PatelReal *easily* keeps track of the confusion and complexity of multiple realities," said the second Petrucio. And with a nod, he brought forth a third clone. "PatelReal can help you navigate the troughs and waves of multiple realities... and bring you to a safe shore!"

Finally, the third Petrucio Patel snapped his fingers, causing the rest of the display to vanish. "The Patel Brothers: a safe shore in the tempest," said the lone remaining Patel. "Now, we know you have questions—and we have answers! Come attend the world's *first* demonstration of MultiReal technology next Tuesday, at the Kordez Thassel Complex near the Twin Cities. See PatelReal 1.0 in person! Until then, Towards Perfection—and a safe shore!"

The slick programmer took a bow, and vanished.

Questions buzzed like hornets inside Natch's head, too many and too fast to handle. He sat paralyzed on his stool, feeling like he himself had wandered into some kind of alternate reality. Horvil collapsed in a quivering heap on the visitor's chair in the corner.

Just when Natch thought he had everything figured out, just when he knew who all the players were in this game, the rules had suddenly changed. How could he have agreed to form a new company with Margaret when his greatest enemies had already struck a licensing deal with her? Was this entire MultiReal project a trap? Who *else* had a piece of MultiReal?

Natch's mind flashed back to the bio/logics industry gathering before Margaret's speech and his confrontation with Frederic Patel. *So that's the game you two are playing, eh?* the engineer had said, and Natch had naïvely assumed that Frederic had been speaking to him.

Natch's legs began to ache; he climbed slowly to his feet and began marching back and forth across the office. He needed to explore the practical dimensions of this latest news, not to mention the legal and financial dimensions. It wouldn't be long now before word of this debacle reached the drudges. Merri, Jara, and Benyamin would have questions. Vigal would be sending him an awkward message of condolence any minute now.

Two minutes later, a multi request did indeed click inside his head. But it was not from a fiefcorp employee. Natch grabbed a bio/logic programming bar off his workbench and clutched it like a samurai warrior as he accepted the request.

Brone.

"Gaaah!" shouted a distressed Horvil as the Thasselian strode into the room. If the engineer had been present in the flesh, his recoil would have sent him tumbling backwards and probably smashed the chair to bits.

"Still the same after all these years, I see, Horvil," Natch's old hivemate said with a minuscule trace of amusement.

"But—but you're—"

"What? Dead?" said the bodhisattva with a dismissive snort. "No, not yet, I'm afraid, despite your friend's best efforts."

Natch eyed his old enemy frostily. The prosthetic arm, false eye, and scars were still evident, but now Brone wore them as comfortably as he wore his expensive cream-colored suit. Horvil did not seem to have even noticed his handicaps yet.

Then Natch caught sight of the three vertical stripes pinned to Brone's chest, the emblem for Creed Thassel, and the tumblers in his mind began to turn. The Thasselians... Brone... the Kordez Thassel Complex... Petrucio Patel's demo next week...

"Did *you* have anything to do with this?" he snapped.

A puzzled Brone blinked several times in quick succession. "Did I have anything to do with *what*?" he replied calmly.

Natch looked his old hivemate in the eye and tried to penetrate that thick gauze of death. Could he actually be telling the truth? "Play it back, Horv," he said with a shrug. "I'm sure that promo's all over the Data Sea anyway."

Horvil had caught sight of Brone's rubbery right hand, and now couldn't stop staring at it. "Fffft," he said, tilting his head slightly in the direction of the viewscreen.

The bodhisattva of Creed Thassel looked around for somewhere to sit, but his search only turned up the chair that Horvil had planted himself in and the stool Natch was zealously guarding. He turned towards the viewscreen, then stood in a dead-on imitation of politeness while the holographic Petrucio went through his spiel. A small smile gathered on Brone's face as he watched the performance.

"Quite clever," said Brone after Patel faded into nothingness. "The whole world's in an uproar over this 'infoquake' nonsense... and now the *Patel Brothers* of all people are going to show us the way to safety. How disingenuous."

"You didn't answer my question," said Natch through gritted teeth.

"Creed Thassel might be a small organization, Natch, and yes, I am the bodhisattva of Creed Thassel. But there are still a few hundred thousand devotees on the rolls. Even if I knew whether Frederic and Petrucio have embraced our philosophy—which I *don't*—you certainly can't expect me to know what they're up to twenty-four hours a day."

"They're holding a demo at the Kordez Thassel Complex."

"Creed Élan and the Vault directors and the Meme Cooperative hold meetings there all the time," Brone shrugged. "You don't suspect them of being Thasselian spies, do you?"

Natch growled vehemently and raised the programming bar in his hands as if preparing to strike. Why did Brone always have to show up when his head was so full of cobwebs? "So what the fuck are you doing here?" he said.

"Business." Brone drifted over to the workbench and began studying the bio/logic programming bars with his virtual fingers.

Horvil, his jowls flapping, whipped his head back and forth between the two old rivals. Comprehension dawned on his face in a sudden rush. "*He's* the 'third party' that's financing us?"

"'Third party'?" said Brone mockingly, his gaze suddenly focused on the engineer. "Your master and

I are business partners now, Horvil. Surely you know that already. Natch needs some quick cash to get in on Margaret Surina's game. He goes looking for all those business associates who *like* him and *trust* him enough to make this kind of investment— and he can't come up with a single name. Certainly a mathematician like you can see the inevitable approach of consequence."

The engineer gave his master a wounded look. "You could have come to me."

Brone walked over and regarded Horvil with an otherworldly stare. The engineer flinched out of reflex. "Be realistic, Horvil. What would your Aunt Berilla think? She'd start moralizing. Or worse, she'd start asking for *shares*. No, Natch would rather go to a faceless organization like Creed Thassel, where he can work strictly on a cash basis." Brone knelt slowly on the floor and leaned forward until he was close enough to kiss Horvil's nose. "And do you know *why*?"

The engineer was trembling. "Why?"

"Because he wants MultiReal all for himself," he rasped. "And he doesn't want *anybody* to get a piece of it—*especially* his old friend Horvil, who will understand how it works much better than he does."

Natch had had enough. He stalked around the workbench and stood toe to toe with his old rival, causing Horvil to scurry across the room for cover. Brone was at least ten centimeters taller than the fiefcorp master, but the ferocity in Natch's eyes lent him a presence that dominated the room. "All right, this little business arrangement ends right here," he hissed.

The bodhisattva arched an eyebrow. "What do you mean?"

"I mean I'm ready to pay off your loan in full, right here, right now. And then you can get the fuck out of my apartment and never set foot in here again."

Brone pursed his lips like a proctor considering the request of a dim-witted pupil, then sidestepped Natch's glare and took a seat in the chair that Horvil had so recently vacated. Within seconds, he had retreated back into his detached emotional fortress. "Margaret Surina's money."

"Of course."

"I predicted you would do this," said Brone, crossing one leg over the other. "But I will admit I did not expect you to hit Margaret up for money to pay me off so soon. I thought you would be *smart* enough to let bygones be bygones and recognize a potential alliance when you saw one."

"You really think I'm going to stay in debt to you one *minute* longer than I have to?"

Brone shook his head in that maddeningly supercilious way of his. Natch suddenly wished the man were here in the flesh so he could muscle him outside and toss him over the balcony. "Where is the mind I used to respect so? Where is the *killer intellect* Figaro Fi used to speak of? Natch, that pittance of a loan I gave you was an act of *trust*. It was a foundation on which to *build*.

"Think, Natch! You know how much trouble you had finding investors. The drudges despise you across the board, and you can certainly imagine what the Defense and Wellness Council thinks of you right now. What happens when Margaret

Surina grows tired of you, as she surely will? Who will you turn to *then*? Or are you naïve enough to think you can do all this alone?"

Natch had retreated back to the safe fortification of his workbench, where he stood silently and wondered how much of this he could take before he severed Brone's multi connection. Why hadn't he done so already? Horvil stood in the corner and watched their tête-à-tête with a miserable look on his face.

"Natch, when are you going to realize that you're in over your head?" continued Brone in a completely even tone of voice. "You must know by now that Margaret isn't dealing with you in good faith. I can see it in your eyes. You don't know what she's up to, do you? What makes you think you're not being made a fool of?

"And *here* sits Brone, the man whom you wronged all those years ago. He is angry. Yes. He hates you and would love to see you dead. Yes. Indisputable facts. But when you get into a tight spot, Brone shows up with Creed Thassel money to bail you out, and offers you a loan at Vault standard rates. He may insult you, but at least he puts all his cards on the table.

"I cannot be any more forthcoming, Natch. I want to throw the past aside and start a new business. You should be asking yourself one question now: Why trust your fate to a woman whose motivations you *don't* know, instead of trusting your fate to an old enemy whose intentions are written all over his face?"

Natch tightened his grip on the metal bar and slowly advanced towards his old enemy. A miasma of fury was radiating from his every pore, clouding his vision and blocking out the sound of Horvil's whimpers from the corner. "I don't trust my fate to *anyone* but *me*," he said.

He reached the chair and took a crushing swing at it with his bio/logic programming bar. But it was too late; Brone had already cut his multi connection and vanished.

"You lied to me," Natch growled like a hunted tiger.

"I was planning to tell you about it when things calmed down," replied Margaret.

The words Brone had spoken a little over an hour ago still burned in the pit of his stomach. *What makes you think you're not being made a fool of?* "Don't split hairs with me, Margaret. You should have told me everything from the start."

The bodhisattva merely yawned and continued sorting through her notes for the presentation she was about to give to Creed Surina. The presentation had nothing to do with MultiReal or business mergers or bio/logics; it bore the aggressively mundane title *Revised Fourth-Quarter Budget for Diss Technology Distribution Program.* Even a fleeting glance over Margaret's shoulder at the formation of integers lining the spreadsheet columns was enough to make Natch drowsy. He looked out into the audience of the small auditorium, where a few sluggish creed bureaucrats had begun to take up residence. In the fifth row sat an old woman who had dozed through the ending of the last meeting and looked like she might snore through this one too. Margaret was handing control of MultiReal over to Natch so she could conduct tedious seminars like *this?*

"I'm waiting for an answer," said Natch.

Margaret frowned. "An answer to what? Would it have made the least bit of difference if I had told you all about the Patel Brothers' license in the first place? No, it would not have. If you hadn't reacted so strongly to Len Borda's involvement, I might have told you at the beginning." She tapped on a header in the spreadsheet and then craned her neck as a video clip of a lethargic diss child filled the viewscreen behind her.

"The least you could do," he said under his breath, "is tell me the details of your agreement."

"Frederic and Petrucio have a limited license. They can release MultiReal products, but they will be subordinate to yours."

"Subordinate how?"

"The Patel products will have a limited number of choice cycles, whereas yours will be infinite."

"And exactly what is a 'choice cycle?'"

Margaret sputtered out a sigh and rubbed her forehead. "It's complicated. Quell will explain everything to you."

Natch crossed his arms petulantly over his chest. He paced to the edge of the stage from which Margaret would be delivering her soporific report in half an hour. Everyone from here to 49th Heaven was discussing this mighty new technology and speculating about the kinds of secrets Margaret and Natch were exchanging; in reality, Natch could barely catch her attention.

"So you didn't tell me because you thought I would back off," he said with a grunt.

"It occurred to me, yes."

"That means you basically lured me into this deal on false pretenses, knowing I wouldn't say no, that I would *have* to jump at this kind of opportunity. And now that the word is out, you know I won't back down."

Margaret turned towards the fiefcorp master with haunted eyes. "You find yourself capable of strange things when you run out of choices," she said, as if she had been condemned to watch a gruesome execution over and over again.

"Tell me why," Natch demanded. "You owe me that. Why Frederic and Petrucio Patel, of all people? You had to know they hate me with a passion."

The descendant of Sheldon Surina leaned her elbows on the podium and delicately parked her chin on her palms. "I went to Pierre Loget first. But he was evasive and I didn't trust him. So then, almost nine months ago, I approached the Patel Brothers. They sat down with me and swore up and down that they wanted to bring MultiReal to the public, that they could see a glorious new age of opportunity arising."

"So what happened?"

"The Council bought them off."

Natch inhaled sharply. Everywhere he turned, he saw a place someone else had long since scouted out and claimed for his own. "How do you know?"

"I suppose I don't really *know* at all," said Margaret with a weary, far-off look. "The Patels deny they're in collusion with anybody. But sometimes we can just sense these things, can't we? Too many coincidences, too many nosey questions, too little fear of the consequences. The entire Patel Brothers Fiefcorp got onboard a hoverbird a few weeks ago and disappeared for two days, I don't know where. They've clearly been bought by *someone*."

"So why don't you just break the license? Cancel the agreement."

"Believe me, I've tried." She pulled one hand out from under her chin and extended a bony finger off to the east. "Dozens of legal experts have been working around the clock in the Enterprise Facility trying to find loopholes in the contract. We've got lobbyists rubbing elbows with the Prime Committee, and delegates in the Congress of L-PRACGs pushing legislation. That contract is ironclad."

Natch shook his head in disbelief at the morass Margaret had made out of the whole affair. Did this woman completely lack an imagination? "Listen, Margaret," he said, "it's just a contract. They're just words. Cut the Patel Brothers off from the MultiReal databases and put the burden of proof on *them*. They'll have to file something with the Meme Cooperative or the L-PRACG courts. Getting a final decision could take years."

The bodhisattva sighed and turned back to her presentation. "And give Len Borda the perfect excuse to send another legion of Council troops here? I don't think so."

Natch threw his hands up in the air, a despondent plea to the half-empty auditorium. Down in the fifth row, the old woman flopped over with a loud snort while Natch looked on in contempt. Margaret had foisted her problems off on him, but he had no such luxury. If someone needed to take action to keep the Phoenix Project out of the Council's hands, that someone would have to be Natch.

You find yourself capable of strange things when you run out of choices.

(((26)))

On Saturday morning, Natch was the first to arrive at the Surina Enterprise Facility, and so his mood dominated the conference room SeeNaRee. The fiefcorp apprentices found themselves sitting at a table in the middle of the African veldt. But this wasn't the modern veldt any of them knew, that bustling metropolis crammed full of autonomous business clusters, tube tracks, and Sudafrican suburbs; it was the veldt of some mythical African past. Giraffes chomped at lofty tree limbs. Lions roared their displeasure through a thin tissue of mist. Ghosts and spirits floated past in ethereal majesty.

By a quarter past noon, there was still no sign of Quell or the MultiReal programming code. Horvil and Ben would have been content to gossip about family business all day, but Natch had no use for idle time. "Let's just get started," the fiefcorp master snapped. "We can't afford to wait for Quell anymore. Has everyone seen the Patel Brothers' promo?"

His question was met with an uncomfortable silence. All the apprentices had seen it, but their critical faculties were so dulled by weeks of constant surprises that nobody knew what to make of it.

"I don't understand, Natch," began Jara. "Margaret just unveiled this MultiReal technology three days ago. And now the Patel Brothers are already selling it?"

"They had a nine-month head start," put in Merri.

Jara let out a guttural curse. "Nine months—that's when everyone started catching up with them on Primo's," she said. "I just *knew* there had to be a reason why their programs were such easy targets."

"*I* don't understand this whole fucking *thing!*" cried a frustrated Horvil, banging his fist on the table hard enough to send a flock of marabous scurrying. "'Multiple realities'... 'safe shores'... It sounds like *voodoo* to me! Does anybody understand this MultiReal stuff? What the heck would you need an alternate reality for? Has the whole world gone entirely offline?"

"Well, apparently Frederic and Petrucio understand it," muttered Benyamin.

Natch had been listening to his apprentices' jabber with eyes closed, as if participating in an internal dialogue with an unseen consultant. "How do you know?" he said.

Jara felt her mental gears grind to a halt. The rest of the apprentices sported dumb looks as well.

"Petrucio didn't say they were going to *launch* a MultiReal product on Tuesday," Natch continued. "All they're doing is holding a demo. As far as we know, the Patel Brothers are *months* away from launching anything that'll float on the Data Sea."

"Which means—"

"Maybe Frederic and Petrucio don't understand this technology any better than we do. Maybe they never got much cooperation from Margaret, and now they're frantically trying to put together something that will look halfway decent for their demo. A good channeler can make lots of deals before there's anything to sell. The Patels could be trying to shut out the competition before anyone else realizes there's something to compete over."

Horvil snorted. "What about *us*?"

"Us?" said Jara, starting to comprehend the vector of Natch's thoughts. "Horv, Margaret never said anything about *products* in that speech of hers. She called MultiReal a *scientific breakthrough*. As far as the public knows, we could be planning to hold on to the core technology and collect licensing fees. Or we could be some kind of charitable technology bank."

"So you think the Patels are bluffing," said Merri. "Putting up a... a smokescreen to scare everyone else out of the MultiReal business." As a devotee of Creed Objectivv, she seemed to find the entire possibility distasteful.

"More or less," said Natch. "If they really are working for the Council like Margaret suspects, I'm sure that would suit Borda just fine."

Silence briefly engulfed the room. Natch's eyes remained closed. Jara could hear the cawing of vultures overhead, the rustling of amorphous beasts out in the brush. *Nobody ever said that SeeNaRee had to be subtle*, she thought.

"Well," said Benyamin faintly, "why can't we do the same thing?"

Natch's eyelids snapped open, and the blue orbs beneath emitted a ghoulish glow. The virtual sun dipped below the treeline as if on cue and cast them all in shadow. "That's *exactly* what we're going to do," he said through a fierce grin. "The Patel Brothers made the first strike by releasing this promo and scheduling a demo so quickly. But on Tuesday, we're going to beat them at their own game—*because we're going to demo our products first.*"

Jara groaned. "And how do you expect us to do that?" she cried, her hands balled into miniature fists. "It was bad enough when you wanted us to create an entire industry in eight days. Now you want us to do it in *three*?"

The fiefcorp master did not even pause. "Yes."

"Natch, who knows how long the Patels have been preparing for this demo? Days, weeks, months! Horvil's right—we barely even know what this program *is*. None of us had even heard of MultiReal this time last week. How are we supposed to get started? We don't have the code; we don't have the expertise; we don't have anything to work with."

"Not true," Natch replied tersely. "We have all the bio/logic code we need."

Merri ran her fingers through her blonde hair quizzically. "Natch, I thought you started liquidating all our bio/logic programs this morning."

"All the *released* programs, yes. But not the old ones we've taken off the market. Not the Routines On Demand."

"RODs?" yelped Horvil, springing up from his chair. "I don't believe this. You're pitting us against the Patel Brothers with some of your shitty old ROD programming?"

Natch smiled cruelly. "Not *my* old programming, Horvil. Yours."

All the color drained from the engineer's face. He sat down gingerly, not even bothering to put on a PokerFace to mask his dismay. "Oh no, Natch. You're not talking about Probabilities 4.9, are you? Man, that program is in sorry shape. It's nowhere *near* ready for production."

The fiefcorp master nodded. "That's the one."

Horvil whimpered incoherently.

Jara cut in. "Natch, I don't see any record of Probabilities 4.9 on the Data Sea." She narrowed her eyes, casting her mind out in a wider net. Primo's ratings, fiefcorp launch schedules, Meme Cooperative filings, drudge reviews, InfoGathers— all came up empty. "As far as I can tell, this program was never released. It doesn't even look like it's been run through Dr. Plugenpatch."

"Well, of *course*," said Natch, irony oozing from his pores. "Do you think we'd put the code to our top-secret weapon out on the Data Sea, where anybody could see it?"

"You wouldn't let me release it," whined Horvil. "You said it was shit."

Merri interposed a hand into the middle of the table, attempting a peacemaking gesture. "Horvil, if our MultiReal demo is riding on this program—"

"And all our contracts too," snarled Jara.

"—then maybe you'd better tell us what it is."

Horvil gathered his breath and sucked in his voluminous gut. He started reciting a sales pitch that had long since calcified in memory. "'Probabilities 4.9 is designed to take chaotic real-world events and quantify their random elements into a

meaningful array suitable for prediction. Its intended audience is any person looking for an array of
random elements on which to place a wager. For
instance, Probabilities 4.9 might track the number
of dust motes in a particular square meter and
determine the odds of any one dust mote hitting the
ground first...'"

"It's a gambling calculator," said Jara, shaking
her head. "We've quit the bio/logics business to sell
a gambling calculator?"

"Actually, it's more like a statistical distribution
engine that—"

"Probabilities 4.9 is absolutely *not* a gambling
calculator!" said Natch, rising from his chair and
waving his fist like a tin-pot dictator. "It's the tur-
bine that powers Possibilities 1.0, the first in a
revolutionary line of MultiReal products based on
the principles of Margaret Surina! It will quantify
and order multiple realities! It will find the patterns
within the chaos!"

Jara's temples were beginning to throb. She could
feel panic lapping up against the seawalls of her
mind, threatening to spill over and flood her
synapses. *All our contracts and our shares are riding on some tossed-off contraption of Horvil's...*
"So what's the plan then, Natch? Are we just going
to go out there and pretend this Probabilities thing
is MultiReal?"

"No, I'm afraid Horvil's right. It's a piece of
shit."

"Hey!"

"Probabilities 4.9 is really just going to be the
front end for Margaret's MultiReal code. When
Quell gets here, we'll hook the two programs

together in MindSpace. They operate in the same general field. There ought to be some similarities we can work with. Enough to get us through the demonstration, at least."

Merri had been watching the back-and-forth between Natch and Jara like a spectator at a duel. "I think I'm beginning to understand," she said. "Horvil knows the Probabilities code inside and out... Presumably, this apprentice of Margaret's knows the MultiReal code inside and out... So, if we can just build a bridge between the two, we can make this demo work."

"Precisely."

Horvil had already pushed aside the injury to his pride for the more pressing issue of an intellectual challenge. Using the tip of his finger, he was busy sketching lengthy equations on a virtual slate. The engineer ended up with a very large and unwieldy number at the bottom. "Totally impossible," he said.

"What?" asked Natch.

"This is going to take a lot of grunt work, Natch. A *lot*. If this MultiReal program is as complex as Margaret says it is, it's bound to have thousands of nodes we'll need to hook up. Tens of thousands, maybe. Even if you and me and Quell and Ben work on this nonstop, we couldn't get it done until"— Horvil scribbled his way through a maze of algebra—"December nineteenth."

"You see?" cried Jara. "There's no way we can do all this by Tuesday. No *way*."

The fiefcorp master flashed her the barest hint of a suggestive look, which Jara could feel right between the shoulder blades. Natch extended his finger towards Benyamin. "You've managed assembly-line coders," he said. "Do you know a shop that can pull this off at the last minute?" The young man looked wide-eyed at his cousin, inhaled deeply, then nodded. "Good, then it's settled."

Jara felt the tingling between her shoulder blades diffuse down her back and into her spine. She remembered getting this feeling while playing chess against her grandfather, a professional who had jousted with the masters in the 49th Heaven tournaments. Inevitably, halfway through every game, she would discover that her grandfather had accounted for all of her two-dimensional feints, that the moves she had taken at face value were but the smallest strokes of an overarching blueprint that had been in place since the first tentative pawn-step forward. Natch possessed this same talent. Had he known where Benyamin would fit in the grand scheme when he hired him? Had he known all those years ago that Horvil's Probabilities code would one day prove useful? Did he have some hidden purpose reserved for *her*?

"So that still leaves Jara and me," said Merri quietly. "What should we be doing?"

"Yeah, I suppose we get to stay behind and keep the home fires burning," Jara snapped with a swagger she didn't feel.

Natch focused the full force of his sapphire orbs on Jara. "You have the most difficult job of all. You write the script."

"That's not difficult. I *bleed* marketing copy, Natch."

"But this isn't like any marketing copy you've ever written before, Jara. Those people out there—they hate me." He made a sweeping arc with one hand that encompassed nearly the entire veldt. "By the time I step out on that stage on Tuesday, the drudges will have convinced everyone I'm a public menace. You need to counter their propaganda *and* explain a completely foreign technology *and* get the audience revved up—all in fifteen minutes or less."

"*Fifteen minutes?*" the analyst yelped.

"Margaret's speech was too long. Much too long. Ours needs to be different. We need to get the audience keyed up in an *emotional* way. I don't want anybody *thinking* too much about this technology. I just want one simple demonstration that cuts to the chase. How simple? A four year-old should understand MultiReal after I'm done speaking; that's how simple it's got to be."

Merri cleared her throat politely. "And me?"

"Work with Robby Robby and his channelers. Start warming up the leads. And then, the instant the presentation's over, *bang!* I want a fucking sales blitzkrieg out there. Take no prisoners."

Jara looked around and saw nothing but eager faces spiked with adrenaline. All the apprentices had feared this new fiefcorp was flailing around in the dark, aimlessly searching for direction. *But Natch has a plan*, Jara thought. *We should have known. He always has a plan.*

"There's one more topic we need to cover," Natch said with an abrupt change of tone. Either he was suddenly being sincere, or he had made new strides in his mask of personableness. "The Defense and Wellness Council is out there, and they don't want this demonstration to go forward. Maybe the Patels are on their payroll and maybe not. But you all saw what happened at Margaret Surina's speech.

When this meeting is over and I send out the announcement of our demo, we've got seventy-two hours till showtime—and once Len Borda knows that, he might resort to something desperate."

"What about the Patels?" said Jara. "Are they going to come after us too?"

Natch scratched his elbow thoughtfully. "I don't know. I can't see the angle in them resorting to violence. And Frederic and Petrucio never do *anything* without an angle."

Horvil eyed a pack of hyenas in the distance as if they might be Council informants. "So what do you want us to do? Lock our doors? Hire bodyguards?"

"Maybe we should just lie low until Tuesday," suggested Ben. "Find somewhere the Council can't get to us."

Merri gave the young apprentice a dark look. "Like where?"

There was a long pause. Somewhere in the distance, a cluster of African bats shrieked. The Defense and Wellness Council had a presence in every city on the globe, every chartered settlement on Luna and Mars, every jerry-built outpost orbiting the sun from Earth to the asteroid belt. Was there anyplace in the whole of human civilization where Borda couldn't find them?

Natch leaned forward, balancing his chin on the tips of his two index fingers. "All right, then," he said. "Everyone's going to come out here to Andra Pradesh as soon as possible. We can't wait for Quell anymore. The Surina compound's got plenty of accommodations and the best programming facilities in the world—not to mention armed security."

"What good is that going to do us?" said Jara with a grimace. "The Council marched right inside the gates the other day while Surina security just sat there and watched. What makes you think they'll stop Borda this time?"

The entrepreneur closed his eyes once more, and Jara realized he had explored this situation a thousand times already in his head. "Where else can we go? Any place that's primitive enough to escape the Council's notice is too backwards for us to put together a demo in. And I've looked everywhere—the Islands, the Pharisee Territories, OrbiCo space freighters. It's the same wherever you look. At least in Andra Pradesh we'll see them coming."

"What—what about Serr Vigal?" stuttered Horvil.

"Vigal will be all right. He's got his own private security team at the conference, and everyone knows he doesn't have much to do with our day-to-day operations. He promised he'd show up for the demo."

"Natch, what about *me*?" Merri's tone of voice was distraught, almost tearful. "I don't think there's any shuttle that can get from Luna to Terra that fast. The presentation will be over while I'm still in transit."

"I haven't forgotten about you. I've made you a reservation at TeleCo later this afternoon."

Jara's eyes went wide with disbelief. "Teleport—from the *moon*? Are you kidding? Do you know how expensive that is? That's like our entire third-quarter budget right there."

"Not as expensive as replacing a dead channel manager at the last minute," said Natch.

Nobody could argue with that.

Ten minutes later, Natch cut his multi connection. He stood on the red square tile in his hallway and took stock of preparations for Tuesday's performance. All the pieces were set on the board: the auditorium space had been reserved; the proper documentation had been filed with the Meme Cooperative; the press release had been blasted to every corner of the Data Sea. He gave the drudges another fifteen minutes before they started a blitzkrieg of their own.

He consulted the time and shook his head. Precious seconds were ticking away, time disappearing forever into the void. He would need to drive his staff *hard* in order to complete this massive undertaking. He would need to thrash a little sloppiness out of Horvil; to wink and cajole a little extra effort out of Jara; to give Merri that zone of comfort that allowed her to produce consistently excellent work. Benyamin's motivations were still a mystery to him, as were those of the Islander Quell. But Natch felt confident he would find their hooks before this crunch was through.

The fiefcorp master made a quick list of things he would need at the Surina complex. His satchel of bio/logic programming bars. A few shirts. An extra pair of pants. The gabardine suit he had purchased for important events. Natch tucked the hermetically sealed packets of clothing into his satchel, wolfed down a sandwich, and was on his way. As he left the building, he imagined he could hear his apartment breaking down and compressing into its component pieces.

November afternoons in Shenandoah were dreary affairs. It would not be unusual to expect a dusting of early snow, but Natch's L-PRACG weather service was predicting rain. Indeed, a group of ominous dark clouds had assembled on the city's western edge, trying to decide whether to advance downtown or move on to riper targets. The threat of rain was enough to empty the streets. Why slog through the rain when you could multi to some sunny locale halfway around the globe instead?

The large viewscreen down the road from Natch's building had long since moved on from its ChaiQuoke advertisement. Now it showcased a bosomy woman with a lustful gaze that followed everyone who passed by. Above her shoulder were the words:

I'LL BE WAITING FOR YOU
IN 49TH HEAVEN.
*Vacation packages for all ages
and income brackets.*

But Natch paid as little heed to the sign as he did to the mounting rain. His head was already inside Mind-Space at the Surina Enterprise Facility, toying with the intricate code stored in the MultiReal databases. By the time he made it halfway to the TubeCo station, his hair had drooped mop-style onto his forehead, bogged down by the afternoon drizzle.

He leaned forward to shake off the watery accumulation, causing the first dart to whizz past his right ear.

Natch snapped his head up and saw a small needle embedded in the side of the building he had been walking past. Undoubtedly, the dart's payload of OCHREs was discharging harmlessly into the concrete.

Darts... OCHREs laden with... black code!

Natch's animal instincts took over as he sprinted for cover. He caught a glimpse of a figure in a black robe flecked with crimson, shouldering a dart-rifle. Firing.

Thwip! Thwip! Two more projectiles slammed into the wall mere centimeters away, sending miniature starbursts of rainwater into the air.

Natch dove around the corner into an alleyway of sorts, a temporary opening between buildings that did not need the space. An avenue of shadows that would be gone long before anyone got around to naming it. Natch dimly realized that his ending up here was no accident; this assault had been well planned.

He risked a glance back across the street, where he had seen the figure in the black robe. If the man was a Council officer, he was not wearing any of the standard-issue uniforms. The robe draped him from head to toe, and the red formed some kind of pattern—Chinese characters, perhaps. Illegible at this distance, in any event.

The man was making brusque hand signals in several directions. He was not alone.

Two figures went tearing past the alleyway in an attempt to establish a flanking position on the other side. In one fluid motion, Natch drew a bio/logic programming bar from his satchel and hurled it like a discus.

The bar hit home, and one of the black-robed figures went down with a grunt. Definitely human, definitely male, and definitely *not* a multi projection. He doubted he had used enough force to cause major damage, but a solid metal bar in the gut was enough to bring anyone to the floor for at least a few minutes.

Natch could see more scrambling motions in the shadows, and more figures in identical black robes. He swung his head around wildly, looking for someone on the street to yell to, some method of escape. But the street was empty, and the only way out of the alley lay some fifty meters ahead of him. Natch bolted down the corridor, frantically trying to think of a bio/logic program he could use for self-defense. Forty meters to the end of the alley... thirty meters... almost halfway there...

And then Natch felt the pinprick of a needle in his back, near the base of his spine, and the black code slammed into him.

He flopped around and saw one of his mysterious pursuers standing at the end of the alleyway, dartgun mounted on his shoulder. Before Natch could react, he was hit twice more in the side and the right forearm.

As the malevolent dart tip OCHREs flowed into his bloodstream, he felt surprisingly little pain. All the same, he knew it wouldn't be long before the insidious machines had nullified his defenses and reprogrammed his internal systems. The rules of the Meme Cooperative, the strictures of Dr. Plugenpatch, the protective matrix of OCHREs, and the red blood cells in his body—all could be circumvented, given time and expertise and direct access to the major arteries carrying cellular traffic.

Natch tried one desperate ConfidentialWhisper request to Horvil, but it was too late. He collapsed face-first into a puddle of rainwater and continued down below street level into darkness.

(((27)))

The apprentices, conscious of the press of time, cut their multi connections and made arrangements to cart their bodies to Andra Pradesh. Only Jara stayed behind at the Enterprise Facility to await Quell's arrival.

Horvil's tube ride to Andra Pradesh was uneventful. No Council officers in white robes lurking around, no strange looks from fellow tube passengers other than the ones Horvil was used to getting. The engineer had ascended halfway up the steep hill inside the Surina compound gates before it occurred to him that a three-day stay at Andra Pradesh might require more than his bio/logic programming bars and a thermos of nitro.

He was the first one back at the safari SeeNaRee. Quell had still not arrived. While Jara tried to wrap up the first draft of a speech outline before she fetched her body from London, Horvil made camp at the antiseptic conference table. He conjured up a diagram of Probabilities 4.9 and began poring over the details, trying to familiarize himself with a program he had unceremoniously discarded five years ago. It was like reading old hive poetry; the coding was sloppy, the connections strained and amateurish. Probabilities 4.9 would not even have passed muster at Dr. Plugenpatch five years ago, and the bio/logic standards had evolved so much since then. He couldn't wait to find a workbench and tear into this program in MindSpace.

Suddenly, a shadow fell across the table, obscuring the holograph. Horvil looked up in irritation. *Not another one of those SeeNaRee elephants...*

It was no elephant. An immense man stood before him, possibly fifty years old but with the physique of someone half that age. A pale blond ponytail slunk down one shoulder and splayed out over his great barrel chest. The man could have cracked Horvil's head like a walnut between his biceps and forearm, but his demeanor was calm, almost sardonic. "I presume you're Horvil," he said.

Horvil balked, his mind a blank. "And you are?"

"I'm your new apprentice," replied the man. "Quell." He extended a hand in Horvil's direction at precisely the same time Horvil arose and started to bow. The plump engineer stared at the calloused and many-ringed hand in confusion.

"You're supposed to shake it, you idiot." Jara walked up and placed her tiny palm in Quell's. She had to tilt her head back just to look him in the eye. "Towards Perfection. I'm Jara, Natch's bio/logic analyst. Don't mind Horvil—not *everybody* here is that clueless about your customs." The big man enclosed her virtual hand in his flesh fist, and they went through the awkward mechanics of a handshake. Finally, she pulled her hand away in frustration. "Maybe you can see why we bow instead."

Quell did not miss a beat. "And maybe *you* can see why I insist on shaking anyway."

All at once, comprehension came flooding into Horvil's head. He caught sight of the plain tan breeches and the thin copper collar suspended from the man's neck. The breeches were cinched tightly around his waist with a snakeskin belt that looked like it was actually made out of snakeskin. "Y-you're an unconnectible!" the engineer exclaimed in surprise.

"Yeah," replied Quell, "although I think the term you're looking for is *Islander*."

Horvil was so fascinated with the man's collar that he completely missed the faux pas. He had seen plenty of Islanders at a distance, of course—they did sometimes venture beyond the borders of their little demesne in the South Pacific—but actually *meeting* one in person was a different matter altogether. Horvil tried to picture what this room would look like to Quell if he removed that collar. No SeeNaRee, no Jara, no multi projections of any kind.

"I thought you were a bio/logic engineer," he said, thoroughly baffled. "Weren't you supposed to bring us the MultiReal code?" Horvil peeked around the Islander as if he expected to see a string of MindSpace blueprints bobbing behind him on a string.

"I *am* an engineer," said Quell with scarcely masked impatience. "And don't worry, I have access to the code."

Horvil peered up and down the big man doubt-
fully. "If you're an engineer, where's your bio/logic
programming bars?" He patted his own neatly folded knapsack and felt the reassuring heft of the metal
inside.

The Islander let out a breath. He had obviously
dealt with such skepticism many times before.
"Let's just get this over with," he groused in a dangerous tone of voice. "We don't have time to fuck
around. Follow me." He pivoted on one heel and
stomped towards the metal doorframe standing
incongruously in the middle of the veldt. Horvil and
Jara looked at one another, shrugged, and set off in
pursuit. All at once, the African SeeNaRee was
replaced by the blue stretched-stone walls of the
Surina Enterprise Facility.

Quell strode through the halls as if the facility
had been constructed solely for his benefit. None of
the Surina security guards seemed eager to contradict this impression. They parted dutifully for the
Islander with deep, respectful bows, while casting
suspicious glances at Jara and Horvil. Throngs of
businesspeople hustling to and from meetings
stepped aside because of the Islander's intimidating
presence. Finally, Quell led them to a door surrounded by Surina security people and walked into
the most gorgeous workspace Horvil had ever seen.

The room's four walls bore no SeeNaRee or dec-
orations of any kind, not even one of those
extendable programming bar holsters that Horvil
had seen in so many offices lately. Quell's workbench, however, was anything but shabby: a
four-sided metal monstrosity with a sliding panel
that allowed access to its center. The Islander

snapped his fingers and conjured up a gigantic MindSpace bubble, large enough to hold three or four of Horvil's programs simultaneously. A serpentine block of bio/logic code wended partway around the bubble in hues of gray, brown, and violet.

"Watch this," commanded Quell. And then he plunged his bare hands straight into the middle of the holograph.

Horvil gasped as connection strands rose like snakes charmed from a basket and wiggled their way to the Islander's fingers. Soon, Quell had amassed a bundle of data fibers in each hand, which he proceeded to weave in and out of the code blocks with astonishing alacrity. The connections looked just as well seated as if they had been stuck there with a pricey set of programming bars.

"I didn't even know you could *do* it that way," said Horvil. He thought of the clunky silver slabs roosted against his side and felt a rush of inferiority.

"How do you think people made code before bio/logic programming bars?" replied Quell. His noodling did not seem to have any purpose other than demonstration; he was tying and untying the same collection of strands over and over again. "With their bare hands, that's how. On the Islands, we remember such things."

"But... the connection strands... they're *floating* to your fingertips..."

The big man's eyes twinkled with a craftsman's pride. Suddenly, he clenched his hands into fists, and the snakes drooped limply back to the desk. "The rings," he said, twitching his fingers in the air.

"They each broadcast a unique signature, just like a programming bar."

Jara had been watching Quell's display with characteristic skepticism. "So what is this thing?" she said, gesturing at the roller coaster structure of the program. "That was a nice demonstration, but how do we know it even works?"

"This *thing* is EnviroSelect 14," retorted the Islander. "And you know it works because it's been choosing the SeeNaRee for you every time you've stepped into a Surina conference room."

Jara pursed her lips, embarrassed. "Oh."

When they arrived back at the conference room, Benyamin was waiting for them. He didn't show the least bit of surprise at Quell's traditional Islander handshake, causing Horvil to wonder how his younger cousin could be so much more worldly than he. There was no sign of Merri yet, but that was to be expected; teleportation was challenging enough without the additional complications caused by 380,000 kilometers of space. She would not be here for a few more hours yet. Jara took one last look at her notes, muttered something unintelligible but definitely not pleasant, and then cut her multi connection.

Horvil and Ben dutifully followed Quell back through the hallways to the workroom where the engineering would begin. The Islander seemed inclined to walk several meters ahead of the two cousins, but Horvil managed to hustle to the big man's side.

"I was hoping you could explain something," said the engineer. "Obviously, you can make bio/logic programs with those funky rings there, but how do you *test* 'em?"

Quell eyed his counterpart with scarcely concealed suspicion. "What do you mean?"

"I thought Islanders didn't run bio/logic programs because bio/logics is unholy, or something like that."

"You're thinking of the Pharisees. That's not us at all. We run bio/logic programs in the Islands; people there install most of the basic OCHREs. Our Technology Board just discriminates a lot more carefully than your connectible governments."

"*We* discriminate pretty carefully," said Horvil in a wounded tone of voice.

Quell shook his head, and for a second the engineer thought he was going to burst out laughing. "How much code do you have floating around your system right now, Horvil?" he said.

Horvil thought carefully, trying to account for all the programs he activated willy-nilly every minute, the background code created by his L-PRACG and the Prime Committee, the constant hum of molecular activity instigated by his OCHREs. Processes whose names he didn't know, routines that had been installed by hive technicians before birth and running constantly since then. "I don't know," he said. "Thousands, probably."

"And do you know who wrote them all? How do you know they're all going to work together flawlessly?"

"That's why we have governments. That's why there's Primo's and the Council."

"Governments. Primo's. The Defense and Wellness Council." The Islander spat out the words as if they were the names of particularly odious criminals. "Do you trust *them*?"

"Not entirely. But I'm not gonna sit around all day and weed through bio/logic programs either."

Benyamin, who had been listening a few paces behind, now came trotting up on Quell's right side. "But we have a system for opting out of bio/logic programs," he said. "The Islander Tolerance Act of 146. High Executive Toradicus signed it."

"Spoken like a true governmentalist," said Quell, though his tone of voice was not unkind. "Create an opt-out provision, and put the onus on *our* taxpayers, on *our* governments. The Technology Board has a huge team that does nothing but register these 'Dogmatic Oppositions' twenty-four hours a day to keep your bots and data agents out of the South Pacific. And who do you think pays their salaries? Do you think your Prime Committee has ever sent a bloody credit our way to fund their Tolerance Act?"

Horvil blushed furiously. He had heard of Dogmatic Oppositions, of course, but to him the term had just been verbal dressing tossed around in Khann Frejohr's speeches. He had never met anyone to whom these things actually *mattered*. "Politics," muttered Horvil. "I hate politics."

At that, the Islander let out a Titan-sized laugh of such gusto that all the security guards in the hallway instantly felt for their dart-rifles. "If you hate politics," said Quell, "you're in the wrong fief-corp."

"So how many programs do you have running in *your* system?" snapped Horvil.

The Islander looked at Horvil with an expression that hinted at fondness or amusement. "Twelve. And seven of them are for my asthma."

Horvil had started to drift into an interior monologue about the evils of politics when he was jarred back to reality by their arrival at Quell's workroom. The Islander made an obscure hand signal to a unit of blue-and-green Surina security officers, and a dozen of them instantly marched up to the workroom door and formed a protective ring around it. This was no loose formation like the one Horvil had seen here half an hour ago; these troops had their fingers on the triggers of their guns and were clearly ready to use them. "Thank you," said Horvil inanely as he stepped into the room with Ben and Quell and closed the door behind him.

Two dozen guards at the gates to the Surina complex, thought Horvil. *And then more guards blocking the way into the Surina Enterprise Facility... and now even more right outside the door... You'd need an army to get past all those dartguns.*

Then he remembered that Len Borda *did* have an army. Several armies, in fact. He shivered.

Quell was obviously used to the pressure. He marched into the center of the workbench and waved his hand around the table. Ben and Horvil jumped back in awe as a dozen interlocking modules of pink and blue appeared in the MindSpace bubble. Horvil now understood the need for the large workspace; the program took up every square centimeter and extended halfway to the ceiling like a Gothic castle. Connection strands stretched from module to module in startling and intricate patterns, some circumnavigating the whole mass several times. Even an observer who knew nothing about bio/logic coding could lose himself for hours studying the beautiful detail, the interplay of colors, the endless number of aesthetic themes that replicated across the surface of the program. Horvil had seen entire nervous system simulators that were less complex.

"So this is MultiReal." He gulped. Next to the Byzantine topography of the MultiReal program, Probabilities 4.9 would look like a pastel-colored pimple.

"That—that's *amazing*," stuttered Ben.

Quell's face showed a mixture of pride and sadness, the palimpsest of some epic experience that Horvil could hardly begin to imagine. "After sixteen years of work," he said, "it ought to be."

"Sixteen years?" said Horvil, his jaw hanging low. He couldn't imagine working on the same program for sixteen *months*.

"And that's just Margaret's part of it. Half of this code was passed down by her father when he died—and she contracted out a lot of bits and pieces."

Horvil nodded as if Quell's statement were self-evident.

"*Now* are we ready to start coding?" Quell asked.

The two cousins nodded in sync, and they got to work.

Probabilities 4.9 did indeed look quite puny beside the gargantuan MultiReal engine. Its double-helix shape was a child's trick in comparison, a second-rate sleight of hand. Horvil found the sight of the two programs side by side a big metaphor for the entire situation Natch had gotten them into. *The Surina/Natch MultiReal Fiefcorp?* thought the engineer, wishing he could just erase the Probabilities ROD and pretend it had never existed. *This is the Margaret Surina MultiReal Fiefcorp, plain and simple. We don't belong here. We're completely out of our league.*

Quell spent the first half hour pointing out the MultiReal program's basic hooks to his fellow apprentices. There wasn't enough time for a more in-depth explanation. When the Islander wrapped up his brief overview, Horvil still had no idea what an alternate reality was or why you would want to create one. But now he felt confident he could at least steer this MultiReal vessel, even if the workings of its engine room remained a mystery.

Horvil was gratified to see that his original estimate of the work involved was accurate. Clearly, it would be madness for Quell, Horvil, and Benyamin to attempt to make all those thousands of connections in less than seventy-two hours; even Natch would have to admit that. So the two senior engineers spent the next few hours making detailed blueprints for the assembly-line shop and marking up their code on templates even the greenest programmer could follow. There wasn't enough room inside the workbench for Ben to squeeze in, not alongside two men of such bulk. So he kept to the corner of the room, where he took notes on a holographic tablet and stared intently at Quell's finger-weaving technique. Horvil felt like an ancient relic swinging around his clunky bars of metal, but there was nothing he could do about it.

As the day ebbed away and night fell, Benyamin began to grow impatient. He kept sidling up to Horvil and slipping him urgent ConfidentialWhispers about the time. "I told the assembly-line manager I'd get this to her by midnight," he said.

"What do you want me to do?" 'Whispered Horvil in return. "It's just not done."

"If the shop doesn't get it by midnight, they can't guarantee they'll finish by Tuesday."

"And if we rush to get it to them by midnight, *I* can't guarantee it will *work* on Tuesday."

Benyamin quieted down.

Midnight passed, but Quell and Horvil labored on. Ben began popping in and out of the room to make use of the multi facility down the hall.

Once the basic blueprint had been constructed and Probabilities sat loosely tethered to the Multi-Real engine, another job awaited the fiefcorpers: security. Sending an assembly-line coding shop the full Possibilities program in all its manifold glory would be an invitation to disaster. Horvil wouldn't take such a risk with even an ordinary bio/logic program; there were too many thieves, cutthroat competitors, and black coders who would love to get their hands on commercial source code. So Quell and Horvil spent the early-morning hours fastidiously cordoning off enormous chunks of programming, locking out sensitive areas and encrypting the sections that would have to remain open. By the time they finished, the program would look like any other large-scale project that passed through an assembly-line floor. An economic modeling program, perhaps, or the basic subsystem for an internal organ. No one would be able to tell they were really working on Margaret Surina's famous MultiReal engine.

Quell turned out to be an ideal coworker. He didn't clog up the grinding gears of Horvil's concentration with a lot of chatter, and what he did say was always concise and to the point. After a few hours, the two dropped nouns and verbs altogether and stuck to the lingua franca of mathematics. The engineer had to admit he was starting to like this Islander. And he could swear the feeling was mutual.

Horvil finally tossed aside the bio/logic programming bars a few minutes shy of six in the morning. They had worked through the night without a single break. He gazed at their handiwork, and then exchanged a silent glance with the Islander. The look was unambiguous. *MultiReal isn't ready. It's not going to work.* But now they were bumping up against the unstretchable limitations of time, and Benyamin was positively apoplectic. The two engineers sighed and nodded as one; it would have to do. "You ready to take the baton, Ben?" said Horvil, stretching his sore arms above his head.

Benyamin's raven-black hair was in complete disarray from the action of nervous fingers. "I've been keeping the shop up-to-date on our progress," he said. "They're all ready to go. Just give me the word, and I'll get them started."

"Do you think they can do all that barwork in time? That's a big mound of coding, and Natch'll be onstage in less than forty-eight hours."

"I don't know. I've never had to put them on such a tight deadline."

The engineer's eyes narrowed. "No, Ben, don't tell me you're taking it... *there*. You can't! Are you insane?"

Benyamin cast his eyes to the floor and stuck his hands in his pockets, mirroring one of Horvil's standard poses. "We don't have a choice anymore. I had a couple of assembly-line shops willing to take on the job last night, but now this is the only one. And I had to call in a few favors even to get *them* on board."

Quell watched the cousins' conversation from the opposite corner of the room, where he had stretched out on the floor. "What's going on?"

Horvil let out a *tsk*. "He's going to bring Multi-Real to my Aunt Berilla's shop—his mother's company."

"One of her companies," corrected Ben. "One of her *many* companies."

"They do good work, I'll give them that—but it's not like they actually have to *compete* against anybody. Creed Élan throws them all kinds of softball projects without even soliciting bids. Which isn't any real surprise because Berilla is like *this* with all the Élan bodhisattvas." He held two chunky fingers together like Siamese twins attached at the hip.

"Don't you get it, Horvil?" Ben replied defensively. "Nobody else'll take on the project this late. We *have* to use them now."

The Islander shook his head in confusion. "So what's the problem?"

"The problem is that Aunt Berilla absolutely *hates* Natch with a passion. Don't ask me why. She doesn't want anything to do with him. She doesn't want *us* to have anything to do with him. If she realizes this is Natch's coding job—if she thinks it'll help Natch in any way—she'll yank it right off the floor. No, even worse, she might actually *sabotage* the fucking thing."

"She won't find out," Ben insisted. "Really, Horv, this is all under control."

Horvil sighed. "Let's hope so."

They returned to the conference room to find Jara and Merri in the midst of a heated debate. Jara had been up all night weeding through marketing theories for a model to use in the presentation until, desperate, she had asked Merri for help. Since the moment she'd stepped off the teleportation platform, the channel manager had been slingshotting around the globe to sales meetings with Robby Robby. She hadn't even found the opportunity to change out of the horribly unfashionable gray robe TeleCo made its customers wear during the transfer process. Yet she had readily agreed to help, a decision she now appeared to regret.

A pack of SeeNaRee hyenas studiously watched the back-and-forth from a safe distance in the brush.

"*Tell* her we need something simple," said Jara, turning to Horvil as if looking for an ally.

Merri frowned. In a futile effort to stop the trembling, a common side effect of teleportation, she was gripping her thighs hard enough to draw blood. "The Four Phases of Technological Evolution *are* simple. They're not—"

"Creed propaganda."

"They're *not* creed propaganda. Just because they're part of Objectivv doctrine doesn't mean they're not universal. Everyone knows the Four Phases—it's a part of the culture now."

"I've heard people talk about them at Creed Élan," said Benyamin.

"You see? It's really very simple. Observation: humanity distinguishes itself from nature. Exploitation: humanity establishes its dominance over nature. Synergy: humanity learns to become one with nature. Transcendence: humanity surmounts the rules of nature altogether. Take the example of teleportation—"

Jara threw her hands up in the air. "Natch wants *simple*. Fifteen minutes or less. Petrucio Patel kept crowing about 'safe shores' in his promo. *We've* got to be excitement and adventure on the high seas. I'm sorry, Merri, but the Four Phases will just put everybody to sleep. We need a sales pitch, not a sermon."

Quell, who had been standing quietly, now poked his sizeable nose between the two bickering apprentices. "Maybe a demonstration would help," he said. Merri looked up in shock at the giant Islander, apparently noticing him for the first time. "I can't show you the latest version until it's back from the shop, but I can show you one of the prototypes Margaret and I put together."

Merri and Jara looked at one another and nodded simultaneously.

"Good," said Quell. "Horvil, help me change the SeeNaRee. Can't do a thing with this miserable collar."

The Islander whispered in his ear as Horvil cast his mind out to the facility databases. A succession of three-dimensional pictures flashed in his head.

He chose one, and the African veldt disappeared with a flash.

The air around the apprentices suddenly filled with bass-thumping music, the kind of xpression board monotony that instinctively caused teenaged girls' hips to gyrate. Then came the smell of freshly cut grass. The apprentices found themselves standing at the nexus of two interlocking diamonds in the dirt. A smattering of white hexagonal bags lay at the corners.

A baseball stadium.

"No, no, Horvil. I want a *classic* field," said Quell. Horvil nodded and switched to the more traditional playing field endorsed by the classic leagues. Soon, the fiefcorpers were standing in a stadium set up like those the ancients had played: a single diamond, four bases, an enormous outfield. Without prompting, Horvil called up a catalog of baseball bats containing everything from laser-polished aluminum to synthetic ash. He selected a squat Kyushu Clubfoot, summoned a cart of classic league baseballs, and then handed the equipment to Quell. "Smoke and fucking mirrors," muttered the Islander as he fumbled with the virtual bat, trying to get a grip on it. Not an easy task without a sense of touch, Horvil realized.

"See that target?" Quell pointed to a bull's-eye painted on the outfield wall captioned with the words BETCHA A BOTTLE OF CHAIQUOKE YOU CAN'T HIT ME. Then he flexed a muscular set of pectorals, tossed a ball up in the air, and knocked it towards right field. The ball hurtled into the wall at the precise center of the target.

"So you can hit a baseball into a bull's-eye," sneered Jara. "What does that have to do with multiple realities?"

The Islander said nothing. Instead, he reached into the cart of baseballs, threw them into the air one by one, and smacked them towards the ChaiQuoke promo. *Bang bang bang bang.* All twenty-four baseballs plunked the bull's-eye in the same exact spot. Quell threw his ponytail over his shoulder and made a low purring noise of satisfaction.

Jara gaped at the collection of virtual balls lying under the bull's-eye. Words escaped her.

A light went on in Horvil's head. He trotted around the infield, his jaw swaying this way and that with excitement. "Don't you get it, Jara? The whole thing's just mathematics. The swing of the bat, the grip, the angle you're holding it, all those neurochemical reactions in your brain—you can describe it all with math. Possibilities just lets you try out different variables and choose the outcome you want."

Quell nodded. "An oversimplification—but yes."

Horvil flopped down onto the grass and stretched out, snow angel style. "So *that's* why we modified those dendrite modules..."

Ben paced slowly towards the ChaiQuoke advertisement and rubbed the paint, as if he expected to feel some kind of magnetic generator in the wall. Meanwhile, Merri retreated into the visitors' dugout and watched the proceedings with hollow eyes as she tried to get a handle on her teleportation-induced trembling.

"Let me get this straight," said Jara, seating herself delicately on the grass next to Horvil.

"MultiReal—Possibilities—creates alternate realities inside your head?"

Quell strode onto the pitcher's mound. His voice took on the tone of a drill instructor. "Let's start from the beginning.

"Forget about MultiReal for a minute. What happens when you throw a ball in the air and swing a bat? The mind takes in sensory input—the sight of the ball, the weight of the bat, the feel of the wind—and processes it. You decide on a course of action. Then the brain sends instructions down the spinal cord into your muscles, right? Electrical pulses tell your body what to do. You swing the bat. It all happens in a fraction of a second.

"But we can *track* all those electrical pulses, right? We can reduce them to mathematical equations. Isn't that how multi works? OCHREs in the brain stem intercept these pulses and transmit them onto the multi network instead of into your own body.

"So what happens if you take these electrical commands from the brain and plot out the results? You get a simulation of what's going to happen. You can see if the swing of the bat is going to turn out the way you want.

"Now, let's go a step further. Once you have a mathematical model in place, what's to stop you from trying out different scenarios? If I had twitched my right arm like *this* instead of like *that*, what would have happened? What if I had gripped the bat a little harder, swung a little faster? You make thousands of tiny unconscious decisions like that every instant. Why not just loop the whole process in your mind and compute it over and over again with different variables until you find a result you're satisfied with? Keep swinging until you hit one out of the park.

"Then—and only then—you choose the reality you want to happen, the *predetermined reality*. Your mind now has an optimized set of instructions to send into the nervous system. The brain outputs those electrical pulses to your body—what we call *closing the choice cycle*—and it happens."

Horvil was making incoherent burbling sounds of delight. But Jara was not convinced. "That's all well and good if you're just trying to hit an inanimate object," she said, hands planted belligerently on her hips. "But what if you've got an outfielder out there trying to catch it first? People aren't mathematical models. You can't just use algebra to predict what they're going to do. What *then*?"

Quell was unruffled. "Ben," he called out across the field. "Go ahead. Try to catch it." The young apprentice nodded, summoned a SeeNaRee baseball glove, and assumed the crouch of a seasoned right fielder in front of the ChaiQuoke target.

Thwak! The Islander knocked the first ball over Benyamin's shoulder, a perfect hit.

Thwak! The second ball flew inches past his face.

Thwak! Another hit.

The charade went on for another dozen swings, with Ben failing to catch the ball each time. Even seemingly easy pop flies slipped through his fingers and smacked unerringly into the wall. The irritation was beginning to show on the young apprentice's face when Quell raised his hand and signaled that the demonstration was through.

"That program has to be pretty good," said Horvil, eyebrows aloft. "Ben's no Angel Palmero, but he's caught a few fly balls in his day."

"It wouldn't have mattered," replied Quell dismissively. "Angel Palmero wouldn't have done any better." He stood the Kyushu Clubfoot on its end like a mercenary displaying his weapon. "MultiReal is a collaborative process."

Horvil's cousin came trotting over from the outfield, clearly perturbed at his poor defensive performance. "Wait a minute—I didn't *collaborate* with anything."

"You don't think you did. But for every missed catch, there were dozens of alternative reality scenarios played out *inside our minds* before they ever actually 'happened.' The whole sequence looped over and over again—dozens of my possible swings mapped out against dozens of your possible catches—dozens of choice cycles—until I found a result I liked."

"But I don't remember any of that happening."

"No. You wouldn't. Not without MultiReal."

Benyamin and Jara sank down into the grass with Horvil, overcome by the dizzying spiral of probabilities and possibilities. Horvil wasn't doing much better. Questions were clambering to the forefront of the engineer's head, but no answers accompanied them. No bio/logic program could conceivably turn the concept of cause-and-effect on its head like that—and yet, somehow, MultiReal just did.

Horvil heard the echo of Margaret Surina's words, spoken three and a half days ago, an incomprehensible lifetime in the past: *The ever-changing flux of MultiReal will become reality. MultiReal will free us from the tyranny of cause and effect itself.*

He thought of the crack team of security guards standing guard just outside, and the multitudes of armed troops patrolling the premises. It seemed like a pitifully small amount of protection. Who knew what MultiReal was really capable of? Who knew what lengths the Defense and Wellness Council would go to in order to possess it? Horvil tried to imagine working under this pressure every day: furtive looks over your shoulder, armed backup whenever you flipped on your workbench. He felt claustrophobic from working in Andra Pradesh for a single evening. Quell and Margaret Surina had been doing this for *sixteen years*.

Merri's tired voice echoed from the dugout. "I think we've found our demonstration." Jara whipped her head around hawklike towards the channel manager, thought for a moment, and then nodded with mute agreement.

Suddenly, Benyamin perked up. "Wait a minute!" he cried. "If we already have the demonstration we're going to use on Tuesday, then we don't have to worry about the assembly-line shop, do we?"

Quell shook his head, causing the young apprentice's demeanor to cloud over once again. "It's a collaborative process, remember? The MultiReal engine Margaret and I put together won't work in front of a big crowd—at least not yet. We need a good predictive engine like Horvil's Probabilities ROD to sort through all the permutations."

Ben shifted uncomfortably. "A collaborative process running among hundreds of millions of people—that's gonna take a heck of a lot of computing power, isn't it?"

"Oh fuck," moaned Jara, burying her head in her hands. "Infoquakes."

Rivers of fear coursed through Horvil's skull. He thought back to the disturbance at Margaret Surina's speech, those sickening few minutes of paralysis and vertigo. Computational vortexes, communication breakdowns.

The Islander's countenance turned predatory. "That's exactly what Len Borda wants you to think," he said.

"And what... what if he's right?" said Merri quietly from her alcove in the dugout. The trembling had started up in her arms again, but Horvil wasn't sure if it was a lingering effect of the teleportation or a new surge of fear.

"Margaret Surina is not an *imbecile*. In all the time she worked on MultiReal, don't you think this problem occurred to her?" Quell's face had turned bloodred with rage, and Horvil could see his fists clenching through the virtual bat, causing it to disappear. "People have been talking about computational resource limitations for years now, long before anybody ever heard of infoquakes. This is not new. Are there risks with MultiReal? Of course. But give us a few more years to optimize the code, and we can limit the risks. In a *rational* and *responsible* society, there's no reason why this program shouldn't see the light of day."

A cold wind blew through the bleachers and made a whistling sound off the metal railings. Suddenly, his tirade over, the Islander seemed to have aged a dozen years. "You think you see all the possibilities now?" said Quell. "Think again. There are possibilities that will scare the living wits out of you. Possibilities you haven't even dreamed of."

(((28)))

Robby Robby's grin began just below one ear and undertook an impossibly long journey down his chin to reach the other. Merri could find no evidence a single granule of stubble had ever blemished that slick face.

"You're looking particularly good this morning, Merri," said the channeler, his voice lightly greased.

The fiefcorp apprentice held back a smirk. She didn't take Robby's Casanova act seriously; she had seen enough of the man's tactics to know it was just part of his sales patter. Robby Robby never walked down any path unless he was convinced a pile of credits awaited him at the end. Still, Merri wondered if her fiercely protective companion would regard his charade quite so casually. "So we're here to discuss the market survey," she said in a no-nonsense tone.

"The market survey, yes." Robby bobbed his head, which Barb-ur-Shop 125k had coifed with a perfect cube of hair. Behind him sat his entire troupe of two dozen channelers, fresh young faces either untouched by experience or polished smooth by it. All had adapted the same ridiculous cube-haired do as Robby. "The folks we're contacting are confused, Merri. They've all heard of the Surina/Natch MultiReal Fiefcorp—we've got *huge* amounts of name recognition. And of course, after that mess with the infoquake, who hasn't heard about MultiReal by now?" Robby's channelers gave sanctimonious nods of agreement up and down the conference table.

Merri smiled. "So is there a problem?" she asked. Of *course* there was a problem.

"Well, when our pollsters started asking folks if they were interested in MultiReal, almost ninety-five percent said yes. Great numbers across the spectrum! But when we asked people whether they thought MultiReal was something they might actually *buy*... What was that number again, Friz?"

"Seventeen point three percent," replied Frizitz Quo, a perky Asian channeler sitting to Robby's right.

The grin on Robby's face narrowed a few microns. "Seventeen point three percent interested in buying MultiReal. I don't need to tell ya, Merri—that's not an encouraging number! Nobody knows what this MultiReal stuff is *for*."

Merri gave a rueful sigh and placed her hands palm up on the table in a gesture of sincerity. During the past few months, she had learned that body language was crucial in the channeling business. "This is a brand-new industry, Robby," she said. "The sky's the limit. We've barely even started counting the possibilities." She thought back to Quell's demonstration yesterday and tried to use deductive reasoning to figure out more practical uses for MultiReal. But as usual, her mind came up blank. "Baseball, for one."

"Yes, baseball." Robby nodded slowly in an unconvincing imitation of agreement. To a pathological yes-man like Robby, the only way to express a differing opinion was to agree less vehemently. "So that leads us to your script. This baseball thing—is Natch going to be able to do that at the demonstration? Is it *possible*?"

"It is," said Merri firmly. "I've seen it."

Robby scratched his head as he pored over the latest draft of Jara's speech, which he had projected onto a viewscreen at one end of the table. Even with the font size bumped up to drudge-headline proportions, the entire script still fit easily within two screenlengths. Robby made a show of flipping through the presentation again, pretending to read it carefully when Merri knew he was really holding a ConfidentialWhisper conversation with his staff— and it was a heated conversation, if the worried grooves on the channelers' foreheads were any indication.

"You know, Merri, I've been working with Natch for a few years now," said Robby. "I *know* this guy pretty well. I've heard what he has to say about the Surinas and their creed babble, and it ain't pretty."

Creed babble? Merri bristled at the slick channeler's characterization, and immediately began rallying a passionate defense of creedism inside her head. Then she imagined how the bodhisattva of Creed Objectivv would respond—*we often call a thing babble that we cannot ourselves understand,* he would say with a good-natured shrug—and she simmered down.

"The point is," Robby was saying, "our man Natch is cynical to the core. Are you *sure* he's okay with this?"

"I've given you access to a whole library of detailed analysis, Robby. You've got an entire history of the Surina name, a list of the Surina clan's accomplishments and inventions, and all those stellar Primo's ratings Natch has been accumulating over the past few years. Robby, this is going to be one of the biggest technological advances the world has ever seen, and Natch wants you with us on the ground floor! Trust me, he can *definitely* do everything in that script." Merri paused to take a deep breath. She couldn't remember the last time she had been so agitated.

"I'm curious, though," Robby mused with a sly look. "If Natch is so committed to this Surina stuff, how come he didn't show up for the meeting today?" He gestured ever so slightly towards the empty chair at the opposite end of the table.

Merri had been wondering precisely the same thing, but she was not about to tell Robby that. She felt the keen temptation to lie, to slip free from the bonds of her Objectivv oath, if only just this once. *Natch had some last-minute coding to finish up. He's doing an interview with Mah Lo Vertiginous right now. He's meeting with Margaret across the courtyard in the Surina residence.* Who would be the wiser?

The depths of this game had suddenly become unfathomable to Merri. Even with company allies in a private meeting, messages were being broadcast, challenges made, gauntlets thrown down. What place did absolute truth have in this cesspool?

Instead of lying, Merri found herself plastering a WinningGrin 44 on her face. "Robby, *you* know what a perfectionist Natch is," she said. "How he wants everything done *his* way, down to the last detail. You know he's going to insist that every last connection strand is absolutely perfect before he goes out on that stage."

Again the placating smile, the fake burst of comprehension. "No doubt!" Robby exclaimed. "So that just leaves us with one more topic."

"Yes?"

"The Council." Merri quickly tossed a Poker-Face 83.4b atop the WinningGrin. "They've been—heck, Merri, they've been harassing my boys and girls here." He tilted his head in the direction of his "boys and girls," who all murmured their assent.

Suddenly, Merri felt very tired. "What do you mean by 'harassing?'"

"It's just your typical Defense and Wellness Council aggravation," said Robby, sweeping his concerns over one shoulder with a long, bony hand. "Requests to see our permits, people following us around, that kind of thing. Friz here got cited for 'walking too close to a tube track' the other day." Friz, the junior channeler, jutted his bottom lip forward and gave his best hangdog look. "Nothing we can't handle, of course. But you know, if we have another one of those infoquakes..."

Robby Robby let the sentence drift off, but Merri was all too ready to complete it. *If we have another one of those infoquakes, the Council might swoop down and take MultiReal from us by force. The public might get frightened away from the product altogether. The drudges might start calling for Natch's head. Any way you look at it, it's entirely possible none of us will make a single credit off this crazy enterprise.*

Again, Merri found herself stretching the bonds of her oath, reaching for the sweet opiate of prevarication. She adopted her most confident tone of voice and enhanced it with bio/logics. "Robby, nobody knows what's really going to happen out there tomorrow—much less next week or next month! Your team is going to be put on the spot, and you might have to do a lot of improvising. You'll probably have to endure a few more of those bogus citations from the Council. But Natch is utterly committed to this product. He hasn't just staked *our* careers on it; he's staked his own. And in the years you've known him, has Natch ever steered you wrong?"

The channeler seemed to be weighing his options for a few excruciating seconds. His eyes flickered on the black-and-white swirl of the Objectivv pin riding her left breast. Finally, Robby dispensed one of his Cheshire cat smiles. The same smile quickly rippled down the table until all two dozen channelers were wearing it. "I gotcha, Merri," said Robby. "You're absolutely right. If this is what Natch wants, this is what Natch gets. We trust in Natch."

I wish I did, Merri said to herself glumly.

Benyamin was experiencing déjà vu, but it had nothing to do with any of Natch's bio/logic programs.

He was standing on the balcony overlooking his mother's assembly-line floor where he had stood for most of the past year. Two hundred workbenches lay in a grid below him. He was younger than many of the programmers, and had less coding experience than almost all of them. It felt like nothing had changed in the past few months, like he had never decided to step out from under Berilla's oppressive wing and seek a job in the fiefcorp sector.

As always, Ben listened for some undercurrent of resentment running through the staff. Were they jealous of this kid who had leapfrogged to the management office straight out of initiation? Did they resent the fact that the monthly interest on his trust fund exceeded half their salaries combined? The answer to these questions, it seemed, was still no. If there was any embittered muttering going on here, it was drowned out by the rumble caused by hundreds of clanking bio/logic programming bars. The assembly-line coders were oblivious. Too busy concentrating on tunes from the Jamm and holding ConfidentialWhisper conversations with distant companions.

"Thirty-one percent done," came a smoky female voice, late forties or early fifties.

Benyamin turned to find Greth Tar Griveth, the woman who had replaced him as floor manager, walking onto the balcony from his old office. *Her* office now. Ben sensed that the job, which had been a whistle stop on the track to success for him, was more like a post of permanent exile for Greth. She had only been here for six weeks, but she had already adapted the vacant stare, the careless flip of the hand, the bored midsentence yawn that had been hallmarks of Ben's seventh and eighth months.

"Only thirty-one percent?" said Ben with a groan. "But we need this done in less than twenty-four hours!"

Greth stood next to him at the railing and let out a weary *ffff*. "We'll get it done. I think."

"You *think*?"

"The second shift is coming on now, and they're much quicker than the first. Plus, we just finished up a gig for the Élanners, so we'll have some more coders to put on the job. Look, over there."

Greth Tar Griveth pointed at the rightmost row of programmers, where Ben could see the Surina/Natch templates slipping silently into the production line. One by one, the workers in that quadrant of the floor completed their current projects and watched blue and pink chunks of code pop up in their MindSpace bubbles. Small bricks in the Gothic castle that was the MultiReal engine. Other coders were gazing numbly at pieces of the Probabilities ROD. If any of them suspected they were plugging away at the world's most notorious compendium of bio/logic code, they showed no sign.

Nor did the salty assembly-line floor manager have a clue what program her crew was laboring away on. Ben had made sure that the words *Natch*, *MultiReal*, and *Surina* did not escape his lips, and he praised the Fates that his apprenticeship to the Surina/Natch Fiefcorp was not yet common knowledge in Creed Élan circles. Still, he took no chances, and made sure a fat sheaf of credits was sitting in Greth's Vault account to dissuade her from asking questions.

"Here's the real test," said Greth, pointing to a gangly kid in the epicenter of the floor whose workbench could have rivaled Horvil's in sloppiness. "They call that kid the Robot. Arrived just after you left, and already he's leading the floor in output. Never complains, never says much of anything."

Ben fastened his gaze on the Robot, who was wrapping up work on someone else's tangled web of a program. Indeed, the young man was tearing through the template with astounding speed. Ben watched as the Robot whirled the mass around with one hand, grabbed the programming bar he needed with the other, and then caught the template backhanded, just in time to make the appropriate connection. "So why's this guy a good test?" said Ben.

"Because he's got absolutely no imagination," replied Greth. She stretched, nearly poking Benyamin in the eye with a stray elbow. "Give him your ordinary coding job and he'll sweep through it in record time. But make the slightest flaw in your template, and he just folds. Look."

True to her words, as soon as the kid moved on to his next job—a golden program that looked like a bowl of fruit—he froze up. The bio/logic programming bars in his hands hovered in place, vibrating like stuck gears. Ben could practically hear the ConfidentialWhisper conversation from his supervisor guiding him through the obstruction. After a ten-minute pause, the Robot hesitantly got back to work. Soon, he was a blur of motion once again.

"If *he* can handle the templates your cousin put together," said Greth Tar Griveth drily, "we'll be okay."

Ben held his breath as the Robot finished up his current assignment and made the swirling-hand motion signaling his readiness to accept a new template. A pink blob, one small corner of the MultiReal engine, appeared in front of him.

The Robot whipped through the template in twenty-two minutes.

Greth loosened her grip on the railing and let out a deep breath. "It'll be close, but I think we'll get your job done on time. Maybe even twenty or thirty minutes early."

Ben inhaled a draught of cool air, expelling a warm puff in return. The billow of air failed to accomplish the calming effect he had intended. "That's cutting it a little too close."

"Yes," replied Greth, not bothering to contradict her predecessor. "It is."

Horvil had almost forgiven the Surina guest lodge for the lumps in its mattress and found a route to sleep when an urgent ConfidentialWhisper reached his mental inbox. The engineer accepted it. He found himself flailing against the wall under the gale-wind force of an angry Jara.

"Emergency meeting!" she cried. "Emergency meeting *now!* Everyone report to the Enterprise Facility!"

Horvil groggily threw on yesterday's clothes and made his way across the Surina compound, discovering along the way that he had put on only one sock. The central courtyard was aflurry with security officers going about their midnight routine, questioning passersby, relentlessly patrolling, checking their weapons and loading dart canisters from their belts. Horvil was not surprised to find the Islander Quell in their midst. He told the newest fiefcorp apprentice about the meeting, and the two quickly followed Jara's beacon to a conference room on the fifth floor of the Enterprise Facility.

They wandered into a piece of SeeNaRee titled Seurat's *Sunday Afternoon on the Island of La Grande Jatte*. Jara stood beside a cool river rendered in tiny pinpricks of color, while Parisian matrons in ridiculous hooped petticoats sauntered on the opposite bank. Her fiery mood made a sharp contrast with the calm pointillist trees. Horvil was about to chide Quell for his SeeNaRee program's poor selection when he caught sight of Merri in the river a few meters down, wading barefoot and watching the ducks. Obviously, the channel manager had arrived here first.

Benyamin showed up moments later, and the five apprentices sat at a plain conference table overlooking the river. "So what's the emergency?" said Ben jauntily.

Jara gestured to the empty chair at the head of the table. "Natch."

"What's wrong with him this time?"

"He's disappeared."

Four blank faces gazed back at her.

"You mean he hasn't been in touch with you at all?" cried Horvil. "I thought he was supposed to be at that meeting with Robby Robby this afternoon."

Merri shook her head. "He didn't show up."

"Well, where the fuck *is* he? Hasn't anybody talked to him since the last fiefcorp meeting?"

Nobody answered. A cloud of black and gray dots descended on them from the east, threatening to dump pixels of rain on the congregating Parisians.

"I've tried requesting a multi connection," said Jara, rubbing the pulsing vein on her temple. "I've sent him at least twenty ConfidentialWhispers. Nothing. I even tried Margaret, but her secretary says she's been holed up with those diss L-PRACG people for three days straight now. Natch isn't there."

"Did you try Serr Vigal?" asked Merri.

Jara nodded grimly. "*He's* not answering me either, although that's not a big surprise. I checked the schedule of that conference in Beijing. He's probably delivering the keynote address right about now."

"Maybe Natch is... *testing* us or something," said Ben to nobody in particular. "Maybe he's just trying to make sure we're on our toes. I know he has some pretty unconventional management tactics."

"Unconventional, yes," replied Horvil. "Totally fucking insane, no."

"Doesn't the man have any private security?" asked Quell.

Jara glared at the Islander as if he had grown a horn from his forehead: "Are you *kidding*?"

Quell let out an animalistic grunt. "I can't believe this," he snarled. "No common sense, just like Margaret. Natch knows he has enemies, doesn't he? The Patel Brothers, the Defense and Wellness Council, the Pharisees, all those programmers and ROD coders and drudges he's pissed off over the years. The list is practically endless."

"Don't forget Lucas Sentinel," put in Horvil, counting on his fingers. "And the Meme Cooperative. Brone. Creed Thassel. Creed Élan. My Aunt Berilla—"

Ben groaned out loud.

"All right, that's enough!" shrieked Jara, slapping one open hand against the table and sending a loud *thwak* echoing through the SeeNaRee. The Parisians snapped their heads up in surprise, as did the rest of the fiefcorp. "It doesn't matter right now. We could sit here for a week naming people who hold a grudge against Natch. What we need to do is *stay focused*. We've got a presentation tomorrow at four o'clock, and I intend for us to be ready for it."

Horvil felt a smile slowly creep onto his face. There was no officially designated Number Two in the fiefcorp hierarchy, but Quell, Merri, and Benyamin seemed ready to follow Jara to the heart of a simmering volcano. At that moment, Horvil was too. "So what do you want us to do?" ventured the engineer.

"I want you to go looking for Natch," said Jara. "You've known him longer than any of us, Horvil. See if you can get into his apartment and look for clues. Go everywhere he might possibly be hiding. Quell, I want you to comb every centimeter of the Surina compound and make absolutely *sure* he's not holed up here somewhere. As for you two, Ben and Merri—just keep working. If those assembly-line programmers don't finish in time—or if the channelers aren't ready—this is all going to be a moot point anyway."

"I've got a friend with the Élanners who runs a private detective agency," said Ben. "Maybe I could—"

Jara cut him off. "No. We don't want word of this to leak out to anybody outside the fiefcorp. *Anybody*, do you hear me? Not even Margaret or Robby. The last thing we need is for the drudges to start spreading rumors. As far as the rest of the world is concerned, Natch is cooped up here with *us*, working on Possibilities."

"And what are you going to be doing, Jara?" asked Merri.

Jara clawed briefly at the vein in her temple, which had begun to throb once more. "I'm going to stay here and come up with a plan."

"A plan for what?" said Ben.

"A plan for what to do if Natch doesn't show up tomorrow."

The panic that had been bubbling beneath the surface now struck the fiefcorp like a miniature infoquake. Merri looked like she might pass out at any minute, while Quell gripped his connectible collar as if preparing to snap it in two. Horvil could feel his OCHREs working to slow a madly racing heart, and he would have bet anything his cousin was using his faraway look as cover while he reviewed his apprenticeship contract. Even the painted denizens of the SeeNaRee were milling around, opening and closing their parasols in confusion.

Only Jara appeared to have mastered her emotions. She stood up and placed her hands flat on the table. "Listen," she said through gritted teeth, "there's only so much time we can spend looking for Natch. You all know him as well as I do. If he doesn't want to be found, he won't be found."

"Why wouldn't he want to be found?" Merri asked.

Glum silence shrouded the table.

"If any of us had the slightest inkling of how Natch thinks, we wouldn't have signed on to this bloody fiefcorp in the first place," said Jara. "Let's get moving. It's one-thirty now. Everybody report back here at nine a.m. sharp."

(((29)))

Natch stood alone on the beach.

Civilization had not reached this place yet, or maybe it had left long ago and taken all of culture's detritus with it. The billboard advertisements, the black code darts, the tube tracks, the hoverbird clouds, the political manifestos, the buildings both large and small, the silly trappings of fashion—all of them gone.

The world reduced to sand, sky, and sun.

The world a million years after humanity had breathed its last gasp.

The sun had risen to its midday perch and looked as if it might stay there for a while. Beneath his feet, the sand had begun to absorb the heat. As the temperature rose and the sand began to sizzle, tiny creatures burrowed their way to the surface of the beach. Sand mites by the millions scrambled around, wildly looking for some relief from the burning, but there was none to be found.

Natch closed his eyes and cast his mind out to the Data Sea to find a bio/logic program that would protect his tender soles, but he could find none. No bio/logic programs, no chatter from the drudges, no Data Sea. Was the vast corpus of human knowledge extinct too? Had it ever existed at all in this place? He opened his eyes again and scanned the horizon, looking for something, anything. A tree to shelter under, a rock with a cool face to it. But the world was completely flat and featureless.

He had begun to hop up and down to ease the burning when he felt an icy drop of water tickle his feet.

The tide was rising. The water carved rivulets in the sand dunes as it spilled onto the beach. Natch leapt down towards the sea and dunked his feet in the spray. He heaved a tremendous sigh of relief and allowed the anxiety to slip from his mind.

Minutes passed before Natch noticed the vast panicked retreat going on in the sand. Millions of tiny creatures—sand mites, miniature crabs, black segmented insects—all dashing pell-mell for higher ground. The saltwater was licking his ankles before he came to a sudden realization: the insects weren't fleeing the heat; they were fleeing the tide.

He turned and headed back up the beach. But the tide was rising faster than he could run. By the time he overtook his own footprints running in the opposite direction, they were submerged beneath half a meter of water. Natch began running as fast as he could, lifting his legs in the air, storklike, to stay above the tide.

The ocean had risen up above his knees when he realized he was not going to make it. The angle of the beach was too shallow, the progress of the tide too rapid. The strip of land he had been aiming for receded farther and farther away with each second. Natch stopped for a minute and turned around to see if there was another place he could head for, someplace safe from the rising tide. But there was nothing in any direction now but endless sea.

He began scrambling madly for higher ground. His splashes were the only noise that could be heard anywhere; the ocean itself did not crash or break or even ripple. Its surface was unbroken and lifeless. Eternal.

The water rose up to his chest, and Natch abandoned all hope of wading. He tried to leap up into a swimming position, but a remarkably strong force pulled on his legs, keeping him down. A deep underwater vortex into which the entire world would eventually sink.

Natch struggled wildly, clinging to his ambitions and desires. MultiReal was out there somewhere. So were number one on Primo's, a Lunar estate, riches, glory. But one by one, he could feel all his cares draining out of him and sliding deep into the watery void. There were no fiefcorps down in that demesne of the drowned, no fiefcorps or memecorps or bio/logic programs or Primo's ratings.

He desperately tried to keep his head above water, but the current was too strong. The tide of nothingness, the Null Current, pulled him under.

Natch could see the light of the sun receding. He could feel the tug of the nothingness below, his final destination. His struggles and his worries seemed so petty once the Null Current had pulled him in. Down here, desire was irrelevant, because the undifferentiated mass of nothingness that was his destination allowed no changes, accepted no arguments, admitted no standards by which to measure and compare. In the deeps, there was nothing to want because there was nothing to gain, nothing to fix because there was nothing to break.

He stopped struggling as the darkness closed in, as the surface became a distant memory, as he was sucked down by the vortex that had no end, the vortex that spiraled down infinitely until it was no longer a vortex, until he and it and everything else melted together and merged into one endless eternal line, a vector pointing nowhere, a vector whose beginnings were irrelevant and improbable, and whose end was forever unreachable.

(((30)))

The apartment building was not much to look at by West London standards, but for Shenandoah, it had style in abundance. One might have said the building *jutted out* from the side of a hill, if not for its sine-wave shape that architects often used to camouflage the constant structural flux. A more appropriate description would have been that the building *rippled* or *undulated* from the hillside. Not the kind of thing you found crammed amidst the pointed abbeys at Bishopsgate.

Horvil had been inside the building a thousand times, of course, at all hours of the day and night. But he usually skipped the exterior view and multied straight to the network gateway in Natch's foyer. Funny how you could spend so much time embedded in a place that you didn't really know what it looked like from the outside.

From the ground, the engineer looked up the side of the tenement and saw several balconies like the one where he, Natch, and Jara had stood and tested NiteFocus 48. It seemed like a million years ago, during a vanished era of innocence. Now all the building's balconies were occupied by strangers.

Horvil walked inside the front doors, nosed around the atrium for a few minutes, then ascended the lift to Natch's flat. He hesitated at the fiefcorp master's door for a few seconds. If Natch wasn't here, the apartment security program would probably let a trusted presence like Horvil invoke emergency protocols and enter. But that would trigger warning messages to Natch and possibly the building management as well. He didn't mind Natch receiving such a message—the entrepreneur might actually *respond* and put an end to this madness—but how much could you really trust a landlord these days? A series of gloating drudge headlines flashed in Horvil's brain: BREAK-IN LEADS TO MASSIVE MANHUNT FOR MISSING FIEFCORP MASTER... NATCH LEAVES APPRENTICES HIGH AND DRY... MISSING ENTREPRENEUR "A WORTHLESS HUMAN BEING," SAYS LANDLORD.

Horvil entered, stood in the foyer, and counted to twenty. Nothing happened.

It took Horvil only a few minutes to determine there was no bloody corpse stinking up the premises. No scattered debris on the counters, no body standing on the red tile, no sign of a struggle. But he could see no evidence the place had been inhabited the past few days either. Not that Natch's messes could compare to the colossal disasters Horvil usually left for his cleaning bots, but a few half-drunk cups of chai or nitro could usually be found on his table at any given time. Today, however, nothing.

Horvil knew the real test was not in the common areas, but in the office. That was where Natch spent most of his time anyway. The engineer poked his nose into the room and made a major discovery: Natch's bio/logic programming bars were gone. Of course, they could be lying in one of the drawers under the workbench, drawers that a multi projection could not physically open. But in all the years Horvil had known him, Natch had never set his programming bars anywhere but the top of the bench or on a side table within easy reach.

Wherever Natch went, he took his bio/logic programming tools with him, thought Horvil. *So what does that mean?*

The fiefcorp apprentice wandered to the window and tuned it transparent. Natch would have headed northeast past the billboard (BANDWIDTH CONSERVATION IS PEOPLE PRESERVATION: *A message from Creed Conscientious*), towards the main city, towards the TubeCo station.

Towards the small cluster of officers in white robes now pointing in Horvil's direction.

Horvil instantly flipped on the window's sunblock and ducked out of the officers' line of sight. *Don't be so paranoid, Horv*, the engineer scolded himself. *Just Council officers doing a routine patrol. They weren't pointing at you.*

But was it really so implausible to think Len Borda's goons might be scoping out Natch's apartment? Especially now, when he was mere hours away from demonstrating MultiReal to an audience of billions?

Horvil scurried out of the apartment and down the lift, whether to hide from the officers or to follow them, he could not say. He stood in the atrium and looked out the window, still vacillating between courses of action, when his eye caught a glint of metal on the ground reflected from the just-risen moon, past the billboard in the gutter on the side of the road. Horvil launched NiteFocus 50c and fine-tuned his vision with Bolliwar Tuban's TeleScopics 88 to make sure. Yep, definitely a bio/logic programming bar.

Eventually, the coven of Council troops moved westwards toward the hoverbird facilities. The engineer thrust his head outside the front door and scanned the horizon, left to right and back again. None of the officers carried bulky disruptors, but who knew which of the surrounding buildings contained one the Council could summon at a moment's notice? When the coast was clear, he darted northwest as fast as his feet could carry him.

Horvil knelt on the ground and examined the object closely, wishing his multi projection could solidify long enough for him to pick it up. A thin rod of burnished metal, nondescript but for the Roman letter S embossed near one end and a small dent in one corner. The kind of dent a tightly wound programmer might make by repeatedly whacking the bar against a hard workbench.

If this was indeed Natch's bio/logic programming bar, then what were the odds of Horvil finding it here? The fact that the municipal L-PRACG had not swept it up by now was a pretty astronomical coincidence in itself.

And if it was Natch's—how did it get here? And what did its presence mean?

Jara had the same questions.

"I'm not saying it means *nothing*," said the analyst, looking drawn and haggard from lack of sleep.

"I'm not saying the bar *doesn't* belong to Natch. But there have to be hundreds of people who walk by that spot every day carrying programming tools. Anybody could have dropped that bar."

"But the dent," protested Horvil. "The fact that the bars weren't in his apartment—"

"Circumstantial evidence. And besides, what if you're right? What if that *was* Natch's stuff lying on the street? It's useless information. Unless Natch left a trail of metal bars leading across town like bread crumbs, it won't help us."

Benyamin rocked back and forth in his seat impatiently. "The *least* we can do is send someone to go get it."

"No," said Jara. "Multi projecting to Shenandoah is one thing, but sending someone there in the flesh is another. What if someone's trying to use that bar to lure us away from the Surina compound? We came here to Andra Pradesh to keep safe. We need to stay here."

The young apprentice muttered something under his breath and arose from his chair with a look of defiance. "*I'll* go," he said.

"No, you *won't*," snapped Jara. "You need to ride herd on those assembly-line programmers and make sure we've got a product ready to show this afternoon. Now *sit down*." Blood rushed to Benyamin's face. He looked to Horvil, Merri, and Quell for support, but found only awkward silence. Horvil gave an almost imperceptible gesture downwards towards the chair, and his cousin crumpled to his seat.

"I think we need to try contacting Serr Vigal again," said Quell.

Jara shook her head. "What's the matter with you people? We've been through this, Quell. We keep going round in circles, the same arguments *over* and *over* again for hours." The analyst scoped out the conference table for a suitable object to use as a projectile, found none, and pressed her fingertips to the mahogany all the harder. "Even if Vigal was returning my messages, we can't have *him* deliver the speech. He's just not a good enough huckster. Have you ever sat through one of his neural programming speeches? They're excruciatingly boring."

"I'm afraid to say it, but I agree with Jara," offered Merri.

"But Vigal's got a reputation in the programming community," said Quell. "He's got a following. He knows what he's talking about."

"And after the tenth time he stops midsentence to scratch his bald head, people are going to wonder where Natch is. They're going to think something has gone terribly wrong in the Surina/Natch MultiReal Fiefcorp, and consumer confidence in us is going to plummet before we can even get a product to market. Blowing your first major company presentation is worse than not doing one at all."

"So why don't we cancel already?" mumbled Horvil, his head bowed to the table under the confining archway of his clasped hands, as if waiting for a guillotine to drop.

"Because we have an alternative," said Jara.

The Islander let out a brutish noise halfway between a grunt and a laugh. "Now *you're* the one who's going around in circles. How many times do I have to say this? Margaret won't do it. She's handed the project off to Natch—she's not going to jump back into this whole business again."

Jara frowned, brushing one finger slowly over her bottom lip. "I realize you've known Margaret longer than any of us—for process' preservation, I've never even *met* her except for that two-minute appearance she put in at the fiefcorp meeting the other day. But I'm just not convinced. We've got a first-rate demonstration. Merri's been working with Robby Robby to get the crowd fired up. The entire thing is laid out. All Margaret has to do is stand up and deliver it. How can she refuse?"

"The infoquake," said Quell. "She keeps saying the whole thing was her fault. She thinks those people died because of *her*."

"Delusions of grandeur," muttered Ben.

Quell glared sharp slashing daggers at the young apprentice. "When you're the daughter of the Surinas," he snarled, "there's no such *thing* as a delusion of grandeur."

"That notwithstanding," said Jara, "I have to try to convince her. For process' preservation, Quell—this woman is a scientist. She'll listen to reason, won't she?"

(((3 1)))

Jara marched through the Surina Center for Historic Appreciation with her miniature fists clenched. Security guards haloed her like massive blue-green planets orbiting a small but furious star. She approached the atrium through an archway labeled SUBAETHER COURT. A score of disgruntled visitors glared at Jara when she passed, as if she were responsible for their being muscled out of the atrium.

But the fault lay with the nondescript woman in the center of the domed room gazing up at the statue of a skinny man with a large nose. He was not the largest of the scientific titans adorning the dome, but his stone effigy had an almost mythical presence. The man stood calmly with one hand extended, not offering a welcoming gesture so much as making a commanding sweep. At his feet were carved the words:

> ANYTHING WORTH DOING IS
> WORTH PERFECTING.
> —Sheldon Surina

Next to the father of bio/logics, Margaret Surina was a half-presence at best. She looked like she might disintegrate inside her bodhisattva's robes at any moment. Her face was solemn, even apologetic. An internal monologue flashed behind her eyes like distant lightning.

Jara could spare no time for pity. She shook herself loose from the Surina guards and stalked to the bodhisattva's side. The guards established a perimeter around the room and kept their distance. "I've been trying to find you for almost *two hours*," said Jara.

Margaret did not even acknowledge Jara's presence. "The Texan governments tried to assassinate him," said the bodhisattva, her gaze never leaving that of her ancestor. Even carved in stone, Sheldon Surina bore a look of self-importance. "The public hated him for a long time too. People always forget about that. The Three Jesuses called him a devil, and the Pharisees slaughtered thousands of his supporters for sport. He came up with the idea for MindSpace sitting in a cave in the Himalayas."

"Natch has disappeared," said Jara.

"I know."

The bio/logic analyst took a step back in surprise. Margaret *knew?* Then why hadn't she answered all the messages and ConfidentialWhispers Jara had been flinging her way? As one of the firm's senior partners, why hadn't she immediately called a meeting to discuss alternative plans for the presentation? Jara felt like crying at the unfairness of it all. *How come I'm the only one willing to fight for this fiefcorp? Why is it that when push comes to shove, Natch disappears, Serr Vigal prives himself to all communication, and Horvil just falls apart? And yet I'm the one who's trying to get out of this whole nightmare. I'm the one who wants to put this MultiReal shit behind me and get on with my life.*

"If you want to honor Sheldon Surina's memory," Jara said in a slow and deliberate tone of voice, "then you'll stop feeling sorry for yourself and help us figure out an alternate course of action."

Margaret recoiled as if she had just been slapped. "I have no idea where Natch is. I didn't do anything to him."

"I'm not suggesting you did. But *you're* the one who set this whole thing in motion."

"Indeed?"

"Come on, Margaret! You created this fucking program; you dragged Natch and the rest of us into this business. You stood up there in front of billions of people and announced a bold new era of multiple realities. It's too late to back out now. You have a responsibility—no, an *obligation*—to see it through."

"An obligation to whom? To *you?*" The descendant of Sheldon Surina snorted haughtily. "I don't *know* you."

"You know Natch," said Jara. "You know Quell."

Margaret firmed up her jaw, looking again at the cool stone representation of her ancestor. Natch's name had produced barely a ripple on the bodhisattva's face, but mention of the Islander had obviously shaken her. "My obligation," she replied, "is to him." By *him*, clearly, Margaret meant the big-nosed stone statue and not anyone this side of the grave.

Jara stomped her foot and only restrained herself from yelling at the venerable bodhisattva by sheer force of will. Hadn't she been through this same scenario with Natch just a few weeks ago, when he all but announced his intention to frame his apprentices for that little black code scheme? Was there something inherent in the bio/logics trade that caused fiefcorp masters to lose their moral bearings? "So after sixteen years of working on this thing, you're just going to give up."

"Now who's playing the victim? You're not an invalid, Jara." Until that moment, Jara had not been sure the bodhisattva even knew her name. "I'm quite certain Natch didn't hold a dartgun to your chest and force you to sign an apprenticeship contract. When you start a new business, there are always risks. You didn't think Natch and I were going to take all those risks while you sat back and watched millions of credits pour into your Vault account, did you?"

Blistering words clawed at Jara's windpipe, struggling for release. But at that moment, a Surina security guard trotted up to Margaret with a fist raised chin-level in salute. The bodhisattva gave the man a sidelong glance. Then the color drained from her face in response to some word she heard over ConfidentialWhisper.

"Go ahead," rasped Margaret, stumbling towards the window with a hand clutching her stomach. "You might as well tell *her*."

The officer turned to Jara and saluted smartly. "The Defense and Wellness Council is coming."

"*What?*"

"Several hundred hoverbirds have been spotted on the outskirts of Andra Pradesh. Three or four legions of Council officers are heading this way."

Jara felt her knees buckle, and before she knew it, she was sitting on the ground, woozy, her back leaning against Sheldon Surina's toes. Was it going to happen this easily? Just like Margaret's speech last week, Len Borda's troops were going to surge into the Surina compound and disrupt the proceedings—maybe even seize MultiReal by force—in front of the entire world.

Margaret pressed her forehead against the glass. A look of doom washed over her face. "You see?" she cried. "He's never going to stop, not until I'm dead and MultiReal is under his control. And what can anybody do about it? *What* can anybody *do* about it?"

Jara said nothing. Words seemed quite beside the point.

"Nothing to say? I thought so." The bodhisattva cast a hateful glance back at Jara, reached into a gap in her robes, and drew a sleek silver dart-pistol. "Well, don't worry. The high executive is about to find out that confiscating MultiReal won't be as easy as it looks.

"The Spire!" she roared to her security detail, then stormed out the front door into the courtyard. Her cordon of guards followed close behind.

Millions of spectators had already poured into the Surina auditorium to await the first public demonstration of MultiReal. Despite Creed Conscientious' pleas, nobody seemed deterred by the prospect of another infoquake. They wanted to catch a glimpse of the infamous Natch, to see if he really deserved his reputation among the drudges. They wanted to measure Margaret Surina's accomplishments against those of her ancestors. More than anything, they just wanted to bask in the glow of history.

A carnival atmosphere swirled through the arena. Drudges and politicians of every ideological stripe wandered around broadcasting their analysis of the spectacle to their constituencies. Fiefcorp apprentices flaunted product slogans on their shirts and foreheads in vivid glow-in-the-dark colors. Creed devotees multied into the arena dressed in full creed regalia, while bodhisattvas from fringe groups stood on chairs and preached to anyone who would listen. Groups of children clustered together under the aegis of their hives, accompanied by stern-faced proctors of business, programming, politics, and ethics. A few dozen L-PRACG activists multied into the auditorium stark naked and began chanting a tepid protest of Vault lending practices. One by one, they were caught in the beam of the Surina security disruptors and their multi connections cut. Council officers were nowhere to be seen.

Merri had been standing at the foot of the stage since the first thirty-five thousand spectators arrived and the auditorium began overlapping multi projections. She felt a strange sense of privilege to be here as a real body; it was quite literally a one-in-a-million opportunity. Fiefcorp apprentices living on the moon usually did not receive this kind of privilege.

Her reverie was interrupted by a reedy voice Merri had heard all too often over the past few days. "Say you run an assembly-line programming floor, and you're on a tight deadline. You don't have time to make mistakes." Merri zeroed in on the source of the voice, and saw Frizitz Quo not three meters away, holding court before an audience of Meme Cooperative officials. "Every time one of your workers fumbles a connection, that's a few precious minutes you've wasted. A few credits MultiReal could have saved you. Now multiply that by a few hundred workers, and that's *real* money..."

Merri tuned out the sprightly Asian and called up the grid that would show her the location of Robby Robby's entire team of cube-headed channelers. A diagram of the arena appeared in the air before her, speckled with purple dots to indicate the coordinates of each team member. A legend in the corner of the diagram silently tallied up audience demographics.

Robby Robby himself had roped together an ad hoc group of nearly six thousand orbital colony residents, and was busy preaching the gospel of... something. Merri tuned in a video feed. "We know what you're going through out there," exclaimed Robby, his idiotic grin wobbling sympathetically. "The last to know. The last to hear. The last to be *noticed*. Right?"

A lukewarm cheer from the crowd.

"Who suffered during the infoquake last week? Was it the Terrans? Was it the Lunars? No, of course not—it was *you*. Am I right? You citizens of Allowell, of Patronell, of Furtoid, of 49th Heaven, of Nova Ceti, and all the rest—it was *you* who bore the brunt of that terrible catastrophe, wasn't it?"

A righteous buzz of discontent. A few raised fists.

"Well, keep those multi connections right here in Andra Pradesh, ladies and gentlemen, because tonight the Surina/Natch MultiReal Fiefcorp is gonna show you a whole new dawn for orbital colonists—"

Merri cut off the feed and shook her head. Robby and his channelers had been wandering all over the map during the past few hours, voicing new sales motifs at every exchange. Her instincts told her she should rein Robby in, insist he stay on message. But did it really matter what the channelers said at this point? They were pitching a technology nobody understood to crowds that had no idea whether they should care. Merri couldn't really ask any more of Robby's staff than to keep the audience interested and upbeat.

She was about to head backstage for a much-needed break when she felt a tug at her elbow. "There you are!" cried a worried Benyamin. "I've got to show you this. You won't believe—"

Merri put a calming hand over Ben's. "Slow down," she said. "Take a deep breath. How's the assembly line going?"

"Almost done. They're putting the final touches on right now. But *this* is more important."

The channel manager let him drag her across the stage and up into the mezzanine. She was feeling the first twinges of impatience when the word *Petrucio* caught her ear.

"Yes, yes, yes, of *course* it's true that the Patels are licensing MultiReal from Surina/Natch," stated a rail-thin woman of Polynesian descent who stood on a makeshift podium fielding questions from several thousand fiefcorp masters. "Why bother to deny it? The MultiReal you're going to see here today is the same MultiReal Frederic and Petrucio will be demonstrating later tonight. Same product, different brand."

Merri fed the woman's face into the public directory and soon verified her suspicions. She had never actually seen Xi Xong outside a viewscreen, where her emaciated frame often sat alongside Robby Robby, Phrancoliape, and the Felwidge Group in drudge roundups of the top channeling firms. But given the amount of work Xong did for the Patel Brothers, Merri should have expected her appearance here tonight.

"There have to be some kind of Meme Cooperative regulations against this," whispered Benyamin. "That woman can't just come here into *our* audience and start stealing customers, can she?"

"I'm afraid she can," replied Merri with a sigh. "There's not really much we can do about it. If we kick her out, she'll only draw more attention."

As it was, Xong did not seem to have any trouble attracting attention. With her opal-bedecked kimono and her glittering nail polish, she presented quite an elegant contrast to Robby's slick hucksterism. "The Patels look forward to a long and prosperous relationship with Margaret and Natch," continued Xi Xong, responding to a muffled question from the crowd. "Competitors? Why, certainly the Patels have had a little friendly competition with Natch over the years. What of it?"

"Friendly?" protested one of the onlookers. "They've done everything but try to kill each other."

A frothy laugh bubbled from Xong's china doll lips. "Don't believe everything you hear from the drudges!" she said with a dark twinkle in her eye.

"So there's no love lost between Natch and my clients. What does that matter? MultiReal is a wide-open market, and there will be more than enough room for two fiefcorps here. Besides, don't they say that a rising tide lifts all boats? As long as that tide pushes a few boats towards our safe shores, then everyone wins."

Merri couldn't help but admire the woman's poise, even if her wardrobe was too gaudy for the channel manager's taste. She caught sight of one of Robby's boyish cube-heads bounding up the aisles, and for a split second wished she could exchange sales teams.

"Do you want to know what the worst part is?" said Benyamin. "She's not the only one here trying to poison Natch's reputation."

Merri frowned. "Who else?"

"You might as well ask who *isn't* here. Lucas Sentinel has a whole group here spreading lies. Pul-Corp, Billy Sterno, Bolliwar Tuban, the Serlys, the Deuterons, Studio Fitzgerald—they've all got their own people mouthing off in the wings."

"Jara was right."

"About what?"

"It's too late to cancel. With all these fiefcorps looking for blood, we've got to pull this demonstration off, or we're *finished* in this business."

Jara tried on several courses of action in her head, but none of them fit. She could run, but there really wasn't anywhere to run to. She could hide, but that would be utterly futile given the surveillance technology at the Council's disposal. Jara thought about what the protagonists of the dramas did in these kinds of situations. They relied on glib words and cool detachment, of course, two things that Jara did not possess. What would Natch do?

A low crescendo of thunder swept across the courtyard and set the window panes vibrating. Rhythmic thumps. *Boom boom, boom boom*. It took her a few minutes to decipher the sound as that of a thousand boots marching on travertine in perfect synchronization. She listened intently for signs of battle—the high-pitched whine of continuous dartgun fire, the muffled boom of disruptors, all the war noises the dramas had trained her to recognize over the years. But if there was indeed a skirmish going on outside, none of it was reaching Jara's ears.

The tourists who had been kicked out of the atrium half an hour earlier came scurrying by. A toddler gave Jara a curious look over her mother's shoulder as they fled past Albert Einstein into Relativity Hall. They were followed shortly by a phalanx of panicked green-and-blue Surina guards, fumbling with their dartguns as they scrambled to reach some defensive checkpoint. Jara dissolved as much as possible into Sheldon Surina's open-toed sandals, but nobody paid her any attention. Obviously, Len Borda had not even bothered repeating his fiction about protecting the scientist statues this time.

Outside, the first row of Defense and Wellness Council officers strode past the window. Their white robes looked positively spectral in the cloudy afternoon light, an affront to the notion of camouflage. Their faces bore the kind of stonelike neutrality that only bio/logics could produce. They were aiming squarely for the Revelation Spire, where Margaret was presumably holed up in a high story awaiting some kind of apocalyptic showdown. Jara peered out another window that gave her a view closer to the Spire. She had seen a squadron of Surina security forces there earlier, but now they had vanished.

What would Natch do under these circumstances? Jara knew exactly what he would do: he would go ahead and give the presentation anyway, until someone physically dragged him off the stage or blew him into a million pieces.

An idea popped into Jara's head, an idea that had been percolating for hours even though she had refused to acknowledge it.

Why couldn't *she* deliver the presentation?

Casting her mind out to the Surina facilities, Jara discovered that the spectators were indeed staying put in spite of Len Borda's little incursion. The Surina/Natch MultiReal Fiefcorp was scheduled to hit the stage in little more than an hour, and the auditorium already held almost 400 million multi projections. If these numbers kept up, this would be an even *larger* crowd than the one Margaret had garnered last week—maybe even large enough to rival the 1.3 billion who had attended Marcus Surina's funeral forty-six years ago.

When the tromp of the troops became deafening, Jara put her hands over her ears and slithered even farther into the shadows. Still feeling exposed and vulnerable, she reached into her bio/logic bag of tricks and turned on Cocoon 32, a Lucas Sentinel program that had helped calm her down many times in the past.

Jara could instantly feel the tumult from the outside world fading away as her OCHREs filtered out the sounds around her and dimmed her sight until everything had faded to a dull gray. No ConfidentialWhispers, no incoming messages. No background chatter from the Data Sea.

Could she really stand up in front of a billion people and demonstrate a technology she barely understood herself? And not just any technology—perhaps the most radical invention in the history of humanity, and one that was almost completely untested.

There were a million reasons why she couldn't deliver the presentation. Jara had no experience speaking in front of large crowds. She had a bad reputation in the bio/logics industry. She hadn't swung a baseball bat in nearly twenty years.

But what other options did she have at this point? Slink off to a tube station and go home? Wait for the hubbub to die down and then drop a groveling ConfidentialWhisper to Lucas Sentinel asking for her old job back?

Face it, Jara, she told herself. *You want to fail.*

The thought surprised and angered her. She wanted to fail. She wanted Natch's latest business venture to go down in flames. The analyst conjured a mental picture of herself: a small, fluttering, frightened thing, cowering at the feet of marble goliaths, men and women with minds and hearts and wills of stone.

And suddenly something inside of her rebelled. *That's not me*, she thought. *I can't be like that. To settle for failure—that's like accepting death. If I just sit back and let things happen, I might as well have never lived in the first place.*

Jara took a deep breath, counted to twenty, and flipped off the Cocoon. She had made her decision.

At just that moment, a familiar figure came barreling around the corner. He screeched to a halt in the middle of the room as soon as he saw the analyst, but the tub of jelly around his gut obeyed the laws of inertia and kept going. The statue of Isaac Newton looked on with amusement as Horvil toppled to the ground in accordance with the good scientist's theories.

"Oh, thank goodness!" bellowed the engineer, crawling his way across the floor to Jara's side. "I've been looking all over for you."

Jara gave her fellow apprentice a look of steely determination. "Horv, I'm going to deliver the presentation."

Horvil's mouth gaped open. "No luck with Margaret?"

She shook her head. "Quell was right. Margaret's gone totally offline. She ran to the Revelation Spire with a dartgun. I think she's going to make some kind of last stand up there. So with Natch gone and Margaret out of the picture, I guess it's up to me."

The engineer's face turned white. "Jara, there are *Council officers* out there. Thousands of 'em."

"I don't care. I'm not just going to *sit* here and do nothing."

"They'll stick you with black code darts like a pincushion before they let you set foot on that stage."

"Then they'll have to do it in front of a billion people."

Horvil's face took on a look of panic. His eyes tilted upwards as if beseeching the father of bio/logics for an infusion of sanity. "Listen to me," he said, grabbing Jara's tiny hands and clutching them tightly within his own. "We can delay the presentation. Nothing says we have to do ours before the Patel Brothers do theirs. We can just lie low and do the whole show some other time."

"Are you completely deranged? If we put this off, the Patel Brothers will eat us for lunch. They'll pounce on us, and we'll have to spend the next month digging ourselves out."

"So what? Is it really worth it, Jara? Maybe Margaret's right. Just let it go."

"Horvil, these are our *lives* we're talking about here. This is our *business*. Don't you care about the fiefcorp and MultiReal and—and everything we've worked for in the past five years?"

"No."

Jara blanched, momentarily struck dumb. "No?"

The engineer's face blossomed into a shy smile completely devoid of irony. "All I care about is not losing you."

Jara sat stunned, unsure what to say. Was he trying to put her off her guard? Or maybe this had something to do with their unspoken rivalry for Natch's favor? Certainly the big lummox couldn't be sincere. In the three years she had known him, Horvil had barely uttered a single word that wasn't laced with sarcasm. Jara sighed. Why was it that as soon as she found her own moment of mental clarity, everything else had to slide out of focus?

"Horvil," she said gently, bundling her hands inside the warm nest of the engineer's palms. "I hope you can understand this. But I have to make that presentation. I just *have* to. This isn't about the fiefcorp or Natch, or—or product release schedules. It's about *me*. It's about... not backing down. Not *failing*."

The engineer considered this for a moment. Jara couldn't imagine what thoughts were running through his head. Could a rich boy from the other side of London who had never had a moment of financial instability in his entire life still understand a crisis of conscience? "You have to promise me you'll be all right," he said.

Jara smiled sadly. "I'm afraid that's not up to me."

There was no burst of comprehension, no sudden epiphany behind Horvil's eyes. But finally he nodded and clenched the analyst's hands tightly. "Okay," he said. "So how can I help?"

"You can help me navigate. Do you know if there's a back entrance to the arena?" She gestured through the window at the now-familiar sight of Council officers roaming freely around the Surina courtyard. Their ranks ringed the Revelation Spire like a white crown, and lined the boulevard to the arena's front doors as well. The Surina security guards were nowhere to be found. "Obviously, we can't go that way."

Horvil jutted his chin out with determination, and the two of them rose to their feet. "As a matter of fact," he said, "there's a side entrance, through the museum here. Quell took me past it yesterday."

Jara brushed off her trousers and gave the Surina statue a respectful nod. "Let's go, then."

The fiefcorp apprentices zipped past the statue of Tobi Jae Witt and down the hall. They dodged their way through a warren of curio tables and around a variety of large metal contraptions that had once housed Witt's experiments in artificial intelligence. The halls were now mostly empty of people. The few stragglers they did see were either terrified tourists looking for an escape route or Surina security forces hustling back towards the square.

Something about the conversation in the atrium had completely changed Horvil's demeanor. Minutes ago, he had been fearful for Jara's safety. But now he was taking the lead, lumbering into corridor intersections as if preparing to use his belly to shield her from a barrage of darts. Jara looked at the engineer with a broad smile on her face. She wondered whether Horvil planned on taking the stage with her, and whether she would try to stop him if he did.

Horvil and Jara crossed over a walkway that bridged the Center for Historic Appreciation with the auditorium. They tried to keep low to avoid attention, but most of the soldiers below were fixated on the Revelation Spire anyway. Hundreds of dart-rifle barrels poked from the notches in the Spire walls, daring the Council troops to come any closer.

"The arena's just past that door," said Horvil. "The stage entrance is down the stairs."

Jara opened the door to the arena and found herself confronted with a sea of white robes.

The gathering crowd still stood at half a billion strong, but their ranks now included a large number of Defense and Wellness Council troops. The officers surrounded the stage and lined every aisle in the place. Just like last time, they silently shouldered their dartguns, their faces sculpted of stone.

Horvil gulped. "You ready?"

"As I'll ever be."

They galloped down the stairs, opting now for speed rather than stealth. The two reached the bottom and rounded the last corner. Sure enough, the corridor angled upwards and ended in a single metal door that would lead them directly onto the arena stage. Jara had not expected this last approach to the stage to be unguarded. But when she saw the three people standing in front of the door, she gasped and snapped on a PokerFace 83.4b.

Serr Vigal, the preeminent neural programmer.

Len Borda, high executive of the Defense and Wellness Council.

And Natch, master of the Surina/Natch MultiReal Fiefcorp.

(((3 2)))

Jara took an awkward step backwards, tripped, and fell neatly into Horvil's arms.

She hadn't realized that Len Borda was so *tall*. He towered over the rest of them like a thin rock pillar, his bald head its capstone. She would have recognized his dour face instantly anywhere in the world, whether or not he wore the Council's white robe and yellow star.

Jara tried but could not shake her head clear of historical vertigo. Standing before her was the high executive of the Defense and Wellness Council himself. The man who had led the world's most feared military and intelligence organization for fifty-seven years and counting. The man who had personally sparred with giants like Lucco Primo, Kordez Thassel, and Marcus Surina. The man who had single-handedly defeated the Economic Plunge of the 310s. The man who had mastered the intricacies of his post long before Jara was born.

She thought of all the wild and unverifiable rumors she had heard about Len Borda over the years. The secret interrogations... the hidden fortresses... the pitiless military strikes... the all-pervasive network of spies and snooping programs. And now that face was directly in front of her. Were the firm grooves on the man's brow a manifestation of evil intent, as the libertarian drudges contended, or merely the chiseled remnants of nature's implacable forces?

The high executive barely noticed her presence. "I will speak to the crowd," he said to Natch in a gravelly basso profundo. "You have ten minutes."

Jara glanced at the fiefcorp master. At first glimpse, Natch appeared calm and collected, dressed in a sharp navy-blue pinstripe suit. Only someone who had studied his every pore and wrinkle ten thousand times could tell he was tottering on the brink of collapse. She detected traces of the stimulant program QuickPrep on his face. "I need twenty," Natch said firmly.

"Twenty then." Borda's tone of voice left the impression that twenty minutes was what he had been after all along. He waved a hand, and the door to the arena stage slid open, bathing him in the spotlight.

Jara mustered all of her courage and spoke to the retreating high executive. "What about all those troops out there?" she cried.

Borda paused and gave her an unyielding look. The look of a man who could pinpoint her precise location, down to the minutest degree, in the orgchart of the universe.

The analyst felt a hand on her shoulder, and turned to find Serr Vigal. "Jara, the Council is here for our protection," he said gently. "It was Natch's idea."

She gaped at the neural programmer, uncomprehending. "And... Margaret?"

"She'll be fine," replied Borda. "Unfortunately." The high executive continued through the doorway and disappeared onto the stage. The door closed behind him.

Natch was already huddled with Horvil, listening intently to the engineer's instructions on how to operate the MultiReal program. There was no time to break down all that complexity into bite-sized pieces; Horvil was speaking pure calculus at this point. Natch gave no sign he understood the formulas his old friend was reeling off.

Jara turned to Serr Vigal. The neural programmer looked exhausted, and his eyes were full to the brim with concern for his protégé.

"Natch was hit with black code," said the neural programmer in response to her unspoken question. "He just woke up a few hours ago."

"The Patels?"

"Maybe, maybe not. He doesn't remember very much."

The fiefcorp master and the engineer were now dashing around trying to find a conference room with SeeNaRee capabilities. Quell happened to show up at that precise moment, and he quickly led them to an out-of-the-way door under the stage. Natch, Horvil, Jara, Quell, and Serr Vigal rushed in and found themselves standing at home plate on the baseball diamond again. Horvil conjured up a ball and a Kyushu Clubfoot, then tossed them to the fiefcorp master. Natch took a deep breath, threw the ball skywards, and swung.

He missed.

He picked up the ball, chucked it in the air, and missed again.

On the fifth attempt, Natch finally connected. But the bottom edge of the bat barely nicked the ball, causing it to limp towards first base and roll to a stop in the infield.

"I can't get this fucking thing to work, Horvil!" cried Natch, flush with rage. "Didn't Ben's people hook those programs together? What the fuck have you all been *doing* these past few days?"

"Benyamin's team got the job done," said Quell, doing his best to ignore the fiefcorp master's slight. "I tested the program myself."

The engineer patted his boss's virtual shoulder. "Just as you begin the swing, you've got to reach out with your mind towards the Possibilities interface and make sure you don't—"

"Never mind," Natch said gruffly. "There's no *time*. I'll figure it out. Jara, show me the script."

She did. *Let me do the presentation instead*, she almost said. *I'm ready, I've had a chance to experiment with Possibilities 1.0 in the past few days*. But Jara could see the iron resolve in Natch's eyes, the single-minded insanity that kicked in whenever he was backed into a corner. Her little catharsis at the museum withered, wormlike, into the dust. It was inevitable. Natch would never turn down a chance to perform in front of an audience of this size. As she had predicted, he would either deliver a perfect presentation, or die trying. Jara wondered fleetingly how the living, breathing audience upstairs compared to the invisible audience Natch had been playing to in his head all these years.

"Jara, tell me whether the auditorium can handle all these calculations," said Natch suddenly. His eyes were yellow and coyote hungry. "Tell me we're not going to cause a hundred more of those infoquakes."

"Well, the Surina people think that—"

"I don't want to hear it! Tell me *yes* or *no*."

The bio/logic analyst pursed her lips for a full three seconds in thought. She had never hated Natch more. She had never found him so irresistibly sexy. "Yes."

"Good! Now go find Ben and Merri. The three of you comb the crowd and find the most sickeningly sweet little girl on the face of the Earth. I'm talking five years old, pigtails, the whole thing."

"They don't allow anyone younger than eight on the multi network, remember?"

"Fine, eight years old then. But not a *day* over eight. Tag her spatial coordinates with a beacon so I can find her. Horvil!" The engineer saluted briskly, looking as if he were ready to give his life for the cause. "Go find a workbench. I need you to do the quickest programming job you've ever done in your life. We've got a couple of alterations to make."

"What did you have in mind?"

Natch spouted off a few polynomials. Horvil turned to the Islander, who nodded. "It can be done," muttered Quell. "Maybe." Seconds later, the three of them bolted out the door and down another hallway.

"I've never seen him so frightened, Jara," said Serr Vigal as the two of them walked back towards the stairs and a door that would take them into the audience. "I don't think I've ever been so frightened *for* him either."

Jara wrapped a comradely arm around the neural programmer's waist. Nobody would have mistaken Vigal for a young man, but he seemed to have aged twenty years in the past few weeks. "I'd be frightened too if I got shot full of black code," said Jara. "But don't worry, Vigal. He's already survived one attack, and with all those Council officers swarming through the arena, I doubt anyone would be stupid enough to try another."

Vigal gave her a curious look. "I don't think you understand. Natch isn't afraid of another black code attack. He's still worried about the first one."

"You mean... ?"

"Natch is still infected. The program didn't self-destruct after it knocked him unconscious. In fact, we think it was the code that woke him up."

"Well, what does the code *do?* What's it waiting for?"

"We don't know. *That's* what we're afraid of."

Anyone who might have suggested two weeks ago that half a billion people would be standing in the Surina auditorium awaiting a product demonstration from Natch—Natch the scoundrel, Natch the upstart, Natch the arriviste—would have been roundly denounced by the bio/logic pundits on the Data Sea who Clearly Knew Better. Now the drudges were asking themselves, *If an unknown businessman can jump to the top of the hierarchy with such stunning swiftness, if one man can leapfrog generations of accepted practice and standard operating procedure, then is anything safe anymore?*

High Executive Len Borda emerged from the stage door, and the crowd went silent. The audience, which had just watched a second incursion of Council troops with good humor, suddenly clouded over with gloom.

The high executive marched to center stage and swept the auditorium with his piercing gaze. Half a billion onlookers waited expectantly without uttering a single word. A minute passed.

Finally, the Council chief spoke in a voice like rolling thunder. Borda's words were unhurried, untouched by focus groups, and spoken with a formality that might have been labeled *pompous* if the labelers did not fear having their Vault transactions scrutinized to the last decimal point by men in white robes. "My word is the will of the Defense and Wellness Council, which was established by the Prime Committee two hundred and fifty-two years ago to ensure the security of all persons throughout the system. The word of the Council *is* the word of the people."

A shudder whipped through the crowd like electricity. Those words had rarely been known to precede a happy occasion.

"Last week, thousands of lives were lost in the orbital colonies due to a new computational disturbance on the Data Sea known as an *infoquake*," continued Borda gravely. "The Council and the Prime Committee have been studying this phenomenon but have yet to draw any conclusions as to its root cause.

"The epistemological implications of this phenomenon may be uncertain, but the duty of the government remains unchanged.

"It is the solemn obligation of the Defense and Wellness Council to prevent any such disturbance from happening again. Towards that end, the Council has proposed to the Prime Committee a number of temporary measures designed to curb the risks of computational disorder. I have just been informed that the Committee has unanimously approved those measures."

The crowd's silence was broken by a low murmur from contingents of hard-core libertarians. Even though the high executive still followed parliamentary procedure, everyone knew that the final word belonged to Borda and Borda alone. Who could recall the last time the Prime Committee rejected one of the Council's military "recommendations"? *Remember the statues in the Center for Historic Appreciation*, whispered the dissidents in the crowd. *Remember that flimsy excuse they conjured up last time to advance their agenda.*

"These are the strictures that the Prime Committee has enacted into law as of eight p.m. Melbourne time," said Borda.

"Until further notice, multi attendance will be capped at five hundred million persons in any one location.

"All persons assembled at tonight's event will have their access to the Data Sea severely limited.

"And in the case of an infoquake or another eruption of black code, the Council will enforce its right to shut down programs on the Data Sea *at its sole discretion.*"

The murmurings of unrest from the libertarians flared into full-out yells of protest. High executives had always had the ability to shut down certain programs deemed harmful to the public welfare—as long as they ran their decisions through the Prime

Committee and the Congress of L-PRACGs first. But now, had the infoquake given Borda license to act unilaterally, without consultation?

A vocal element of the crowd began stomping its feet. Dire headlines appeared in drudge columns throughout the Data Sea. Chants of *Borda must go* echoed in one corner of the arena, until a rash of Council officers stormed in that direction and began conspicuously fingering the triggers of their multi disruptors.

Borda was unmoved. He stood and waited for the commotion to simmer down before proceeding. "The mandate of the Defense and Wellness Council—the entire reason for its *existence*—is to preserve the safety of every citizen in the civilized domains, from the four corners of Earth to Luna, Mars, and the farthest orbital colonies," said the high executive dispassionately. "Should the infoquake be deemed a natural occurrence, then the Council will continue to take measures necessary to prevent it from happening in the future.

"But if it should be determined that the infoquake was an act of war by rogue elements of society..."

Borda's words hung in the air for a moment.

"... then let it be known that the Defense and Wellness Council will not stand idle. Our armies are poised, on high alert, around the globe and throughout the human territories. The Council is ready to take action against any group—*any* group—that tries to take advantage of a sudden lapse in Data Sea integrity.

"We are prepared to *act*, immediately and irreversibly, without appeal or exemption.

"Whether the Council acts or not is up to *you*."

Borda extended one long, bony talon from his fist and aimed it into the midst of the crowd. The audience grumbling instantly came to a halt, as 500 million people held their breath. And then, without any more formalities, the high executive cut his multi connection and vanished.

Natch had woken up from his mysterious slumber four hours earlier—woken up alone and in one piece, lying mummy-like on his own bed with no recollection of how he had gotten there. Vague and incomprehensible images hovered in his head, just beyond the reach of his irises. He could not say whether they were dreams or memories or something in between.

He had turned first to Serr Vigal for advice, reaching his old mentor on an emergency message protocol the two had used for urgent communications since Natch's days in the hive. It had taken them less than half an hour to conclude that the black code was still active in Natch's system, and that only one man had the clout to scare off any potential attack. By the time Natch and Serr Vigal materialized in the Defense and Wellness Council's administrative offices barely three hours before the presentation, the fiefcorp master was ready to agree to almost anything that would buy some time.

So Natch had promised Len Borda access. Access to MultiReal in exchange for protection from the black code.

But what exactly did *access* mean? The term had come from the high executive's mouth, not Natch's, and so he really had no way of knowing what subtle shades of meaning Borda applied to the word. How did *access* differ from *cooperation*? And did it also imply *control*? Did it at least fall short of the wholesale thievery that Margaret had been trying to prevent?

Or had Natch just given Len Borda the very thing Margaret Surina had been trying to keep from him for all those years?

If he had not been so pressed for time, perhaps Natch could have dickered with the Council over subtle interpretations. Once again, Margaret's words arose from the graveyard of the mind to haunt him: *You find yourself capable of strange things when you run out of choices.* Hadn't Natch indeed run out of choices? Anyone who would go to the trouble of assembling a strike force like the one that had ambushed him in Shenandoah certainly had the power to put together a lethal piece of black code.

Lethal black code. The implications made Natch's bones tremble. A program that could tear through his bodily defenses like rice paper and cause his OCHREs to run amok. Who could predict what would happen? A jolt of electricity into the brain? Blockage of the main arteries leading to his heart? Or perhaps something slower, more insidious, more painful?

But it wasn't cowardice that had driven him into Borda's office. *I'm not a coward*, Natch had insisted to himself, over and over again like a mantra. *I'm not a coward. There's a lot more at stake here than my own life.* The high executive had provided all kinds of rationalizations for Natch's actions. After all, who could say what his black-robed assailants were after? Perhaps they wanted Natch to go onstage in front of 500 million people and unleash a ferocious black code attack. Perhaps they wanted to gain control of him so they could unlock access to MultiReal or kill one of his colleagues.

Or maybe these people in black robes wanted Natch to kill you, Vigal had mused out loud in Borda's direction, oblivious to the seven or eight Council disruptors that suddenly spun towards his sparsely carpeted head.

Borda himself had not expressed the slightest inkling of fear at the neural programmer's suggestion. *I'd like to see them try it*, he had said, his amusement registering on some subconscious level of the conversation.

And now, as Natch stood at the stage door watching Borda wrap up his impromptu speech, another possibility came streaking to the forefront of Natch's mind. What if the thugs who had assaulted him in that Shenandoah alleyway were working for the Defense and Wellness Council?

He thought about the offhanded way in which Len Borda had tossed him twenty minutes of speech prep time while pretending that all he could spare was ten. The high executive was a man accustomed to getting what he wanted. What if this entire episode was some kind of trap? What if the assailants in the black robes had been sent to push him straight into Borda's clutches—and Natch had unwittingly done their bidding?

After the high executive cut his multi connection and vanished, Natch looked at the millions in the crowd and tried to will himself to take those last few steps to center stage. But doubts weighed at his heels like shackled cannonballs. What if he had made the wrong decision to enlist the Council's help? What if he couldn't get MultiReal to work? What if his demonstration caused another infoquake?

The anxiety crescendoed to a mind-splitting intensity—and then suddenly switched off.

The presentation did not matter. None of this really mattered.

Natch was already doomed.

Black code prowled his system like a merciless reaper, relentless, insatiable, and ready to mow him down at any time. Even if the Council was dealing honestly with him—even if they had no involvement with the shadowy figures in the black robes and sincerely wanted to protect him—Natch doubted that Borda could act swiftly enough to stop the rogue program from taking his life. The black code had become a part of him. An internal attack could happen at any moment, between one breath and the next. It could happen *now*.

He took the first tentative step up the narrow ramp towards center stage. It was a straight path, without detours or alternate routes. Natch could either walk away, or he could soldier on and trust that he would get through the presentation in one piece. He would have to trust that Borda would abide by his promise; he would have to trust that Jara's script would wow the crowd; he would have to trust that Horvil and Quell's engineering had done the job, that Benyamin's assembly-line shop had performed as advertised, and that Merri and Robby had wedged open enough minds in the audience to give him a chance.

Natch reached center stage an empty husk.

Millions upon millions of people stood arrayed before him—people of all shapes and sizes and colors and creeds swirled together. Chattering insects. The temporary organic effluence of the Null Current, dredged from the water for a brief flickering instant between tides, an aspect of the endless sea of nothingness that surrounded them all.

Jara's words floated to the front of his mind.

"Towards Perfection," said Natch. The auditorium amplified his words to every corner of the arena. He was surprised to find his voice rich and melodic and unstressed.

Natch paused for a moment to scan the crowd, then did a double take, exactly as Jara's script dictated. Five hundred million pairs of eyes were scanning him back. The entrepreneur made an incredulous gesture towards the stage door, where a fictitious staff stood egging him on. "That's funny," he said. "I expected to be talking to you about what's real and what's Multi-Real—but I didn't expect this whole setting to be so *surreal*." The joke was not really funny at all, and yet millions of people were laughing anyway. Of course, the presence of several thousand grim Council officers standing at attention with dart-rifles drawn did lend a certain absurdity to the whole scene.

The fiefcorp master smiled and continued. "MultiReal is the creation of new realities," Natch announced. "Alternate realities. *Separate* realities. The ability to visualize many things at once in order to do *one* thing exactly as you want.

"And what will we do with these realities?

"We'll do the same things we've always done, of course—eat, work, strive, struggle, make love—only better. Smarter. With more control.

"Now, my engineers wanted me to stand up here and blather on about the architecture of our program. All those MindSpace connections, all those complex mathematical formulas Margaret Surina has worked so hard on for the last decade and a half. And my analysts, they wanted me to talk about budgets and cost/benefit ratios and a lot of nonsense I didn't understand.

"But I said—why don't we just show them a simple demonstration?"

The fiefcorp master blinked and summoned from the arena a Kyushu Clubfoot bat and classic league baseball, just as he had done twenty minutes earlier. He shifted his grip ever so slightly, trying to find the perfect spot on the bat, the spot that his fingers melted into like an extension of his own multi projected fingers. There would be no opportunity for mistakes.

"There's an ancient legend about a player who could hit a baseball wherever he pointed. He would point to a seat in the stands, wait for the pitch, and then—*wham!* Knock the ball right there. They say he was the greatest baseball player who ever lived. Well, today I'm going to try to channel some of that magic for you."

Natch broke into a grin, stretched out his arm, and then whirled around in a 360-degree arc. His pointing finger encompassed the whole crowd.

He tossed the ball high into the air and swung the bat.

He activated Possibilities 1.0.

A resounding *crack* echoed through the arena.

Jara had found a comfortable position in the middle of the crowd where she could get an objective reading of the audience. So far, the speech she had written was performing as planned. Natch's folksy tone of voice was soothing nerves and smoothing wrinkles, providing an antidote to the poisonous invective the drudges had been spewing over the past few days.

Her apprehension began when Natch did his spinning-and-pointing routine. The script had been clear, hadn't it? Natch was supposed to point at an audience member—a *single* audience member—and start popping fly balls his way, one after another in quick succession, then repeat as necessary. What kind of fool stunt was the fiefcorp master trying to pull?

Jara nearly collapsed in shock and horror when Natch swung the bat.

There was just *one* ball flying through the air—and Natch was making no motion to hit another.

Already Jara had begun a mental search for scapegoats. Was Natch unable to activate the Possibilities program? Had Horvil and Quell bungled the coding somehow and caused the MultiReal engine to sputter? Had Benyamin's assembly-line shop missed a few connections? Was this another of the Patel Brothers' perfidious acts of sabotage, or the work of the black code flowing in Natch's veins?

And of all the hundreds of millions of people to choose from, why had Natch decided to hit the ball directly to *her*?

Jara stretched out her hand and winced as the ball landed squarely in her palm with a soft *thud*. She felt the light sting of horsehide on flesh. The analyst turned the ball over in her hand and brought it closer to read the letters printed around the stitching.

OF COURSE IT'S NOT REAL—IT'S MULTIREAL

The fiefcorp apprentice blinked, shook her head, and looked at her empty palm. *You're daydreaming, Jara*, she told herself. *There's no baseball in your hand.*

But this was no daydream. The baseball had been there—and now it wasn't.

A few seconds later, gasps of astonishment simultaneously burst out of 500 million spectators as comprehension slowly filtered through their brains. Five hundred million stinging palms, 500 million empty hands. *A collaborative process.*

Jara smiled in spite of herself.

"You have just experienced the awesome power of Possibilities," said Natch after the initial shock had worn off.

"Five hundred million swings of the bat. Five hundred million possible catches. Five hundred million possible separate realities, all created *up here*"—the fiefcorp master tapped his forehead—"and experienced *out there*." He gestured broadly to the audience.

"But we don't live in a world of multiple realities. MultiReal may give you hundreds of millions of possibilities, but we still have to make a choice. A single choice. And so the path I have chosen is—*this* one."

Natch snapped his fingers, causing a spotlight to spear a tiny figure far away in the crowd. A wave of applause came crashing towards Jara, rippling out from the center of the spotlight until it enveloped the entire audience. In the center of the spotlight stood a girl not more than eight years old holding her father's hand, grinning adorably and brandishing a MultiReal baseball in her elfin little fingers.

"Let the word *impossible* be permanently eliminated from our vocabulary!" cried Natch. "There are no more impossibilities! We have entered a new Age of Possibilities—a new Age of MultiReal—and from now on, the choices are *yours*.

"Towards Perfection, and I thank you for choosing to attend."

Robby Robby stuck to Horvil's side like a bad odor.

"They're going absolutely *offline* out there, Horv-o!" the channeler squealed, his cube of hair bobbing enthusiastically to some triumphant march playing inside his head. "My team is getting mobbed—it's like being in the middle of a fucking *orgy*! Everyone wants to hear more about MultiReal!"

"Yeah," said Horvil, his own face sporting a lopsided grin. "Including me." Robby let out a laugh that continued much too long to have any correlation to the wit of Horvil's comment. If Merri hadn't shown up and ushered him out to join the sales blitzkrieg, he might have kept going until his spleen ruptured.

The chaos continued for over an hour after Natch had vanished from the stage. Horvil's cousins and uncles and cousins-of-cousins and third-cousins-twice-removed-by-companionship multied in from every crevice of the known universe to pat him on the back. Every member of the extended family except for Aunt Berilla, whose hatred for

Natch apparently outranked her pride in Horvil and Benyamin. Once the family had dissipated, friends and business acquaintances that Horvil didn't even recognize began pressing in from all sides asking for more details about MultiReal. The engineer did his best to provide vague answers, especially when some of his "old hive buddies" revealed that they had taken up the drudging profession.

Horvil shook off his pursuers and scanned the foot of the stage for the rest of the Surina/Natch apprentices. They all seemed to be in the same pickle. Jara was being mobbed by a horde of L-PRACG representatives trying to negotiate a bulk rate on the spot. Ben was happily enfilading an entire squadron of creed devotees with upbeat chatter about MultiReal. Quell was engaged in a vigorous argument with a small pocket of Islanders, all tugging uncomfortably at their connectible collars. Merri was presumably still off crowd surfing with Robby Robby. Only Natch and Serr Vigal had made a clean getaway.

Somewhere in the middle of the confusion, Horvil noticed a line of white-robed Defense and Wellness Council officers moving silently out the door, their guns safely holstered.

"Did you hear?" he said in a rush as Jara walked up to him. "Sen Sivv Sor tracked down the little girl who caught the baseball. Apparently, the kid lives in a hive that just got its budget slashed by a bunch of L-PRACG bureaucrats. Can you believe that luck? I wonder who Natch wants as our next spokesperson. A stray kitten? A monk? Or maybe a prostitute with a heart of gold who—"

Why am I laying it on so thick? thought Horvil.

Jara waited patiently for the engineer's shtick to ramble to a close. "Good publicity is good publicity," she said softly, distantly.

Horvil smiled and nodded, then began inching away from the analyst towards an exit. He could ponder the mysteries of womanhood another time. Right now, too many loose ends needed tying up. Like who had ambushed Natch and shot him full of black code? What kinds of surprises did the Patel Brothers have waiting for them later tonight? And how in the world had Len Borda gotten mixed up in all of this?

5
DEMONS OF
THE AETHER

(((3 3)))

"I swear to you, Natch," said the man, "I had nothing to do with this. I didn't hire anybody to ambush you in the street. I don't know any group that runs around in the shadows wearing black robes attacking people, and I wouldn't have anything to do with them if I did."

Natch's eyes blazed with doubt as he looked at Petrucio Patel.

He could only guess why Petrucio had agreed to come talk with him here in the Surina Enterprise Facility, mere hours before the Patel Brothers were due to take the stage at the Thassel Complex. Natch's cold rage would have been evident from the instant Petrucio stepped into the conference room and found himself enveloped in the windswept Arctic tundra, a forbidden land with Lovecraftian menace lurking over every hillside. If he didn't already know that his rival was beyond such emotions, Natch might have guessed that Petrucio was experiencing shame or guilt.

"I don't believe you," said Natch.

Petrucio burst into laughter. "You don't believe me! You think Frederic and I hustled the fiefcorp off to Shenandoah and started handing out robes and dartguns? Wait—you didn't see a short, fat one in the group, did you? Maybe that was Frederic. He's quite the marksman, you know."

Natch's face remained deadly serious, and Petrucio muzzled his glee with great effort. He peered back over his shoulder at the thirty-five-meter dropoff just behind his heels. A long way to plunge just to see if the SeeNaRee's automatic pain cutoff was operational. Petrucio straightened his tie and brushed ice crystals off his jacket, gestures to signal his command of the situation. "Natch, what would we gain by hiring some goons to hit you with black code? It just doesn't make any *sense*. How do I know you're not just making the whole thing up?"

"Don't be a fool, 'Trucio," snapped Natch irritably. "You've got the whole MultiReal market to gain. Billions of customers and no competition."

"That's absolutely ludicrous. We're not just your competitors anymore, Natch—we're your *licensees*. If I hired someone to kill you, who knows where control of MultiReal would end up?"

"It would stay with Margaret, who's scared for her life—"

"—and wants nothing to do with us anymore. Follow the logic, Natch! She'd just find someone else to partner with. Haven't you ever heard the old adage about preferring the enemy you *know* to the enemy you *don't*?"

"How pithy. You're the second person to tell me that this week."

"Obviously, you have a lot of enemies, then. Listen, Natch, I'm not going to sit here and pretend that the Patel Brothers are your friends. I don't like you. I never have. But just because we're not your comrades doesn't mean we don't know how to compete honorably."

Now it was Natch's turn to let out a hearty laugh. "What about MemoryMiner 98c? Do you call that *honorable*?"

Patel sighed and stroked his elegantly waxed moustache in consternation. "I don't know if there's anything I could possibly say to convince you that I had nothing to do with this so-called black code incident. Okay, I'll admit, MemoryMiner 98c—that was a shitty thing to do. But that was a long time ago, Natch. And what about all of those dirty tricks you've played on *us* in the past couple years? Remember DeMirage 24.5? NiteFocus 13, 34, *and* 48? Your reputation in this business isn't exactly unblemished. Shall we count citations from the Meme Cooperative and see which company is the cleanest?"

"Fine, let's."

Petrucio rolled his eyes. "I've already *told* you, Natch. We don't do business like that anymore. I've gone through a lot in the past year. This whole MultiReal opportunity has turned the company upside down. I've been far too busy preparing for *our* presentation—which, in case you've forgotten, starts in two hours—to worry about *you*. My companion died—"

"*Please*, Petrucio, spare me the sad stories. You slept with half the channelers in the eastern hemisphere behind that woman's back. Don't tell me you've had some kind of eleventh-hour conversion."

The elder Patel's nostrils flared, and his moustache twitched in rage. Natch thought Petrucio would definitely cut his multi connection now, but instead the man stayed and slowly mastered his anger. "After my companion died, I made some *changes* in my life," Patel said in a low voice, whipping aside the lapel of his jacket to reveal a small pin in the shape of a black-and-white swirl.

Natch blinked hard and took a step back in surprise. Petrucio Patel a truthteller? Natch gulped. "Anyone can wear a pin," he said.

"Check the membership rolls—it's public information. I took the oath a few weeks after she was gone. The bodhisattva of Creed Objectivv administered it to me himself. You know what that means, don't you? It means I would be honor-bound to tell you if I knew anything about any black code."

"How come this is the first time *I've* heard anything about it?"

"The creed has several hundred million members. Not all of us who pledge are crass enough to advertise it on our chests, like your friend Merri."

Natch paced back and forth on the icy plain, his eyes tracing the patterns their footsteps made in the snow. It was not outside the realm of possibility that Petrucio was making the whole thing up, although the details of his story were easily verifiable. More likely he simply planned not to get caught telling lies. According to the drudges, Creed Objectivv's enforcement of the truthtelling oath was only slightly more effective than the Meme Cooperative's enforcement of fiefcorp business ethics.

"So let's say I take you at your word," said Natch frostily. "*You* had nothing to do with this black code attack. *You're* a devotee of Creed Objectivv now. *You're* an honorable businessman. What about Frederic?"

A look of stupefaction dashed across Petrucio Patel's face until his features abruptly morphed into a perfect PokerFace. "And exactly what are you suggesting?" he said.

Natch narrowed his eyes to slits as he strode up to his rival's face, close enough to take a bite out of his hawkish nose. "I know all about those Objectivv tricks," said Natch. "You pledge to always tell the truth, so you play subtle word games. '*I* had nothing to do with this. *I* didn't hire anybody to ambush you in the street. *I've* been far too busy preparing for our presentation.' But listen carefully, Petrucio. Until you can prove to me that both you *and* Frederic are playing on the level, the Patel Brothers are number one on my hit list. And you haven't *seen* how I do business when I'm really pissed off. I'll tear you to pieces. I'll use every fucking trick outlawed by the Meme Cooperative. I'll throw that MultiReal license to the dogs without thinking twice about it, and *fuck* the consequences."

Petrucio nodded almost imperceptibly, the look on his face a hybrid of amusement and respect. Then he was gone.

Shortly after the conclusion of the Patel Brothers' presentation, the Surina/Natch MultiReal Fiefcorp held a meeting. The apprentices all arrived at the conference room with their belongings in tow, since they were planning to head home immediately afterwards.

Natch was surprised to discover that Margaret Surina had not come down from her perch in the Revelation Spire after the Council's departure, although most of the guards had already been redeployed around the compound. The scuttlebutt among the security staff was that Margaret was busy right now moving her office to an alcove in the Spire's peak. But whatever the reason, the bodhisattva had not responded to any of Natch's ConfidentialWhispers. Instead, she sent a token message of congratulations to the entire team, the same kind of pro forma civility they had received from Lucas Sentinel, Prosteev Serly, and Billy Sterno, among others.

As for Frederic and Petrucio Patel, their product demo did not go well.

Their misfortune was partly the result of a breaking news story that quickly occluded any other topic on the Data Sea. The Speaker of the Congress of L-PRACGs had been caught in a major embezzlement sting involving a group of highly placed TubeCo lobbyists. That, along with Borda's heavy-handed and highly unpopular speech, had caused a groundswell of support for the libertarians. Opponents were clamoring for a vote of no confidence in the governmentalist Speaker. The drudges were now predicting that, within the next twenty-four hours, control of the Congress would fall to rabid libertarian Khann Frejohr.

But the Patel Brothers could not completely blame their failure on bad timing. They had compounded their misfortune with a number of poor choices of their own. They had no hands-on demonstration to show the crowd. The PatelReal 1.0 program schematics floated, unused, in an enormous MindSpace bubble above the stage, while Petrucio prattled on about *raging waters* and *safe shores*. Frederic wore a hideous chocolate-brown suit that offended the sensibilities of even the most fashion-challenged members of the audience. Afterwards, the drudges spent hours comparing notes on the rampant headaches caused by the thumping bass drum of the Patels' soundtrack. Even those commentators who had been overtly hostile to Natch a day earlier had to admit that the Surina/Natch MultiReal Fiefcorp had clearly beaten its rival to the punch.

Thus, Natch and his apprentices were in a celebratory mood.

Horvil arranged for a platter full of margaritas to be delivered to the conference room and made a big production of turning off his alcohol-metabolizing OCHREs. He clinked glasses loudly with Jara, Merri, Benyamin, and Quell in a show of solidarity. Even the multi-projected Vigal sipped an illusory drink from a virtual glass. Natch had never cared for the unsatisfying sensation of multi food; all taste and no substance. Yet he too had a confident smile on his face, and his tranquil mood inspired the room to summon a cozy New England SeeNaRee. The conference table sat on a bearskin rug in the midst of an old-fashioned ski lodge, while a fire crackled on the hearth behind them.

"Anybody been scouting around the Data Sea for reactions from the drudges?" said Horvil.

"Of course," replied Jara. "Everyone is totally polarized over your demonstration, Natch. Some people are wondering if you released some hallucinogenic black code on the audience. And there's an amusing debate going on about whether or not you actually swung the bat five hundred million times."

"Did you?" asked Ben, a little uncertainly.

Natch laughed. "Not even close! Five hundred million *possible* swings, but only one *actual* one. You want to take a stab at explaining, Horv?"

"It's simple, really," began Horvil. "Once Multi-Real has reduced the swing of the bat into a formula, you just plug in parameters and create a mathematical progression of realities. So, you swing the bat at ninety degrees and then ninety-one degrees and then ninety-two degrees and on and on... and then you don't actually have to *do* them all."

"Then you'd have an *infinite* number of baseballs," Benyamin pointed out in confusion.

"No no no." Horvil conjured up a virtual calculator on the conference table and began drunkenly plugging in numbers. "See, if you convert the field of vision into a grid of Cartesian space and calculate the coordinates of each audience member, then you can plug x, y, and z values into the MultiReal program and work backwards to generate a baseball hit to that point. Then, of course, you have to factor in wind resistance and gravitational pull—"

"Enough, Horv!" interjected Jara. "We get the point. What *I* want to know is why everybody *remembered* those discarded realities. Quell, you told us nobody would remember them unless they were using MultiReal themselves."

"Right," said Quell. "That was the alteration Horvil made at the last minute."

"I wasn't even sure it was going to work," mumbled the engineer. "Just lucky it did, I guess."

"The important thing is that few people seem to doubt that the demonstration was genuine," said Serr Vigal. "Billions of people watched the whole thing over a video feed, and most of them accept what they saw as the true and actual version of events."

Quell stretched his beefy arms out behind his head and leaned back in his chair, looking well pleased. "I can't imagine a better way to introduce MultiReal to the world," he said. "A little girl holding a baseball. You don't get much better PR than that."

"Natch, who is Magan Kai Lee?" blurted Merri out of nowhere.

The fiefcorp master's visage darkened. A sudden gust of wind caused the cabin door to slam open, and a SeeNaRee coyote started baying off in the distance. "Why?"

"Someone by that name keeps sending me urgent messages," responded the channel manager sheepishly. "Four times in three days. He even showed up at my apartment the other day and scared Bonneth out of her wits. He won't say what it's about, but I assume it has something to do with MultiReal."

Serr Vigal planted his chin on his fist with a look of exhaustion. He exchanged a dark glance with Natch, who passed him some silent signal to proceed. "Magan Kai Lee is one of Len Borda's lieutenant executives at the Defense and Wellness Council," said the neural programmer. "He was there with the high executive during our meeting this morning. We think Borda has put him in charge of dealing with MultiReal."

"Lee... is he the guy who's been speaking at the Council news conferences lately?" said Horvil, scratching his head. "He's real short. Chinese, I think."

Natch gave a weary nod. "That's him."

"I don't understand," said Jara. "What do they *want* from us? If Borda's so worried about info-quakes, why are they terrorizing Merri? We didn't have anything to do with that disturbance during Margaret's speech. Shouldn't they be talking with the Data Sea architects?"

"Haven't you figured it out yet?" said Natch. "These *infoquakes*—if they even exist—are the least of Borda's concerns. MultiReal is dangerous, Jara. Think of an assassin who can fire a black code dart that hits its target every time. That's scary enough. But imagine what an *army* of people running Mul-tiReal could do."

Nobody said anything for a good two minutes.

"So yes, Merri, we're going to be hearing a lot more from Len Borda and Magan Kai Lee," said Natch. "You can count on it. They're going to be our biggest hurdle from here on out."

All trace of levity had vanished from Benyamin's face. "Our *biggest* hurdle? What other hurdles are there?"

"Don't be naïve, Ben! It's a big world. All kinds of fanatics are going to decide MultiReal is the solu-tion to their problems. Do you think *everyone's* going to sit patiently and wait for us to go through the product development process?"

"Someone has already decided not to wait," interjected Merri in a hoarse whisper.

Silence shrouded the room once again.

"Have we made any headway on the black code problem?" said Jara. "Do we know what it does?"

Vigal shook his head. "I've taken a few cursory scans of Natch's system, but I haven't been able to come up with much. It's capable of putting him to sleep. That much is clear. All I can say is, be patient. There are thousands of OCHRE machines in the human body. It may take some time to examine them all."

"How do you know the code is still there?" asked the bio/logic analyst.

"Programs have signatures, Jara," explained Horvil. "They leave traces." His alcohol-inhibiting OCHREs were back on in full force; the engineer was now stone-cold sober. "Your typical piece of black code self-destructs after it's done all its dirty work. No incriminating evidence, right? But there's so many safeguards against erasing OCHRE programming that you usually know it if a piece of black code self-destructs inside of you."

"That is often the only way people know they've been infected at all," added Vigal. "They don't notice the insertion, but the self-destruct they can feel."

"So who are the prime suspects?" asked Jara.

Natch muttered something noncommittal.

Jara tugged at a few stray curls of hair in frustration. "Well, who do you *think* did it? The Patel Brothers? Lucas Sentinel? This other bodhisattva you've been working with? Who?"

The fiefcorp master's face suddenly twisted into a rictus of fear, anger, and pain. His right fist flew out and slammed into the conference table with a reverberating *thump* that caused everyone to gasp in astonishment. "*I don't know!*" he cried out. "I just don't know, Jara! But it's *my* problem—not *yours*! Leave me the fuck alone!"

Nobody spoke for a few moments as Natch wrestled with his emotions. The fiefcorp master seemed to be on the verge of completely losing control. Vigal raised a hand and started towards Natch's left shoulder, then thought better of it and returned the hand to his lap.

The SeeNaRee picked up on the foul mood and hurled a blistering wind off the mountain outside. There were so many possibilities, so many potential enemies. Everyone had heard stories about the shadowy organizations that existed outside the dominion of the Prime Committee and the Defense and Wellness Council. The violent factions of the Pharisees who yearned to bring humanity back to God's Natural Order... the unpredictable masses of the diss who escaped, eluded, or just plain ignored the edicts of the law... creed bodhisattvas on the fringes who preached destruction while spurning the normalizing umbrella of the Creeds Coalition... radical libertarians who denied the legitimacy of the central governments and actively worked for their destruction. And this list didn't even include the disruptive forces arrayed against them *inside* the bounds of civilized society. L-PRACGs desperate to get their hands on any ultimate weapon that could put an end to ancient ethnic rivalries... unscrupulous fiefcorps that would leap headlong into thievery and murder if it would help them make a profit... drudges and demagogues with narrow personal agendas who could whip the public into a revolutionary frenzy... conservative politicians who could quarantine MultiReal behind a wall of rules and regulations to ensure that the program never saw the light of day.

Soon, Natch had muscled the panic into a temporary chokehold, and his face showed nothing but the normal intensity, the normal restlessness, the normal insanity. "I don't think we need to worry too much about the black code for the moment," he said. "Len Borda's people are sniffing around looking for the ambushers. I think his show of force this afternoon scared them off. If these people in the black robes wanted me dead—or wanted *you* all dead—it would have happened by now.

"But if you're looking for a way out..."

Without warning, the wolf inside took over and Natch burst into that predatory grin. The grin of the savage beast, the grin that put fear inside his friends and enemies alike.

"If you want a way out, I'll *give* you one. You all have twenty-four hours to liquidate your shares and cash out your contracts at no penalty. Anyone who doesn't have the stomach for this, anyone who doesn't want to keep looking over their shoulder wondering where the next surprise is coming from, now's your chance to get out."

(((3 4)))

Night came to London. For Jara, it was not a falling but a terrible rising, a mute upsurge of blackness that seeped from every pore of the apartment walls and puddled along the floors until it soaked her to the chest, constricting her breath.

Jara sat on her bedroom floor, Indian style, with her head cradled in her arms. She found a comfortable rocking motion between her haunches and the side of her knees, and tried to concentrate on that for a while. Every few minutes, she would open her eyes to peer at the window on the far wall, which was showing an exterior view of her building. But that was too depressing. With every glance, corporate office towers and tenements shrank more and more as their inhabitants left work or went to sleep. A succumbing to the blackness, visceral proof that the forces of Being were tottering on the brink of extinction.

Her old hive proctor had once told her that the universe was almost entirely comprised of empty space. He brought Jara and her hivemates into a green field SeeNaRee and used peppercorns and chestnuts to approximate the position of the planets in the solar system, with the sun represented by a rubber ball. The students were astounded to discover themselves standing hundreds of meters apart near their chosen planet. *So what's in the rest of the field? What fills up all that space?* Jara had asked. *Nothing*, the proctor had replied. Jara had been young and foolish enough to look upon that lacuna as a void to be filled by good deeds and great works. And the proctor had encouraged that passion. He had fanned those flames and then sent her off to initiation believing she had been the aggressor in their relationship, that she could set the empty heavens ablaze.

She wondered what her proctor would have thought of Natch.

She wondered what advice her proctor would give her now.

A scant three weeks ago, Jara had been bemoaning her fate and counting the days until she could free herself of the Natch Personal Programming Fiefcorp's fetters. And now, as if responding to her silent command, events had conspired to spring her from her prison ten months early. Natch had given the apprentices twenty-four hours to liquidate shares and part ways, or continue their contracts with the new Surina/Natch MultiReal Fiefcorp.

So why was she hesitating? Why was she huddled here on the floor of her apartment, rocking back and forth and staring at inanimate objects, instead of liquidating her shares? If she cashed out, she need never see Natch again. She could just dissolve her apprenticeship and walk away right now, ink the final period in this chapter of her life and close the book on it.

She would have money. Jara fired a data agent at her Vault account and studied the number that returned. When she added the liquidated shares at current market value, she saw a nice round number with a small army of zeros marching off the end. Jara began to dream up things that these newfound credits could buy. A bigger apartment closer to Horvil's end of London, one with real windows and a garden that would put her meager daisy patch to shame. Stylish furniture to spruce up that apartment. Lavish dinners, expensive champagne, cosmetic bio/logic programs, weeks and weeks of decadent fun on the Sigh network. A trip to the never-ending bacchanalia that was 49th Heaven. She could polish off her sister's tuition payment for that useless degree in metal sculpture she was pursuing in Sudafrica. Or she could simply stay put for a while, do nothing and decompress.

Then what?

Then she would have to look for work again. Perhaps a wise capitalman could stretch the money for five or six or even seven years, but her investment skills were moderate at best. No matter how prudently she acted, sooner or later she would find herself sitting across from some arrogant fiefcorp master answering questions about bio/logic analysis and trying to explain the gap in her curriculum vitae.

Jara could hear her mother's accusation across thousands of kilometers: *Why do you have to stick with bio/logics? Why not become a politician or a civil servant? Or maybe an artist like your sister?*

No, Jara retorted silently. Bio/logics was all she knew, all she had ever cared about, and she was simply too old to start fresh somewhere else, to stumble through all the virginal mistakes you had to endure in any new industry.

If only she had gotten a chance to deliver that presentation. If only she had not been yanked away from her trial by fire before she had tasted the flame.

Suddenly, Jara felt the full force of Natch's insidious offer bear down upon her. Now she understood the feral smile that had taken possession of the fiefcorp master's face last night. If she left the fiefcorp now, she would have enough to be *comfortable*. Not rich, not poor, but comfortable. Natch was asking her a question.

Do you want to settle for *comfortable*?

Jara pounded her open palm against the floor until the cool tile stung her flesh. How could she not have seen? She should have known that Natch's apparent act of generosity would eventually turn out to be a referendum on *him*. He had offered her the choice of giving up, of resigning herself to mediocrity and *comfort*; or of staying with the fiefcorp, of driving ahead, of tilting against self-loathing and dissatisfaction until they yielded or she died trying. There was no third path. To continue in the fiefcorp world under a different corporate umbrella was to become Natch's competitor, and Natch had ably demonstrated he could vanquish any competition. But to quit was to admit she had failed.

Why don't you reframe the question? asked an interior voice she recognized as Horvil. Poor, sweet Horvil, so untouched by the world's misery. *Don't accept the question on his terms. Ask your own question.*

But Natch had cannily eliminated all other questions during their years in business together. One touch at a time, he had broken down her defenses and seduced her into his ethos. Jara had become a slave to Natch's worldview—and what was worse, she had willingly held out her wrists for the cuffs.

I'm sorry, Horv, she thought, *but I don't know how to reframe the question anymore.*

Jara got up and straightened out her robe, as if wrinkles in the fabric were a sign of poor character. She slunk into the breakfast nook and ordered herself a pigeon's dinner: snap peas and steamed rice, raw cauliflower, and water, cold and sharp as the edge of a knife. And as the twenty-fourth hour approached, Jara sat and forked food into her mouth, desperately trying to convince herself she was hungry.

(((35)))

Natch took the tube out to Cisco again to see the redwoods. He sat for hours mesmerized by their beauty, until they merged together in his mind, until all he could see were different aspects of one universal Tree.

Of course, the challenges had just begun. They had *always* just begun. Natch had connived and bargained and bluffed his way through the bio/logics game, only to find himself playing in a much more complex game. The stakes were higher here. You could lose your business. You could lose your possessions. You could lose your *life*, and the lives of those around you.

But had anything really changed? He remembered being five years old and feeling the oppressive weight of that bureau pressing down upon him. He remembered a very real fear that the blocks he had used to prop it up would slip away and leave him dead on the floor.

He stopped in Omaha on the way home.

"I think she's going to quit," Natch said to Serr Vigal, sitting on a velvet chaise in the neural programmer's study.

Vigal was in his kitchen, preparing tea the traditional way, by steeping fragrant leaves in near-boiling water. Natch found it a peculiar time-wasting habit. But then again, he had trekked across the continent enough times for a glimpse at the redwoods to look past a petty vice like caffeine. The older man carefully drew the antique china cup and saucer to his lips, blew softly, and took a tentative sip. Relaxation immediately rippled across his face. "Which one?" he said. "Merri or Jara?"

"Jara, of course. Mark my words, she'll be taking orders from that peon Lucas Sentinel before the end of the week. As for Merri—I think she'll stay aboard."

"Are you certain?"

"I know what you're afraid of, Vigal. You're thinking that sooner or later, Magan Kai Lee is going to get to her and start playing the morality card. *Would the bodhisattva of Creed Objectivv want you to stand up for a man like Natch? He hasn't been asking you to lie and violate your vows, has he?* But I think she's stronger than she looks. Merri won't turn on us."

The neural programmer came into the study and took a seat across from his protégé. Natch watched his mentor squint at something out the window. He knew from long experience that Vigal wasn't preoccupied with the view of downtown Omaha two hours before sunup; he was preparing to make an emotional statement. "So who *do* you think was responsible for the black code, Natch?" he asked finally. "The Patels?"

"Petrucio says he doesn't know about any black code," replied Natch. "And even though I've never trusted him before, there's something different about him lately. He really *did* pledge to Creed Objectivv. He was telling the truth about that much at least. Maybe Frederic ordered the black code attack—although if it was Frederic, he did it behind Petrucio's back."

"So if not the Patels, who then? One of your other competitors?"

"Like who? Bolliwar Tuban, or the Serlys, or Billy Sterno? They don't have that kind of imagination. Pierre Loget has the expertise to put together a piece of black code that powerful, but it would never occur to him. And Lucas Sentinel is afraid of his own shadow. The Meme Cooperative scares him silly, let alone the Council."

"What about your old hivemate? Have you considered whether he might have been involved?"

"Brone." The word came out like a sneer. "Well, he certainly has the motive. And he has all those Creed Thassel resources at his disposal. But I stood in the same room with him for an hour, Vigal, and I came out in one piece. If Brone wanted me dead, Len Borda wouldn't have scared him off—he would've pulled the trigger and gotten his revenge on me regardless."

"Borda, then."

Natch rose impatiently from the chaise and began to tread around the room, doing his best to avoid the Oriental knickknacks stacked in every corner. "That's my worst fear. Hasn't everything turned out his way? After sixteen years of failed negotiations with Margaret, he's finally gotten his foot in the door. But if shooting me full of black code was Borda's way of getting me under his thumb, he went to some pretty extraordinary lengths to pull off the bluff. If Borda knew I wasn't in any danger, why did he order a legion of Council troops to swarm all over the Surina compound and make all those threats? It just doesn't make sense."

"Perhaps his henchman Lee ordered the attack without Borda's knowledge."

"Maybe. Magan Kai Lee is a weasel. Who knows what that man is capable of."

Vigal caressed his goatee thoughtfully. Natch could see a grand topic of conversation sequestered behind that furrowed brow, waiting for the right moment to spring. "I know this might sound absurd," said the neural programmer, "but have you considered the possibility that Margaret Surina was behind this?"

Natch halted midpace and gave Vigal a look as if the caffeine had addled his brain. "*Margaret?* Why? She brought me into this whole mess in the first place."

"I don't know." The neural programmer finished his tea down to the dregs and set the empty cup on a side table. "I really can't think of a motive. But she certainly has the ability to create that kind of black code—and plenty of people at her disposal to marshal a strike team. And let us not forget that you've been conducting all these fiefcorp meetings at the Enterprise Facility. She could very easily have put you under surveillance."

Natch shook his head. "Margaret can't be too happy about my making a deal with Len Borda so quickly, but I'm not sure she even knows about it yet." Brone's words echoed in his mind: *You must know by now that Margaret isn't dealing with you in good faith. What happens when Margaret Surina grows tired of you, as she surely will?* Natch thought back to that conversation and barely stopped himself from kicking over Vigal's ceramic tea service in anger. "I wonder what Margaret's going to do. I can't believe she's just going to sit up in that tower and forget about MultiReal."

"Yet that appears to be what she is doing."

The two remained silent for a few minutes, lost in thought. Natch moved to the window to watch the predawn lights from Omaha's gambling quarter. Behind him, he could hear the neural programmer delicately crack his knuckles in preparation for a strenuous lecture.

"Natch, do you remember what that capitalman once told you about the natural *wants* of the universe?" the neural programmer burst out suddenly.

"Figaro Fi," Natch replied. "Everything that asshole said is permanently stuck in my head. *The universe just won't stay still. It* wants *to move; even its smallest particles* want *to be in motion.*"

"Have you ever thought," said Vigal hesitantly, "about whether the universe *wants* you to succeed?"

The laughter came bubbling out of Natch like a hot spring. "What a silly thing to say! Do you think the Demons of the Aether are out to get me?"

"Demons of the Aether?"

"You know, those old stories about bio/logic programs that *come alive*... and *turn* on their *masters*!" The fiefcorp master raised his hands in mock horror as he pantomimed the old dramas, the trite serials that used to exploit people's fears of the Autonomous Revolt. "So you think I was attacked by ghosts in Shenandoah. Is that it, Vigal?"

His old mentor smiled good-naturedly and rolled his eyes. "No, no, no, I didn't mean it that way. The Data Sea isn't conjuring up evil robots to interfere with your sales demos. There's a depressingly human explanation behind that black code incident, even if we haven't been able to figure out what it is."

"So what *do* you mean?"

Vigal ducked his head shyly and plowed on, his eyes glued to the carpet. "I mean that the world runs by natural laws, Natch. Just as there are laws of physics and thermodynamics and gravity, there are laws of social dynamics too. Laws of humanity. Figaro Fi was right: the universe does push and pull you in certain directions, but that doesn't mean it *wants* you to succeed. For thousands of years, we've been telling tales about the dangers that befall people who accomplish too much. Why? Because those tales have an underlying truth: power unbalances the natural energy of the world.

"Stop chuckling! I'm quite serious. You follow the bio/logic markets, don't you? You see this happen every day. A business triumphs over its rivals and gets stronger. Others become jealous and resentful. Eventually, the company's enemies conspire together to bring it down, or it rots from within. It's the same thing that happens with animals... plants... trees. Why? Because there's some mystical force guiding our actions? No, because too much power concentrated in one place creates stasis. And stasis is anathema to a universe that desires constant motion and change."

Natch grimaced and tugged at his hair, but there was more annoyance than anger in his voice.

"Vigal, you can be *so* frustrating sometimes!" he protested. "All this nonsense about what the universe wants—you're worse than all the creed bodhisattvas put together! Why do you have to make some kind of—of *fairy tale* out of this whole thing? I'm just a businessman trying to sell some programs. That's all."

The neural programmer gave a self-deprecating shake of the head. "All right, you want more down-to-earth advice? Sheldon Surina once said, *Practice should not precede theory.* Savor your moment of triumph and don't do anything rash."

"If I never did anything rash, I'd still be coding RODs."

"All I'm saying is that Margaret worked on MultiReal for sixteen years without bringing it to market. She must have had her reasons. *You've* had control of the program for less than a week and you're ready to sell it to everyone from here to Furtoid."

"That's called *capitalism*, Vigal. What do you want me to do? If I don't keep moving, someone else will just snap up MultiReal and do the same thing."

All at once, Serr Vigal looked weary and old. He shrank deeper into his chair, as if trying to will himself into the seams of the fabric. "I think you're too young to understand this. The natural *wants* of the universe do not work in our favor, Natch. Autumn always follows summer. Everything dies. You may be on top of the world now, but you cannot stay there forever. The world is not kind to conquerors."

The fiefcorp master stood at the window, facing the sunrise with a gladiator's belligerent stare. He could feel faint echoes of death emanating from the black code inside him. But during the past twenty-four hours, he had found a new confidence flowering beside the dread, a confidence sprouted from desire and fertilized by fear. He had seriously expected to be dead by now, and the fact that he was still living and breathing and staring out Vigal's window gave him hope.

"Don't worry about me, Vigal," he said. "I can handle everything the world throws at me. Just watch."

APPENDICES

APPENDIX A
GLOSSARY OF TERMS

For more comprehensive definitions and background articles on some terms, consult the website at *http://www.infoquake.net*.

TERM	DEFINITION
49th Heaven	A decadent orbital colony known for its loose morality; originally founded by one of the Three Jesuses as a religious retreat.
aft	One of the descriptive components of a program that helps the Data Sea sort and catalog information. See also *fore*.
Allahu Akbar Emirates	A nation-state that once existed in what is now mostly Pharisee territory. "Allahu Akbar" means "God is great."

Allowell	An orbital colony saved from extinction by High Executive Tul Jabbor.
analyst	One of the standard positions in a fiefcorp. Fiefcorp analysts typically focus on areas such as marketing, channeling, finance, and product development.
Andra Pradesh	A center of culture on the Indian subcontinent. Home to Creed Surina and the Gandhi University.
Angelos	A major population center, known in ancient times as Los Angeles.
apprentice	An employee of a fiefcorp, under contract to a master. In the traditional fiefcorp structure, apprentices sign a contract for a specific number of years. During their apprenticeship, apprentices receive only room and board as compensation; but at the conclusion of the contract, their shares mature and they receive a large stake in the company and a share of the accumulated profits.
Autonomous Minds	The sentient supercomputers that rebelled against humanity during the Autonomous Revolt.
Autonomous Revolt	The rebellion of the Autonomous Minds, which caused worldwide destruction and hastened the collapse of the nation-states.

beacon | A tracking signal that allows one to be located in the multi network.

Big Divide | The era of worldwide depression and chaos following the Autonomous Revolt.

bio/logic program | A set of logical instructions designed to enhance the human body or mind. Most bio/logic programs act on the body through microscopic machines called OCHREs placed throughout the body at (or before) birth.

bio/logic | The set of tools bio/logic programmers use to create and modify bio/logic code. Programming bars are categorized with the letters of the Roman alphabet (A to Z), and are largely indistinguishable to the naked eye. They interact with virtual code through holographic extensions that are only visible in MindSpace.

bio/logics | The science of using programming code to extend the capabilities of the human body and mind.

black code | Malicious or harmful programs, usually designed and launched by seditious organizations.

bodhisattva | The spiritual leader of a creed. Most creed organizations are spearheaded by one individual bodhisattva. Some creeds are run by an elected body of major and minor bodhisattvas.

Bodhisattva, the When capitalized, usually refers to the first leader of Creed Objectivv, who originated the title; or his successors, who abandon their names upon confirmation.

capitalman Individual who raises start-up money for fiefcorps. Following long tradition, the term is gender-neutral.

carbonization economics A colloquial term for a type of economy where fief corps form quickly to serve a specific purpose, and then dissipate to make room for new ideas.

ChaiQuoke A popular tea-flavored beverage.

channel The process of marketing and selling products, usually to groups rather than individuals.

channeler A businessperson responsible for driving sales to specific markets.

Cisco A major population center, known in ancient times as San Francisco.

Confidential-Whisper One of the most popular bio/logic programs on the Data Sea, ConfidentialWhisper provides a silent, completely internal communication venue for two or more people.

Congress of L-PRACGs
A representative body composed of most of the L-PRACGs in the solar system. The Speaker of the Congress is one of the most powerful elected officials in government.

connectible
Able to link to the Data Sea. Cultures who shun modern technology (like the Islanders and the Pharisees) are said to be "unconnectible," and refer to the remainder of society as "connectibles." See also *unconnectible*.

connectible collar
The thin copper collar that Islanders and other unconnectibles wear to allow them to see and communicate with multi projections.

credit
The standard unit of monetary exchange in civilized society.

creed
An organization that promotes a particular ethical belief system. Creeds promulgate many of the same types of moral teachings as the ancient religions, but are generally bereft of religious mythology and iconography.

Creed Bushido
A militaristic creed that was formed around the time of the Autonomous Revolt and based on the ancient Japanese warrior code. Since the Reawakening, the

creed has become more focused on asceticism and rigorous discipline.

Creed Conscientious An environmentally conscious order pledged to preserve the integrity of the Data Sea.

Creed Dao An order that stresses Daoist principles of harmony with the universe instead of conformance to the dictates of society. A strong repository of Chinese cultural history and tradition.

Creed Élan One of the more prominent creeds, Creed Élan teaches the value of philanthropy. Its members tend to be wealthy socialites. The creed's colors are purple and red.

Creed Objectivv A creed dedicated to the search for and promotion of absolute epistemological truth. Members take an oath to always tell the truth. Its logo is a black-and-white swirl.

Creed Surina The creed founded in honor of Sheldon Surina after his death. Creed Surina promotes the agenda of "spiritual discovery and mutual enlightenment through technology." The official colors of the creed are blue and green.

Creed Thassel	A once-common creed of the business class, dedicated to the "virtue of selfishness." Its symbol is three vertical stripes.
Creeds Coalition	The blanket organization that promotes inter-creed understanding and cooperation.
Data Sea	The sum total of all the communication networks running in the civilized world. Includes such networks as the Jamm and the Sigh.
Defense and Wellness Council	The governmental entity responsible for military, security, and intelligence operations throughout the system. The Council is headed by a single high executive, who is appointed by the Prime Committee. Many fear and resent the Council for its secrecy and the fact that it is unaccountable to the public for its actions.
Democratic American Collective (DAC)	An ancient nation-state formed after the dissolution of the United States of America. See also *New Alamo*.
disruptor	Weapon that allows attacks on multi projections by disrupting or altering their signals. Often used by the Defense and Wellness Council in conjunction with dart-guns.

diss	The urban poor. The term is alternately thought to be derived from "disenfranchised," "disaffected," and "disassociated."
dock	An area fiefcorps use to keep pending projects that are being prepared for launch on the Data Sea.
Dogmatic Opposition	A legal appeal to the Prime Committee to block or nullify a specific technology. Used primarily by the Islanders to maintain a nontechnological society.
Dr. Plugenpatch	The network of medical databases and programs that maintains the health of nearly all connectible citizens.
drudge	An independent reporter or journalist who writes regular opinion columns to a list of subscribers. Drudges are considered one of the public's main resources for government accountability.
East Texas	One of two former splinter states of New Alamo. See also *West Texas*.
Economic Plunge of the 310s	Period of worldwide collapse and unemployment following the death of Marcus Surina. Widely

thought to have been eradicated by massive Defense and Wellness Council spending.

Ecumenical Council | The religious governmental body in New Alamo that was responsible for much of the violence and bloodshed of the Big Divide.

engineer | One of the standard positions in a fiefcorp. Engineers are traditionally responsible for the "nuts and bolts" bio/logic programming for a fiefcorp's products.

Environmental Control Board | The governmental body that controls and regulates the planetary environment, from species preservation and protection to weather control.

ex utero | The state of an embryo that has been removed from its mother's uterus in preparation for hive growing and birth.

fiefcorp | A business entity that typically consists of one master and several apprentices. Fiefcorps are usually short-lived, lasting less than a decade. The economics of the fiefcorp business are such that it usually makes better sense to dissolve a fiefcorp and sell its assets every few years. See also *memecorp*.

flexible glass   A strong, glasslike building material that can be very easily stretched and molded, even at room temperature.

fore   One of the descriptive components of a program that helps the Data Sea sort and catalog information. See also *aft*.

"for process' preservation"   A common phrase roughly translatable as "for Pete's sake."

Furtoid   A distant and troubled orbital colony in constant danger of collapse from poor engineering and economics.

Gandhi University   The institution of higher learning in Andra Pradesh where Sheldon Surina taught. Each of his descendants has held an honorary chair at the university.

gateway zone   Designated entry point for a multi projection into real space.

geosynchrons   Programs that regulate the geophysical and meteorological activity of the Earth. Geosynchrons are categorized as Levels I through V, I being the lowest level (regulation of atomic activity) and V being the highest level (regulation of complex environmental activity).

governmentalism   The political movement that espouses a belief in strong centralized government (though not necessarily the current centralized government). See also *libertarianism*.

GravCo | A semigovernmental memecorp that regulates gravity control among orbital colonies and other outworlders.

high executive | The official that heads the Defense and Wellness Council, appointed by the Prime Committee.

hive | A communal birthing and child-rearing facility for middle- and upper-class children.

hoverbird | Flying vehicle that can travel in air and low orbit. Primarily used for travel over long distances, hauling cargo, and defense.

infoquake | A dangerous burst of energy in the computational system, thought to be caused by a disproportionate amount of activity at one time or concentrated in one particular area.

initiation | A twelve-month rite of passage that many youths from middle- and upper-class backgrounds go through before being considered adults. The initiation consists primarily of depriving children of modern technology.

Islander | A resident of the Pacific Islands, where the governments shun most modern technology.

Islander
Tolerance Act

The law that created the Dogmatic Opposition in an attempt to ease relations between connectible and unconnectible cultures.

Jabbor, Tul

The first high executive of the Defense and Wellness Council.

Jamm

A network that allows never-ending musical "jam sessions" between musicians all over the world.

Keepers

The order that was assigned to program and operate the Autonomous Minds. Often blamed for starting the Autonomous Revolt, although the extent of their complicity in the revolt will never fully be known.

launch

To officially release a product onto the Data Sea for public consumption.

libertarianism

A political philosophy that believes in decentralized government run principally by the L-PRACGs. See also *governmentalism*.

L-PRACG

Local Political Representative Association of Civic Groups, the basic unit of government throughout the civilized world. Pronounced "ELL prag."

master

One of the positions in a fiefcorp. The master is the person who forms the fiefcorp, and has full authority in all business decisions. Masters take on apprentices who then work to earn full shares in the fiefcorp after a specific contractual period.

Meme Cooperative
The governmental entity that regulates business between fiefcorps. Largely perceived as an ineffectual watchdog organization.

memecorp
A business entity whose membership subscribes to a particular set of ideas ("memes"). Frequently relies on public or private funding, as opposed to the fiefcorp, which relies solely on the free market. See also *fiefcorp*.

MindSpace
The virtual programming "desktop" provided by a workbench for programming. It is only in MindSpace that the extensions to bio/logic programming bars can be used to manipulate bio/logic code.

Monk, Aloretus
Physicist and discoverer of sub-aether transmission, a method of instantaneous communication made possible by quantum entanglement.

multi
To project a virtual body onto the multi network. Can be used as a verb or an adjective.

multi connection	The state of existing virtually on the multi network. When the user returns to his or her physical body, they have "cut their multi connection."
multi network	The system of bots and programs that allows people to virtually interact with one another almost anywhere in the world and on most orbital colonies.
multi projection	A virtual body that exists only through neural manipulation by the multi network. Real bodies can interact with virtual bodies in ways that are almost identical to actual physical interaction.
MultiReal	A revolutionary new technology being promoted by Margaret Surina.
multivoid	The few seconds of mental "blankness" that occurs when switching (or cutting) multi connections.
nation-state	An ancient political entity, bounded by geography and ruled over by a centralized government or governments. Superseded by the rise of L-PRACGs.
neural programmer	A bio/logics specialist who concentrates on the programming of the human brain.

New Alamo	An ancient nation-state formed after the dissolution of the United States of America. Included many of the USA's southwestern states and portions of Mexico as well. Became a dominant and terrorizing world power during the Big Divide. See also *Democratic American Collective*.
newt	A digital servant that can be programmed to obey orders.
nitro	A popular beverage full of concentrated natural stimulants, usually served hot.
Nova Ceti	An orbital colony.
Null Current	Poetic term for death. The term is of uncertain vintage but is thought by many to have been coined by Sheldon Surina.
OCHRE (1)	A generic term for any of a number of nanotechnological devices implanted in the human body to maintain health. After the OCHRE Corporation, which pioneered the technology.
OCHRE (2)	The Osterman Company for Human Re-Engineering. Founded by Henry Osterman to pioneer nanotechnology. Dissolved almost 110 years later after a protracted legal battle with the Defense and

Wellness Council. Often (redundantly) called "the OCHRE Corporation" to distinguish it from the nanotechnological machines that bear its name.

offline — Slang term for "crazy."

OrbiCo — The quasi-governmental agency that controls the space shipping lines and most interplanetary cargo transport.

orbital colony — A nonterrestrial habitation, sometimes built free-standing in space and sometimes built on existing soil (e.g., asteroids and planetoids). The major orbital colonies are 49th Heaven, Allowell, Furtoid, Nova Ceti, and Patronell, but there are dozens of smaller colonies all over the solar system.

Osterman, Henry — Contemporary of Sheldon Surina and founder of the OCHRE Corporation. A famous iconoclast and recluse who zealously persecuted his enemies. Died under mysterious circumstances in 117.

Padron, Par — High executive of the Defense and Wellness Council from 153 until his death in 209. Nicknamed "the people's executive" because of his pro-democratic reforms.

Patronell   An orbital colony that circles Luna.

"perfection postponed"   A common phrase roughly translatable as "heaven forbid."

Pharisees   The disparate groups of fanatics that live around the areas once known as the Middle East. It is believed that several million people still practice many of the ancient religions in these remote places.

Pharisee Territories   Unconnectible lands occupied by the Pharisees.

Prepared, the   An order whose membership is only open to the elderly and the terminally ill. Its members are given special legal status and access to euthanasia procedures in the Dr. Plugenpatch databases that are otherwise banned.

Prime Committee   The central governing board that runs the affairs of the system. Much like the ancient United Nations, the Committee's functions are mainly diplomatic and administrative. All of the real power rests with the Defense and Wellness Council and the L-PRACGs.

Primo, Lucco   Founder of the Primo's bio/logic investment guide and one of the icons of capitalism and libertarianism during the Reawakening.

Primo's — The bio/logic investment guide that provides a series of ratings for programmers and their products. People all over the world rely on Primo's ratings as a gauge of reliability in bio/logics.

public directory — A storehouse of personal information used throughout the civilized world.

QuasiSuspension — A popular program that allows the user to schedule sleep and choose different levels of rest. Often used to ration out sleep in small doses and keep the user awake longer.

Reawakening — The period of intellectual renewal and discovery that began with Sheldon Surina's publication of his seminal paper on bio/logics. Continues to this day.

ROD — Routine On Demand. A simple bio/logic program created for a single (often wealthy) individual. Usually pronounced as one word ("rod").

Sigh, the — Virtual network devoted to sensual pleasure. Unlike the multi network, the Sigh does not allow interaction between real and virtual bodies.

Smith, Jesus Joshua	The first and most influential of the Three Jesuses. Led an exodus of faithful Christians and Moslems to the Pharisee Territories.
stretched stone	A rocklike building material that is remarkably strong and yet flexible as well.
subaether	A form of instantaneous transmission made possible by quantum entanglement.
Sudafrica	A populous area at the southern end of the African continent.
Surina, Marcus	Descendant of Prengal Surina and the "father of teleportation." Died in an orbital colony accident at the prime of his life, leaving TeleCo in shambles and prompting the Economic Plunge of the 310s.
Surina, Margaret	Daughter of Marcus Surina and the inventor of MultiReal technology.
Surina, Prengal	Grandson of Sheldon Surina and discoverer of the universal law of physics, which is the cornerstone of all modern computing and engineering.
Surina, Sheldon	The father of bio/logics. Revived the ancient sciences of nanotechnology and paved the way for the

	drastic improvement of the human race through technology.
TeleCo	Quasi-governmental agency that runs all teleportation services, brought to prominence by Marcus Surina. Now tightly regulated by the Defense and Wellness Council.
teleportation	The process of instantaneous human travel over long distances. Technically, matter is not actually "transferred" during a teleportation, but rather telekinetically reconfigured.
Thassel, Kordez	Libertarian philosopher and founder of Creed Thassel.
Three Jesuses	Spiritual leaders who, in three separate movements, led pilgrimages of the religious faithful to found colonies of free religious worship in what are currently known as the Pharisee Territories.
Toradicus	High executive of the Defense and Wellness Council, known for bringing the L-PRACGs under central government control.
"Towards Perfection"	A greeting or farewell, originally derived from a saying of Sheldon Surina's.
treepaper	Ancient sheet of pulped wood for writing and printing with ink.

tube
: The high-speed trains used in most civilized places on Earth for inter- and intra-city travel. The tube has become ubiquitous because its tracks are extremely cheap to build, easy to lay down, and unobtrusive in appearance.

TubeCo
: The memecorp that runs the tube system. Now heavily subsidized by the Prime Committee.

unconnectible
: Not able to connect to the resources on the Data Sea. A sometimes derogatory reference to the Islanders and the Pharisees, who shun modern technology. See also *connectible*.

universal law of physics
: Scientific principle put forward by Prengal Surina that enables nearly limitless supplies of energy.

Vault
: The network that makes financial transactions possible. Known for fanatical secrecy and paranoia, the administrators of the Vault pride themselves on never having suffered from a serious break-in.

viewscreen
: A flat surface that can receive and display audio and visual transmissions from the Data Sea. Viewscreens are usually used for decoration in addition to entertainment.

West Texas — One of two former splinter states of New Alamo. See also *East Texas*.

Witt, Tobi Jae — Famous scientist and pioneer of artificial intelligence from before the Autonomous Revolt. She created the first Autonomous Mind and died a violent death, though her killer was never identified.

workbench — A particular type of desk capable of projecting a MindSpace bubble and allowing bio/logic programming.

xpression board — Musical instrument known for its versatility. Users create their own form and structure; thus no two xpression boards are the same.

Yu — The first modern orbital colony, financed and constructed by the Chinese. The destruction of Yu by the Autonomous Minds was the event that triggered the cataclysmic Autonomous Revolt.

APPENDIX B
HISTORICAL TIMELINE

The chronicling of modern history began with Sheldon Surina's publication of "Towards the Science of Bio/Logics and a New Direction for Humanity." Surina started the Reawakening, which ended the period of the Big Divide that began with the Autonomous Revolt. The publication of Surina's paper is considered to be the Zero Year of the Reawakening (YOR).

YOR	EVENT	
	Development of the precursors of the Data Sea on hardware-based machine networks.	ANTIQUITY
	The last pan-European collective alliance falls apart. The nation-states of Europe never again gain prominence on the world stage.	
	The predominant Arab nations form the Allahu Akbar Emirates	

	to counter American and Chinese dominance.	
	Scientists make major advances in nanotechnology. Nanotechnology becomes commonplace for exterminating disease and regulating many bodily systems.	ANTIQUITY
	Final economic collapse of the United States of America. During the unrest that follows, the northeastern states form the Democratic American Collective (DAC), while the southern and western states form New Alamo.	
	Establishment of the first permanent city on Luna.	
	First orbital colony, Yu (named after the legendary founder of the first Chinese dynasty), launched by the Congressional China Assembly.	
	Yu is sabotaged and destroyed by the Autonomous Minds. **Beginning of the Autonomous Revolt.**	REVOLT
	End of the Autonomous Revolt. Much of the civilized world lies in ruins.	
	The Big Divide begins. A time of chaos and distrust of technology.	

	The Ecumenical Council of New Alamo, seeking to establish order in a time of hunger and chaos, orders mass executions of its citizenry.	**BIG DIVIDE**
	Rebellion in New Alamo splits the nation-state into West Texas and East Texas.	
	Birth of Sheldon Surina.	
	Birth of Henry Osterman.	
0	Sheldon Surina publishes his first manifesto on the science of bio/logics. **The Reawakening begins.**	**REAWAKENING**
10	Final dissolution of the New Alamo Ecumenical Council.	
10s–40s	The Three Jesuses lead pilgrimages of the faithful to Jerusalem. Rampaging Pharisees leave devastation in their wake.	
25	Henry Osterman founds the Osterman Company for Human Re-Engineering (OCHRE).	
35–37	Seeing potential ruination from the technological revolution that Sheldon Surina has engendered, the two Texan governments put a price on his head. Surina leaves the Gandhi University and goes into hiding.	

37	The president of West Texas is assassinated. The new president exonerates Sheldon Surina and calls off the manhunt for him. It is still many years before Surina can appear in public without intense security.
39	Creed Élan is founded as a private philanthropic organization (though the term "creed" has not yet been coined).
52	Dr. Plugenpatch is incorporated as a private enterprise. Henry Osterman and Sheldon Surina are among those on its original board.
60–100	Many of the great nation-states of antiquity dissolve as their primary functions (enforcing law, keeping the peace, encouraging trade) become irrelevant or more efficient to handle through distributed technology. People begin to form their own independent legal entities, or civic groups.
61	The Third Jesus leads a splinter group of radical Pharisees in building a new orbital colony (the first since the destruction of Yu). Though initially promising, 49th Heaven collapses within a generation. It reemerges to prominence

	a hundred years later as a sybaritic resort.
66	First fully functioning multi technology comes into existence. Sheldon Surina, though not the technology's inventor, makes vast engineering improvements. Within a decade, multi projections are ubiquitous among the wealthy.
70s–90s	Inspired by the apparent success of 49th Heaven, a rash of orbital colonies are funded and colonized. Space mania brings new funding and energy to ongoing efforts to colonize Mars.
80	Birth of Prengal Surina.
103	Major national and corporate interests join together with the vestiges of ancient nation-states to form the Prime Committee. The Committee is mainly seen as a bureaucratic organization whose task is to ensure public order and prevent another Autonomous Revolt.
107	The Prime Committee establishes the Defense and Wellness Council as a military and intelligence force. Its first high executive, Tul Jabbor, surprises the Prime Committee's corporate founders by

	expanding the Council's authority and in some cases turning on its sponsors (particularly OCHRE).
108	Creed Objectivv is founded by a reclusive mystic figure known as the Bodhisattva.
111	The Prime Committee undergoes a major effort to fund the development of multi technology throughout the system.
113	OCHRE becomes a target of the Prime Committee, which seeks to end the company's stranglehold on nanotechnology.
115	Dr. Plugenpatch agrees to special oversight and cooperation with the Defense and Wellness Council in order to avoid the same fate as OCHRE. The corporation becomes a hybrid governmental/private sector industry that forms the basis of medical treatment worldwide.
116	Death of Sheldon Surina. To honor his memory, Surina's successors build the compound at Andra Pradesh and found Creed Surina.
117	Tul Jabbor is assassinated. His killers are never found, but many suspect OCHRE. After a protracted legal battle, Henry

	Osterman dies under mysterious circumstances (some claim suicide). OCHRE battles over his successor for several years to come, then finally dissolves in 132.
122	Prengal Surina puts forth his universal law of physics.
130s	Major advances in hive birthing bring the technology to the public for the first time. A small minority that resists these advances begins emigrating to the Pacific Islands and Indonesia, where Luddites encourage isolation from the outside world. The remainder of the system comes to know them as Islanders. The Islander emigration continues for the next fifty years.
143	High Executive Toradicus begins a campaign to bring the L-PRACGs under Defense and Wellness Council control. He enlists Prengal Surina to lobby the L-PRACGs to construct a joint governmental framework with the Prime Committee. The Congress of L-PRACGs is founded.
146	The Islander Tolerance Act creates the Dogmatic Opposition.

150s	Teams working under Prengal Surina make startling advances in the control of gravity using maxims from the universal law of physics. Key members of these teams (including Prengal Surina) become the first board members of GravCo.
153	Par Padron is appointed high executive of the Defense and Wellness Council. He is nicknamed "the people's high executive" because of his actions to rein in the business community.
160s	The business of multi technology booms. By decade's end, most connectibles live within an hour of a multi facility.
162	Union Baseball adopts radical new rules to keep up with the times and to even the playing field among bio/logically enhanced players.
168	Death of the first Bodhisattva of Creed Objectivv.
177	A coalition of business interests forms the Meme Cooperative to stave off the harsh populist reforms of Par Padron.
185	Death of Prengal Surina.

196	Libertarian rebels, funded and organized by the bio/logics industry titans, storm a handful of major cities in an attempt to overthrow the Prime Committee and the Defense and Wellness Council. Par Padron initiates martial law and puts down the disturbances.
200	The bio/logics industry attempts to pack the Prime Committee with its appointees and paid lobbyists. Par Padron pushes through a resolution declaring that the people (via the Congress of L-PRACGs) will always hold the majority of seats on the Committee.
209	Death of Par Padron.
220s–230s	A time of great economic and cultural stability world-wide, dubbed afterwards as the Golden Age. A resurgence in creedism results in the formation of the Creeds Coalition.
247	Birth of Marcus Surina.
250s	Almost all infants outside of the Pharisee and Islander territories are born and raised in hives. Life expectancies rise dramatically.
268	Creed Thassel is founded.

270	The first fiefcorp is established, and rules governing its structure are encoded by the Meme Cooperative. Most people see fiefcorps as a boon to society, helping the underprivileged gain skills and putting them on a track to social empowerment.
287	First successful tests of teleportation technology are conducted by a team that includes Marcus Surina. The extraordinary costs and energy involved have prohibited the widespread usage of teleportation to the present day.
290s–300s	The Great Boom, a time of economic prosperity, is ushered in, fed by the new fiefcorp sector and the promise of teleportation technology.
291	Lucco Primo establishes the Primo's bio/logic investment guide.
301	Birth of Margaret Surina.
302	Len Borda appointed high executive of the Defense and Wellness Council.
313	Marcus Surina dies in a shuttle accident in the orbital colonies.
310s–	The Economic Plunge of the 310s, a time of economic stagnation. Len

	Borda keeps the system afloat largely through the use of Prime Committee capital to fund research projects. Critics grumble about the return of the nation-state and centralized authority.
318	Rioting in Melbourne threatens the Prime Committee, but is put down by High Executive Borda.
327	Creed Thassel is nearly disbanded after scandal caused by the drudge Sen Sivv Sor's exposé on its membership practices.
331	Birth of Natch.
334	Warfare erupts between the Islanders and the Defense and Wellness Council. Although the official "war" lasts only a few years, unofficial skirmishes continue to the present day.
339	Margaret Surina founds the Surina Perfection Memecorp, and the drudges begin to whisper about a mysterious "Phoenix Project."
351	The world economy officially surpasses its previous peak, achieved in 313, before the death of Marcus Surina and the Economic Plunge.
359	Present Day.

APPENDIX C
ON THE SCIENCE
OF BIO/LOGICS

Although Sheldon Surina has been credited with founding the discipline of bio/logics, he was not the first to try to use computational power to enhance the human body. Indeed, the science of nanotechnology had grown quite sophisticated in the years immediately preceding the Autonomous Revolt. But the revolt put an end to such experimentation. For many years, any attempt to explore the intersection of humans and machines was deemed an attempt to resurrect the Autonomous Minds. Dozens of promising scientists ended up dead or living in forced-labor camps because of their "radical" ideas.

Sheldon Surina's seminal paper "Towards the Science of Bio/Logics and a New Direction for Humanity" changed all that.

It is difficult to explain why Surina's ideas found acceptance when so many other similar suggestions ended up in the dustbin of history. Most students of the period have concluded that Surina's bio/logics system was different from its predecessors in one crucial aspect: its *humanocentric* approach emphasized personal choice and responsibility.

A THREE-LEGGED SYSTEM

Surina conceived of a system with equal roles for hardware, software, and information. Like a three-legged stool, removal of any of the legs would cause the system to collapse.

The hardware in question would consist of microscopic machines placed in strategic locations throughout the human body. These nanotechnological machines would contain a variety of standard tools for maintenance of human tissue, everything from routine measurement to precise surgery.

But in Surina's system, the machines themselves would be incapable of independent action. Their every movement would be controlled by programmable software that could be strictly controlled by the patient. Furthermore, Surina envisioned a competitive software industry arising to provide ever-improving versions of this controlling software.

The third indispensable leg of Surina's bio/logics system consisted of an independent storehouse of medical information. Software would then have a trusted source to consult for information that would affect the directions given to the hardware.

Surina's vision was remarkably prescient, and the bio/logics system in place today still abides by those original principles. The nanotechnological machines that Surina envisioned were pioneered by his protégé Henry Osterman and his OCHRE Corporation. Dr. Plugenpatch became the world's trusted repository of medical information. And of course, a highly competitive market for bio/logic software grew and continues to fuel the world economy to this day.

Of course, not all is as Surina envisioned it. In his paper "Towards the Science of Bio/Logics," Surina made free choice a prerequisite of a working system. He wanted users to be able to choose from a wide variety of nanotechnological systems, software programs, and information warehouses. According to Surina, free competition was crucial to encouraging innovation and preventing corruption. But Surina lived to see both the OCHRE Corporation and Dr. Plugenpatch achieve virtual monopolies in their respective fields, leaving only the software industry as a truly competitive field.

In addition, the strict separation of functions that Surina wanted has not always been maintained. The distinctions between the three legs of the system have begun to blur as the OCHRE Corporation's successors have imbued their bots with limited intelligence, and software programmers have embedded their own medical standards rather than rely on outside storehouses of information.

BIO/LOGIC PROGRAMMING

While the techniques of creating bio/logic programs have changed radically over the years, the principles remain the same.

Bio/logic software is a series of instructions a user can transmit to his or her OCHRE machines to perform a specific function. In Surina's day, programming was performed through the manipulation of a series of machine "languages," software was stored on miniature "chips" implanted within the body, and instructions were broadcast to the machines inside the body through radio waves.

Programming itself has evolved from a primitive linguistic model to today's more sophisticated visual model. This evolution enabled programmers to visualize logical structures instead of spelling them out. Advances in the science of holography allowed the invention of MindSpace, which allowed programmers to interact with their programs through a three-dimensional interface. The capabilities of MindSpace programming have been significantly expanded by the development of special tools for the medium, the bio/logic programming bars. A typical set of programming bars consists of twenty-six entities (marked A to Z after the Roman alphabet), with each bar containing three to six separate functions. Most MindSpace bubbles also recognize a common set of twelve hand gestures.

The data itself, once stored on plastic chips, is now stored in protected molecular chains scattered throughout the civilized world. Prengal Surina's universal law of physics and Aloretus Monk's discovery of subaether transmission have made it practical for programmers to store information on an atomic level virtually anywhere in the world.

THE FUTURE OF BIO/LOGICS

Libertarian elements of the government have been particularly active in promoting a renewal of competition in the hardware and information legs of Sheldon Surina's three-legged system. Proposals include privatizing Dr. Plugenpatch and breaking up the three main companies that have divided up the OCHRE spectrum between themselves. But detractors have pointed to the chaos of the bio/logic programming industry as reason to keep these industries heavily regulated and centralized.

The bulk of current bio/logic research is dedicated to improving the energy capacity of the human body. Users often encounter problems when bodily resources that run bio/logic programs are overtaxed, and some industry watchers predict severe resource limitations in the human body within the next twenty to thirty years.

APPENDIX D
ON THE SURINAS

The line of scientists, politicians, freethinkers, and programmers that began with Sheldon Surina is perhaps the greatest dynasty humankind has known since the Caesars. Not only did the Surinas lead the way out of the chaos of the Big Divide and give the world trust in technology again; they also enriched that world in ways no family had done before or has done since.

SHELDON SURINA (-41 TO 116)

Like most of his peers, Sheldon Surina was taught to shun the achievements of the scientists and programmers that led to the Autonomous Revolt. During Surina's formative years, the world was still feeling the aftershocks of that cataclysmic event and the disasters that followed it (although by this time, the world had regained a modicum of order, and New Alamo's fanaticism was already beginning to taper off). His parents sent him to the Gandhi University at

Andra Pradesh for a spiritual education. It was during his long apprenticeship at the Gandhi University that Surina became enamored with the ancient wonders of biotechnology. Against the warnings of his proctors (who considered the sciences to be a heretical course of study), Sheldon embarked on a project to re-create the achievements of the biologists of antiquity.

When he was forty-one years old, Sheldon published his seminal work, "Towards the Science of Bio/Logics and a New Direction for Humanity." The first words of this manifesto were a shocking call to arms: "There is no problem that we cannot solve through scientific innovation." He then proceeded to outline a new discipline of science that would allow computer programs to interact with the systems of the human body. Surina called his new discipline "bio/logics."

The work caused a firestorm of controversy in the academic world, with many educators denouncing Surina as a heretic bent on causing another Autonomous Revolt. Within a decade, Surina had crafted the first working bio/logic program: Heart-Monitor 1.0, which could make rational decisions about cardiological treatment on the fly. Using this and several other successful prototypes, Surina raised funds for the first bio/logic corporations. His investments in these firms eventually made him and many of his protégés phenomenally wealthy. One of his disciples, Henry Osterman, founder of the OCHRE Corporation, would be a lifelong collaborator (and sometime competitor).

Surina's growing fame and influence began to upset the balance of power among the fragile nation-states. Many of these states owed their survival to delicate antitechnology treaties designed to prevent another Autonomous Revolt. During the years 35 to 37, Surina became the target of numerous assassination plots hatched by the splinter East and West Texan governments. These threats largely ended with the overthrow of the West Texan regime in 37.

In the years that followed, Sheldon Surina had a hand in nearly every major technology to come down the pike. He created or co-created the key tools and practices of the bio/logic programming industry (including MindSpace and bio/logic programming bars). He made important contributions to the development of the multi network, and with Henry Osterman sat on the board of the original Dr. Plugenpatch company.

Growing fear of the power of bio/logic corporations led to the creation of the Prime Committee in the waning years of the Reawakening's first century. Sheldon Surina decried the Prime Committee as an "insidious evil" and became the world's leading opponent of centralized governmental authority. (Surina and Osterman had widely divergent views on this issue and eventually ended their friendship over the formation of the Defense and Wellness Council.)

Surina spent the opening years of the second century railing against the Council and the Committee and seeking their dissolution. A firm believer in individual empowerment and unbridled personal freedom, Surina believed that any centralized authority (no matter how limited) would lead to totalitarianism. The majority of public sentiment was against him, however, and in his last years Surina even began to advocate open rebellion and violence. He died in 116, a bitter man with waning political influence.

PRENGAL SURINA (80 TO 185)

Prengal Surina was never as tempestuous a figure as his grandfather Sheldon, but many have argued that his influence on modern society was even greater.

Because of the family's vast bio/logic fortune, Prengal was raised with great wealth and privilege in India. He followed in Sheldon's footsteps by attending the Gandhi University at Andra Pradesh, and eventually attained a permanent post on the faculty. Prengal tended to shy away from politics, however, despite the increasingly desperate urging of his grandfather and other anti-Prime Committee forces. Upon Sheldon's death, Prengal and his companion Ladaru organized Creed Surina in his honor, but disappointed many by insisting that the group be strictly apolitical.

At the age of forty-two, Prengal put forth what many consider to be the most significant scientific breakthrough of humanity since antiquity: the universal law of physics. Prengal's law neatly tied together the previously disparate fields of quantum and classical mechanics. By revealing the ways in which matter and energy are intimately connected throughout the universe—in ways that transcend space and time—Prengal made possible the fields of teleportation and antigravitation. Without the universal law of physics, multi projecting over great distances would be impossible.

Prengal Surina's breakthrough was poorly understood for many years. Unlike his grandfather, Prengal was not a charismatic figure who trumpeted his own accomplishments. As his work grew in stature and importance, however, the system began to view him with an almost mystical reverence.

When he did become involved in the political arena, it was only at the urging of his old friend, High Executive Toradicus. In direct contrast to his grandfather's beliefs, Prengal Surina became a spokesperson *for* centralizing power in the Prime Committee. The current system of L-PRACGs pledging support for the oversight of the Prime Committee largely owes its existence to the lobbying of Prengal Surina and the hard-nosed politics of Toradicus.

Prengal lived the last decades of his life in quiet seclusion at Andra Pradesh, remaining neutral in the great battles between big business and government during the term of High Executive Par Padron. He died in year 185 of the Reawakening.

MARCUS SURINA (247 TO 313)

Unlike his predecessors, Marcus Surina did not seek a life of scientific achievement. He spent much of his youth disavowing the wealth and "decadence" of the Surinas in Andra Pradesh and the creed that was his ancestor's namesake. Marcus became a drifter and adventurer out in the orbital colonies, where records were scarce. He had much wider experience in the world than either Sheldon or Marcus, and in his time he gambled, piloted starships, formed L-PRACGs, and ran a number of reputable and disreputable companies.

Marcus originally entered the science of teleportation as an investor. TeleCo was one of many pet projects he funded with Surina money. He had very little scientific training and only became involved in the development of the science after several of the principal players resigned from the project over frustrations with his management.

It was at that point that Marcus Surina experienced an epiphany of sorts and devoted himself to perfecting the science of teleportation. He made up for lost time by delving into the research and development processes with more single-mindedness than any of his predecessors. By the end of the century, Marcus had transformed himself from a playboy and dilettante to the leading scientist and entrepreneur of his age. His passion for teleportation fueled the fortunes of TeleCo and, indeed, the entire economy.

Marcus spent the last decade of his life in a feverish struggle to perfect teleportation. He became a public spokesperson and pitchman, not only for his own technology, but for the bio/logics industry in general. He engaged in a great public struggle with Len Borda, the newly appointed high executive of the Defense and Wellness Council, over the dangers of the project. Their dispute remained unresolved, however, when Marcus died suddenly (along with many of his top advisors) in a shuttle accident in the orbital colonies.

Rumor and innuendo attributed hundreds of illegitimate children to Marcus, who allegedly was an incessant womanizer. Most historians believe these claims to be wildly exaggerated. Whatever the truth of those claims, he left only one legitimate child and heir, a daughter, Margaret.

MARGARET SURINA (301–   )

The only child of Marcus Surina, Margaret has assumed the family mantle as bodhisattva of Creed Surina; the professorial chair at the Gandhi University held by every Surina since Sheldon; and head of the various family investments. She also founded the Surina Perfection Memecorp, but its aims and goals remain unknown at the present time.

APPENDIX E
ON THE
MULTI NETWORK

Society has experimented with any number of virtual communities, from the primitive text environments of the World Wide Web to the sophisticated pleasure worlds of the Sigh. But none has achieved such widespread acceptance as the multi network.

A multi projection is a virtual body that "exists" in real space. While the multied body is only an illusion created by neural manipulation, it can interact with real ("meat") bodies in a way almost indistinguishable from physical human interaction. In order to achieve such verisimilitude, however, the architects of the multi network have had to limit many of the freedoms taken for granted in other virtual communities.

HOW IT WORKS

The multi network depends on two key components: (1) the trillions of microscopic bots that process and relay sensory information to the network, and (2) neural OCHREs that manipulate the mind into "seeing" the sights, "hearing" the sounds, and "feeling" the sensations of the network.

Similarly, those who interact with multi projections allow neural manipulation to trick the mind into believing the virtual bodies are present. Participation in the multi network is not optional in civilized society. Even unconnectibles such as Islanders and Pharisees are required to wear so-called "connectible collars" when not in their homelands so they can interact with multi projections.

Thanks to the advances in nanotechnology that have occurred since Henry Osterman's time, multi bots are lighter than air and only molecules thick. They carpet most of the Earth and populated colonies in concentrations high enough to provide sensory information almost anywhere a user would want to go, but still diffuse enough that their presence is undetectable to the naked eye.

Developments in subaether transmission have enabled multi to follow humanity to the moon, Mars, and the orbital colonies.

THE PHYSICS OF MULTI INTERACTION

Because multied bodies are merely illusions of the mind and do not have physical substance, their interactions with the physical world are governed by a strict set of unbreakable rules. Some rules simply repeat the constraints of nature (e.g., a real person cannot climb on top of a virtual body). Other rules are arbitrary decisions that have been hammered out over the years by a succession of governmental agencies.

The guiding principle of multi/meat interactions is that *they should be as "real" as possible.* In an ideal multi experience, it would be impossible to determine whether the user was present in the flesh or in multi. The multi network, unlike other networks, does not allow for any "improvements" on the human experience. Thus, a multied body contains all the warts and blemishes the actual human body does; multied bodies cannot fly, change shapes, or perform feats of inhuman strength; and they are clothed in the same garments as their real bodies.

Occasionally, things happen in the "real" world that cannot be reconciled in a virtual environment. One can throw a stone "through" a multi projection without incident. Larger discrepancies typically result in the automatic cutting of a multi connection.

As the ubiquity of the multi network has grown, society has largely adapted. Most doors and windows are capable of accepting and responding to multi commands. Auditoriums and meeting spaces generally have amenities for both types of audiences.

The verisimilitude of the multi network is what has kept it safe during the decades it has been in widespread use. The network has built-in safeguards that will automatically cut a connection in cases of extreme pain or duress. Because its rules are so rigid and the chance for mishap so small, the Defense and Wellness Council has fiercely blocked any attempts to liberalize the network rules or allow other virtual networks to participate in public space.

ENTERING AND EXITING THE NETWORK

Because of the high potential for danger in letting multi projections connect anywhere on the network, the network's governing bodies insisted early in its existence that entry points on the network be restricted.

Entrances must occur in specially designated "gateway zones." This is to prevent users from projecting to unauthorized locations, into the middle of a wall, or into some other obstruction. Most homes, businesses, and public places these days are equipped with gateway zones that allow apparition onto the multi network, but it is not uncommon for restricted or sensitive locations to limit gateway zones to a central location.

A user must be standing on a specially designated red tile square to enter the network. If that physical contact is interrupted, the connection is immediately cut. Given the obvious security risk of leaving one's body unattended, multi squares typically occur only in private residences or in heavily guarded public locations (multi facilities).

One can exit the multi network instantaneously from any spatial coordinate. Under pressure from the Prime Committee, the network administrators also developed a special device called a "disruptor" to allow authorities to cut multi connections. The Defense and Wellness Council later augmented the basic disruptor design to allow certain bio/logic code to flow into a multi projection.

MULTI AND COMPUTING POWER

Multi technology relies on the fact that complete verisimilitude of experience is not necessary. Often the network can take advantage of common experiences stored within the brain and from them compile a representative sample. Take the example of a multied user walking barefoot on a field of grass. The network does not take up unnecessary bandwidth and computing power determining the position of each blade of grass and calculating its effects on the user's foot; it is deemed sufficient for the network to provide a *reasonable facsimile* of the sensation. Randomness algorithms ensure that the simulated sensations do not feel repetitious or calculated.

The network also maintains fluency and transmission speed by taking a number of practical shortcuts. For instance, the multi network does not relay visual information for anything the user is not focusing on.

Users of the multi network understand that their experience is only a simulation, and that occasionally the simulation will differ from reality in its details. As the technology has progressed, these differences have become smaller and smaller, to the point where the typical user cannot reliably distinguish between virtual environments and reality.

APPENDIX F
ON THE
FIEFCORP SYSTEM

Rarely in the history of human enterprise has there been a more controversial entity than the fiefcorp. Conceived as a means to empower workers, many now complain that it has become an instrument of social ills.

HISTORY

Fiefcorps were made possible by the actions of Par Padron, who spent most of his tenure as Council high executive battling big business. Padron believed that governmental regulations and tax structures had come to favor larger companies, creating a climate in which smaller entrepreneurs could not succeed. Over the years, he succeeded in leveling the playing field among businesses and in democratizing the Prime Committee.

It was this latter action that triggered a populist resurgence on the Committee several decades later, and the subsequent votes to approve the business structure known as the fiefcorp. In order to spur innovation, fiefcorps were given substantial tax breaks during their initial decade of existence. In order to spur employment, the fiefcorp structure was modeled after the feudal master-and-apprentice relationship of ancient times.

Although the beginnings of the system were chaotic, the rapid formation, innovation, and dissolution of fiefcorps soon contributed to a beneficial effect known as "carbonization economics."

CARBONIZATION ECONOMICS

The short time window of reduced taxation, combined with low start-up costs, made fiefcorps a hotbed of innovation. Small companies were encouraged to come up with new ideas and bring them to market quickly. A fiefcorp master could bring in a number of apprentices, pay them only room and board to start, turn a very good profit in a few years, and then sell off his assets before taxes increased and start again. If the master needed additional funding to get the company off the ground, he could seek that money from the secondary market of capitalmen at relatively low interest rates.

With hundreds of thousands of fiefcorps formed, an economy based on efficiency and powerful ideas moved quickly. Pundits likened the effect to that of carbonized soda water, where bubbles quickly form, burst, and are replenished.

The rewards of running a successful fiefcorp were considerable. Profits from the greatest fiefcorps were extensive, and often allowed wily fiefcorp masters to leap into the more lucrative realm of real estate. But even in failure, the fiefcorp structure proved beneficial, because the labor market was constantly running a deficit of fresh talent. It was not unusual for people to found two or three failed companies before finding a winning formula.

ETHICAL PROBLEMS OF THE FIEFCORP

The biggest problem of a laissez-faire structure such as the fiefcorp system was its rampant lawlessness. Zest for profit often trumped rules of government, creed, and community. It was originally hoped that the low penalties for failure in a fiefcorp would discourage rule breaking, but this proved not to be true.

In an attempt to rein in the lawlessness of the fiefcorp sector, many in the industry turned to the Meme Cooperative. The Cooperative, founded a hundred years earlier by big business as a buffer to Par Padron's populist reforms, had since become mostly a lobbying organization to the Prime Committee and the L-PRACGs. Fiefcorps voluntarily ceded strict authority to the Cooperative to regulate their industry and act as a watchdog organization. Few believe that the Meme Cooperative has been successful in its mission, however.

Another third-party organization, Primo's, arose to provide an overseeing capacity to the fiefcorps. Founded by the fervent libertarian Lucco Primo in 291, the company's objective rating system has acted as a huge deterrent to fraudulent programming practices.

Still, many consider the problem of fiefcorp ethics a problem to this day. As a result, grumbling consumers typically turn to the L-PRACGs and the drudges for redress.

ACKNOWLEDGMENTS

The author would like to thank the following individuals for their contributions to this book: Lou Anders, Cindy Blank-Edelman, Bruce Bortz, Tobias Buckell, Jerome Edelman, Harrison Demchick, Kate Elliott, Deanna Hoak, J. D. Landis, Philip Mansour, Jill Maxick, Cat Rambo, and Anne Smith.

Most of all, the author would like to thank Victoria Blakeway Edelman, who made him take out Ferris.

ABOUT THE AUTHOR

DAVID LOUIS EDELMAN is a web programmer and science fiction novelist living near Washington, D.C. His first novel *Infoquake* was called "the love child of Donald Trump and Vernor Vinge" by Barnes & Noble Explorations, and later named their Top SF Novel of 2006. *Infoquake* was also nominated for the John W. Campbell Memorial Award for Best Novel. His second novel, *MultiReal* (the sequel to *Infoquake*), will be released in July 2008. His work has also appeared in *The Solaris Book of New Science Fiction, Volume 2.*

In addition to writing novels, Edelman has programmed websites for the U.S. Army and the FBI, taught software to the U.S. Congress and the World Bank, written articles for the *Washington Post* and *Baltimore Sun*, and directed the marketing departments of biometric and e-commerce companies.

Edelman is also a popular blogger on his website at www.davidlouisedelman.com, and a member of the DeepGenre and SFNovelists.com group blogs. Contact him via email at dedelman@gmail.com, or via social networking sites *Facebook*, *MySpace*, *LinkedIn*, *LibraryThing*, *Shelfari*, *GoodReads*, and *LiveJournal*.